The corridor of the county rest home smelled of Lysol and was littered with the same abandoned walkers and gurneys Owen had seen on his last visit. There was no answer when he knocked on Dolores Cantrip's door, but he heard a small scraping noise inside the room. The door was unlocked, and he opened it far enough to peer inside.

The blinds were drawn, and the only light in the room came through the half-opened bathroom door and fell slanting across the bed. The plastic bag hanging beside the bed swung like a slow metronome in and out of the sliver of light. Clear tubing ran from the feeder into Dolores Cantrip's thin, speckled arm. Her face was obscured by a pillow scrunched at an awkward angle between the bed and headboard. Owen stepped forward to adjust the pillow when a blow from behind sent him tumbling into the tangled tubing and knocked him senseless.

★

HIGHWAY ROBBERY

JOHN BILLHEIMER

W🌐RLDWIDE.

TORONTO • NEW YORK • LONDON
AMSTERDAM • PARIS • SYDNEY • HAMBURG
STOCKHOLM • ATHENS • TOKYO • MILAN
MADRID • WARSAW • BUDAPEST • AUCKLAND

For Wayne and Mildred,
and the sons and daughters of their sons and daughter

HIGHWAY ROBBERY

A Worldwide Mystery/December 2001

First published by St. Martin's Press, Incorporated.

ISBN 0-373-26404-6

Printed in U.S.A.

...you quiver and you clutch
For something larger, something unfulfilled,
Some wiser kind of joy that you shall have
Never, until you learn to laugh with God.
—E. A. Robinson, *Captain Craig*

PROLOGUE

The Carniverous Caterpillar

JIMMY JOE CRESAP put the last of the orange traffic cones in front of the detour sign and drove his pickup back up Gobbler's Grade to the construction equipment. The patchy morning fog broke at the peak of the grade, where a backhoe and a bulldozer were parked beside an asphalt paver. Someone had painted gigantic eyeballs on either side of the backhoe bucket, turning the machine, with its protruding white teeth, into a crook-necked monster with a severe overbite. The same artist had drawn glowering black eyebrows oversquinting eyes on the cab of the bulldozer and covered the dozer's blade with two rows of snaggled yellow teeth. Both the backhoe and the bulldozer were coated with a fleshy pink paint that made them look like refugees from a Saturday-morning cartoon.

Jimmy Joe opened the door of his pickup, inhaled the damp river air, and poured black coffee into his dented thermos cup. He swung his long legs outside of the pickup and cradled the cup in his scarred hands while he waited for the rest of his crew to arrive. They would come from the Barkley side of the river, through the first DETOUR signs he'd set up.

The DETOUR signs kept traffic off the winding two-lane roadway, leaving Jimmy Joe alone with his coffee and the shrill cackling of two hell-diving loons. The loons suddenly went silent and flapped away, frightened by something coming up the hill. Jimmy Joe couldn't hear anything coming, but as he watched, a wiry woman with slate-gray hair shouldered aside the fog and pushed a bicycle up the slope toward him. The construction foreman swore under his breath, flung the remainder of his coffee over the ground, and went to meet the woman.

"Mary Jewel," he called. "What the hell are you doing here?"

The woman waited until she cleared the top of the hill to answer. "Thought I'd get up at dawn to see the sun rise over the river. Nothing quite like a West Virginia sunrise."

"Well, dawn's about the right time to see the sun rise, but the river's a mile behind you, past the DETOUR signs."

Mary Jewel Robertson set her bike on its kickstand across the road from the construction equipment. "Why, my goodness, Jimmy Joe, I know where the river is as well as you do. I've just come from there."

"We're not going to have trouble with you today, are we?" Jimmy Joe asked.

Mary Jewel took off her backpack, sat down on it, and stared back down the fog-bound road. "Trouble? Whatever do you mean, trouble?"

"This is the first dry day we've had in two weeks," Jimmy Joe said. "I'd like to be able to get some work done today."

"I suppose that means you'll be using those monstrous machines to knock down that stand of birch over there."

"We're widening the road from two to four lanes. You can't have birch trees standing right beside a four-lane highway."

"Barkley doesn't need a four-lane highway."

Jimmy Joe kicked at a shallow dent in the roadway, loosening a chunk of asphalt. "Barkley doesn't need potholes and blind curves."

"If you'd built the road right in the first place, you wouldn't be cutting down trees now."

"I wasn't around when this road was built, Mary Jewel."

"Well, your boss was."

"You are fixing to make trouble, aren't you?"

From down the hill, Jimmy Joe recognized the rattling roar of the Blatt brothers' pickup. It crested the grade, followed by a navy-blue minivan he hadn't seen before.

The pickup swerved to the side of the road and Sonny Blatt jumped out, gesturing over his shoulder at the minivan, which was filled with women. "They followed me through the barricade, boss. I couldn't stop them. Honest."

Two older women climbed down from the minivan, carrying peck baskets full of tomatoes. Jimmy Joe recognized one, Pluma Wilcox, from his mother's sewing circle. She avoided his eyes and carried her basket of tomatoes over to Mary Jewel.

Phil Blatt joined his brother and Jimmy Joe. "It's true, boss. They just followed us through."

"It's all right," Jimmy Joe said. "Better call Sheriff Reader and get him up here."

"Hell, it's just a bunch of old ladies," Sonny said. "How come we need the sheriff?"

"Just call him."

The van emptied and six women gathered around Mary Jewel. The driver of the van was younger than the rest and carried an infant in a papoose pack. "Good stewing tomatoes," the driver told Mary Jewel. "Pearl Tharpe knocked down the price when she heard why we wanted them. Four-twenty a bushel. It comes out to a dollar and five cents apiece, not counting the gas."

Mary Jewel lined up six peck baskets by the side of the road and covered a seventh with a checkered cloth from her backpack. "What happened to Claire Marie and her van?"

"Dougie took sick," the woman with the baby answered.

"Well, we'll just have to make do," Mary Jewel said. She knelt on one knee as if she were outlining football plays on her backpack and the other women huddled around her.

The fourth member of the day's crew, Butch Muth, pulled up in his battered Dodge Dart. He was followed by a yellow van with a scanning antenna on its roof and the call letters WSAZ-TV on its sides.

Butch joined Jimmy Joe and the Blatt brothers by the backhoe. "We gonna be on TV?" he asked.

"TV's gonna be on us, I'm afraid," Jimmy Joe said. "All over us, like sweat on a fat boy."

Two men climbed down from the yellow van. Jimmy Joe recognized the first as Russell Oliver, the evening news anchor for Huntington's Channel 3. The second man carried a portable camera and a battery pack.

Mary Jewel left the huddle and jogged over to the news anchor. They talked briefly, with Mary Jewel pointing first at the construction equipment, then at the road, and finally at the roadside trees. Then the cameraman lined up Mary Jewel with the backhoe and bulldozer in the background, and the news anchor began an interview. From where he stood, Jimmy Joe could make out the repeated words "no growth," and "pollution." Each time she said the word "growth," Mary Jewel clapped her fist into her tiny palm.

"That's the guy from Channel Three, isn't it?" Sonny Blatt asked. "What's he doing with that old lady?"

"She brought him here," Jimmy Joe said.

"We gonna be on TV?" Butch Muth asked again.

"Whether we want to or not," Jimmy Joe said. "Not much we can do about it. Might as well get to work. Butch, you take Attila. Sonny, you take the backhoe." He watched as the cameraman and the news anchor, left Mary Jewel and walked toward him. "Better work the downhill side of the slope. There aren't any trees to level there."

The news anchor set the cameraman up off his left shoulder and thrust his microphone under Jimmy Joe's chin. Jimmy Joe knew he should look at the camera or the interviewer, one or the other, but he didn't know which. His eyes darted from the camera to the microphone and back again.

The first question the interviewer asked was about the monster faces painted on the equipment.

Jimmy Joe watched the bulldozer clear a swath in the berm by the side of the road, then looked into the camera. "The boss did that," he said. "His outfit in Korea painted faces on all their planes, like the Flying Tigers." When he got out and started his construction company, he did the same thing with his equipment. His little kids thought it was funny, so he kept it up every time he bought something new. Now the kids run the company, but they still paint faces on all the backhoes and dozers."

"The boss would be Charley Hager?"

"That's right."

"And what does he think about the movement to stop your construction?"

Jimmy Joe looked from the camera to the microphone. "You'll have to ask him that."

"What about you?" the news anchor asked. "Do you think Barkley needs wider roads, with all the growth and pollution they bring?"

"Barkley's population is, what? Twenty-five thousand? I'd say it could stand to do a little growing."

"And you're willing to cut down trees to bring that growth?"

Jimmy Joe looked away from the camera to his equipment. "There's maybe twenty-five trees in that stand we're cutting down. There's hundreds on the hill behind us, and hundreds more on the next hill over. We're leaving lots more than we're cutting, and the state needs jobs lots more than it needs trees."

Over the interviewer's shoulder, Jimmy Joe saw a fusillade of tiny red spheres. Mary Jewel and her cohorts were pelting the bulldozer with tomatoes.

"Hey, cut that out," Jimmy Joe yelled, running toward the bull-dozer.

The interviewer turned the cameraman around and pointed him toward the protesters. "This is great stuff," he said, trailing after Jimmy Joe. "Get all of it."

By the time he reached the bulldozer, the eyes painted on the cab were teary with tomato juice and the teeth on the blade dripped red with puree. The driver had climbed down to take cover behind the blade.

With the bulldozer stopped, the women loosed a volley of tomatoes at the backhoe behind it. All but one fell short and splattered on the roadway.

Instead of shutting down the backhoe, Sonny Blatt steered the cat-erpillar treads onto the roadway and headed for the women. As the backhoe neared the protesters, the tomatoes grew more accurate, rain-ing down on the driver and all but obliterating the word CATERPILLAR on the side panel.

Sitting exposed in the driver's seat, Sonny pulled at the controls and the backhoe bucket reared into the air, its painted teeth and fierce eyes glaring down at the women.

Six of the seven women retreated down the roadway. Pluma Wilcox threw two more tomatoes at Sonny and ran to her basket to reload.

Jimmy Joe climbed up behind Sonny and pulled the keys from the backhoe's ignition. The treads ground to a halt and the fierce teeth froze at the end of the crook-neck crane.

"For Christ's sake, Sonny, you're on TV," Jimmy Joe shouted. "You can't be taking after women with a backhoe."

"That short bitch hit me with a tomato," Sonny shouted back.

The women regrouped and linked arms. When they were unable to span the roadway elbow to elbow, they separated, held hands, and began chanting, "Hell no, we won't grow!"

From where he stood on the backhoe, the seven women clasping hands and shouting looked to Jimmy Joe as if they were playing a geriatric game of Red Rover. He imagined they would look more impressive on the evening news, a human barricade staring down a mechanical monster.

Jimmy Joe signaled his crew members to stay put and climbed down from the backhoe. The interviewer approached across the asphalt, his cameraman close behind. Jimmy Joe turned away from the interviewer's extended microphone and walked toward the chanting women.

A siren sounded in the distance, coming up the grade. A few of the women faltered in their chant. Holding hands in the center of the roadway, Mary Jewel and Pluma stood strong and shouted, "Hell no, we won't grow!" over the wailing siren.

The sheriff's white squad car pulled to a stop behind the line of protesters. Sheriff Thad Reader emerged, cinched the chin strap of his Mountie's hat, separated the hands of the two women at the end of the line, and stepped through the human barricade.

"What the hell's going on here?" he asked Jimmy Joe.

Mary Jewel left the line and joined them. "It's a peaceful demonstration, Sheriff."

"Peaceful, my ass," Sonny Blatt said. "That short bitch hit me with a tomato."

The sheriff reached out and swung the lens of the TV camera so it pointed away from the protesters toward the birch trees. "Turn that thing the hell off."

The cameraman looked to the news anchor for guidance. Seeing the news anchor nod, he lowered his camera.

The sheriff stepped forward and closed his fist over the camera mike. "Boy," he said to the cameraman, "either you're unfamiliar with the operation of this gadget or you think I was just hatched yesterday. When I say turn it off, I mean turn it off. Don't just lower it."

The cameraman flipped a toggle switch and the red light on the camera face blinked off.

"That goes for your mike, too," the sheriff said to the news anchor.

When both the camera and microphone were turned off, the sheriff said, "Mary Jewel, this here is either vandalism or a hell of a sloppy picnic. If you don't want me to call it vandalism, you'd best pack up your crew and be on your way."

Mary Jewel turned to the TV interviewer. "You got everything you need?"

The interviewer gave her a thumbs-up sign.

"Let's go then, girls," Mary Jewel said. As her protesters broke ranks, she raised her fist toward Jimmy Joe and said, "We'll stop you for good at the bridge."

Jimmy Joe gave the backhoe keys to Sonny Blatt, who climbed

back into the driver's seat and turned the treads toward the side of the road.

Mary Jewel uncovered the basket of tomatoes she'd protected with her checkered cloth and put it in the hamper on the back of her bike.

As the rest of the women loaded the minivan, Pluma grabbed a basket of tomatoes and advanced on Sonny and the backhoe. "You can't call me a bitch, you tree-cropping lowlife."

Sonny ducked two tomatoes and the backhoe bucket slewed back and forth, its painted head sniffing the wind.

Pluma set the basket down, gathered a handful of tomatoes, and closed in on Sonny. She caught him full in the face with a tomato and the backhoe bucket crashed to earth, digging its teeth deep into the asphalt.

Another tomato sailed by Sonny's head. The backhoe reared, and the bucket tore loose a mouthful of asphalt, gravel, dirt and debris.

Pluma screamed.

Jimmy Joe ran to Pluma's side. Along with the gravel and debris, a bleached human skull peeked through the teeth of the backhoe. The Caterpillar had turned carnivorous.

ONE

The Return of the Native

OWEN ALLISON'S PLANE from San Francisco was two hours late landing at the Cincinnati airport, which was as close as he could get to his home town of Barkley, West Virginia, without changing to a small propeller plane and making a knuckle-whitening hop to a glorified driveway set precariously on a lopped-off mountaintop. The Greater Cincinnati Metropolitan Airport had signs everywhere apologizing for the ongoing construction that was designed, as nearly as Owen could tell, to make it look like ninety percent of the other airports in the country.

Since most major airports looked alike, right down to their UNDER CONSTRUCTION signs, Owen had a theory that it was easier to tell where you were by studying the people than by looking for telltale signs in the structure itself. The first clue that he wasn't in California anymore came from the bib overalls, which weren't on teenage girls, but rather on older men who looked as if they'd worn them all their lives. The older men's faces weren't smooth and tanned, but lined and weathered by work and worry. The younger men leaned toward sideburns rather than spiked hairdos, and the rage for self-mutilation through lip-, nose-and eyebrow rings hadn't yet spread to the entire teenage population.

One face that Owen didn't see as he scanned the airport crowd was that of his older brother George, who was supposed to meet his plane and drive him to Barkley. His consternation must have shown in his face, because a passing flight attendant stopped and asked, "Can I help you, sir?" He took the "sir" and the easy, open offer of help as another clue he must be somewhere in middle America. Since Owen's flight was two hours late and George wasn't at the gate, he reasoned that his brother had probably staked out a booth in the nearest bar.

When he asked for directions, the flight attendant smiled, nodded in the direction of the Baggage Claim area, and said, "Just down the hall a piece." She stretched the word "down" to nearly two syllables with a soft twang that Owen knew would return to his own speech after a few days in West Virginia.

The airport bar was called the Rhinelander Lounge, and the bartender wore a Cincinnati Reds jersey, a dead giveaway to the airport's location. Owen saw his brother George on a barstool staring vacantly over the beer taps at the bottles stacked on glass shelves. A cigarette drooped from his lips, and his right hand clutched a nearly empty beer mug. At first, George's left hand appeared to be keeping time to the Hank Williams tune playing on the jukebox, but as Owen approached from the rear he was concerned to see that the hand was shaking to some other, internal, beat.

Owen covered the shaking hand with his own. "Been waiting long?"

"Couple of beers, is all."

Owen put his right arm around his brother's shoulder and gave it a quick squeeze. "Good to see you."

"You too. See you've still got the beard and all your hair."

"You've still got the mustache and half of yours. Mom didn't come along?"

"No, she's waiting at home. At her age, three hours to get here and another three back's more than she could take."

Owen nodded. His mother had asked him to come, saying George was close to the edge. She probably thought the two of them would be able to talk on the drive back to Barkley. She hadn't figured that George would have a two-hour wait with a bar nearby.

George drained his beer, swiveled on the barstool, and pointed at the garment bag at Owen's feet. "That all your luggage?"

Owen nodded and watched as his brother braced himself on the bar and stepped down from the stool. His eyes were puffy and his graying mustache was damp with beer or perspiration. He'd gained twenty pounds and aged that many years in the two or three years since Owen had last seen him, but he didn't appear to be drunk.

Owen shouldered his garment bag and followed George out of the lounge and into the flow of airport travelers. He watched his older brother closely as he shambled along the moving walkway leading to the parking garage. He wasn't weaving or slurring his speech. He wasn't even using the moving handrail on the walkway. But it was always hard to tell with George.

When they arrived at his brother's Pontiac, Owen laid his garment bag on the backseat and said, "Maybe I ought to drive."

His brother took a last drag on his cigarette and waved him off. "I'm all right. Besides, there's a new freeway along the river in Kentucky. Want you to see it."

Owen shrugged, giving his brother the benefit of the doubt. He strapped himself into the passenger seat and watched as George cautiously edged the car out of the airport parking lot, following the signs to Kentucky Route 546.

"Wait'll you see this road," George said. "They know how to build 'em in Kentucky." He gunned the engine entering the freeway, blowing by a semi and a van in the right-hand lanes.

Owen braced his hand against the dashboard. "For Christ's sake, George," he said. "You're pushing ninety."

George eased back on the accelerator, and the car's speed slacked off to 75 miles per hour. "Sorry," he said. "Give a West Virginia boy a straight stretch of road and he's off to hell and gone."

"Hell and gone is farther than I want to go today." Owen shifted under his seat belt. "Let's just try to make Barkley in one piece."

"I told you, I'm all right."

"I didn't say you weren't. But you're going to attract a lot of attention at ninety and being a Highway Commissioner in West Virginia won't cut much ice in Kentucky."

George slowed to seventy and drove on in silence. An early-afternoon shower splatted against the windshield. George turned on the wipers, still not saying anything.

Owen wasn't used to seeing his brother sullen and silent. He tried the one topic of conversation that always worked. "So what's with the Reds?"

"Shit, if there were a sub-cellar, they'd be in it. They don't have the payroll to keep up with the big-market teams."

"The faces change so fast, I don't recognize half of them."

"Maybe we can catch a game while you're around. How long are you in for?"

"Don't know," Owen said. He'd stay as long as he was needed, but he had no clear idea yet how he could help.

George peered intently through the windshield wipers. "Been a while."

"I stopped off to see Mom on my way from D.C. to California last summer, just after I left the Transportation Department. You were busy in Charleston."

"So you're back to that failure stuff again?"

"Failure and Risk Evaluation. Same as before." He hoped it wouldn't turn out the same as before, when he'd lost a string of clients by telling them things they didn't want to hear: telling lawyers the problem was their client's blood alcohol content, not the brakes on his car or the slope of the roadway; telling the city fathers of Santa Clarita they'd never get enough riders on their proposed light rail system to justify the federal subsidy they were pursuing; telling an architect friend that his walkway collapsed and killed two people because he'd stretched it too far with no support. There was no reason to believe his restarted business wouldn't have the same problems that had sunk him before. But dropping it to work for the federal bureaucracy had proved to be an even bigger disaster.

George pointed his glowing cigarette at a riverside factory that belched fire from three smokestacks. "Those guys just laid off two hundred plant workers," he said. "How's it going with your business?"

"I'm hanging on," Owen said. "Just barely. The big problem with consulting is you're never sure where the next six months' worth of work is coming from." Or the next three months, he thought, which was about how long his nest egg would last. "Sometimes I miss the regular government paycheck."

The car sped by a sign saying SLOW, CROSS TRAFFIC AHEAD.

"Take it easy, George," Owen said.

"Hell's bells, little brother. I taught you to drive. Remember?"

A stop light materialized in the mist ahead of them. George hit the brakes. The Pontiac slewed, skidded, and came to a stop halfway through the intersection. Brakes squealed and horns blared as cars stacked up behind them.

"Goddamn road's supposed to be a freeway," George said.

Owen reached over the gearshift and pulled the keys from the ignition. "That's enough," he said. "I'm driving."

Owen hustled around the outside of the Pontiac and shouldered George from behind the steering wheel over into the passenger's seat. He shook the rain from his eyes, started the car, and drove it on through the intersection, leaving the blaring horns behind.

George slumped against the passenger door. "Fucking light in the middle of the fucking freeway. Nobody knows how to build freeways anymore.''

"It's a construction zone," Owen said. "Looks like they're building an overpass."

"Goddamn Green Gestapo won't let you build freeways anymore," George mumbled.

"What the hell are you talking about?"

George waved loosely at the trees lining the side of the road. "Not here. Back home in West-by-God-Virginia. Bunch of little old ladies tying my Highway Department in knots. Don't want us to build anymore freeways."

"It's the same all over," Owen said. "Been that way in California for years. You want to widen a road, you've got to lay a paper trail longer than the road itself and hold at least one hearing for every cubic yard of concrete."

"Well, it hasn't been that way in West Virginia. We've been running roads wherever we wanted ever since Dad laid out the first interstate." George shook his head. "That's all over now, thanks to a bunch of shrub cuddlers. The old man must be spinning in his grave."

"If he had a grave," Owen said.

"Well, wherever he is, you can bet the mud around him's scorched some."

In Owen's mind's eye, he saw a grasping hand reaching upward through a slogging sea of mud. The image had haunted him since childhood, and he blinked his eyes twice to clear his head. "You're the Highway Commissioner," he said. "Don't you have the last word on design?"

"Not anymore. We've got a Transportation Department now. Highways are just a part of it. The head of the Department has the final say."

"Who's that?"

"Name's Alicia Fox. Came in with the new administration. She's an old college buddy of the new Governor. Not even an engineer. And she's in with the Green Gestapo. She's killed half the freeway projects on my drawing board." George edged forward. "Watch this interchange coming up."

The freeway ebbed and flowed with the hilly landscape, then dipped under an elevated roadbed that soared and curved gracefully into a bridge approach.

"See that," George said. "They left it all on one column."

"Steel poetry. That's what Dad used to say."

George slumped back into his seat. "Those jobs Alicia doesn't kill she fucks up. Remember Gobbler's Grade? That old road was so narrow you'd have to widen it to paint a stripe down the middle. Before the new administration took over, I approved a plan to stretch it to four lanes. Make it a freeway. Straighten out a few kinks. The greenies objected, but I pushed it through anyway. Beat those buttinskies right out of their Birkenstocks."

George shook his head and fished another cigarette from his rumpled sport coat. "Trouble is, the Fifth Street Bridge sits right in the middle of the job. It takes a separate contract, because it's part state and part local. I figured we'd just widen the bridge to four lanes as part of a retrofit, but Alicia wants to hold it to two lanes."

"Shoehorn a four-lane freeway into a two-lane bridge? You're bound to have accidents where the road narrows."

"My guys figure one or two extra fatals a year."

"It doesn't make any sense."

"The greenies aren't looking for sense. They're looking for symbols. Their pitch is antigrowth." George let his wrist go limp and raised his voice an octave. "'We don't want Barkley to become another Pittsburgh, do we?'"

Owen laughed. "Jesus Christ. Barkley could triple in size and it still wouldn't be another Charleston, let alone Pittsburgh."

George flicked ashes out the window. "It's not funny, Owen. Alicia's threatened to shit-can me if I don't approve the two-lane design."

"What'll you do?"

George sucked in a lungful of smoke and let a little escape. "I don't know. Maybe I'll give Alicia her two-lane design. What the hell, maybe I'm being too careful. I've always overdesigned. Built wider lanes, bigger buffers. Drivers kill themselves no matter what."

"That's no reason to make it easier for them to have accidents." Owen cracked his window enough to expel the cigarette smoke. "Look on the bright side, though. You're lucky they only want to keep the bridge narrower. They could have asked you to make it shorter, too. Now that'd be a real symbol."

George's laugh shook ashes onto his lap. He raised a finger in front of his lips. "Shh," he said. "You don't want to give those damn tree huggers any ideas."

George laid his head against the passenger window, closed his eyes, and fell asleep. Owen turned his full attention to the freeway, which curved gently along the Ohio River. The rain had stopped, and he opened his window wider to let in the damp river smell he remembered from his childhood. His mother had been vague about George's problems on the phone. ("Just come home, Owen. It'll be better if you're here.") After listening to his brother, though, he didn't see how he could help with his predicament at work; and nobody had ever been able to help George with his drinking problem. The river air filled Owen's nostrils and cooled his forehead. In his forty-five years, he couldn't remember his mother asking anyone but his father for help. Maybe she was really worried about problems of her own.

The freeway played tag with the Ohio River for about an hour and then drifted inland, leaving Kentucky and crossing the Big Sandy on a steel-truss bridge with a sign welcoming them to WILD AND WONDERFUL WEST VIRGINIA. Owen left the freeway after crossing the bridge and picked up a newly paved state route that followed the contours of the hilly countryside. Shallow cuts bulldozed along the side of the road were covered with chalky gravel patches that formed small white islands in stands of stiff beech trees. Isolated homes sat in half-hidden hollows and stood on cleared knolls. Satellite dishes and separate garages marked the houses of the well-to-do, while hoodless cars lined the driveways of the less fortunate. From time to time the fresh roadway spanned creekbeds and side roads with graceful arcs that reminded Owen why his father and brother had wanted to build highways.

The fresh pavement ended and the road narrowed to follow a series of tightly angled turns and sharp switchbacks cut into the steep slopes of the jagged mining country. They were getting closer to home, and Owen remembered his father telling him that the roads around here were "so twisty you'd meet yourself coming back." When he'd first heard that as a child he kept watching the road ahead, hoping to be the first to see the radiator grill of their old Nash as it turned back on itself. Now he wondered if the mountain roads would wind deep enough so that he'd come face to face with the young, hopeful Owen Allison.

George stirred in the passenger seat. "The Reds are in town this week. Maybe we can take in a game."

Was he too drunk to remember we already talked about that, Owen thought, or is he just sobering up and looking for a safe topic of conversation? "Sounds like a plan. Looks like the Reds finally solved the Marge Schott problem."

"Hell, she was no problem. The rest of the owners are no better and no brighter. She just mouthed off more."

"What was that crack she made about Hitler?"

"She said he wasn't so bad when he started out. The reporters jumped all over that one. Pulled it out of context and hung her out to dry."

"Is there some context that doesn't make her sound like an idiot?"

"It's all relative," George said. "Attila the Hun didn't start out bad either. He was fourteen before he killed anybody."

"And the *Titanic* had a few sunny days," Owen said.

"Damn straight. Hitler didn't do much harm when he was still hanging wallpaper."

"So you think Marge got a raw deal?" Owen asked.

"Not really. I'd be happy to see a lot of the other owners go too. Baseball's way too important to be left in the hands of nincompoops. It's not only baseball, though. The whole world's being run by those dumb kids in the rear of your third-grade classroom who couldn't get past the fours in their multiplication tables."

"Or by their widows," Owen said.

"Or by their college buddies or idiot children," George said. "Guess who's running Hager Construction now?"

"Not whiny little Eddie Hager?"

"The same. Running it into the ground, too, I hear. They've got the Gobbler's Grade contract. Between the weather and greenie demonstrations, he's six months behind schedule. Penalties are costing him five grand a day."

"They still paint their equipment like cartoon monsters?"

"You know it. Titty-pink bodies and bulging eyeballs. Earth-moving circuses all around the state."

"They weren't so bad when they started out," Owen said. "Whatever happened to Eddie's sister Robin?"

"Divorced and living high off the hog in White Sulphur is what I hear."

"She'd make a better construction boss than Eddie."

George reached across the seat and faked a punch to Owen's shoulder. "You should know, little brother."

Owen ignored the jab. Robin had been his first failure. Robin, and then baseball. Both in his freshman year in college. He supposed the first thing most men failed at was either love or sports. Or both. But he didn't want to talk about his failures with George. Instead he asked, "How's Mom?"

"I'm glad you're coming home. I'm a little worried about her."

"Her cancer hasn't come back, has it?"

"No, it's not her 'little upset.'"

"Amazing, isn't she?" Owen said. "She's survived scarlet fever, buried a still-born child, and fed hot meals to divers dragging the river for her husband, but she still uses code words for anything the least bit unpleasant."

"Like your divorce being your 'situation.'"

Owen wanted to say, "Or your drinking being your 'problem'" but thought better of it and just nodded.

"Yeah, well, I've got a budding 'situation' of my own," George said. "Barb's talking about divorce."

The news saddened Owen without really surprising him. "I'm sorry to hear that. What's the problem?"

"She's got a whole litany of complaints. I'm too tough on Billy. Too long at work. Too short with her. We've had some pretty big blowups."

"How long has this been going on?"

"Hell, I don't know. We've been seeing a counselor for six months, trying to work it out. Nothing's settled yet. Don't mention it to Mom. She's got enough on her mind."

Mom must know already, Owen thought. She'd known about his own troubles with Judith almost before he was aware of them. But she wouldn't have called him home to work out George's marital problems. He'd made too much of a mess of his own.

"Getting back to Mom, why are you worried about her?"

"You better talk to her about it."

"You're as bad as she is. How can I talk to her if I don't know anything?"

George lit a new cigarette with the glowing butt of the one in his mouth. Then he grimaced, picked a stay strand of tobacco from his tongue, and snubbed the used butt in the cluttered ashtray. "One of Hager's road crews found a skull and a bunch of bones under the asphalt on Gobbler's Grade. They'd been there quite some time."

"How long?"

"Nearly thirty-five years. As long as the road's been there."

"What's that got to do with Mom?"

"She thinks it's Dad's body."

Owen oversteered around a tight curve and swerved into the on-coming lane. He crossed back over the center line, found a turnout, and pulled the car off the side of the narrow roadway. "How could it be Dad's body? He drowned when the Eight-Pole Creek Dam burst."

George's cigarette hand traced a series of circles, trailing spirals of smoke. "I know it sounds crazy. You better talk to Mom about it. Get it firsthand."

The steep slopes and tightly packed beech trees had brought an early darkness to the winding mountain road. Owen turned on his headlights and checked his rearview mirror. "Let's go by Gobbler's Grade and take a look." He edged back onto the roadway and picked his way around a series of hairpin turns, alert for anything that might be coming from the opposite direction.

TWO

Gobbler's Grade

THE SUN HAD SET behind the jagged hills and the light of the quarter moon glinted off the yellow crime-scene tape when Owen pulled up beside the construction equipment at the crest of Gobbler's Grade. George unlimbered himself from the passenger seat, leaned against the door of the Pontiac, and tapped a Camel free from the pack in his coat pocket.

"Don't light that," Owen whispered. "I smell gasoline."

George pocketed his cigarette and squinted into the blackness.

Owen took a flashlight from the glove compartment and played its light over the yellow tape, which had been stretched between four sawhorses and tied to enclose a shallow, shadowed gouge in the asphalt. The quiet of the night was punctuated by a slow, steady drip. Owen pointed the flashlight in the direction of the sound. One of Hager's painted backhoes stood next to the tape, leaking liquid into a dark, spreading pool. The backhoe's neck was crooked and its head was bowed, as if it expected a beating for staining the asphalt.

Owen focused the flashlight beam on the leak. "Somebody drove a rail spike into the gas tank."

"Who'd do a thing like that?"

"Maybe your greenies are sore losers."

"Never done anything like this before," George said.

"Let's check the rest of the equipment."

In the dim moonlight, they could make out the hulking shapes of a bulldozer and a pickup parked on the gravel berm farther down the road. As they approached, Owen's flashlight beam reflected off the glowering eyeballs on the bulldozer cab. Just under the cab, some of the letters in the trademark CATERPILLAR had been painted over to leave the word ATTILA. A ten-pound sack of sugar was overturned beneath the bulldozer's gas tank. The cap to the tank was nowhere to be seen.

"Looks like somebody had an idea for an additive that would keep the engine from polluting," Owen said. "Keep it from doing anything else, too."

George toed the overturned sack gingerly. A stream of ants shifted its course on the mound of sugar. "Must have left in a hurry."

A rifle shot exploded and a branch fell from a roadside tree. Owen dived for the ground. George, still standing, turned toward the sound and asked, "What the hell's going on?"

Owen lunged and tackled his brother. "Somebody's shooting at us." He pulled George into the shelter of the bulldozer blade and switched off the flashlight. "From somewhere down the hill."

George poked his head over the bulldozer blade. "We haven't done anything wrong."

Owen tugged at George, bringing his head back under cover. "Whoever's shooting at us doesn't seem to be interested in debating right and wrong."

Below them, twigs snapped beneath running footsteps. "We better make a run for it," Owen said. "Stay low and I'll try to bring the car around."

Owen left the shelter of the bulldozer and ran, hunched over, toward their parked car. Another shot rang out, and he scrambled behind the backhoe that stood leaking gasoline beside the asphalt grave.

The footsteps following him reached the roadway and crunched on the gravel berm. Owen squirmed under the backhoe as the footsteps paused, then started slowly in his direction.

"Come on out of there, motherfucker," a hoarse voice said. "And come out real slow."

Owen clenched the unlit flashlight as the footsteps approached, coming closer to him, but farther away from George. The smell of spilled gasoline burned his nostrils.

"Real slow, now." the voice repeated. "I've got more buckshot here than you've got hide."

George's voice sounded in the distance. "Jimmy Joe. Is that you, Jimmy Joe?"

The footsteps stopped. The hoarse voice said, "Commissioner? What the hell are you doing here?"

Owen heard footsteps receding, then George's voice shouting, "Come on out, Owen. It's all right."

Owen crawled out from under the backhoe, trying to avoid the pool of gasoline. He turned on the flashlight. George was standing with a tall man in blue jeans and a plaid work shirt. The man cradled a shotgun under his arm.

George introduced the man as Jimmy Joe Cresap, foreman of Hager's construction crew.

"I'm real sorry I fired on you two," Jimmy Joe said. "I thought you were the same guys who were spiking our gas tanks. I surprised them when I drove up to drop off tomorrow's work order. They hightailed it down the hill and I grabbed Old Reliable here and hustled after them." He hefted his shotgun. "Never caught them, though. They disappeared down an old fire trail. When I saw your flashlight, I thought they'd doubled back on me."

Jimmy Joe jacked open his shotgun to show two empty chambers. "Just as well you weren't the spikers, he said. I only had two loads with me and I used them up firing blind."

"Yeah, well, my flashlight wasn't loaded either," Owen said.

"I said I was sorry," Jimmy Joe said. "I aimed high enough to miss you."

"The way that buckshot sprays, you could have aimed at the treetops and still clipped us," George said.

"It's okay, George," Owen said. "No harm, no foul." He turned to Jimmy Joe. "Did you get a look at the guys you were chasing?"

"No. It was too dark and they were too quick." Jimmy Joe jerked the spike out of the backhoe's gas tank. "Looks like they dumped sugar into the tanks they could open and spiked the ones they couldn't. This is gonna cost us more down time."

"What'll you do?" George asked.

Jimmy Joe shrugged. "Patch up what we can. Bring in equipment from upstate. We've had a lot idle lately." He hefted his shotgun. "I'll stick around for a while in case those guys come back."

"We better get on home," Owen said. "Mom will be expecting us."

"Maybe I better drive the rest of the way," George said. "You look a little frazzled."

Owen pulled the Pontiac's keys from his pocket, then hesitated.

"Don't worry," George said. "It's been at least four hours since I had anything to drink. I napped while you drove, and it's less than five miles to Mom's house."

"Most accidents happen within five miles of home," Owen said.

"Well, we must be all right then. You're over two thousand miles from your home, and I'm at least fifty away from mine."

Owen handed over the keys. "Let's hope logic isn't part of the local sobriety test."

THE ROAD NARROWED as they drove downhill and the car moved in and out of patches of fog. "This is the part they haven't widened,"

George said. "It's miserable when the fog moves up from the river."

They emerged from a patch of fog to see a bicyclist in the road dead ahead of them. George hit the brakes and the car slewed to a stop, but not before its front fender bumped the bike's rear wheel. The bike wobbled, but the rider regained control for a moment before spilling off into a roadside ditch.

The rider wore black spandex pants over a black leotard, a black leather jacket, and a black backpack. Tufts of graying hair puffed out under a black helmet, and a black scarf hid half of the rider's face. The scarf slipped as the rider sat up, and George recognized her.

"Mary Jewel," George said, scrambling down into the ditch. "Are you all right?"

"What the hell?" Mary Jewel said, picking gravel out of her jacket sleeve. "What the hell?"

Owen retrieved the bike, tested it tentatively, and rolled it back up the hill. Mary Jewel stood, dusted off her spandex pants, and grabbed the bike from Owen. "Gimme that," she said. "Why'ncha watch where you're going?"

"You've got no headlight, no reflectors, and you're dressed like a ninja nun," Owen said. "How do you expect anybody to see you on a night like this? I'm standing right next to you and I can barely make you out."

"Damn cars think you own the road."

George put one hand on the bike's handlebar and the other on its seat. "Let us run you by the hospital. Saint Vincent's just up the road."

"I'm all right," Mary Jewel said. She tugged at the bike's other handlebar. "Gimme my bike."

George held fast. "At least let us drive you home."

Mary Jewel squinted at George. "That you, Commissioner?" She shrugged and released the bike. "Might have known it."

As George loaded the bike into the Pontiac's trunk, he asked, "You sure you don't want to stop by the hospital?"

Mary Jewel's backpack clanked against the door handle as she slammed herself down in the car's backseat. "I told you, I'm all right. Just take me home."

Mary Jewel passed the drive in angry silence. After they had dropped her off and were pulling away from her house, Owen observed, "All the charm of a constipated cobra."

"She's the head of the local tree huggers," George said. "A real lumber-loving Luddite."

"Think she might have been up on Gobbler's Grade spiking gas tanks?"

George checked his rearview mirror. "No, it's not her style. She would have staged it at high noon, with at least two reporters and a cameraman on hand for the ceremony."

"You'RE SURE Mary Jewel wasn't hurt?" Ruth Allison asked her sons for the second time.

"I barely bumped her, Mom," George said.

Ruth removed her eyeglasses, blinked twice, and replaced them on top of her head, just in front of her silver-gray bun. "That awful woman. She wants to stop progress somewhere between indoor plumbing and the telephone. She won't be happy until we're all riding bicycles."

George set his empty coffee cup on the kitchen table. "Well, as long as I've still got a car to drive, I'd better get back to Charleston." He bent over to hug Ruth, whose head barely came up to his breastbone. "Good to see you, Owen. Come on up to the office while you're here. I'll introduce you to the Dragon Lady."

After his brother had left, Owen helped his mother gather up the dinner dishes. They were the same dishes he and George had eaten from as children. His mother's only concession to modern times was a portable dishwasher that was tethered to the sink by two hoses, one attached to the faucet, the other emptying down the drain.

As they loaded the dishwasher, his mother asked, "How's your situation with Judith? You're both in California again."

"It's a big state, Mom."

"I can read a map. You're both in the same half."

"We see each other from time to time."

"That's all? From time to time?"

"Maybe a little more. She's taking care of Buster while I'm gone."

"After she helped you out of that mess with the buses and the law in Contrary, I had hopes you'd get back together."

"It could still happen. We're taking it slow."

"The time to take it slow was before you split up."

"That's blood under the bridge, Mom. You didn't bring me across the country to tell me that."

"You're right, I didn't." She turned on the faucet and water gurgled through the dishwasher hose. "I'm worried about George. His work's going sour, he's got a bad situation with Barb, and his old problem's back."

"I know about his problem. He spent sometime in the bar waiting for me. What about Barb and his work?"

"His work's eating him alive. I think that's what's causing his other problems. He won't knuckle under to his boss on some bridge plans, and it could cost him his job."

"What can I do?"

"You understand these things better than George. You've had troubles yourself. You got out of them. You know about the bridge. You're family. He'll listen to you."

The dishwasher made a loud sucking noise.

Owen felt slow, as if his mother were still holding the answers to his homework problems and he couldn't work through the arithmetic. "Listen to me tell him what?"

His mother took his hands in hers. "You've got to tell him to approve the bridge."

"I can't do that. He's right. It's a travesty."

Ruth Allison shook her head. "You boys. You're just as bull-headed as your father. It's a lost cause. The Governor wants it. The Transportation Commissioner wants it. The press wants it. Mary Jewel and her harpies want it. They've got the clout. The deck's stacked and dealt. George can't win."

"But it's stone-dumb. It'll kill people."

"Nobody believes that but George."

Owen pulled his hands free of his mother's grasp. "But George is right."

"Your father died of being right."

"Wait a minute." Owen held up one hand, palm outward. "How'd Dad get into this? He drowned trying to control the flooding when Amalgamated Coal's makeshift mining dam let go."

"That's what the papers said."

Owen moved his hand slowly back and forth, as if erasing an invisible blackboard. "You're telling me that's not what happened?"

"You were only ten."

"I'm older now. And it feels like I'm aging fast. Isn't that what happened?"

"Oh, Owen. I wish I knew. Lots of people wanted to see your father dead."

The statement stunned Owen. "What people? Why?"

"Contractors. Highway Inspectors. Asphalt layers. Concrete mixers. Back then, West Virginia roads were paved with bribes and kickbacks, and your father was the state's first honest Highway Commissioner. When Eisenhower started handing out Interstate money, people wanted to build roads from no place to nowhere just to line their pockets. But they couldn't buy your dad.''

Owen tried to sort through his mother's information, but it was coming almost too fast to process. From George's drinking and the bridge design, she'd suddenly jumped to his father, with hints of attempted bribes and possibly more. ''Let me get this straight. Are you saying Dad didn't drown?''

The dishwasher sighed and began cranking slowly. ''Oh, Owen. I don't know. They never found his body. Only two people saw him go under. Ray Cantrip and Sammy Earle. And Sammy was the only one who survived.''

''But Mom. Nobody planned the dam break. It was like Buffalo Creek. There are bodies still missing from that too.''

''I know, Owen. Don't you think I know that? I just have…I don't know…a feeling, is all. Your dad was upset the whole week before the dam burst. And I'll never forget Sammy Earle standing there in our doorway, dripping mud. I knew something was wrong before he opened his mouth.''

Owen had replayed that night a thousand times. He remembered his mother's fear-whitened face, hurried hugs, pelting rain, and a terrifying night alone with George before they were told their father wasn't coming home.

''I knew something wasn't right that night,'' Ruth said. ''And now they've found a body.''

''Under the asphalt on Gobbler's Grade. That's high ground. Nobody drowned there.''

''Gobbler's Grade was paved the same time the Eight-Pole Creek Dam broke. It was Chuck Hager's first big job. He bribed an inspector. Maybe others, too. Your dad was outraged.''

''You're saying the body under Gobbler's Grade might be our dad? Is there any reason at all to think he didn't drown?''

''I don't know, Owen. I just don't know. But they never found his body, don't you see? And now this body turns up that must have been shot about the same time.''

''Shot?''

''Sheriff Reader says there's a bullet hole in the skull.''

Owen blinked as if a flashbulb had exploded in his face. ''Good God.''

''After your dad died, the interstate money flowed like water to anybody willing to grease a palm or bribe an inspector. Chuck Hager had more jobs than he could handle. Those fool backhoes and bulldozers he painted were all over the state.''

"Have you talked to the sheriff about any of this?"

"Lord, no. I was hoping you'd look into it. You've had experience dealing with law officers."

"Mom, law officers put me in jail for a murder I didn't commit. That's not exactly the kind of experience that inspires confidence or camaraderie."

"But it's what you do, isn't it? Find out what went wrong? Why things failed? How everything went bad?"

"With structures, Mom. Or networks. Not with people's lives. And we're talking about something that happened thirty-five years ago."

"Your dad had been dead fifteen years when you proved Amalgamated was responsible for the dam failure."

"That was different. It was easy to reconstruct the dimensions of the dam and show it wouldn't hold."

"But you nailed Amalgamated. It was fifteen years later and you nailed them good."

Owen couldn't remember ever refusing his mother anything. And he knew he wouldn't start now. But he didn't want to get her hopes up, either. "It was the mid-seventies, Mom. The environmental movement was in full swing. People were ready to convict the coal companies. And fifteen years is a lot less than thirty-five years. People who were around when Dad disappeared will have died or retired."

"I know it sounds foolish. And I hate pulling you away from your business. But I don't know where else to turn, Owen. George has all those problems of his own. And outsiders take advantage of old people like me."

The dishwasher whined and clanked to a stop. Ruth Allison slapped its side with an open palm and it chugged into its rinse cycle.

God help anybody who tries to take advantage of you, Owen thought. He reached out and squeezed the hand that had just belted the dishwasher. "All right. I'll look into it. If the flood didn't kill Dad, we'll find out what did." He released his mother's hand and held up a warning finger. "There's just one thing, though."

"What's that?"

"Do you want me to find out about Dad before or after I sober George up, save his marriage, fight off the evil harpies, and widen his bridge?"

Ruth Allison rose and patted her son's hand. "Oh, Owen. It's good to have you home."

AFTER HIS MOTHER had gone upstairs to bed, Owen roamed the downstairs, touching and reacquainting himself with the furnishings he'd lived with growing up. The gateleg table in the dining room, covered with crocheted tablecloth and surrounded by stiff wooden chairs whose seats were upholstered with his mother's needlepoint; the ceiling-high corner bookcase filled with carnival glass that belonged to his grandmother; the spool cabinet in the sewing room that his father had found at a back-country auction, which now held columns of spools displaying a rainbow of threads. The only furnishings that he could say for sure had been installed after he had left for college were a nineteen-inch color TV and, in the living room, standing side by side on a marbletop table, wedding pictures of George and Barbara and Owen and Judith.

The sewing room had been Owen's special refuge growing up. It had an overstuffed chair where he used to sit to do his homework and a card table that had always held both his mother's current sewing projects and his current jigsaw puzzle. Now the card table held a half-finished needlepoint of Dorothy, the Tin Woodsman, the Cowardly Lion, and the Scarecrow on the Yellow Brick Road to Oz. A few jigsaw puzzles still sat collecting dust on the shelves under the spool cabinet. Owen could see that the top puzzle was a map of the London subway system. He remembered the puzzles as the battleground of an ongoing war with George, who liked to hide puzzle pieces when Owen wasn't looking. Instead of complaining, Owen made a game of it, trying to figure out which piece was missing and work around it. As soon as he'd successfully outlined the absent piece by surrounding it with interlocking pieces, it would mysteriously reappear and another piece of the unfinished puzzle would disappear. Owen assumed his brother never realized he knew the pieces were being filched, and he remembered the London subway puzzle as a landmark in their cat-and-mouse game.

Owen searched through the stack of records on the shelf under the old 33-1/3 rpm record player, found a few that had once belonged to him, and put on a collection of Patsy Cline's greatest hits. He turned down the volume on "Faded Love" so that it wouldn't disturb his mother and looked through the drawers under the spool cabinet. He found what he was looking for in the top drawer. It was a leather-bound copy of his Ph.D. thesis, "An Investigation into the Failure of Eight-Pole Creek Dam."

His thesis shared the drawer with blank sketch pads, a tablet of graph paper, and two unopened packs of college-lined loose-leaf paper. Owen took his thesis and the graph paper to the overstuffed chair that had been his homework seat. Between the chair, Patsy Cline, and the work facing him, he felt as if he'd never left home.

He made a horizontal line across the center of the top sheet of graph paper, labeling it with the date he'd never forget—June 4, 1962, the date the gob pile of mine leavings heaped across the Eight-Pole Creek Valley had let go, killing thirty-four people including, he'd always believed, his father. He stared at the black line crossing the green graph paper and tried to sort through the other dates he'd need to nail down, the information he'd need to assemble. His approach in investigating structural failures had always been to collect as much information as possible, lay it out in an orderly fashion, and try to make sense of it, to find the weak link, the missing piece, the fact that didn't fit.

With the Eight-Pole Creek Dam, the weak link had been the hundred-year flood. The Amalgamated Coal officials had claimed the '62 flood had been an Act of God, stating publicly that "...there was nothing wrong with the gob pile, except that the Almighty had poured more water behind it than you'd expect in a hundred years." Owen had calculated the dimensions of the dam from old photographs and showed that it wouldn't have held back the high waters of 1925, 1937, or 1942, let alone the lesser rains of 1962.

Local lawyers had taken his thesis and run with it, arguing that Amalgamated's out-of-state officials knew the dam was unsafe even when they were pumping sludge-filled water into the lake behind it. Owen calculated that a safe dam could have been constructed for as little as $40,000, and the lawyers showed that the refuse heap Amalgamated had piled into the valley violated at least three state laws.

Amalgamated's absentee owners agreed to an out-of-court settlement of two million dollars, roughly ten percent of their yearly earnings. The award brought checks for $39,000 apiece to Owen's mother and other survivors, and considerably greater rewards to their local lawyers, who skimmed a third of the settlement off the top. The award also brought unemployment to many local miners. Carrying through on threats they had made before and during the trial, Amalgamated's owners closed down their local mines and reopened old shafts across the border in eastern Kentucky.

The award and Amalgamated's tacit admission of guilt made Owen a hero to half the county. To the other half, miners and people whose livelihood depended on the mines, he was a traitor who had caused the biggest local employer to leave town. Even now, twenty years after the trial and thirty-five years after his father's death, there were still neighbors who wouldn't speak to Owen and shunned his mother.

Owen's thesis contained the names of the thirty-four people who had died when the makeshift dam burst. Bodies of twenty-eight of the thirty-four victims had been found, one floating forty miles down-stream in the Ohio River. The other six bodies, including his father's, had never turned up. Owen copied down each of the names, along with the names of the Highway Department officials who'd succeeded his father and two state inspectors who were convicted of taking bribes to approve the faulty dam.

When he'd gotten as much information as he could from his thesis, Owen rooted around the sewing room for a scrapbook he remembered from his childhood. He hadn't looked at it in over twenty-five years, but it was still in the same place, on the bottom shelf of a bookcase, under a stack of old civil engineering textbooks. The black scrapbook had silver filigree at the edges of the cover and the first page read "June 30, 1946: HAPPINESS AHEAD," in paste-on silver letters.

The second page of the scrapbook held his parent's wedding pic-ture. It struck him now that his mother had been a beautiful woman. Beautiful in the fashion of the times, with full cheeks and a serene expression that reminded him of Ingrid Bergman, but also beautiful for anytime. He didn't recognize the slim young man standing beside her, half hidden by the cascading train of her wedding dress. In Owen's clearest memories, his father wore construction boots, a hard-hat, and a full, open smile. The smile in the sepia picture was tight-lipped and formal, and there were no construction boots or hardhats to trigger Owen's memory.

The next page of the scrapbook held neatly labeled photographs of the wedding party, mostly members of Owen's mother's family. Her father, Owen's grandfather, stared uncomfortably out at the camera from a too-tight tuxedo that encased his slight frame like a sausage skin. He'd died of a heart attack driving a tractor that went on plowing in looping circles until it finally ran out of gas. The field he was plowing had belonged to his father before him. Until Owen had come along, he reflected, jobs had always outlasted the men in his family.

His mother's three sisters had served as bridesmaids, while her two brothers, both wearing army uniforms, had been ushers. The only non-family member in the picture of the wedding party was Sammy Earle, his father's best man, the co-worker who'd been with him the night of the flood. All the wedding party except Sammy, a bachelor, had posed with their respective spouses. Like jobs, marriages had always lasted in Owen's family until he'd come along. His aunts and uncles had taken their troubles to priests instead of marriage counselors. Or they'd lived with them. Owen and Judith had tried neither priests nor counselors, and he hadn't been smart enough, or big enough, to try to live with their trouble.

After the wedding pictures, most of the early scrapbook pages were filled with childhood pictures of Owen and his brother posed with one parent or the other. Owen leafed quickly through photos of George and himself opening Christmas presents, sitting on a Flexible Flyer, feeding ducks at Fleisher's Pond, standing in white first-communion shorts. All the early pictures were neatly organized, lined up in corner mounts, and labeled with the date and occasion in his mother's precise handwriting.

The pages in the back half of the scrapbook weren't organized at all. The binding bulged with loose yellow envelopes filled with unsorted pictures. In the center of the scrapbook, separating the neatly pasted pictures from the helter-skelter envelopes, were a batch of folded newspaper clippings. He unfolded the largest of the clippings, the front page of the *Charleston Gazette* for June 5, 1962. He knew the headline by heart.

HIGHWAY COMMISSIONER, AIDE, LOST IN DAM COLLAPSE

The picture was as he remembered it. It was one of those he'd used to derive the dimensions of the dam for his thesis. Murky water ran through a gap in the jerry-rigged levee. Downstream from the gap, the water surged against the shingled roofs of a half dozen clapboard dwellings. A bulldozer sat on the surviving slope of the levee above the gap. Two huge painted eyes glowered from the cab of the bulldozer at the scoured gouge in the useless embankment.

THREE

The Last of the Least Bitterns

THE ASPHALT ON Gobbler's Grade was shimmering in the noonday sun and swarming with people when Owen returned the next day. Jimmy Joe Cresap was helping a man in grimy blue overalls hook a tow truck up to the spiked backhoe. Two deputy sheriffs harnessed to metal detectors swept them slowly outward in a spiral centered on the shallow grave. Owen remembered running the math in graduate school to prove that a spiral search pattern minimized the distance you had to travel to cover a particular area.

Beyond the deputies, about a dozen civilians were poking straight sticks into the earth in no discernible pattern. Spread out between the road and a stand of white birch trees, they pushed pointed sticks deep into the damp soil, withdrew them, and examined the sticks with varying degrees of interest. Some barely glanced at the withdrawn sticks before they poked again, lurching forward as if limping on too-short canes. Others scrutinized the sticks carefully, some even sniffing the points, before reinserting them. Owen recognized Mary Jewel Robertson wielding a stick at the edge of the birch trees. She wandered in and out of the trees, poking the soil at random intervals, apparently paying little attention either to the stick or the path she was following.

A yellow van with the call letters WSAZ-TV was parked where the sugar-fed bulldozer had stood the night before. The bulldozer was nowhere in sight. A cameraman with a portable battery pack stood beside the van, capturing the search on videotape.

On the other side of the van, a short sandy-haired man with a hint of a potbelly wagged his finger under the nose of the sheriff, who stood with his arms folded, imperturbable as a baseball umpire standing by his decision. Owen approached the pair, stopping far enough away so he wouldn't interrupt, but close enough to hear what was being said. The sandy-haired man was complaining that the commotion was costing his company five thousand dollars a day and demanding that the sheriff find the vandals who had spiked his equipment. The sheriff's Mounted Police hat tilted forward to shade his face so that Owen couldn't make out his expression, but he barely moved through the finger-wagging diatribe.

The man's finger ran out of steam. He lowered it and said, "Goddamn it, Thad. You've got to do something."

The thin whine in the man's voice struck a chord in Owen's memory, and he recognized the pleader as Eddie Hager, who George said had taken over Hager Construction from his father.

Without unfolding his arms, the sheriff scratched at his biceps. "Let me set you straight on my priorities, Eddie." He stopped scratching and raised his index finger. "First off, there's been a murder here. That's my number-one worry. If my people find something that points to your spiker, we'll pursue it. But I'm not going to compromise a crime scene just so you can pour your asphalt a little faster."

"My God, Thad. Your deputies have been poking around for two days now. You've got civilian volunteers tramping all over the berm and the woods. If that's not compromising the scene, I don't know what is."

"The people want to help, Eddie. If they weren't poking sticks looking for anything else that might be buried here, they'd be standing around gawking. Put 'em to work and we'll all be done faster."

"If you kept them the hell away, I could get on with my work."

The sheriff tightened the cinch on his Mountie's hat. "You telling me how to do my job, Eddie?"

"I wouldn't do that, Thad."

"I'm right glad to hear that, Eddie. Because if you were telling me how to do my job, I might start fretting that I'm not doing it right. I might start worrying over every little detail, taking my time, making sure I don't miss anything. Maybe do a few things twice, just to be sure. That could take some time. Could be quite a while before I finish here and you're spreading asphalt again."

"Oh, for shit's sweet sake." Eddie Hager turned away from the sheriff and charged off past Owen, giving no sign that he recognized, or even noticed, him.

The sheriff watched Eddie Hager go, then turned his eyes on Owen. His right eye, which had a starburst of wrinkles at its corner, seemed to lag the left eye in focusing on Owen's approach.

Owen shifted the manila folder he was holding into his left hand and introduced himself.

The sheriff's handshake was firm and dry. "You're George Allison's brother," he said. "You were out here last night. See anything unusual?"

Owen shook his head. "We were too busy dodging buckshot."

The sheriff nodded. "Jimmy Joe said he was a little quick on the trigger. That's not like him. He's usually cool as a well digger's behind. His boss has everybody jumpy, though."

Owen fingered the manila folder. "That's not why I came up here. My mother..." He knew it was going to sound strange, but there was no easy way to say it. "My mother thinks the body you found here might be my father."

The sheriff squinted under his Mountie's hat. "Thought your dad died when the Eight-Pole Creek dam let loose."

"That's what I thought, too. But they never found his body. And the dam broke about the same time that this road was going in. My mother thinks there might be a connection."

The sheriff pushed his Mountie's hat back on his head, uncovering a long forehead and a receding blond hairline. With the hat pushed back, he looked less like a drill sergeant and more like a thoughtful professor. "Any reason she thinks that?"

"She said Dad had a lot of enemies because he wouldn't trade state contracts for bribes."

"That was some Highway Department back then. Your dad stood out like a silver dollar in a dung heap. But you don't murder a person just because he won't take a bribe. Not when you can go down the hall and find a bribe-taker behind every other door."

Owen shrugged. "The missing body has always left Mom wondering. I think she just wants some kind of closure."

"'Closure.' Now there's an upstate word. Just what is it you'd like me to do?"

Owen handed him the manila folder. "My dad's dental records are in there, along with his weight, height, and medical history. I'd like you to check it against the body you found. See if there's a match."

The sheriff leafed through the papers in the folder. "Easy enough to do. Might take a day or so, though. You're the one blew the whistle on Amalgamated, aren't you?"

"I thought I was getting back at Dad's killers. Now I'm not so sure."

"My brother-in-law hasn't worked since they shut down."

Owen sighed. It wasn't the first time he'd heard that complaint.

The sheriff rolled the manila folder into a tube and slapped it against his palm. "Hell, it's not your fault. He's so lazy he leaves his fly at half-mast so he won't have to unzip. The trip to the welfare office is closer than the mines across the river. You did the right thing, shutting them down."

"Appreciate your saying so. And thanks for—"

"Over here, everybody. Over here," a voice cried out at the edge of the birch trees.

The cameraman began running toward the sound of the voice, checking his viewfinder as he went. The civilian searchers uprooted their sticks and crowded around, while the two deputies unbuckled their metal detectors and hurried toward the trees. Owen and the sheriff joined the stampede.

Owen followed the sheriff to the center of the crowd, where Mary Jewel Robertson, flushed and excited, pointed to something at the edge of a small puddle of standing water.

Mary Jewel's backpack bounced as she bobbed up and down. "Look here. Look here."

Owen peered over the sheriff's shoulder. Mary Jewel was pointing at a dilapidated nest filled with four small brownish eggs.

"It's a red-backed bittern's nest," Mary Jewel said.

"What the hell, Mary Jewel," the sheriff said. "We're not on some damn field trip here."

"It's the rarest of the least bitterns," Mary Jewel said. "It's an endangered species."

"It's no wonder it's endangered if it's way the hell up here." Owen knelt and examined the nest, which looked disconnected from its surroundings. "They usually nest along the river."

"That's right," the sheriff said. "The bittern's a marsh bird, isn't it, Mary Jewel?"

"We've had a wet spring," she answered. "It's damp all over. That's a bittern's nest all right."

"A little bitty bittern," said a woman wearing a quilted vest.

"That's what makes it rare," Mary Jewel said. She tilted her head back and looked up at the sheriff. "Well, Thad Reader. I'd say your duty is clear."

The sheriff tilted back his Mountie's hat and scratched at his receding hairline. "How's that, Mary Jewel?"

"Why, stop the road building, of course. This here's an endangered species."

The sheriff took a handkerchief from his pocket and wiped the sweat from his forehead. "Mary Jewel," he said, refolding the handkerchief carefully. "I've got a dead body that needs to be identified. I've got a bunch of vandals running free and spiking construction equipment. I've got a tax-paying contractor who thinks I ought to find those vandals. I've got an election coming up in November. And I've got a lot of voters who think all incumbent sheriffs are crooked 'cause that's what they see on TV." He pocketed the handkerchief. "Now, with all that, I'm not about to reroute a freeway just because some fool bird got lost and couldn't find a riverbank."

Mary Jewel's face flushed crimson under the blue headband that confined spikes of her gray hair. "Well, we'll just see about that," she said, stomping off through the crowd.

The civilian volunteers dispersed and the two deputies retrieved their metal detectors and adjusted each other's harnesses.

"You know," Owen said to the sheriff, "my brother and I saw that woman riding her bike down from here last night."

"Mary Jewel? You reckon she spiked Hager's backhoe?"

Owen shook his head. "George didn't think that was her style. No TV cameras around, for one thing. Wouldn't surprise me, though, if she planted that nest."

Mary Jewel had retrieved her bicycle and stood talking to the TV cameraman.

"She'll make the six-o'clock news with her little discovery," the sheriff said.

Owen smiled. "I'll bet you right now there's a homeless bird looking for that nest down by the riverbank."

"Price of fame," the sheriff said. "Mary Jewel probably figures he'll line up at the welfare office like the rest of the homeless."

ON HIS WAY BACK from Gobbler's Grade, Owen saw that downtown Barkley was nearly empty of people and that once-familiar landmarks had changed or disappeared. The Keith-Albee Theater, where he'd ushered and changed the marquee every Thursday night, was now a multiplex; Bailey's Cafeteria, where his mother had treated them to fish dinners every Friday, had become a Burger King; the corner of Fourth and Adams, where he'd had his first traffic accident, was part of a pedestrian mall.

A few of the downtown storefronts were boarded up, victims of the exodus to a big new shopping mall on the road between Barkley and Charleston. Ashbury's, where he'd bought his first sport coat, was closed, and Charley's Place, where he'd used a fake ID from George to buy his first drink, had evidently changed its name to the Bottle-Cap Bar before shutting its doors for good. He remembered Jake Ashbury, who took such care and pleasure in fitting him that Owen had put off buying suits until he came home to West Virginia just so he could visit Jake's. And Charley Anderson, the black Korean War Vet who made sure all the drunks had a safe ride home at closing time, even if he had to drive them himself. Owen wondered if they'd seen failure coming. Had it been like a sudden traffic accident? Or like a lingering cancer that tortured them for years before killing their businesses? For the sake of his friends, he hoped that it had struck quickly, and that they'd managed to salt away enough to retire comfortably.

Owen felt pangs of regret for the displaced friends missing from the stores and streets of his hometown. But he found he felt little for the stores and streets themselves. The places had changed, and so had he. His memory registered the once-familiar sights, but the changes blocked any emotional response. He felt no more for the altered landmarks than he might for a remembered but meaningless TV jingle.

Owen headed out of town along the river road, looking for a place he was sure could still charge his memory, Sammy Earle's home on the banks of the Little Muddy River. Sammy had worked with his father, and was with him the night he disappeared. And Owen remembered playing hide-and-seek in Sammy's overgrown yard and fishing off Sammy's pier with his father and brother. He wasn't sure of the address because his mother or father had always driven him there, but he knew he'd recognize the grounds on sight. He spotted a familiar wall of hedges and slowed his mother's Toyota when a scene in front of a dilapidated house caught his eye. A spare white-haired man wearing a navy-blue windbreaker and gray corduroy cap was using a retractable tape measure to record the height of the crumbling stone steps leading to the two-story house. A bent older man in a frayed cardigan stood hunched over a wooden cane watching the measurement.

The white-haired man was so short he had to stretch to reach the porch with his tape measure. His height and the precision of his movements triggered Owen's memory, and he parked his car and approached the two men.

The man with the cane watched Owen approach, but the white-haired man went on taking measurements and jotting figures in a tablet fastened to a clipboard.

"Sammy?" Owen said. "Sammy Earle?"

The white-haired man squinted at Owen, looking him up and down. A smile creased his weathered face and he retracted the tape measure with a solid *thwack*. "I'll be damned," he said. "It's Wayne's other boy. You've growed a couple of feet and a beard, but I'd know those eyes anywhere."

He shook Owen's hand firmly and turned to his companion. "Feldon, you remember Wayne Allison? This here's his youngest boy, Owen."

Feldon touched the bill of his grimy Cincinnati Reds cap and held out his hand. "Right pleased to meetcha."

"What can I do for you?" Sammy asked.

"I came out to talk to you about my dad."

"Happy to oblige," Sammy said, unleashing the tape measure. "Just let me finish up with Feldon here."

Owen watched as Sammy measured the steps and sketched an iron railing on his pad with small precise strokes of his pencil. He didn't use a ruler, but the lines of the railing and the steps were laser-straight.

Sammy tapped the concrete steps with his level. "Should be able to anchor the railing here and here."

"'Preciate it," Feldon said.

"Can't have you and the missus slipping when these steps get slick." Sammy took Owen by the arm. "Come on next door."

The house next door was surrounded by a maze of hedges and gnarled oak trees that shaded the whole property. "I remembered these hedges," Owen said. "That's how I knew it was you next door. Bobby Cantrip, George and I used to play kick-the-can and hide-and-seek here."

Crickets sang in the shade, reminding Owen of long-dead arguments about fast counts, no peeking, and base-hugging. He started to wander down a narrow path toward a remembered home base when Sammy tugged at his arm. "The house is this way."

The living room of Sammy Earle's home was cooled and shaded by the oaks and hedges outside. An Oriental rug covered the parquet floor, and photos of bridges in various stages of construction hung on one wall. Sammy had just settled in an easy chair and gestured for Owen to sit on the sofa when a slim woman with gray close-cropped hair appeared in the doorway. Owen judged that she was closer to his age than to Sammy's. She carried herself with the air of a woman who had once been beautiful and was still beautiful to someone.

Sammy stood. "Elizabeth, this here's Wayne Allison's boy Owen. You wouldn't remember Wayne. He was before our time together. Owen, this is Elizabeth Jackson."

Elizabeth smiled. "Pleased to meet you, Wayne Allison's boy. Can I get you something to drink?"

"No, that's all right."

"Better let me bring you something. When Sammy settles in that chair and talks about people that were before our time together, you're in for a long listen."

"Tea, then. Thank you."

Sammy watched Elizabeth leave, then eased himself back into the overstuffed chair. "How's your mom?"

"Seems fine as ever." Owen scratched at his beard, hesitated, then decided to plunge right in. "That body up on Gobbler's Grade upset her. She thinks it might be Dad."

Sammy shook his head. "Not a chance. Ray Cantrip saw him go under. Black water just swallowed him up."

"Mom says you're the only one Ray had a chance to tell about it." Owen took a notebook from the pocket of his sport coat. "I've never heard a firsthand account of his story."

Sammy ran his tongue around the inside of his mouth, then began. "The storm was a real toad strangler. When we got word the dam broke, your dad and I took a Highway Department pickup and drove out to see if we could help."

Owen interrupted to ask, "About what time did you leave?"

"Around four-thirty in the afternoon, I guess. It was just before quitting time. By the time we got there the water was way over its banks. Chairs, tables, outhouses, uprooted trees, anything that wasn't nailed down was running with the river. Your dad organized a sandbag brigade and I took over one of Chuck Hager's painted bulldozers."

Sammy pulled himself up to the edge of his chair. "I lost sight of your dad for a while. Maybe fifteen minutes went by before I crested a little rise and Ray Cantrip come running up to me, out of breath and babbling. I had to work the story out in little pieces. He said a little boy had ridden a tabletop into a barbed-wire fence. Your dad tethered himself to a fence post with a rope and was edging his way into the floodwater to get at the boy when the posts ripped loose. Your dad, the boy, and the barbed wire all went down the river.''

Owen fought to shove aside the image of his father shackled by barbed wire in a raging river and tried to focus on the notebook in his lap. ''There's no chance Dad made it out?''

''Don't see how. That river was running too fast to give anybody up.'' Sammy seemed to stare through a picture of a highway bridge on the opposite wall. ''It's a damn shame. Your dad was the finest road builder ever to come down the pike. Used to lay out roads by dead reckoning. Hardly ever touched a transit. He'd just hop in his jeep, yell 'Follow me, boys!' and bust off next to a creekbed. We'd lay the road right in his tire tracks.''

Elizabeth returned with a tray holding a teapot, a plate of lemon wedges, and three mugs full of hot tea. She set the tray on the coffee table in front of Sammy and took a seat on the footstool next to his chair.

''Thanks, darlin','' Sammy said. He lifted his pink mug, which had two round eyes flanking the handle and bore the logo of Hager Construction. ''Except for your brother George,'' he said, ''there's nobody left in the Highway Department who cares a damn about roads. Hell, the woman running the show now would rather build birdbaths.''

Sammy sipped his tea and continued. ''You know, there's still spots in the Mingo County hills where roads get so muddy after a bad storm, folks can't make it out. Well, they were scheduled to pave those roads last year when somebody found a nest of rare old spotted owls in one of the hollows. Stopped the road right in its tracks. Now the folks are living with muddy ruts so the owls don't get any rarer.''

''I saw something like that today,'' Owen said. He described Mary Jewel's excitement over the bittern nest and offered his theory that the nest had been transplanted.

''But that's awful,'' Elizabeth said. ''What will become of the poor bird who built the nest?''

''Maybe he could get a room at the Holiday Inn,'' Owen said. ''Then they could offer to let people take the suite with the bittern.''

Elizabeth groaned and said, ''I think you've got it backwards. It's 'take the bitter with the sweet.'''

Sammy ignored their exchange. His face had tightened at the first mention of Mary Jewel's name. He spat it out, saying ''Mary Jewel Robertson. Her and that Fox woman in the Department of Transportation. Now there's a pair to draw to. Give them their head and they'll have us all slogging to the welfare office up to our ears in owl shit.''

"They're not that bad," Elizabeth said.

"The hell they're not." Sammy set his mug down so hard the lemon wedges bounced on their plate. "Now you know I love animals as much as the next man—so long as the next man isn't Walt Disney—but you got to put people first. Trouble with those two women is, they got no sense of proportion. Hell, I never knew a woman who did.''

Elizabeth straightened on her stool, extended her little finger, and shook it under Sammy's nose. "That's because you men are all the time telling us a dick the size of your pinky measures eight inches.''

She blushed and returned her hand to her lap. "Excuse me," she said to Owen. "But he says things like that about women just to get my dander up.''

"It's the truth, though," Sammy said. "Hell, we got real environmental worries in this state. I mean, we got strip mines, dams that won't hold water, bone piles that still burn sulfur, and chemical runoff that'll rot your socks. But that woman in the Transportation Department worries about owl sanctuaries and biodegradable traffic cones.''

Owen laughed. "Biodegradable traffic cones?''

"Oh, yeah," Sammy said. "Now there's a combination that's about as useful as whitewalls on a wheelbarrow. The Fox woman figured that if she got biodegradable traffic cones they wouldn't clog the landfills when the state was done with them.

"Well, you can imagine what happened. After one wet West Virginia winter, all the cones pitted, tilted, and turned the color of rotting pumpkins. Everyone of our construction sites looked like a witches' graveyard.''

"You've got to be kidding," Owen said.

"It's true, so help me God," Sammy said. "They tried to hush it up, but you can ask your brother about it. Cost the state millions.''

Owen shook his head in disbelief. He could see that George would have a hard time working with a woman responsible for such a fiasco.

Sammy waved his hand, as if dismissing the million-dollar losses. "But that don't bother me near so much as what they're doing now. Half our downtown's boarded up and they're building birdhouses instead of roads. You can't jack up the state's economy that way. You know West Virginia's got the oldest population in the U.S.? Older even than those geezer gardens down south. That's because young folks have to leave to find work and old farts like me can't afford to go anyplace else.''

Elizabeth patted Sammy's arm. "Now, Sammy, you know you love it here.''

"That I do. That I do. That's why it pains me to see them trade highways for high-minded horseshit." Sammy pointed a nicotine-stained finger at Owen. "Your dad never would have stood still for it. And you and George shouldn't neither.''

BACK HOME IN HIS sewing-room sanctuary, Owen broke out his graph paper and added the few facts he'd gleaned from Sammy Earle. The dam had burst at 4:05 p.m., and Sammy said he'd left the office with Owen's father around four-thirty. That all made sense. Ray Cantrip must have left about the same time, since he helped organize a sandbag brigade. If his father really had been shot and buried on Gobbler's Grade, though, either Ray Cantrip or Sammy Earle had lied about the drowning. Owen found it hard to believe that either of the two men would lie. What would they have to gain? Ray Cantrip had been Owen's scoutmaster, and Sammy had been his father's best friend and best man.

While Owen was staring at the spare chronology he'd logged on the graph paper, the doorbell rang. The sheriff was on the front porch. "Is your mother home?" he asked, fingering the manila folder Owen had given him at Gobbler's Grade.

Owen stared at the folder and swallowed hard, trying to clear the taste of dread from his mouth.

"It's all right," the sheriff said. "It's not what you're thinking.''

"Who is it, Owen?" his mother called, coming downstairs from her bedroom. When she saw the sheriff, she stopped, gripping the banister.

The sheriff took off his Mountie's hat and stepped inside the house. "We've identified the body," he said, moving to the foot of the stairs. "It's not your husband, ma'am.''

He handed the manila folder to Owen. "Your worries got me to thinking, though. Your dad wasn't the only body missing after the flood. I got me a list and went through it.''

Owen's mother sat down on the stairs.

"Turns out the dead man was on the list," the sheriff said. "Fellow name of Cantrip.''

"Oh, God," Ruth Allison said. Owen moved to the staircase and put his arm around his mother's shoulder.

"You know him, ma'am?" the sheriff asked.

"He worked for my husband."

"Any kin still living?"

Ruth's face went pale and one hand fluttered near her chest. "His wife Dolores. She's in a rest home in Mingo County. And there's Bobby."

Owen took his mother's hand to still the fluttering. "Bobby's their son. He and I went to high school together. I hear he just moved back to West Virginia. Over in Huntington."

"I better notify the wife," the sheriff said. "What's the name of the rest home?"

"Dolores only understands half of what you tell her, if that," Ruth Allison said. "Best you tell Bobby and let him break the news to his mother."

"I've been meaning to look Bobby up anyhow," Owen said. "I'll take care of it."

"I'll drive if you like," the sheriff said.

"It's all the way to Huntington."

"I don't mind. Part of my job, notifying the next of kin." The sheriff put his hand on the doorknob. "Hope you don't mind my asking, ma'am, but did your husband own any firearms?"

Ruth Allison's shoulder stiffened under Owen's hand. "Wayne? A couple of hunting rifles. They're put away in the attic."

"But no pistols?"

"No."

The sheriff opened the door and put on his Mountie's hat. "We better get going if we want to make it back at a decent hour to see the wife."

Ruth Allison patted Owen's hand. "I'll be all right, Owen. You go with the sheriff. Stop by on your way back if you need help with Dolores."

The sheriff cinched his hat tightly around his chin.

Owen was reluctant to take his arm from around his mother's shoulder. He wanted to ask why she'd thought the body under the asphalt might be his father's and how his father had gotten along with Bobby Cantrip's dad. Mostly, though, he wanted to ask her why she'd lied about the pistol that his father had always kept in his sock drawer.

FOUR

SHERIFF THAD READER whipped around the winding country roads with the assurance of someone who wasn't subject to speed laws but still respected the laws of centripetal force. After surviving the first two hairpin turns, Owen relaxed and leaned into the curves. "Breaking bad news to the next of kin can't be a pleasant business."

"Goes with the territory."

"I don't see that you'll learn anything from Bobby Cantrip. He was only ten when his father was killed. Same age as me."

"Almost always learn something. Never sure what till after." The sheriff downshifted into a curve. "Sometimes not even then."

Owen wondered how much the sheriff had learned in his mother's living room. Had he seen through her lie about the gun? "Why all the interest in a thirty-five-year-old murder?"

"Made the front pages of the newspaper. Big local mystery. People expect you to solve it, just like the TV lawmen."

"Seems like people'd be more worried about current crime."

"There's no statute of limitations on murder. It's always current."

"Coming in thirty-five years late, though, it has to be tough to pick up any kind of trail." It was the same problem that had worried Owen when he thought the body might be his father's.

"We'll see. There are bound to be a few people around who still remember Ray Cantrip."

"Have you seen a lot of murders?"

"Don't get that many. Those we do get mostly solve themselves. Bar stabbings with a dozen witnesses. Wives who shoot their husbands and want to tell the world why. Nothing that says 'Reelect Thad Reader.'"

"So you're worried about reelection?"

"Always."

"Tough competition running against you?"

"Small county like ours, anybody with a pretty face and a copy machine's tough competition." The sheriff tilted his Mountie's hat backward and scratched his forehead. "Used to take a pot of money, too. Back when Jack Kennedy was campaigning, cost him fifty cents a pop to buy a vote in the presidential primary. A vote for sheriff, though, that went for as much as five dollars. Difference was, the sheriff had jobs to give away back then and people wanted work."

The sheriff shook his head. "County budget's so strapped now, I can't even afford to buy my wife's vote. And people'd rather go on the dole than take a county job. It's not like you're beholden to anybody if you're bellying up for givement money."

The sheriff skidded around a freeway ramp and sped by a Corvette whose driver left the fast lane when he saw the patrol car bearing down on him. After overtaking a clump of freeway traffic, the sheriff slowed to sixty-five and held that speed.

Owen laughed. "You were going faster on the backwoods curves."

"Nobody to see me there. I'll hammer down again when we leave the county."

The sheriff's head swiveled slowly from side to side as he drove. "You're watching my right eye," he said to Owen.

"No, I'm watching you adjust for it."

"Same difference." The sheriff tucked his right thumb under his index finger and flicked it against his right eyeball as if he were shooting a marble.

Owen winced as the thumbnail clicked against the surface of the eye.

"Glass," the sheriff said. "Fragged by a grenade in Vietnam. Took out two guys standing next to me."

"It doesn't match your other eye."

"Doesn't quite fit, either. I got potluck from the spare parts at the field hospital. Never had it replaced, though. I keep it to remind me how lucky I was. Remind others, too. There's folks in the deep hollows think I can see into their hearts with it."

"It pays to advertise." Owen watched in the rearview mirror as traffic clumped up behind them, afraid to pass the squad car. "How long were you in Vietnam?"

"Lost my eye a month before my year was up."

"Get caught in the draft?"

"Hell, no. I was teaching high school over in Mullens. History, Civics, coached JV football. Marines came to the school recruiting our seniors. Made it sound so good they landed me and two of our football players. I'm the only one made it back."

"But you didn't go back to teaching."

"Truth to tell, it was me recruited those two senior boys. I figured I'd done enough damage to the next generation."

"They might have gone without you. Lots did. West Virginia lost more men per capita than any other state."

"You get called up?"

"No. I rode out a graduate school deferment."

The sheriff trained his glass eye on Owen. "Smart."

The eye seemed to penetrate Owen's being. He could understand why county residents might feel the sheriff's right eye could see more than his left.

"So what brings you home?" the sheriff asked Owen.

"Just visiting."

"Come all of a sudden? Or you been planning it for sometime?"

Something in the sheriff's tone made the question seem like more than idle conversation. "Had a break in my work," Owen said, not wanting to admit his mother had called him after the body had been uncovered on Gobbler's Grade.

The sheriff turned his glass eye on Owen again. "Tell me about the other night on Gobbler's Grade. What did you see there?"

Owen recounted the events of his first night home, from ducking Jimmy Joe's buckshot on their way up Gobbler's Grade to bumping Mary Jewel Robertson on the way down.

After Owen finished, the sheriff asked, "Was Mary Jewel carrying anything on her bike?"

"Just a backpack. Nothing else."

"Any idea what was in the backpack?'

"No. But I remember it clanking when she got into George's car. Why do you ask?"

The sheriff blinked both eyes and swiveled his head toward the road. "Eddie Hager's gas tanks weren't the only thing to get spiked that night. Eddie had no sooner started his roadwork again when one of his boys took a chain saw to a spiked tree. Chain whipped loose and ripped into the fellow's arm. Looks as if he may lose it. Lose the use of it for sure."

"Pretty extreme protest just to stop a road widening."

"Eddie's shut down again while they look for more spiked trees. Kind of ups the ante in the whole game. I want to find the spikers. Give them a little time behind bars to ponder legitimate forms of protest."

It wasn't the first time Owen had seen principled opposition slip through unreason into fanaticism. But it always baffled him. "You think Mary Jewel might have spiked the trees?"

"She denies it. And she's never done anything like that before. But she's been getting pretty feisty lately. Courting the TV cameras. Staging tomato-tossing protests. I wouldn't put it past her."

The road signs announced they were leaving Raleigh County and entering Boone County, and the sheriff floored the accelerator and pulled away from the pack of cars. "So," he said, "you and this Bob Cantrip were good friends?"

"The best. We went through grade school and high school together. Lost our fathers at the same time. We thought then they'd both drowned."

Owen remembered their fathers' joint memorial service. He and Bobby Cantrip had served as altar boys at the funeral mass offered by old Father Hampton. When the mass ended, there were no coffins to be interred, and everyone drifted away, leaving Bobby to snuff the candles. Instead, he brought a lit candelabrum and the big black leather missal into the sacristy where Owen was dressing.

Bobby set the candelabrum down, grabbed Owen's hand, and held it over the missal. Then he fished a Boy Scout knife from under his cassock, opened it with his teeth, and ran the blade through the flame of the nearest candle. "Swear we'll be friends till death, Scout." With his white surplice and curly blond hair, he looked like one of those angels that flitted around saints' heads on holy cards. But no angel was ever so wild-eyed.

He ran the thumb of the hand holding the knife over its blade, drawing a thin line of blood. "Swear it. Till death."

Owen tried to pull his hand back, but Bobby held it fast over the open missal. "I swear," he said.

Bobby slashed Owen's thumb with the knife, then pressed his own slit thumb against it. Blood dripped onto the missal page, mingling with the painted red curlicues and ornate Latin letters.

Bobby tore the blooded page from the missal, ripped it in two, and gave Owen half. It was the Our Father, in Latin.

"Till death," Bobby said again. Then he slammed the missal shut and hustled it back to the altar, dripping candle wax all the way.

Bobby always claimed that the next time Father Hampton used the missal for a requiem mass he'd had so much altar wine that he rumbled right past the Our Father without missing it. But Owen had a hard time believing it. The outcome of Bobby's pranks grew more preposterous with each recounting. Itching powder in the jockstrap of an obnoxious outfielder became a team-wide epidemic in the retelling.

Jumbled flashcards in the basketball team's cheering section became an orchestrated display reading up yours. But there was no end to the pranks. And, one way or another, most had involved Owen.

After their junior year in high school, Bobby had talked his way into a job with the local radio station, doing the "Junior Disc Jockey" show six hours every weekend. He called himself the Tripper, and ended each show with a request number billed as "One from the Tripper." It was the first time any of the rest of the kids really paid attention to him. But the job didn't last the summer. The station had promotional records made by a variety of stars who recorded standard answers and left blank spaces for local interviewers to interject questions. The local dee jays would get scripts to follow so it would sound like a live interview. But Bobby would make up his own questions. One Saturday he asked Elvis—or, rather, the record of Elvis—whether it was true he'd diddled Robin Hager on his last trip through Barkley. And Elvis, or the record Elvis, answered, "Yes, I was quite excited about it."

The interview cost Bobby his job and drove a wedge between Owen and Robin, who went from steady dating to an off-again, on-again relationship their senior year before going their separate ways in college.

One of Bobby's pranks their senior year could have landed them both in jail. It was his idea to walk out to the middle of the Fifth Street Bridge wearing a moth-eaten woman's coat and a pair of high-heeled shoes. Owen agreed to follow in his '64 Chevy. When there were no other cars around, Bobby planned to shuck the coat and shoes and duck back into the Chevy, leaving the clothes behind as if their owner had jumped.

They got to the bridge around midnight, and the wind was whipping streamers of rain through the support cables. There was so little visibility that Owen argued they should just leave the coat and shoes without going through the charade of wearing them. Bobby insisted on following his plan, though. He got into the coat and shoes and started walking. Owen gave him a head start and followed in the Chevy. When they could see no other cars on the bridge, Bobby hobbled over to the iron guardrail. Instead of dropping the clothes, though, he grabbed the support cable and climbed up on top of the rail. Then he began swaying and shouting into the rain.

Owen braked the Chevy, shoved open the passenger door, and yelled "Get your ass back in here."

Bobby pretended not to hear. As soon as Owen was out of the car, he could hear Bobby shouting.

"Fuck you, world," he shouted and swayed out toward the river.

Owen grabbed him around the knees.

"Fuck you, world," Bobby shouted again. He let go of the cable and slid down through Owen's arms until his feet caught the bridge ledge on the other side of the rail.

"My God, Scout, hold me."

Owen held tightly to Bobby's waist, but he was still on the other side of the rail.

Bobby squirmed around and wrapped his arms around Owen's shoulders. "Hold me, hold me," he said again.

As Owen wrestled him back over the rail, the big coat buckle caught and something ripped around Bobby's waist. He kicked out and lost one high heel.

Just as Bobby's feet hit the bridge, he kicked off the other high heel and shucked the coat. Owen shoved him in the driver's side of the car, jumped in himself, and hit the gas. They tore away with the passenger door flapping open in the rain.

As soon as they were off the bridge, Owen pulled over to the curb.

Bobby shook with laughter. "Had you going, didn't I, Scout? Admit it, I had you going there."

The next afternoon, newspaper headlines read "DID OWNER OF COAT, SHOES FOUND ON BRIDGE END LIFE?" Crowds lined the riverbank, and the sheriff announced his intention to drag the river. That was when Owen called it off, against Bobby's protests.

"They have to drag," Owen explained. "They can't help themselves. Even if they're ninety percent sure it's a prank, they have to drag. They've got no choice. It's no joke if they've got no choice." He placed an anonymous phone call and admitted it was all a prank. A dumb kid's prank.

Owen watched the sheriff's head swivel as he negotiated the winding backcountry road. He hadn't thought about that night on the bridge in years. He took out his wallet and leafed through credit cards, library cards, and video-club memberships until he found his half of the missal page that Bobby had filched after their fathers' memorial service. Maybe what his dad said about these roads was true. When the turns got tight enough, you met yourself coming back.

OWEN RECHECKED Bobby's address to make sure they had the right place. The frame house would need two coats of paint before it could be described as dilapidated. The front porch was covered with soiled Astroturf, and whatever was supporting the Astroturf creaked and wobbled under their feet. Owen winced for his friend and tried to clear his face of any concern as he rang the doorbell.

The woman who answered the bell needed as much renovation as the house. She wore a tattered gray housecoat and rubber flip-flops and looked as if she was not too pleased to be torn away from the *National Enquirer* she carried. She squinted past Owen at the sheriff's cruiser and waved the tabloid toward the garage at the rear of her driveway, saying, "Bobby rents the room over my garage. But he's not here right now, and I won't let you in 'less you've got a warrant."

"Do you know what time he'll be home?" Owen asked.

"It's Tuesday," the woman answered.

Owen nodded and waited for more.

"He teaches traffic school down to the Y on Tuesday," she said to the sheriff, as if he ought to know that, at least. "You hurry, you can still catch him there."

THE CORRIDOR at the YMCA smelled of liniment and wet sweat socks. A cardboard sign posted outside the door of a small classroom read.

JUST 4 LAUGHS
TRAFFIC SCHOOL

Owen and the sheriff entered the classroom and took seats in the back row. Owen barely recognized Bobby Cantrip, who paced in front of the blackboard wearing an orange fright wig and a red clown's nose. He was going over the answers to a multiple-choice test.

"All right," Bobby said. "How many thought it was illegal to drive barefoot?"

A smattering of students raised their hands.

"Well, you're wrong. This is West Virginia, after all. You can even drive buck-naked if you want to." Bobby pulled the red clown's nose out and let it snap back onto his face. "Just let me know when and where you plan to do it and make sure you've got your license with you."

Bobby paused and pointed a white-gloved finger at the sheriff. "I direct your attention to the rear of the room." Heads turned to look at the sheriff. "And remind you that the best speed-control device in your car is your rearview mirror—with that man in it."

Bobby waved the multiple-choice test to reclaim the student's attention. "All right, last question. Two cars arrive at the same time at an intersection with four-way stop signs. Who goes first?"

A teenager in a black leather jacket two rows ahead of Owen answered, "The car on the right."

"That's right," Bobby said. "Those of you who thought the right answer was the pickup with the gun rack and the NRA bumper sticker got the question wrong." He snapped his red nose again. "But you're likely to live longer than the rest of the class."

Owen joined in the general laughter.

"Okay," Bobby said. "Anybody get all ten questions right?"

The teenager in the black leather jacket raised his hand, as did a short blond woman and a balding man wearing bifocals.

"That's great," Bobby said. "Bring me your tests and certificates and I'll sign them so you can leave first. It may not sound like much of a prize, but think about it. Won't you be happy to be out of the parking lot before the rest of these negligent operators start their engines?"

The sheriff leaned over and whispered an explanation to Owen. "People take this class to get a violation removed from their driving record."

The three students with perfect test scores got Bobby's signature, gathered their belongings, and left the classroom. After they were gone, the rest of the students formed a line in front of the teacher's desk, where Bobby sat stamping forms and signing certificates. He glanced up from his signing a few times to stare at the sheriff. If he noticed Owen at all, he clearly didn't recognize him. Owen picked up a blank form from a stack on a desk in the last row and went to stand at the end of the line.

By the time Owen worked his way to the front of the line, he, Bobby, and the sheriff were alone in the classroom. Owen slid the blank form onto the desk for a signature.

Without looking at Owen, Bobby yelled to the sheriff at the back of the room, "What the hell is this? You guys audited me just last week."

He shoved the form back toward Owen. "You know I can't sign this. You weren't here for the class."

"I only had a small accident," Owen said. "I shouldn't have to take the whole class."

"What the hell's going on here?" Bobby asked, still addressing the sheriff.

"I ran over a beer bottle," Owen said.

Bobby grinned widely. If he didn't recognize Owen's face, at least he remembered the line. "Didn't you see it?" he asked.

"Guy had it under his coat," Owen said.

Almost before the punch line was out, Bobby had left the desk and wrapped his arms around Owen. "Jesus, Scout, I didn't recognize you with the beard. Why don't you give a guy some warning?"

Bobby stepped back. "Let me look at you. Hairline's going, but those killer brown eyes are still there. Handsome as ever, I must admit." He tapped Owen's midsection. "Little pudge down below, though. Probably can't go nine innings anymore. But, hell, you never threw hard enough to work up a sweat anyhow."

Owen reached out and pinched the red clown nose. "At least you haven't changed a bit. I'd know that hair anywhere."

Bobby took a quick breath and pointed at the sheriff, who stepped forward between a row of desks. "What's with the law? They finally got you, huh?" He held up his white glove, palm outward, toward the sheriff. "I don't care what he told you, Sheriff. I was the one who planted the coat and shoes. Me, not him." He pounded his breast once. "Mea culpa."

Bobby positioned himself between Owen and the sheriff and extended both arms as if barring a door. "I was the one who scrambled the flash cards. Me, not him. And I was the one with the fake Elvis broadcast." He dropped to one knee and beat his breast three times. "Mea maxima culpa." He interlaced his white-gloved fingers and pleaded, "This man is innocent. Of those things, anyhow."

Bobby's orange wig shifted as he looked from Owen to the sheriff and back again. "It's not that, huh? Well, if it's about that sixteen-year-old girl, Scout, I'm afraid I can't help you." He rose from his knee and put his hand on the sheriff's shoulder. "But you've got to realize, Sheriff, he was barely sixteen himself at the time."

By now, Owen knew, Bobby's routine should have gotten at least a few laughs. But the sheriff stood silently, hat in hand, and all Owen could manage was a tight smile.

Bobby wound down. "This isn't just a friendly visit, is it?" He stepped backward and took off his orange wig, revealing a sparse gray crew cut. "It's Mom, isn't it?" Without the wig, he looked a foot shorter. "Something's happened to Mom, hasn't it?"

Owen stepped forward and took his arm. "No, Bobby, your mom's all right. It's about your dad..."

BOBBY SAT IN the rear of the patrol car on the drive back to Barkley. "You're sure it was my dad's body?" he asked after they got underway.

"No doubt about, it. Dental records match," the sheriff said. "Let me ask you, if you don't mind, what you remember about the night your father disappeared.''

"It was a long time ago," Bobby said. "There was thunder and lightning. Lots of noise. I remember Dad tracked a lot of river mud into the house and he and Mom argued about it. She spent a lot of time vacuuming it up.''

"Your folks argue a lot?" the sheriff asked.

"How much is a lot?" Bobby asked. "They never came to blows. I have more arguments with the state over my course material." He tapped Owen on the shoulder. "They won't let me do the beer-bottle joke.''

Bobby slid forward and let his hands dangle over the front seat between Owen and the sheriff. "You've probably got some good stories I could use in class," he said to the sheriff. "What's the dumbest excuse you ever got from somebody you ticketed?''

The sheriff smiled. "Funniest I remember is a guy I pulled over for DUI. He'd been weaving all over the road. When I ask him for his license, he hands me a rolled-up piece of tinfoil and says, 'Perhaps this silver bullet will let you know who I am.'''

"That's good," Bobby said. "I can use that. Did he have a license?''

"No. Lots don't. I'd guess maybe a third of the DUIs we collar don't have a valid license. The guy with the tinfoil was a caution, though. Back in the station he blew a point two-eight on the Breathalyzer and then turned a perfect standing back flip in front of the booking camera.''

"That reminds me. Hear about the blonde who got pulled over for speeding?" Bobby asked. "She looks in her rearview mirror, sees the approaching officer unzipping his fly, and says, 'Oh, no. Not another Breathalyzer.'''

Owen shook his head. "They probably won't let you tell that in class, either.''

"You know it," Bobby said. "Humor is dead in this country.''

A NURSE IN A starched white uniform and nubby gray cardigan led the sheriff, Bobby, and Owen through the back corridor of the county home, which smelled of fresh green paint and was littered with abandoned walkers and gurneys. The nurse stopped at a closed door, knocked once, opened it, and stepped aside. Bobby's mother sat in a wheelchair in a narrow, dimly lit room, staring out the single window into darkness. When Bobby turned the wheelchair to face the room, the woman's appearance shocked Owen. Her once red hair stuck out from under a shower cap in sparse gray wisps, and she seemed to have shrunk inside a faded blue dressing gown.

Dolores Cantrip pointed a bony finger at Sheriff Reader. "You're not Sheriff Brennan. What have you done with Sheriff Brennan?"

The sheriff retreated along the wall to the edge of a pockmarked sink. "I worked for him, ma'am. He died sometime ago."

"Mom, you remember Owen Allison," Bobby said.

Dolores's chapped lips creased into a thin smile. "Of course. Always liked you, Owen. You were such a good-looking boy. Took after your dad. You should shave that beard, though."

Bobby bent over the wheelchair and took his mother's hand. "They found Dad's body, Mom."

"How could they?."

"He was buried on Gobbler's Grade."

Dolores Cantrip shook her head slowly. "Your dad was never buried."

Still holding his mother's hand, Bobby knelt beside the wheelchair. "He's not buried now, Mom. A backhoe dug him up. We're going to have to bury him properly."

"You said he was buried."

"A backhoe dug him up."

The sheriff stepped forward, holding his Mountie's hat in both hands. "I'm afraid your husband was murdered, ma'am."

Dolores Cantrip's slate-gray eyes turned to the sheriff. "I was expecting Sheriff Brennan. You're not Sheriff Brennan."

"No, ma'am."

"Where is Sheriff Brennan?"

Dolores shifted in her wheelchair. Owen smelled the acrid scent of urine.

The nurse left the doorway and stepped into the room. "I'm sorry, I've got to help Mrs. Cantrip now. I'm going to have to ask you to leave."

Bobby shrugged and kissed his mother's sallow cheek. She patted his hand in return.

As they backed out of the narrow room, Dolores Cantrip called out in a cracked voice, "Owen? I always liked you, Owen."

MOONLIGHT GLINTED off the metal batting cage of the baseball diamond behind the orange brick high school Bobby Cantrip and Owen Allison had attended. Bobby took two more beers from the six-pack between his feet on the portable bleachers and handed one to Owen.

"Sorry you had to see Mom like that. What she said was true, though. She always did like you."

"I liked her, too."

"Dad always liked you, too. You were better than I was at that scouting stuff he was into." Bobby took a long pull at his beer. "Remember how we used to pretend our dads weren't dead? That they had amnesia and would come back someday?"

Owen swallowed his beer without responding. He couldn't remember ever believing his father had amnesia.

"I guess I never really stopped believing Dad might return," Bobby said. "Until you showed up with the sheriff today. But, my God, I still can't believe someone shot him."

Owen recalled his own disbelief when his mother had been sure the body on Gobbler's Grade was his own father. "I know what you mean."

"I mean, really. It's like thinking you grew up in Mayberry, and all the time it was really Peyton Place. Who would want to kill my father?" Bobby leaned forward in the bleachers, cradling his beer between his feet. "I want to find out who did it. Will you help me, Scout?"

"Isn't that the sheriff's job?"

"You saw him. Blind in one eye, and I doubt if he sees very well out of the other."

"I had a long talk with him driving to pick you up. He seems pretty solid to me."

"All the same, how much attention is he going to give to a thirty-five-year-old murder? You and I know all the people Dad knew."

"We didn't know everybody. We were only ten."

Bobby held up his right thumb. "But we were blood brothers. Remember?"

In high school, Owen had always been happy to agree to whatever scheme Bobby hatched on these bleachers. By morning, he knew, it would be replaced by two or three others. But this was different. Still, he couldn't shake the feeling that his own father's death was somehow tied to Ray Cantrip's. Owen matched Bobby's thumb with his own. "Sure, I'll help."

"Good. That's settled." Bobby leaned back and let his legs stretch out over two rows of bleachers. "Jesus, how often did we come here to drink? Seems like two lifetimes ago."

"Seems like just yesterday to me. We still know each other's punch lines."

Bobby curled his lip and produced his best Elvis drawl. "Yes, I was quite excited about it."

"What the hell was that all about anyway? Of all the girls we knew, why'd you pick the one I was going with for your fake interview?"

"Well now, if you were the King, who would you have diddled?"

"It was never the same with Robin after that."

"Fuck her if she couldn't take a joke." Bobby handed Owen another beer. "You were better off with Judith anyhow. Now there was one classy lady. Whatever happened with her?"

"My consulting business went belly-up when I wouldn't tell my clients what they wanted to hear, so I left California to work for the feds in D.C. Judith didn't care to leave the law practice she was building, and we couldn't make a bicoastal marriage work."

"Can't quite see you as a bureaucrat."

"Neither could the head bureaucrats. When my findings didn't support their politics, they banished me to the backwoods. Had me counting buses. Just up the road in Contrary."

"Contrary. What a great name."

"They had five names to choose from, but the city founders couldn't agree on any of them. So they called it Contrary. You'd love the guys in charge there now. They ran a two-bus system, charged the feds for twenty, and claimed they were saving the town with the excess profits."

"My kind of guys, all right."

Owen picked at the label of his Bud Light. "They couldn't keep it up. When the shit hit the fan, it splattered all over me."

Bobby sniffed the air around Owen. "Seems like you cleaned up pretty good."

"Judith helped bail me out."

"See. Robin never could have pulled that off. I did you a real favor by breaking it up."

"Anyhow, I'm back where I started. Consulting in California." Owen didn't tell him that, in northern California, "consultant" was a not-so-secret code for "currently unemployed," and that the code was close to being true in his case.

"Failure and Risk Evaluation. FARE. Right?"

"Right. You remembered."

"Always thought you and I could put together a pretty good slogan. Like, maybe, 'Only the Brave Deserve the FARE.' or 'It's Always FARE Weather.'"

"FARE Exchange, No Robbery." It felt good to be riffing with Bobby again.

"'I stayed too long at the FARE.' No. That doesn't work."

"FARE Enough."

"Too bad you didn't call it Failure and Risk Testing. Now that's an acronym people wouldn't forget." Bobby leaned over and patted his rump. "I could really get behind that."

Owen screwed his face into a mock frown. "'Only the Brave Deserve the FART?' 'It's Always FART Weather?' I don't see that's any better."

Bobby reached out and nudged Owen with his beer bottle. "Well, life just isn't FARE." He puffed out his cheeks and made a loud farting noise.

They beat the bleachers with their hands as laughter resonated between them and built like waves amplifying in the clear night air. Owen knew that their exchange wasn't nearly as funny as they were making it sound, that it would barely rate a smile in the light of day. But he also knew that, right now, the bleacher-banging laughter was therapeutic. For both of them.

When the laughter had subsided to random sputtering, Owen wiped his sleeve across his teary eyes. "But enough about me. What about you? How'd you get back where you started?"

"You mean entertaining the criminal cognoscenti with my rapier wit?"

"I meant back here in West Virginia. I figure you could always get another job."

"What, and leave show biz?"

"Sorry, I didn't mean it as a put-down."

"Hell, it's all right. It's not what I thought I'd be doing either. It probably won't last anyhow. The state's trying to give all its traffic schools to a single bidder."

"Could that be you?"

"Not likely. They've been auditing me to make sure I don't even qualify. I hear this bitch in Charleston has the winner all picked out."

"What bitch?"

"Name's Alicia Fox."

"The Dragon Lady? She's giving George trouble too."

"Then I feel for him. That woman's so tough she rolls her own tampons."

"What did bring you back? I sort of lost track when you left the seminary for the Air Force."

"Nothing seemed to be working out. Mom was failing. I'm all she's got."

"I always figured you wouldn't leave the seminary without pulling the Jesuits' chain pretty good."

"Oh, yeah. There was a cosmic chain pulling, all right. I flushed myself right out."

When Bobby didn't elaborate, Owen said, "So you just mustered out of the Air Force and came straight here?"

"I didn't exactly muster out." Bobby set his beer bottle aside. "They asked. I told."

Owen looked up. Bobby didn't sound as if he were joking.

Bobby half smiled, half shrugged. "I'm gay, Scout."

Owen set his beer down carefully. "Why didn't you ever tell me?"

"I wasn't sure until the seminary. That was the cosmic chain pull. I was willing to be celibate. They weren't willing to let me be a celibate homosexual."

Owen shook his head. "I can't believe I never knew."

"By that time we only heard from each other at Christmas. I couldn't seem to find the right card. What was I supposed to say?" Bobby snapped his fingers and intoned in a singsong voice.

"Jingle bells, jingle bells, jingle all the way,
Merry Christmas, Happy New Year,
By the way, I'm gay."

Owen laughed in spite of himself.

"You okay with this?" Bobby asked.

"Oh, sure, sure." Owen raised his hand and was surprised to find it shaking. "What you do with your genitals is your own business. It's just...You're my oldest friend...And I didn't know."

"You didn't ask. I didn't tell."

Owen drained his beer. He remembered the dismal room over the dilapidated garage. "Are you living with someone?"

Bobby handed Owen the last beer from his six-pack. "No. I get off on mail-order porn videos. No emotional entanglements, and the neighbors don't suspect a thing." He toed the empty six-pack onto its side and raised his eyebrows at Owen. "Of course, I get a hard-on every time I pass a VCR."

Owen grinned. "I can see where that would be a problem."

"Turns out it's not my only problem." Bobby took a deep swallow of his beer. "The real reason I'm living alone is, I not only do the deed that makes Jesus puke, I've got the bug that makes Magic quake."

Owen felt as if he were drowning. He inhaled deeply. "AIDS?"

"I've got AIDS." Bobby nodded toward the six-pack between Owen's feet. "And I'm out of beer." He twisted his mouth in a W.C. Fields imitation. "Godfrey Daniel. It's time to crack your cache." His gravel-voiced mimicry stretched the last word into two syllables: cash-shay.

Owen bent forward. His arms felt heavy, as if he were moving under water. He picked up a beer and tried to twist off its cap. "Shit. Cap won't twist off."

"Lemme see." Bobby took the beer from Owen and squinted at it in the dark. "Amstel Light. My, aren't we putting on airs."

Owen took the beer back, stood, and stepped deliberately down the bleachers toward the batting cage. "Used to be able to do this without a church key."

"A church key," Bobby laughed. "Now that dates you."

Owen lodged the beer cap on a kink in the wire-mesh backstop with one hand and brought his free hand down sharply on the neck of the bottle. Nothing happened.

"Guess we need a new backstop," Bobby said.

Owen raised his hand and brought it down hard again. The bottle neck cracked and gashed his palm. Beer spritzed through the backstop as Owen dropped the bottle and grabbed at his hand. He doubled over, pressing his palm, trying to stop the bleeding.

Bobby hurried down from the bleachers. "Let me look at it."

Owen took a step backward, turned his back on Bobby, and dropped to one knee. "It's okay, I can manage."

Bobby stopped in his tracks.

Owen looked up, still holding his bleeding hand. "Jesus, Bobby. I didn't mean..."

Bobby raised both hands, palms outward. "It's okay, Owen. It's okay."

Owen fumbled in his pocket for a handkerchief. "It's not okay." Why the hell had he turned his back? Was it instinctive? Was he afraid of contamination? "It's not okay. I know better." He felt as if it would be a long time before anything would be okay again. "I shouldn't have turned away. I feel fucking useless."

"Hey, look. I blame the brewery. Maybe we ought to sue. Them and the backstop people."

Owen patted his bleeding palm with the handkerchief. "What was the name of that catcher, used to stanch his cuts in the home-plate dirt to show how tough he was?"

Bobby shook his head. "I don't know. You're the baseball nut."

Owen wrapped the bloody handkerchief around his palm, then

dabbed his knuckles in the dirt. "I'm not feeling very tough right now." He pressed his wounded hand hard against his belt.

"It's okay, Owen."

Owen rose and took a step toward Bobby. "Tell you what. Why don't we drive over to the AllNighter and pick up some peroxide and a real bandage?"

Bobby smiled. "Maybe even a bottle opener."

"That too." Owen stared at Bobby's smile until he saw the boy who'd been his best friend, and was still his oldest friend. He smiled back. "You know, Anderson Appliance is on the way there. He's having a sale. Must be a dozen VCRs in his window."

Bobby grinned. "Multi-orgasmic."

Owen put his free arm around Bobby's shoulder and pulled him close. "That's what I thought you'd say."

"You sure you're okay with this?"

"God, Bobby, don't worry about me. You're the one in trouble. I just wish I could help."

Bobby returned his friend's hug. "Listen, you've got nothing to be ashamed of. Some of my best friends are straight."

FIVE

Polishing Turds

CARDBOARD FILING BOXES stacked three-deep lined two walls of George's office in Charleston and crammed the space under the drafting table. The room smelled of stale tobacco smoke, but Owen didn't see any ashtrays.

"That used to be Dad's drafting table, didn't it?" Owen asked. "This isn't his old office, though."

George sat on a stool at the drafting table. "No, Alicia took his office and moved me in here." He waved at the cardboard boxes. "My stuff doesn't quite fit my new digs."

"Pitch some of it."

"Hell, I can't throw anything out."

"Then take it home."

"Barb's already bitching there's not enough room left in the garage for the cars."

Owen ran his hand over the surface of the antique wood drafting table. Cigarette burns scalloped the left edge where the T-square slid. An image of his father's long, slender fingers came to him. "I remember sitting on Dad's lap at this table while he stamped his approval on rolls and rolls of road plans."

George nodded. "I can tell you, he never would have approved that travesty of a bridge design."

"You approved it then?" Owen tried to keep the disappointment out of his voice.

George shrugged. "I sent the papers to Alicia this morning. Along with an impact report that should give her something to think about."

"It's done then. Stop worrying about it. It's not the end of the world."

"It will be for one or two drivers every year the bridge stands."

A picture of their father wearing a hardhat and holding a roll of highway plans hung on the wall behind George. Owen realized that the picture had shaped his memories of his father. "Any idea why Mom thought the body on Gobbler's Grade was Dad's?"

George shifted on his stool. "She wouldn't talk to me about it."

"Is there someplace in this building where I can find out what he was working on when the dam burst?"

"Why would you want to do that? The body wasn't Dad's."

"Mom says there were threats. Besides, Ray Cantrip worked for Dad. And Bobby's a friend of mine."

George patted one of the cardboard filing boxes. "Alicia cleaned house when she came in. I salvaged some of Dad's stuff. But it's not organized. This place has no institutional memory."

The office door swung open and banged against a packing crate. A woman in a brown suit stood stiffly in the doorway. Her russet hair was pulled back in a severe bun and she clutched a dun-colored report to her chest.

"I'm sorry, George," the woman said. "I wasn't aware you had a visitor."

"It's all right, Alicia," George said. "It's my brother, Owen. Owen, this is Alicia Fox."

Alicia stepped just far enough into the office to shake Owen's hand. "I'd like to see you in my office, George."

"We can talk here."

She wrinkled her nose. "This place smells. You know smoking's forbidden in state offices."

"You didn't come here to tell me that. What do you want to talk about?"

"It's about your report." Alicia glanced at Owen. "It's better if we talk privately."

"It's a public report, Alicia. Owen's a part of the public. Besides, he already knows about it."

"I'll decide when our reports go public, George. And yours isn't ready yet."

The woman reminded Owen of his fourth-grade teacher, Sister Mary of the Upraised Ruler.

"Although your report is commendably thorough," Alicia went on, "it will have to be revised."

Alicia had the same glint in her eye that Sister Mary used to have before the ruler came down on the palm of his hand.

"These accident statistics," Alicia said, ignoring Owen and speaking directly to George, "Strictly speaking, there's no requirement for accident projections in an environmental impact report. Is there, George?"

"You're right, Alicia, there's no legal requirement."

"Well, then," Alicia said, "there's no need to include them, is there? They could mean untold liability for the state." She tapped the report with a long frosted fingernail. "And about these energy calculations. You show no significant fuel savings, even though fewer cars will be using a two-lane bridge."

"It's the congestion," George started to explain, "stop-and-go—"

"I'd like you to recalculate that," Alicia interrupted, smiling.

"My numbers are right," George said.

"Your numbers are just numbers. The other side has numbers, too. Everyone's entitled to their own numbers. We need better ones. In time for Thursday's hearing." She handed George his report. "After all," she lectured, "We don't want Barkley to become another Pittsburgh."

Owen had heard George ridicule the idea of comparing Barkley's pollution to Pittsburgh's, and was surprised when his brother didn't respond. He finally broke the silence himself, saying, "Is that really likely? Barkley would have a long way to go just to become another Charleston."

Alicia ignored Owen's remark. She stepped forward and picked a thread from George's tweed jacket. "I understand your father built that bridge. We'll put the press to work on that angle. 'SON PRESERVES FATHER'S DESIGN'—that sort of thing."

George stepped backward and inhaled deeply. Owen could see that his brother was fighting to control his anger. He imagined the headlines running through George's head.

ENGINEER SON OF WAYNE ALLISON KILLS TWO OR THREE COMMUTERS, SAVES BARKLEY FROM STEEL CITY THREAT. FATHER, COMMUTERS UNAVAILABLE FOR COMMENT.

"It's too bad our father isn't around," Owen said.

Alicia misread Owen's comment and George's silence. "Good, it's settled then. You'll revise the report and polish up the two-lane design for Thursday's hearing."

Alicia turned and started for the door.

"You can't polish a turd," George mumbled.

Alicia turned back. "What?"

George stood up. "It's an old saying of my father's." Owen grabbed George's arm. "Let me go," George fumed. "I want no misunderstanding here." He jerked free. "You can't polish a turd," he repeated. "It means—"

"I assure you I understand what it means." Alicia pivoted on a spiked heel and strode out the door.

George grabbed a half-full cup of cold coffee and gulped it down.

"I think you made your point." Owen patted his brother's back, trying to steady him. "Did our dad really say that?"

"No. Dad said 'you can't shine shit.' But he never would have said it to a lady."

"That was no lady. That was your boss."

GEORGE PARKED HIS Pontiac next to the mailbox at the head of his driveway and retrieved a handful of letters and a few catalogs. Then he and Owen walked down the driveway toward his white frame house. A half-inflated soccer ball lay limply beside the driveway. On one side of the sliding garage door, rows of faded yellow chalk marks stretched upward like dried wheat stalks against the white siding. Another row grew at the other side of the door.

Owen ran his thumb over the nearest chalk mark. "Some sort of outdoor art?"

George stopped beside the soccer ball and leafed through the letters in his hand. "Expandable soccer goal. Billy's first soccer coach complained he wasn't aggressive enough on offense. I made him a goalie by chalking off sections of that door and letting him defend it against my kicks. As he got better and better, I made the goal wider and wider. He finally got to be a pretty fair goalie."

George shouted "Heads up," slammed his foot into the ball, and sent it skimming toward Owen.

Owen caught the ball inches in front of his face. The impact stung his hands.

"Nice stop," George said. "Want to try best two out of three?"

Owen underhanded the ball back to George and crouched in front of the chalked-off goal, flexing his knees. "You'll never get it through the Iron Duke."

George toed the ball from one side of the driveway to the other, readying his shot.

Owen shifted from side to side, cutting off the angle of attack. Whatever gene combination made some men attackers and others defenders, he'd always felt more at home on defense. "Take your best shot," he told George.

George took a quick, graceful step and angled a kick toward the corner of the goal. Owen lunged and deflected it past the garage door.

"You always did have pretty good reflexes," George said. He turned his attention to the mail, swore softly and held up a thick envelope. "Letter here for Billy from Marshall University. He's been talking about transferring out of WVU. I didn't know it had gone this far."

Owen retrieved the soccer ball and rolled it back to his brother. "Maybe he just wrote them for some information."

"Just writing them's a big step for Billy." Another envelope caught George's eye. He opened it and slapped his hand against the letter. "That bitch got my license suspended."

Owen took the letter from his brother. "Alicia?"

"Mary Jewel Robertson. She reported our accident, filed an insurance claim."

"So?"

"If one person reports a five-hundred-dollar accident and the others involved don't file a report within ten days, their licenses are automatically suspended."

"So you didn't report hitting her?"

"Of course not. You were there. The only way that could have been a five-hundred-dollar accident was if her bike were studded with diamonds." George grimaced. "Or if her butt were."

"Can't you tell them that?"

"I could kill the bitch." George slammed his foot into the soccer ball. The ball splatted off the corner of the garage. Two strips of wood siding sprang loose and vibrated. Nails shook, dangled, and dropped to the ground, along with a corner of the siding.

Owen stopped the ball before it rolled into the street. "You must know somebody at the DMV. Tell them what happened."

George limped in a tight circle as if the kick had hurt his ankle. "That'll take time. Meanwhile, the suspension's automatic."

A horn honked and a blue VW hatchback pulled into the driveway. George's wife Barbara got out, hurried to Owen, and took both his hands in hers. "What a surprise. It's good to see you, Owen." A foot shorter than Owen, she raised up on her toes and kissed the air between them. Then she dropped his hands and turned to George. "What happened to the garage?"

George stopped limping and stood still, a pained expression on his face. "I'll fix the damn garage."

"While you're at it, get your boxes out. There's still not room enough for two cars."

"Your car fits. Mine's okay in the street."

"Tuesday is garbage-pick-up day. If you can't empty those boxes, I will."

"Barbara, those boxes are valuable to me. Some of them are Dad's."

"Well, they look like trash to me."

"Why don't I take Dad's stuff back to Mom's?" Owen said. "I'd like to look through it anyhow."

"What'll your mom do with it?" Barb asked.

"Save it for our biographers," Owen said.

George held up the thick college envelope that had come in the mail. "Why didn't you tell me Billy was applying to Marshall?"

"You've been too busy to ask. You can't make him an engineer by drawing chalk marks around the WVU campus."

"That's not fair. I've been busy with this bridge business."

"There's always some bridge."

"This one is different."

Barbara picked up the split piece of siding and examined it. "They're all different. I'm tired of hearing about it. Stop dithering and do something about it."

"I did something today. I told off Alicia."

Barbara dropped the siding and dusted off her hands. "That's great. That's a good move. Get yourself fired. Then maybe you'll have time for your family."

As if he'd just remembered Owen was listening, George turned to his brother. "Welcome to Casa Allison."

Barbara stood in front of the garage door, legs planted, one hip cocked toward her husband. "I'm sorry, Owen. Why don't you stay for dinner? You can referee the next round."

OWEN'S NEPHEW Billy joined them at the dinner table. He slouched behind his plate, moving his water glass and the salt and pepper shakers in defensive positions between himself and his father.

"You haven't given engineering a chance," George said.

"Dad, I'm barely scraping by."

"The first year is always the toughest. They're trying to weed out the wannabes."

"Well, they're doing a good job of it."

"You'll catch on," George said. "Remember the tough time you had in the fourth grade? Then with your fifth-grade teacher you could do no wrong."

"It's not like that anymore."

"It's always like that. If you hang in there, your grades will improve." George turned to his brother. "Isn't that right, Owen?"

Owen wiped his napkin across his mouth, considering the question. "Actually, one of the shocks of my adult life has been finding out that nobody cares what my college G.P.A. was."

"You had to graduate to find that out, though," George said.

"I don't hear Billy talking about not graduating," Owen said. "What major do you want to switch into?"

"Poly Sci," Billy said. "I had this great teacher last—"

"Political Science," George interrupted. "That's such a do-nothing, go-nowhere major. You'll never get a job with that on your résumé."

"Doesn't Alicia Fox have a Masters in Political Science?" Barb asked.

George shot her a dark look.

"That's your boss, isn't it?" Billy asked, looking from one parent to the other.

"She's a political appointee, for Christ's sake," George said. "A friend of the Governor. And she's damn near ruined Dad's old Department."

"Speaking of Alicia Fox," Owen said, happy to change the subject. "What's this I hear about biodegradable traffic cones?"

"Now there's an example of sheer imbecility," George said. "She cost the department millions with that hare-brained scheme and has been trying to cover it up ever since. Wasted a year's worth of contingency funds. Managed to hush it up pretty good, though. How'd you hear about it?"

"Sammy Earle."

"Sammy Earle. That old renegade. Is he still around? Remember how the folks used to take us out to his place on the river for birthday celebrations? Is the maze still there?"

"Still there."

"While we're on the subject of birthday celebrations," Barb said, "Billy has one coming up. Billy, maybe you'd like to invite Uncle Owen to go down the Gauley with you and your dad."

"Yeah, sure," Billy said. "Come on along. We do it every birthday. The rapids run really high this time of year. It's a blast."

George offered more wine to Barbara, who declined and glared at George as he refilled his own glass and topped off Owen's. George raised his glass. "Here's to the Gauley River. Didn't you and Bobby Cantrip get an award for saving some capsized kayakers there one year?"

"We only managed to save one," Owen corrected. "One boy drowned."

"Well, it's a lot safer now," George said. "They've got professional guides and equipment and a lot of companies competing for the tourist dollar."

"Sounds like Owen may not want to go," Barb said.

"Oh, hell. He didn't say anything like that," George said. "Come on, Owen. It's a family tradition."

Owen smiled. "In that case, count me in." Maybe seeing the river again would help erase the memory of the clutching hand. Staying away certainly hadn't helped.

THE BARKLEY council chamber, a converted courtroom, was packed for the bridge hearing. Placards reading KEEP BARKLEY BEAUTIFUL dotted the audience, and a banner announcing HELL NO, WE WON'T GROW was draped over the wood railing separating the speakers and council members from the spectators. Alicia Fox and two men Owen didn't recognize sat on a raised platform across from the miked and placarded tables occupied by the council members.

Owen and his mother were lucky to find two seats together toward the rear of the auditorium. Owen looked around for his brother, but didn't see him. He did see Mary Jewel Robertson, who stood on the other side of the wood railing chatting with the council members. She wore a white plaster neck brace and clutched an armful of manila folders close to her quilted vest. Something Mary Jewel said made the head of the council, a balding man wearing a short-sleeved dress shirt and a bright yellow necktie, laugh and point the end of his gavel toward a TV camera draped with a KEEP BARKLEY BEAUTIFUL placard.

"You've got to hand it to Mary Jewel," Ruth Allison said. "Before she got involved with her environmental movement, the only people likely to attend council sessions were the secretary of the League of Women Voters, a few crackpots, and the bare minimum of council members."

"Let's hope the ratio of council members to crackpots has improved," Owen said. "And that we can tell one from the other."

Owen felt a hand on his shoulder and turned to see Sammy Earle.

Sammy doffed his navy-blue beret to Ruth and extended his hand to Owen. "Good to see you both."

Ruth nodded curtly as Owen shook Sammy's hand.

"I declare, this boy's the spitting image of his father. Don't you think so, Ruth?"

"I've always thought so," Ruth said.

"Enjoyed your visit the other day," Sammy said to Owen. "Hope you'll stop by again. I'm always open for business."

"I will. I'd like to find out more about Dad and Ray Cantrip."

"Well, I got to find me a seat before the fur starts to fly." Sammy patted Owen's shoulder and continued down the aisle.

Ruth watched Sammy take a seat with a group of senior citizens. "Why did you go to see that old reprobate?"

"He was with Dad the night he drowned. Why call him a reprobate? I thought you liked Sammy."

"He's pushing eighty and living with a woman who barely qualifies for AARP."

Owen smiled at his mother's characterization of Elizabeth Jackson. "So?"

"So they're not married."

"Well, I hope when I'm eighty I have the energy to chase young chippies who are just starting to draw their social security checks."

"Oh, Owen. Nobody calls them chippies anymore."

"What are they called? Just in case I happen to meet some."

Ruth pursed her lips and shook her head. Then she nudged Owen with her elbow and nodded toward the side of the council chamber. George had just entered, lugging a slide projector under one arm. He opened a gate in the railing and walked up to the head of the council, who was still talking to Mary Jewel.

Mary Jewel and the council chairman ignored George and went on talking. Owen watched his brother shift the slide projector from his right hip to his left hip, trying to get their attention. The council head finally turned from Mary Jewel to George. As he did, Mary Jewel said something that clearly upset George. His face turned crimson and his jaw jutted out. He stepped toward Mary Jewel, causing the council head to move between the two of them.

Owen left his seat and hurried toward the front of the room. As he approached, he could hear his brother say "...nothing but a goddamn fake."

The council head folded his stubby arms across his chest and stood his ground like a blocking back as George sputtered over the man's shoulder at Mary Jewel.

Owen could see that his brother was close to losing control. He stepped over the wood railing and clamped his hand on George's free arm. "Let's back off a little so these people can get their meeting started."

"I'll give her a real injury," George said. But he didn't try to fight free of Owen's grip.

Owen wedged himself between George and the blocking chairman and took his brother by the shoulders. He could smell liquor on George's breath.

"Typical macho driver response," Mary Jewel said.

Owen felt his brother stiffen. "Back off, George," he said again. "This isn't the place. I'll help you set up your slide projector."

George stepped back and handed the projector to Owen. Then he strode to the wall behind the council members' table and yanked down a projection screen, nearly pulling it free from its roller.

The chairman took Mary Jewel's arm and led her to a seat in the front of the auditorium, whispering in her ear as they went.

Alicia Fox joined them as George tested the slide projector by focusing an aerial view of the existing bridge on the wall screen. "You refused to represent the Department at this meeting," she said. "What are you doing here?"

"Providing a little input as a private citizen."

Alicia put her hand over the lens of the slide projector. "We've got to talk."

George switched off the projector. "No, we don't."

"We'll talk now or we'll talk tomorrow at my office," Alicia said. "And it'll have to be my office, because you won't have one."

"You do what you have to do," George said. "I won't shill for your two-lane design."

The chairman gaveled the meeting to order. Alicia glared at George and stalked back to the speaker's platform.

Owen returned to his seat beside his mother, while George stood behind the last row of seats in the rear of the auditorium.

The chairman turned the meeting over to Alicia, who took the podium to explain that the Transportation Department had reconsidered its four-lane design in the light of the environmental considerations and was submitting a two-lane design that would simply reinforce the existing structure without widening it.

This announcement brought loud cheers and a smattering of boos from the audience.

Alicia nodded her acknowledgment of the cheers and introduced a young engineer from George's Design Branch, who unrolled blueprints for the two-lane bridge and taped them to the wall behind the council members.

Owen's mother tugged at his sleeve. "Why isn't George doing this?"

"No stomach for the two-lane design," Owen whispered. "He'll talk later."

Ruth Allison frowned.

The young engineer fumbled with a retractable pointer and retreated to the blueprints he'd taped to the wall, where he spent time talking to the wall, rattling off structural details that could only have been of interest to the contractors, riveters, and the engineer's immediate family. Owen wondered why engineers had so much trouble organizing public speeches. The *Challenger* engineers had one whole day to convince NASA to shut down the ill-fated launch. They had all the evidence they needed to prove that the O-rings lost resiliency in cold weather, but they organized and presented it so poorly that they couldn't stop the disaster.

The engineer finally returned to the podium and held up a thick report that Owen recognized as the one Alicia had carried into George's office. Riffling the pages of the report, he announced proudly that it showed that the design produced no adverse environmental impacts, bringing more cheers from the audience.

Owen checked his watch. Alicia and the engineer had spent fifteen minutes without mentioning traffic patterns or accident rates, and it looked as if they weren't going to talk about either one. He glanced over his shoulder at his brother, who was pacing the rear of the auditorium, shaking his head, and muttering to himself.

Alicia thanked the engineer and introduced the contractor responsible for the bridge renovation, Rudolph Slater of Slater Construction. Slater, a tall man with wavy gray hair, began by saying his firm could easily accommodate the change orders needed to reinforce the bridge without widening it.

Owen's attention began to wander when his mother tugged at his sleeve again. "That's Robin Hager's ex-husband," Ruth whispered. "He left Hager Construction about the time they split up and formed his own firm. Doing quite well, I hear."

Owen watched Slater with new interest. The man exuded an air of slick competence, speaking confidently without referring to notes or the blueprints taped to the wall. He looked older than Owen would have expected Robin's husband to be. But then, both he and Robin had aged over twenty years since they'd last seen each other. He wondered if Robin would look as old to him as her ex-husband did. And whether he'd look old to her.

Slater ended his short pitch by saying he'd be happy to build whatever design the council approved. "The bridge has stood for forty years," he concluded, "and we'll make sure it will stand for at least forty more."

When Slater finished, Alicia returned the floor to the chairman, who opened the meeting to comments from the audience, asking that those wishing to speak fill out a card with their name and affiliation and limit their remarks to two minutes. While some members of the audience scrambled to fill out cards, those who had already done so lined up behind a podium at the front of the auditorium.

The early comments from the audience held few surprises. Developers spoke in favor of progress, wider lanes, and bigger lots. Commuters wanted a wider bridge so they could lower their travel times. A retiree speaking after a commuter got a good laugh by observing that "It don't matter how fast you go if you're on the wrong road." A lawyer recalled the past history of corruption in the Highway Department and asked for a round of applause for the enlightened leadership of Alicia Fox. Neither Owen nor his mother joined in the clapping. Owen glanced over his shoulder at his brother, who looked as if he wanted to rip up the back row of chairs and fling them one by one at the podium.

Homeowners on the far side of the bridge wanted more lanes. Those on the near side wanted less traffic. Sammy Earle took the podium to reminisce about building the bridge forty years ago and observe that trying to force traffic across a narrower bridge would be like "...trying to pour four pounds of potatoes into a two-pound sack." A wispy, white-haired woman recalled how pleasant it had all been when there was no bridge at all. Then she pumped her fist in the air and squeaked, "Hell, no, we won't grow," to loud applause.

A gaunt-faced man in bib overalls with his right arm in a sling took the microphone in his left hand to say "My name's Sonny Blatt. I work for Hager Construction. Or I did until four days ago. That's when I took my chain saw to a tree somebody drove a spike into. Somebody who didn't want us cutting down any trees. Probably somebody here tonight." He rubbed the microphone against his sling. "So I don't see where anything you vote on tonight is worth a pitcher of warm spit. A year ago, right here, you decided that we could build out Gobbler's Grade to four lanes. But for the last year a lot of people, and I see some of you here tonight, have been making it hard for us to do our job. You've been waving signs, throwing tomatoes, making speeches, and spiking equipment to protest something that was decided fair and square."

Sonny Blatt blinked his eyes and looked around as if he'd forgotten where he was. "I just want to say it's some sorry world where people think a tree is worth a man's job." His voice trailed off. "Or his arm." He looked around the auditorium again. "That's all I got to say."

The audience was silent. Then Owen started to clap and applause built slowly as the speaker stepped down from the podium. The chairman broke into the applause with his gavel. When the auditorium was quiet again, he called George's name. Owen could feel his mother grow tense beside him. George strode to the front of the auditorium, explained that he was speaking as a native of Barkley, not as the State Highway Commissioner, and projected his first slide onto the screen behind the council members. The slide showed a row of vertical bars of equal height stretching from the year 1985 to the present day.

"This slide shows that the carbon monoxide emissions on the five worst days of the year haven't changed since 1985," George said.

"Oh, George," Owen's mother whispered. "Nobody cares about numbers."

The next slide showed the spans of the Fifth Street Bridge on a bright clear day. "In fact," George said, "this is a picture of the bridge during the worst air pollution we experienced last year."

Ruth Allison relaxed and smiled. Owen marveled at his brother's ability to perform lucidly with a few drinks in him.

George flipped through two more slides of the bridge in sparkling clear sunshine. "And here are the second and third most polluted days," he said. "So we don't really have an environmental problem here in Barkley. But we do have traffic problems." He switched to the next slide, an aerial view of bumper-to-bumper traffic on the bridge. "This is a typical rush hour." George paused. "But it's not the worst traffic day we had on the bridge last year."

George clicked the slide projector, and another aerial view appeared showing bumper-to-bumper traffic in both directions. In one direction, though, there was a gap in the stream of traffic as three police cars surrounded an accordioned auto impaled on the bridge abutment.

"This is the worst traffic day we had last year," George said. He pushed a button and the image on the screen showed a close-up of the crash scene, with a highway patrolman peering into the smashed window of the mangled automobile.

"Oh, God," Ruth Allison whispered. "That's the Rennart boy's car."

The room was suddenly silent.

"Two people died in this wreck," George said. "It was one of two fatal accidents on the bridge last year. And if you try to run a four-lane freeway into this bridge without widening it, my engineers tell me there will be twice as many fatalities next year."

A woman left one of the front rows and hurried back down the aisle toward the rear of the auditorium, holding a handkerchief to her mouth.

"That's Mrs. Rennart," Ruth Allison whispered. She climbed over Owen and caught up with the woman, putting her arm around her and leading her out of the auditorium.

A gavel sounded. "That's all, Mr. Allison," the chairman said. "Your time is up."

"I only have two more slides," George said.

"I did announce the two-minute time limit earlier," the chairman said. "If we extend it for you, we'll have to do it for everybody." His tone of voice left no doubt that he wasn't about to extend the time limit for anyone, least of all George.

"You gave the Highway Department more time," George said.

"But you're speaking as a private citizen, Commissioner," the chairman said. "Your two minutes are up."

A few boos sounded around the auditorium. Frustrated, George switched off the slide projector and hauled it with him down the aisle, trailing a bouncing extension cord. He turned and stood behind the last row of seats, wrapping the cord tightly around the projector as if he wanted to strangle it.

As the next speaker walked to the podium, the moderator reissued his two minute warning. The meeting has the look and sound of democracy, Owen thought, but it was beginning to feel like a pat hand dealt from a stacked deck.

Two speakers later, the chair called Mary Jewel Robertson's name. Mary Jewel took the podium to a smattering of applause, which she stilled by raising both her hands.

Ruth Allison returned to her seat. "At least Mary Jewel took off her backpack," she whispered. "For her, that's a real fashion statement."

There was someone like Mary Jewel at every public meeting Owen had ever attended, but he'd never learned to deal with their evangelical fervor. He relied on verifiable facts to predict a future that was necessarily couched in probabilities and uncertainties. They seemed to reason from past uncertainties to a future that was bound to be catastrophic if their prescriptions weren't followed. It was like arguing physics in public with Chicken Little. And losing more often than not. Owen wished he were as sure of anything as the Mary Jewels of the world were of everything.

Mary Jewel launched into a rambling discourse that somehow related potholes and a lack of civility to the need for bike paths and control over the rampaging automobile. Owen found it hard to follow and was glad to see that the moderator stopped her when her two minutes had elapsed.

Mary Jewel smiled and nodded at the information that her time was up, but she didn't leave the podium. The chairman called the name of the next speaker, Pluma Wilcox. Pluma stood in the front row and announced, "I yield my time to Mary Jewel Robertson."

"Oh, for pity's sake," Ruth Allison said.

Mary Jewel smiled slightly, lowered her eyes, and nodded her thanks to Pluma Wilcox.

"What an act," Ruth whispered. "That woman's about as bashful as a bulldozer."

Mary Jewel kept smiling and resumed her rambling discourse somewhere near where she had left off.

"That's a game more than one can play," Owen whispered to his mother. He rose and walked to the railing separating the council members from the audience, where he filled out a speaker's card. Before handing it in, he turned and looked for his brother, who was pacing behind the last row of seats, clutching the slide projector in a stranglehold under one arm. Owen held the speaker's card aloft for George to see, using his free hand to point from the card to his brother and back again. George stopped pacing long enough to nod grimly in Owen's direction.

Mary Jewel used her second two-minute stint to remind the audience that the federal government had first contributed funds to building experimental roads in 1893 because bicyclists had complained about ruts. "So you see," she concluded, "we bicyclists are the reason you drivers have roads to run us off of."

The audience applauded, the moderator called time, and the next scheduled speaker rose to yield her two minutes to Mary Jewel. She used the time to remind the listeners of their duty as the planet's caretakers to pass on a clean, unsullied environment to the next generation. "It's our job to speak for the trees and the birds, since they can't speak for themselves." As an example, she cited the plight of the red-backed bittern, an endangered species whose nest she had found on Gobbler's Grade directly in the path of the highway leading to the Fifth Street Bridge.

Owen could see that there weren't many speaker's cards left in the hands of the moderator, and it dawned on him that the man had set aside the cards of Mary Jewel and her cohorts so that they could be the last to speak. If nothing else, his last-minute volunteering had foiled that plan.

Mary Jewel smiled graciously as another speaker yielded her time. "Finally," she said, "it's been insinuated tonight that a two-lane bridge will cause more accidents. In the first place, I don't see how that can be, when the bridge we have now is two lanes. If anything, the faster speeds on a four-lane bridge would seem to me to be more dangerous. But the Highway Commissioner, pretending to speak as a concerned citizen, has brought grisly pictures to convince us that we'll have more accidents."

Mary Jewel took a sip from a plastic water bottle. "Well, excuse me for saying so, but we all know that the driver in those accident pictures had a blood alcohol content that was twice the legal limit. Now, I don't need to tell you that no bridge design—two lanes, four lanes, or even six lanes—is going to stop those kind of accidents. The only design that will work is no lanes.''

The noise of a heavy metal object dropping caused heads to turn toward the rear of the auditorium. Owen looked as well, but he couldn't see the source of the noise.

Mary Jewel waited until she had regained the attention of the audience, then cleared her throat and touched her neck brace. ''Believe me, I know about drinking drivers. A little over a week ago, I was nearly killed by one.''

''Bitch,'' Ruth Allison whispered. Owen started. He had never heard his mother say anything stronger than ''Oh, for pity's sake.''

Mary Jewel stepped back from the podium and the audience stood and applauded. When the applause died down, the moderator called Owen's name.

Owen stood and announced, ''I yield my two minutes to Highway Commissioner George Allison.'' He turned toward the rear of the auditorium, expecting his brother to come forward. But George was nowhere to be seen.

SIX

Swimming in Concrete

THE MODERATOR SMILED at Owen's discomfort. "It appears that George Allison is no longer here," he announced. "Do you wish to yield your time altogether?"

Owen took a last look at the back of the auditorium where his brother had been standing, shook his head, and advanced to the podium.

"My name is Owen Allison," he said into the microphone. "Like my brother, I grew up in Barkley, and like him I'm a registered civil engineer." Owen scanned the sea of faces in the auditorium and focused on his mother.

"As Highway Commissioner, my brother has stayed in contact with this community. He knows the Rennarts, whose son died in that horrible crash he showed you earlier. And I know that, like most of you, he can't drive over the bridge without thinking of the Rennart boy. The accidental death of a young person leaves a hole in the fabric of society and to suggest, as one speaker did, that we should accept some deaths because people drink and drive is harsh and unfeeling." He looked for Mary Jewel in the audience, but couldn't find her.

"Unfeeling," Owen repeated, still searching the crowd for his brother's face. "And to approve a bridge design that adds two fatalities a year to this community's death toll is more than unfeeling. It's irresponsible. It's not only drinking drivers who will die, but also your non-drinking friends and neighbors who just happen to be in the wrong place at the wrong time when the road narrows. And it's all the more irresponsible because the extra pollution from the traffic jams you create will wash out any environmental benefits you might hope to gain. This state has significant environmental problems. But let me tell you, this bridge isn't one of them."

Owen swept his eyes over the crowd again and locked them on his mother. "In my lifetime, West Virginia has had more than its share of catastrophes from poorly built structures. My father was one of the thirty-four people killed when the Eight-Pole Creek Dam burst in 1962. Five years later, forty-six people died when the Silver Bridge between Point Pleasant and Gallipolis collapsed during rush hour. In 1972, the worst flood in the state's history killed one hundred twenty-four people who lived downstream from the Buffalo Creek Dam. All these examples of poor design, neglected maintenance, and human failure cost enough lives to get us national headlines.

"Well, my brother has told you the bridge you're asking him to build will cause two deaths a year. In twenty-five years, that's more deaths than either the Eight-Pole Dam break or the Point Pleasant Bridge collapse. But you won't see any national headlines. Because unless you're unlucky enough to wreck a busful of people, none of the deaths will make page one of the *Charleston Gazette*. They'll happen one at a time, in car wrecks that are only newsworthy to the victim's family and friends. But those deaths will have been preventable. Just as preventable as the deaths at Eight-Pole Dam, the Silver Bridge, and Buffalo Creek. You made Amalgamated Coal and Pittsfield Coal pay for the damage they caused when their dams broke. But tonight you booed my brother for saying he wouldn't build a bridge that would kill two extra people a year for as long as it stands." Owen paused, looking one more time for George's face. "Let me tell you, you should have been cheering him."

Owen relinquished the microphone to a smattering of applause and hurried down the aisle toward the rear of the auditorium, still searching for his brother. George's projector, its slide tray missing, lay on its side next to the door to the men's room. Owen checked the men's room, found it empty, and scanned the parking lot for George's car with no luck. He returned to the meeting in time to hear one final speaker and see the council vote four to three in favor of the two-lane design.

Two of the dissenting council persons said their minds had been changed by the presentation of the Highway Commissioner and his brother. Good strategy for a rigged game, Owen thought. Keep the contest close enough so that the losers go on shoveling their money into the pot.

Owen sat behind the wheel of his mother's Toyota as they waited for the parking lot to empty. When the last car had left, there was still no sign of George.

"He must have gone home early," Ruth Allison said. "It'll take him at least an hour to get back to Charleston." She sighed audibly. "I feel like a drink. Can we stop at the Oasis?"

Owen glanced sideways at his mother. He'd never heard her say she needed a drink. "Sure, Mom," he said, turning on the ignition.

The Oasis was a college hangout near the council chambers, with wooden booths bearing the carved initials of fifty years' worth of underclassmen. Ruth Allison led the way past a row of occupied booths, then stopped in her tracks. Mary Jewel Robertson stood hoisting a pitcher of beer and laughing with a crowd in the last booth.

"That awful woman," Ruth said. "She's enough to gag a maggot. Let's not stay here. There's a nice new place just across town."

Back in their car, Ruth directed Owen along a circuitous route that meandered between dark side streets and gaudy neon-lit avenues. Owen finally realized that she wasn't looking for a particular bar, but for some sign of George's car outside any bar.

Ruth reached over and touched Owen's arm. "This is it, let's stop here." They were outside a long brick building next to a bowling alley. Over the door, a militiaman and a British grenadier flanked old-English lettering advertising the Rebels and Redcoats Tavern.

When they'd been seated in a booth inside the tavern, Owen asked, "Were you expecting to find George here?"

"It's funny. I was hoping he'd be here. But I'm relieved he's not."

"Why don't I just take you home? Then I'll tour the bars on my own."

Ruth shook her head. "Oh, no. I'm sure George went home to Charleston. We'll just wait awhile and call Barb."

"Has he done this before? Disappeared, I mean?"

Ruth ran a napkin over a damp bottle mark on their table. "Two times. But once it was just overnight."

"What about the other time?"

"Oh, Owen. I'm sure he'll turn up at home if we just give him time to get there."

A barmaid in a tri-cornered hat and pantaloons came to their table and they ordered two draft beers. As the barmaid disappeared with their order, Ruth Allison barely parted her lips to say, "Cute."

Owen raised his eyebrows.

"I mean her outfit," Ruth said.

"Mom, I've been meaning to ask you. Why'd you tell Sheriff Reader we didn't have a gun in the house?"

"We don't. There's no gun in our house."

"Not now, maybe. But Dad always kept that automatic in his sock drawer."

Ruth pursed her lips. "I must have misunderstood the sheriff."

Owen knew better, but he didn't contradict his mother. "What happened to Dad's gun?"

"Oh, Owen, I don't know. I looked for it after he..." She raised her hands as if she were trying to mold the right word out of the air in front of her. "After he disappeared. The gun wasn't there."

The barmaid returned with their drinks. Ruth took a sip from her beer and winced as if it tasted bitter. "Do you think I should tell the sheriff I misunderstood his question?"

"I think he knows."

Ruth wiped a fleck of foam from her lips and held her handkerchief to her mouth for a short time, considering Owen's observation. When she returned the handkerchief to her purse, all she said was "Oh, my."

They sipped their beers in silence, stretching out the time. When Owen drained his glass, his mother still had more than half of her beer left. "George should have made it home by now," Owen said. "Why don't I call Barb?"

Ruth nodded absently, anticipating the outcome.

Owen could hear the sleep in Barb's voice when she answered the phone.

"George isn't here," she said. "What time is it?"

"Eleven-thirty. He left the hearing sometime ago."

"Have you checked the bars?"

"We're doing that." Owen propped his notebook on top of the pay phone. "Is there anyone in particular we should try?"

"Just those with up-to-date liquor licenses."

"That's not much help."

"I'm sorry, Owen, I thought I was through with this."

"Mom says it's happened before."

"Oh, God. Does Ruth know? She nearly drove me crazy the last time."

"She's with me now."

"It's good you're with her. Try to keep her calm."

Owen stepped out of the phone booth to check on his mother. Her head was buried in her hands.

"I'm going to take her home. Call if George shows up."

"How did the hearing go?"

"We lost four to three."

"That's closer than George thought it would be."

"We got a couple of runs in the bottom of the ninth."

"But not enough. Close but no cigar. That's the story of George's life. He pissed off his boss and still lost."

"He did the right thing."

"That must be why he's off drinking somewhere."

"Give the guy a break, Barb. I'll find him and bring him home."

"I've been through this too many times, Owen. There's a lot of bars between here and Barkley."

When Owen got back to their booth, his mother had spread six dollar bills on the table and was closing her purse. She stood to leave before Owen could sit down. There was no need to tell her George hadn't returned home.

OWEN TOOK his mother home and bar-hopped until the 2 a.m. closing time looking for some trace of his brother. The next morning he called Barb to make sure that George hadn't returned and learned that Alicia Fox had called to demand that his brother appear in her office as soon as he arrived at work. Then he resumed his search, crisscrossing Barkley's streets trying to find George's Pontiac. By the end of two hours he'd covered the center-city grid in both directions and heard three renditions of John Denver singing "Take me Home, Country Roads" on local radio stations. The fourth time he heard Denver sing "I've got a feelin' that I should have been home yesterday," he punched the radio's seek button, hoping to find a station playing Kathy Mattea or Patsy Cline.

Owen found a station playing Kathy Mattea's "Walk the Way the Wind Blows" and stuck with it until the disc jockey promised to bring on John Denver after the next station break. By that time, he'd worked his way to the other side of town without spotting his brother's Pontiac, and found himself on the river road that passed Sammy Earle's house. The first time Owen had visited Sammy, he thought his father might be the body on Gobbler's Grade. Now he knew the body was Ray Cantrip's, but Sammy had worked with Ray Cantrip as well as Wayne Allison, and Owen had promised Bobby he'd look into his father's death. He turned off the radio and headed down the road toward Sammy Earle's maze.

Elizabeth met him at the door. "Nice to see you again," she said. "Sammy's in his office."

She escorted Owen to a back room of the house, where Sammy sat on a high stool hunched over a drafting table. He waved Owen toward a seat in a leather-covered swivel chair in front of a rolltop desk that had been wedged between two upright wooden file cabinets.

"With you in a minute," Sammy said as Owen seated himself in the swivel chair. Owen could see that Sammy was inking a plan view of the railing on his neighbor's porch. His tongue showed between his lips as he moved a plastic triangle along a T-square and drew his drafting pen along the triangle to sketch a series of short parallel lines.

Owen smiled. "They have computers that do that now."

"They have movies of people screwing, too, but it'll never replace the real thing." Sammy wiped off the nib of the drafting pen and returned it to a black leather kit which he snapped shut.

"My dad had a kit just like that," Owen said.

"Your dad would have been proud of you and George at the hearing last night. Damn shame those eco-weenies are fretting over haze that's not even there. They want to set the clock back to when the streets were full of horse turds. Hell, I was here then. Babies died of typhoid. Now that's pollution worth fretting over."

"One of the speakers at the hearing said the Commissioner's Office had always been corrupt."

"Not under your dad. Before him and after him. But not while he was in. It wasn't easy to keep straight, neither. Especially when the Interstate money started flowing and every son of a bitch in the state tried to funnel some into his own pocket." Sammy climbed down from his drafting stool and perched on the edge of a short wooden file cabinet. "Your dad used to say there was no shortage of sons of bitches in West Virginia. In fact, there was always at least one more than you counted on."

Elizabeth brought a teapot and a large plate containing an assortment of cheese and crackers. She set the plate on the desk next to Sammy and poured each of the men a mug of tea.

"Thanks, darlin'," Sammy said. After Elizabeth had left, he took a long sip of tea and edged forward on his file-cabinet seat. "Before the Interstate money started flowing, the corruption was mostly penny-ante stuff. Bribes, short counts, kickbacks, watered concrete. Contractors would sell the state asphalt by the ton and keep their thumb on the scale. Or sell it by the truckload and run the same truck by an inspector two or three times. Every contractor worth his salt had an inspector or two on his payroll.''

Sammy shaved a thin slice off a small wedge of cheese and put it on a cracker. ''Before the feds started pouring Interstate money in, everybody was taking little shavings off a small chunk of tax money.'' He handed Owen the cracker with its sliver of cheese. ''Hell, some governors even left office without a nest egg. It's hard to believe now, but there was a time when West Virginia had three living ex-governors in dire straits. It wasn't for want of trying. There just wasn't enough money to go around. One was in jail, one was in the state funny farm, and one was driving a cab in Chicago.''

''Hard to know which one was worse off.''

''It was Governor Banning appointed your dad. The previous Highway Commissioner got caught invoicing the state for stones when he didn't have a quarry to piss in. The Governor figured your dad would make a good, straight interim appointee until the heat died down and he could reappoint one of his cronies. About that time, though, the Interstate money started to pour in. Ninety federal dollars for every ten the state put up. A man could live for a lifetime just by cutting himself a little piece of that big hunk.'' Sammy took a knife and cut a large slab from the biggest block of cheese on the plate. ''I tell you, none of our governors left office hungry after that. A few went to jail, but none went hungry.''

The slab of cheese Sammy had cut off was too large for any of the crackers, so he munched it like a carrot. ''Well, it was a real circus for a while. Everybody figured they were in hog heaven. They started planning roads to nowhere, buying up rights-of-way and reselling them to the state at premium markups, invoicing for spare parts that never left the inventory shelf. Inspectors even jacked up their buy-off fees for looking the other way. Then your dad clamped down. He fired inspectors, kicked contractors off the gravy train, insisted that Ray Cantrip personally review all right-of-way appraisals. Sent Otie Crabtree and the Mingo County Five to jail for taking kickbacks from contractors.

''The papers was full of the scandals. Course, it wasn't only West Virginia. Same kinds of things were happening on a smaller scale most places the Interstate was going in. The feds set up a House Committee to investigate, run by some Congressman named Blatnik from Minnesota. Your dad was scheduled to testify before the dam broke and he went under.''

"Could anyone else testify?"

"Ray Cantrip was next in line."

Owen frowned. "That's a mighty convenient flood. The top two witnesses disappear in one night. Didn't that raise any eyebrows?"

"Everybody thought they both drowned. Nobody connected the deaths to the hearing."

"Was there any other reason somebody might have wanted to shoot Ray Cantrip?"

Sammy scratched at the side of his face. "He didn't make many friends turning down hope-hyped appraisals."

"Any particular enemies you remember? Anybody who might have wanted Ray dead? Or Dad, for that matter?"

"None come directly to mind."

"What happened in the Commissioner's Office after Dad died?"

"The Governor put his old cronies back in charge. It was business as usual. Only the kickbacks and right-of-way graft that used to be penny-ante turned into grand larceny. They ran the first Interstate from the capitol to the Governor's hometown in the middle of nowhere. Your dad had fought against the route. And against the design. Hell, there was places in the hills where they only had room for three lanes, so they put a passing lane in the middle of the Interstate." Sammy shook his head. "You give mule-headed mountaineers a lane like that and you're just asking for head-on collisions. Might as well have labeled the three lanes northbound, southbound, and hellbound."

Owen laughed. "That's a good one. I'll have to remember it." Bobby could use it in his class.

"Eventually, the Governor and his buddies piled the shit so high it smelled all the way to Washington. There was one scandal after another and the whole bunch got themselves indicted." Sammy leaned forward and tapped the largest block of cheese with his knife. "But not before they managed to slice off enough to keep them fed and fat for the rest of their winters."

Sammy set the knife back on the cheese plate. "When the new batch of cronies came in after your dad drowned, I quit and went to work for Chuck Hager."

"I never knew that."

"Old Chuck wasn't above greasing a few palms, but he didn't skimp on materials. Shit fire, some of those other contractors poured concrete so thin you could swim in it." Sammy raised one foot and hiked up his pant leg. "And I once saw an inspector sink up to his shoetops in asphalt laced with sand instead of crushed stone.

"Old Chuck Hager would build you a good road, though," Sammy continued. "I stayed with him until he turned the company over to his boy Eddie. I'll never understand why he did that. He had Rudy Slater waiting in the wings, and Eddie couldn't tell a transit from toe-jam. Still can't. Anyhow, I retired and Rudy left and started bidding against Eddie."

Sammy reached out and tapped the drawing on the drafting table. "Still keep my hand in, though."

"What about Alicia Fox and the current crowd in the Transportation Department?"

"You've met the woman. She's a real tight ass. You could stuff a lump of coal up her butt and mine her privy for diamonds. I don't envy your brother working for her."

"He may not be working for her much longer," Owen said. "Is there any hint she's on the take?"

Sammy shook his head. "She's not getting kickbacks from any of the contractors I know. And I'd be surprised if she's fiddling with right-of-way values. Hell, she's barely buying any new right-of-way. It's like she doesn't want to build any new roads."

Elizabeth appeared in the doorway. "I declare, Sammy, you could talk the ears off an acre of corn. Can I get you more tea, Wayne's boy?"

Owen stood, thanked Sammy for his time, and declined the offer. For the first time in thirty-five years, he'd started thinking of himself as Wayne's boy, and he needed to find out more about what that meant.

FROM OUTSIDE, the Barkley Library seemed smaller than Owen remembered, and the stone steps needed to be scoured free of coal dust. Inside, though, there was the same musty smell of books he recalled from his childhood. Except for a row of computer monitors sitting next to the file cabinets, the interior hadn't changed much since he'd been gone.

The face at the reference desk had changed. The librarian was still middle-aged, but attractive, with high cheekbones and a forthright smile.

"Is Mrs. Sink still around?" Owen asked.

The smile gave way to a short, tinkling laugh. "She was here when

I was in high school. I don't think she's been in for years. Can I help you?''

"I'm looking for information on some highway scandals in the early sixties.''

"Oh, Lord. There were so many of them. Do you have the dates? I can get you copies of the *Star*.''

"I don't know the exact dates. There was an Otie Crabtree involved.''

"I'm afraid the *Star* isn't indexed. None of the West Virginia papers are. Is there some way you can narrow down the time period?''

"Well, the Governor was indicted. And there were hearings at the House of Representatives. Run by a Congressman Blatnik.''

The smile returned. "Oh, well. We would have made the *New York Times* with that. We can work backward from their index. Just have a seat and I'll bring you all the news that's fit to print.''

The librarian stood, and Owen watched her fit her wrist through the cuff of a metal walking cane.

"Let me help you with the newspapers,'' he said.

"No, that's all right.'' She paused. "I saw you at the hearing last night. You don't remember me, do you?''

"No. Should I?''

She held out her free hand. "I'm Mary Alice Hogarty. I was two years behind you in high school. Well, I was Mary Alice Varva then. I used to watch you pitch.''

Owen took her hand. "Your brother played third.''

"That's right. You were good on the mound. Did you go on with it?''

Owen was conscious that she was still holding his hand. "I wasn't nearly that good. I didn't even pitch in college.''

"You were plenty good enough for Barkley.'' She released his hand, smiled, and disappeared into the reference stacks.

While Mary Alice was sorting through the newspaper files, Owen phoned George's home and office. There was still no sign of his brother. He would pick up the search again when the library closed and the bars opened.

Mary Alice returned with microfiche copies of the *New York Times* and *Barkley Star* and showed Owen how to use the viewing machine.

"There's a lot on the Governor's indictment and a little bit on the Blatnik Hearings,'' she said as she threaded a reel of miniature *New York Times* pages into the machine. "Your best bet is to look at the hearings themselves. I can get a copy from the Marshall Library, but it'll take a couple of days. How long will you be staying?''

Owen was conscious of her perfume as she leaned over his shoulder to adjust the focus. Lilacs, he thought. ''I don't know.''

''I'll order it just in case. It'll be here if you need it.'' She turned a knob and the headline EX-GOVERNOR OF WEST VIRGINIA INDICTED IN BRIBE swam into focus. ''Just push that button to make a copy. If you need anything else, you know where to find me.''

The *New York Times* reported that the ex-Governor and five others, including the Highway Commissioner who had succeeded Owen's father, had been indicted for bribery and trading state contracts for payments to front organizations. The local papers printed the full text of the indictments, but were generally skeptical of the charges. One editorial warned that ''the accused should not be prejudged,'' while another pooh-poohed the earlier investigations of the Blatnik Commission, claiming that the ''Bleatnik probe'' findings were puffed out of proportion by the national press and gossip-mongers like ''keyhole-peeper Jack Anderson and scandal columnist Drew Pearson.''

Owen decided that the best source for an unbiased treatment of the Blatnik hearings would be the transcripts themselves, and he told Mary Alice he'd be back for them. Before leaving the library, though, he stopped to look up the nesting habits of the least bittern.

Birds of West Virginia confirmed that the least bittern, also known as the slough pup, buttermunk, and barrel-maker, nested in marshes and riverbeds. Only the red-backed bittern appeared to be at all rare.

A shadow fell across the pages of the book and the voice accompanying the shadow said, ''How are you, Scout?''

There was no mistaking the voice. Owen took a quick second to prepare himself and looked up into the hazel eyes of the woman who once made him believe there were no heights he couldn't scale, no wrongs he couldn't right, no mysteries he couldn't solve.

He tested his voice with the two syllables of her name. ''Robin.''

''Mary Alice said you were back here. What are you researching?''

He risked a few more syllables. ''Endangered species.''

''Why, that's me.''

''Only because you're one of a kind.'' There, he got out a whole sentence. Not a bad one either, he thought.

''Thank you, kind sir.'' She stepped back from the library table. ''I like the beard. You look great.''

''That's nice to hear. So do you.'' It was true, he thought. Her hair was shorter and lighter than when they'd been teenagers together, but he could still see the beauty she had been in the tanned and stately beauty she'd become.

"I'm about to drive out to Gobbler's Grade to see how brother Eddie's coming with his roadway," she said. "Want to ride along?" Owen had a sudden vision of his teenage fumblings with Robin on Gobbler's Grade and looked down at his reference book.

She misinterpreted his downward glance. "As a certified endangered species, I can tell you whatever you haven't already found out from that book."

Owen closed the cover of *The Birds of West Virginia*. "Gobbler's Grade with you? How can I refuse?"

"You never did before."

"Actually, that was the first place I went when I got back to town." He didn't tell her why.

"Did it bring back old memories?" Robin touched the back of his head and ran her hand lightly through his hair. "I lost my virginity there, as you well know."

Owen rose from the table. "That was sometime ago," he deadpanned. "I doubt if we'll be able to find it today."

Robin lifted her head and laughed out loud. Owen had always loved her laugh. She threw everything into it, holding nothing back.

A pinch-faced woman two tables down glared at the two of them.

"Oh, Owen," Robin said. "You could always make me laugh. I've missed that. I'm beginning to believe a good laugh is better than a good orgasm."

"I don't know about that. There's probably no such thing as a bad orgasm. But I'm happy to report I'm still good for three loud laughs a night."

Robin laughed again and linked her arm through his. The familiar gesture made him feel buoyant, and he winked at the pinch-faced woman as they smiled their way out of the library.

RUTH ALLISON'S Toyota was parked at the foot of the library steps. "Why don't we take my mom's car?" Owen said. "My two hours are about up."

"Gobbler's Grade in your parent's car? I may not be able to restrain myself."

As she buckled herself into the Toyota, Robin said, "Oh, Owen. Whatever happened to us?"

"I don't know." He tried to recall the wild emotional swings. "Bobby's broadcast. A lot of silly stuff I barely remember. Then college happened. I went to Marquette. You went to WVU."

"But weren't the summers wonderful?"

"We had a few good summers, yes."

"Honeysuckle evenings and wildflower afternoons." Robin shook her head and Owen could see flecks of gray in the dark hair floating over her shoulders. "We were so lucky. What would you have done if I'd gotten pregnant?"

"I'd have married you. I was a dutiful young man."

"And are you still? Dutiful, I mean?"

Owen smiled. "Absolutely." That's one of the things that brought me back here, he thought.

"We could have done worse. I did, at any rate."

Owen drove on without responding, uncertain of his feelings.

Robin broke the silence. "Your mother told me you're divorced too."

"Yes. But we may get back together."

"Oh."

Why had he said that? He and Judith had never actually agreed to get back together. And Robin was only asking about their breakup. "We were living in California," he said. "My consulting business went belly-up, and I moved to Washington to work for the feds. My wife stayed in California to climb the corporate-law ladder. We both thought the separation would be temporary. It turned out to be permanent."

"But now you're back in California."

"For a while, anyway."

"And your ex-wife's still there."

"Still there. Still practicing law."

Robin shifted in her seat and straightened her skirt. "I can't imagine getting back together with my ex."

"I saw your ex just last night. He looked prosperous."

"He is." Robin braced herself against the dash as Owen cornered sharply through a caution light. "He was the first man I ever met who could stand up to Daddy. It took me quite a while to realize that wasn't necessarily the basis of a lasting relationship."

A siren sounded behind them. Owen saw the flashing lights of a patrol car in his rearview mirror. He swore and picked his way to the curb.

Sheriff Thad Reader appeared at the window. "Sorry to startle you." He fixed his good eye on Owen. "I'm trying to find your brother."

"So am I."

"That's what your mother said. Let me know right away if you find him."

"Did Mom call you?"

"No, I went to see her. They found Mary Jewel Robertson dead in her apartment this morning. Apparently as a result of head injuries she suffered when your brother hit her."

"He barely nudged the woman."

"Evidently it didn't take much. He's facing a charge of vehicular manslaughter."

SEVEN

Sam Spade's Mom

OWEN ASKED the sheriff to follow him back to town. Then he apologized to Robin and requested a rain check on their trip to Gobbler's Grade.

"How about dinner instead?" Robin asked.

"I'd like that," Owen said. He made a U-turn and watched in his rearview mirror as the sheriff lit up his flasher and turned around as well. "Not tonight, though. We're still trying to track down George."

"Is that why you want to talk to the sheriff?"

"Not really. I just can't believe George hit Mary Jewel hard enough to kill her."

They drove in silence until Robin pointed to a cream-colored Mercedes parked a block from the library. "That's my car."

"Nice."

"Part of the divorce settlement."

Owen pulled up behind the Mercedes. "My compliments to your lawyer."

"I'll call about dinner," Robin said. "I hope you find George real soon." She swung her legs out of his car and blew him a kiss.

Owen took the parking place Robin vacated and walked back to the sheriff's cruiser, which sat waiting with its lights flashing.

"That was Chuck Hager's daughter, wasn't it?" the sheriff asked as Owen slipped into the cruiser. "Sorry to interrupt."

"That's all right, we weren't going anywhere important," Owen said, wondering if that was true. "Thanks for following me back. I wanted to talk to you."

The sheriff eased his cruiser forward, looking for a place to park. "What about?"

"That Robertson woman," Owen said. "I was with George when he hit her."

"I know. I saw her accident report."

"Like I told you, George barely nudged her. She had to be faking those injuries."

"Pretty good fake, wouldn't you say? To stop breathing for good?"

"Nothing George did could have caused that."

The sheriff pulled his cruiser into a loading zone. "Brain injuries are funny things."

"She never hit her head. She landed on her butt in the ditch. If that's where she kept her brains, I could understand it."

The sheriff allowed himself a smile. "No need to drag the conversation down to that level."

"You think her doctor could tell butt bruises from brain trauma?"

The sheriff seemed to give the question more thought than it deserved. "Never seen Doc Johnston with his medical texts upside down," he said, finally.

"Will there be an autopsy?"

The sheriff bridled at the question. "Of course."

"Who'll do it?"

"Doc Johnston's got coroner duty this year."

"The same doctors that treated her? Isn't that a little incestuous?"

"Welcome to West Virginia."

"Now who's dragging the conversation down?"

The sheriff shook his head. "I'm sorry. You're right. I'll try to get somebody to backstop Johnston." He reached across Owen and opened his passenger door. "Meantime, let me know if you locate your brother."

OWEN CALLED Bobby Cantrip and they agreed to split up the local territory in searching for George. Bobby would make the rounds of the bar in Charleston, where George lived, while Owen would do the same in Barkley, the last place he'd been seen. Once they'd checked all the likely spots within the city limits, they'd start working their way toward one another by visiting the roadhouses along the Interstate linking the two cities. The plan was far from perfect, Owen realized, but it was the best he could do with the limited manpower he had available.

Owen started visiting Barkley's bars at seven o'clock. He remembered a few from his days as a teenager, but most were new to him.

By eleven-thirty, he'd been to everyone in the phone book, and he started on the road to Charleston. By the two-o'clock closing time, he'd made it twenty miles north on the Interstate, just short of halfway. There was no sign of George, no bartender who remembered him. He gave up and started home.

BOBBY CANTRIP called Owen at home the next morning to say he'd just found George's car outside a run-down motel near Cabin Creek, about twenty miles south of Charleston on the Kanawah River.

"Is he alone?" Owen asked.

"Can't tell. His car is the only one near his unit, though."

"Keep an eye on the car and unit. I'll be there as soon as I can."

"What if he comes out?"

"Ask yourself what Sam Spade would do. Follow him."

"Do I get Sam Spade pay for this?"

"Spade made twenty dollars a day. I can probably swing that."

"Isn't there some inflation adjustment?"

"There's no mention of one in *The Maltese Falcon*. Leave a message with my mom if George takes off before I get there."

Owen hung up and walked to the breakfast room, where his mother was reading the morning paper. "Bobby's located George's car," he said. "I'm going to try to bring him home."

Ruth removed her reading glasses and reached for her purse. "I'm coming along."

"Mom, the car's outside a motel room. We don't know what we're going to find."

"Nothing you find will be worse than what I'll imagine if you leave me here."

"I'll tell you all about it later."

Ruth was already slipping her arms into a navy-blue coat. "You'll take me now. If George is blotto, you'll need somebody to drive his car."

THE INTERSTATE had missed the Creekside Cabins by about two miles. It was far enough off the beaten path so that Owen guessed George must have found it before. The tin VACANCY sign had rusted in place, and an uneven row of cabins covered with peeling gray paint marched unsteadily back from the road along a dry creekbed. Swarms of gnats clustered in front of the screen doors which hung askew in front of each unit. Bobby had parked his weathered Dodge Dart about halfway down the dusty driveway linking the motel office with the row of cabins.

When Owen and his mother pulled into the driveway, Bobby left his car and climbed into the backseat of their Toyota. He pointed down the driveway at George's Pontiac, which sat between the last two cabins along the creekbed.

"I see it," Owen said. "Which one of the two units is he in?"

"Don't know," Bobby said. "Nothing's moved in either of them since I called you."

"How'd you ever find this place?" Owen asked. "It's pretty far into the boondocks."

"I'd heard about it from a friend. It caters to a special clientele."

The screen door on the unit nearest them swung open and two young men with buzz cuts and tank tops stepped through it. While the taller of the two fought off the gnats, the shorter man put his hand into the hip pocket of his friend's cutoff jeans. The morning sun glinted off the tall man's nose ring as he nuzzled the top of the shorter man's head and they strolled off arm in arm toward the motel office.

"Good Lord," Ruth said.

"A mother's worst nightmare," Bobby said.

Ruth twisted in her seat to face Bobby. "No, Bobby, my worst nightmare is that my firstborn son will end his days a boozed-up drunkard."

"So what's our next move, Scout?" Bobby asked.

Owen didn't want to burst in on his brother and find him in bed with another man. Or another woman, either. "It's nine-thirty," he said. "Let's wait a bit and see if anything stirs in one of the two units."

Ruth shifted in her seat so she could face both Owen and Bobby. "That was terrible news about your father, Bobby. That must have been an awful shock."

"Hell of a way to die," Owen said.

"Yeah, I want to die peacefully in my sleep like my grandfather," Bobby said, pausing a beat before delivering the punch line. "Not screaming like the passengers in his car."

Owen laughed in spite of himself.

"That always gets a laugh out of my driving class," Bobby said. "The state doesn't like me to tell it, but there's always a way to work it in."

Five minutes passed. Ruth twisted at the handle of her purse. "We can't just wait here."

"Ask yourself what Sam Spade would do," Bobby said.

"Slip a buck or two to the night clerk," Owen said.

"Better adjust that for inflation," Bobby said.

"What the hell," Owen said. "You two wait here." He left the car and marched down the gravelless driveway, stirring up dust with each step. Guessing that the last unit must be George's, he strode through the gnats and pounded on the screen door.

"George, open up. It's me, Owen."

There was no answer. He pounded harder, and the screen door popped free of its lower hinge. Still no answer. He began to worry that he was too late, that he shouldn't have waited in the car at all. He ran to the unit on the other side of the Pontiac and pounded on its door, shouting George's name. There was no answer at that door, either.

He turned toward his mother and Bobby and shrugged, then hurried to the motel office. The clerk on duty was a tall bony man with a small silver hoop piercing his left eyebrow and a grimy red bandanna knotted around his neck.

"My brother's in one of your end units. He doesn't answer when I knock."

The clerk wet his lips with his tongue and cocked his hooped eyebrow. "Maybe he doesn't want to talk to you."

"I think maybe he's in trouble. Can you give me a key to the unit?"

The clerk lifted a cardboard file box up onto the counter. "What'd you say your name was?"

"I didn't, but it's Allison. Owen Allison. My brother's George Allison."

The clerk pulled a card from the file box. "Nobody by that name registered here."

Owen grabbed the man's thin wrist and jerked the card from his hand. Unit 14, the end unit, was registered in the name of Gene Freese.

"There's no need to get physical," the clerk said.

Owen handed back the card. "Gene Freese played third base for the Reds in the early sixties."

"Ooh, a celebrity. And I've got his autograph right here."

"My brother played third in high school back then. Gene Freese was his hero. That's my brother's signature. That's his car outside the unit."

"That still doesn't entitle you to a key."

Owen took a ten-dollar bill from his wallet. "What if I put down a deposit?"

The clerk took the ten and smiled coyly. "That helps some. But how do I know you're not a jilted lover about to create a scene?"

Owen took another ten from his wallet and held it out of the clerk's reach. "Here's another ten so you don't care what I am."

The clerk eyed the ten and turned to take a key from the hutch behind him.

"What time did my brother check in?" Owen asked.

"Night before last, just after I started my shift. About three o'clock."

"Was he alone?"

The clerk's eyes didn't leave the bill in Owen's hand. "What kind of a place do you think I run?"

Owen handed over the ten and took the key. "One with a hefty key deposit."

OWEN SHOVED ASIDE the dangling screen door and fitted the key into the lock of the end motel unit. Inside, the close, curtained room stank of sweat and stale vomit. Owen groped for the curtains and pulled them back, spilling light onto a narrow, swaybacked bed. His brother lay tangled in the bedsheets, wearing a T-shirt flecked with brown stains and a pair of plaid boxer shorts open at the fly. He was snoring softly.

On the floor in front of the bed was a cardboard carton holding a half dozen fifths of bourbon. Three empty fifths lay beside the carton, alongside an overturned ice bucket that had puddled onto the soiled linoleum floor.

Owen looked down at George, trying to recall the third baseman he'd idolized from the bleachers years ago, or even the worried Highway Commissioner who'd met him at the airport nearly two weeks earlier. He kicked aside the carton of booze and shook him hard by the shoulders.

Bleary eyes blinked open, shut, and blinked open again. "Owen? What the hell?"

"Wake up, George. You're going home."

George rolled over and burrowed his face into a lumpy pillow. "Like hell. Not ready yet."

The screen door slammed behind them. "Ready or not, George

Allison, you're coming with us." Ruth Allison stormed into the room, followed by Bobby Cantrip, who gave Owen a shrug that said, "I couldn't stop her."

George sat bold upright. "Mom? What are you doing here?"

Ruth shut the door and moved the room's only piece of loose furniture, a ladder-back chair with a missing slat, in front of it. "I'll tell you what I'm doing."

She wedged the ladder-back chair under the doorknob and sat in the chair. "I'm sitting here until you agree to commit yourself to Saint Vincent's for treatment."

George pulled the pillow onto his lap to cover the gaping fly of his boxer shorts.

"Just as long as it takes," Ruth said.

George doubled over the pillow as if his stomach hurt.

"Well?" Ruth said.

"I'll be all right. I don't need any help," George said.

"Horse puckey," Ruth answered.

George looked from Owen to Bobby. They both shrugged. He hung his head. "All right. You win."

Ruth Allison rose and moved the chair out from under the doorknob. "Good," she said. "I'll call Sister Monica at Saint Vincent's to make the arrangements. Then we'll call the sheriff and tell him where we're taking George. You boys help him get cleaned and dressed and into my Toyota." She left the unit and headed for the pay phone outside the motel office.

Owen and Bobby watched Ruth go. "How old's your mom? Seventy?" Bobby asked.

"Seventy-five."

Bobby whistled silently. "Amazing."

Owen gathered the discarded clothes strewn around the room. He looked at George, who still sat on the bed, staring down at the pillow in his lap. "What do you suppose Sam Spade would do now?" Owen asked Bobby.

Bobby shrugged. "I don't know. I don't think he ever took his mother along."

Owen dumped George's clothes on the ladder-back chair. "Maybe he should have."

THE SMILE ON Ruth's face as she brought the phone to Owen after they'd returned home stopped just short of a self-satisfied smirk. It was the same giggle-stifling grin she'd sported when girls had called him up in high school.

"Somebody wants to talk to you," she said, singsonging the words while covering the mouthpiece with her hand.

Owen took the phone and watched his mother back out of the room, wiggling her fingers in a short good-bye. When she had gone, he raised the receiver and said, "Robin?"

The voice of his ex-wife startled him. "No, it's not Robin. And who the hell's Robin, anyhow?"

"Judith." Owen's mind flip-flopped like a gaffed fish. "Mom didn't tell me it was you."

"Evidently."

"Listen. It's great to hear your voice." It's true, he reflected. He was glad to hear from her. Although his stomach wouldn't stop churning. Was it just because of his mistake, or was it disappointment that Robin wasn't the caller?

"How are things going there?" Owen could hear the edge in Judith's voice.

"We've got George in a treatment center. But a woman he hit with his car just died. And his boss is talking about suspending him."

"He can't do that. Not legally."

"She. She can't do that."

"His boss is a woman?"

Owen smiled at the surprise in Judith's voice. "Does that change your opinion?"

"Of course not. Why would it?"

"You always give your gender the benefit of the doubt."

"Only when I know the woman and when she deserves it. Which is most of the time."

"I know. You never met a woman you didn't like. But you haven't met Alicia Fox. There's a chance George will need legal help. Are you pretty busy?"

"We just took on a big new antitrust case."

"That's McKenzie's area. You're not still working with him?"

"He's still the senior partner. That was part of the deal."

Owen felt a familiar pang. It was Judith's brief affair with the senior partner in her law firm that had sealed the end of their marriage. When their divorce brought the affair to light, McKenzie had tried to fire Judith. She responded with a sexual harassment suit that paved the way for her own partnership. Owen lowered the phone and stared at it. He had first learned of the affair in the middle of another, much different, long-distance call.

Judith's voice came faintly from the lowered receiver. "It's all right, Owen."

Owen returned the phone to his ear and changed the subject. "How are you and Buster the Third getting along?"

"He's a joy. But he won't come in from his walk until I throw him a tennis ball at least ten times."

"You're spoiling him. I can get him inside after five tosses."

"You throw it farther than I do."

"You're raising his expectations."

"Then you better get back here soon."

"This thing with George is still up in the air." Owen checked to make sure his mother was out of earshot. "And they uncovered the body of a friend of Dad's. He'd been murdered the same time Dad disappeared. It's really upset Mom."

"Well, you do what you have to do. But the proposal requests are piling up on your desk back here. And you've had a couple of calls about collaborations. At least answer your phone messages."

"Nag, nag, nag. You sound just like my first wife."

"There's a good reason for that."

"Look. I really appreciate your looking after Buster and dropping in on my office from time to time. I'll get back as soon as I can."

"I hope so. I miss you."

"I miss you too." The words came easily, and he realized they were true.

IN HIS MOTHER'S sewing room that evening, Owen retrieved his graph paper and tried to resurrect his research into his father's death. He'd promised Bobby he'd expand his investigation to include Ray Cantrip's murder as well, but the spare chronology laid out on the tight green graph squares didn't yield much in the way of new insights. Nor was Bobby's admonition to "ask yourself what Sam Spade would do" much help. Owen doubted that Sam Spade ever tried to follow a thirty-five-year-old trail of clues. He knew that Philip Marlowe pondered chess problems to focus his mind, but sitting in a fabric-filled room pondering graph paper and dust-covered jigsaw puzzles didn't make Owen feel like much of a detective.

Maybe he should quit trying to glean inferences from graph paper and talk to the people who'd been there the night their fathers disappeared. Ray Cantrip had seen Owen's father go under. Ray had reported that to Sammy Earle, who tried to find some sign of the missing man. But Ray must have talked to his wife as well. That was one of the facts about that night that bothered Owen. His own father had left to fight the flood and never came back. But Bobby Cantrip's dad had left and then showed up at his house while the flood was still raging. Bobby said he remembered his father tracking water into the house the night he disappeared. Why would Ray Cantrip return home in the middle of the fight to control the floodwaters?

He picked up the phone and dialed Bobby Cantrip, saying "I want to see your mother."

"That's fine with me," Bobby said. "But isn't she a little old for you? I mean, she likes you and all, but—"

"No, I want to talk to her about the night my father drowned. Your dad must have said something to her about it."

"Oh, hell, Owen. She barely remembers what happened last week."

"I know, but I've got to try."

"Well, I've got a class in a half hour. Visiting hours are seven to nine, if you want to go out by yourself. I was planning to drop in on her tomorrow, if you want to wait."

"Maybe I'll wait and go out with you. Give me a call before you come."

"Hey, what's the last thing that goes through a bug's mind when he hits your windshield?"

Owen laughed once and shook his head. "I don't know. What?"

"His asshole."

"They probably won't let you tell that one in class either."

"No. But isn't it great? I've tried to clean it up by saying 'anus' or 'rectum,' but those words just don't get the same laugh."

"Try 'heinie.' It's a funny word."

"No, there's just no substitute for 'asshole.'"

"Well, hang in there. And give me a call tomorrow."

Owen was fixing a turkey sandwich when it occurred to him that neither Sam Spade nor Philip Marlowe would be likely to postpone an interview for a whole day just so a friend could keep them company. He checked his watch. If he hurried, he could still see Dolores Cantrip before visiting hours were over. He took the sandwich and a Coke in the car with him and headed for the Shady Acres Rest Home.

THE CORRIDOR of the county rest home smelled of Lysol and was littered with the same abandoned walkers and gurneys Owen had seen on his last visit. There was no answer when he knocked on Dolores Cantrip's door, but he heard a small scraping noise inside the room. The door was unlocked, and he opened it far enough to peer inside.

The blinds were drawn, and the only light in the room came through the half-opened bathroom door and fell slanting across the bed. The plastic bag hanging beside the bed swung like a slow metronome in and out of the sliver of light. Clear tubing ran from the feeder into Dolores Cantrip's thin, speckled arm. Her face was obscured by a pillow scrunched at an awkward angle between the bed and headboard. Owen stepped forward to adjust the pillow when a blow from behind sent him tumbling into the tangled tubing and knocked him senseless.

EIGHT

Just in Time to Be Too Late

OWEN AWOKE TO the strong smell of Lysol. He was lying on a gurney in the corridor of the nursing home. Sheriff Reader and a clone were standing over him. He blinked twice and fought hard to bring a single sheriff into focus.

"How are you feeling?" the sheriffs asked.

"Like I can't deal with one of you, let alone two."

"You've had a mild concussion. The doctor says it's nothing to be concerned about."

"I'm glad *he*'s not concerned." Owen pushed against the wall, trying to sit up. "What about Dolores Cantrip?" The gurney rolled away from the wall, and he fell back onto its pillow.

The sheriff steadied the cart. "Someone smothered her."

"Oh, Jesus."

"Did you see anything?"

Owen started to shake his head, but the movement caused his temple to throb. "The room was dark. The pillow was off-center. Someone hit me from behind." He touched the back of his head gingerly and felt a gauze bandage. "I guess I was a step slow."

"Just in time to be too late."

"Sounds like a bad country-and-western song. Has anyone told Bobby?"

"We're trying to notify him. What brought you out here?"

"Mrs. Cantrip saw her husband the night of the flood. I thought she might know something about his murder."

"Best you leave the investigating up to us professionals."

"If you were doing your job, why aren't you the one with the headache?" Owen's voice cracked under the weight of pain and frustration. "And why is Dolores Cantrip dead?"

"Your hunch was probably right. It seems likely she knew something about her husband's murder."

"And I got here too late to save her." Owen closed his eyes and saw a clutching hand sucked into a whirlpool. "Story of my life."

"Don't beat yourself up too much. Even if you'd come earlier, the killer probably would have waited until you'd left."

"But at least I would have talked to her. I might have learned enough to stop the killing."

"I doubt if you would have learned much. I talked to her yesterday afternoon."

"Too early to be just in time. Did you learn anything?"

The sheriff shook his head. "She was barely lucid. She kept confusing me with old Sheriff Brennan. She couldn't keep it straight whether Bobby's father had been shot, shot someone, shot himself, or was still alive."

"So she didn't tell you anything?"

"Nothing."

"But someone killed her anyhow."

"Someone who couldn't be sure she wouldn't talk."

From two doors down the corridor came a barely human wail that sounded like a model airplane engine whining to a standstill. No one moved in response to the wail, and it started again.

"Staff was just as alert last night," the sheriff said over the wail. "Nobody saw anything. They don't even remember seeing you come in."

"So we don't know anything we didn't know before Bobby's mom was killed."

A door slammed and the wail wound down.

The sheriff looked in the direction of the slamming door, then turned back to Owen. "We know there's a killer running loose. And there's a good chance the same person that killed Dolores Cantrip killed her husband."

THE COUNTY DOCTOR'S pain killers caused Owen to sleep until one in the afternoon. He awoke with a mild headache and a parched mouth that felt as if a herd of desert camels had been foraging on his tongue. He chased the camels with three glasses of water and tried to call Bobby Cantrip. When no one answered, he went downstairs in his stocking feet to find his mother sitting on one end of the living-room couch, picking through a shoebox of unsorted photographs.

Ruth looked up as Owen entered. "My God, you could pass for a corpse yourself."

"That's probably why the sheriff brought me home. He didn't want me tempting the embalmers."

"Can I get you something to eat?"

Owen sat gingerly on the other end of the brown corduroy couch. "I don't think I could keep anything down."

"Poor Dolores. The sheriff said you interrupted her killer."

"Not before he finished. And he heard me coming."

"So you didn't see who it was?"

Owen shook his head. The action seemed to cause his brain to wobble from side to side.

Ruth sighed. "The way Dolores was slipping, death must have been a blessed relief."

"It was a relief for somebody. The sheriff thinks she knew something about her husband's killing."

"Surely not. Why would she have kept quiet all these years?"

Owen didn't want to risk shaking his head again, so he shrugged his shoulders, causing his brain to wobble back and forth again.

"Dolores was always such a...troubled woman." Seeing that Owen didn't seem to want to talk about the murder, Ruth changed the subject. "Wasn't it nice to hear from Judith yesterday?"

Owen blinked his eyes and picked up a scrapbook that contained clippings and photos from the time of his father's death. "It was quite a surprise. Did she call us, or did you call her?"

"Oh, does that really make any difference?" Ruth reached into the shoebox and showed Owen a photo of his brother smiling and leaning on a bat before a high school baseball game. "Maybe the treatment will bring the old George back to us."

"Let's hope so."

"Judith said your work has been piling up. Will you be wanting to get back to California now?"

"God no, Mom. There are too many loose ends lying around."

Ruth returned George's picture to the shoebox. "One of those loose ends wouldn't be Robin Hager, would it?"

"I don't know that I'd call Robin a loose end."

"She left a phone message saying she'd pick you up and take you to dinner. At the country club, no less."

"I get the feeling you don't approve."

"The woman broke your heart. Don't think I don't remember."

"And you think Judith didn't? Is that why you called her?"

"You and Judith just got crosswise to one another and couldn't get squared around again. I was only trying to help out."

Owen rubbed his temples, trying to squeeze out his headache. "Crosswise is a pretty mild euphemism for divorce."

"You and Judith are right for one another. You felt enough for each other to get married. That never happened with Robin Hager."

"What do you have against Robin?"

"Her father was no friend of your father. Chuck Hager was trying to bribe his way into state construction jobs. Your father wouldn't stand still for it. There were threats."

"Threats?" Owen recalled the news photo of the broken dam. Chuck Hager was there that night. Or at least his painted equipment was on the scene.

"Your dad was going to testify before a House Committee."

"The Blatnick Committee. I know."

"About bribes and bribe offers."

Owen hefted the scrapbook in his lap. "There aren't any clippings in here about the Committee. But it was big news at the time."

"The news reports weren't very kind to the State Highway Commission. It hurt me to read them. They lumped your father in with the bribe-takers. But he was putting a stop to all that. That's why the threats started."

The mention of threats had made Owen forget his headache. "Who threatened him?"

Ruth bit her lip. "I don't know. I don't think they left their names."

"Then how do you know Robin's father was behind them?"

"He was one of the ones your dad had hard evidence on."

"Just one of them? There were more?"

"Your dad was worried. He started carrying that gun to work with him."

"The gun that disappeared?"

Ruth nodded.

"Why didn't you tell that to the sheriff? Maybe Dad had the gun on him when he drowned."

"Why would you take a gun to fight a flood?"

"Why would you take it off if you were in a hurry?"

"I never thought of that." Ruth pulled a large glossy photo from the shoebox. "Remember this?"

The picture showed Owen's high school baseball team, posed in

front of bleachers bearing a banner reading "1969 STATE CHAMPI-
ONS." Owen stood slightly apart at the edge of the back row, cradling
his glove, his head cocked slightly toward the center of the group.

"Seems like a long time ago," Owen said.

"You always cocked your head like that in group pictures. Who
does that remind you of?"

"I don't know. A poster boy for spinal scoliosis?"

"No, silly." Owen's mother picked up the "Denison Commoner,"
his father's college yearbook. The leather-bound yearbook fell open
to the page she was looking for, and she showed it to Owen. His
father stood off to the side of the back row of the basketball team,
wearing a tank top that hung like a loose smock on his skinny frame.
His head was cocked toward the center of the group.

"You're saying my malformation is hereditary?"

"The way you stood reminded me of your father is all. I see a lot
of your father in you."

"Well," Owen said. "I've always thought there was a lot to be
said for heredity. I mean, if your mother and father didn't have any
children, there's a good chance you won't either."

Ruth reached over and pinched her son's biceps. "You're just like
your friend Bobby, making a joke out of everything." She withdrew
her hand as if she'd burned herself. "Oh, God. Poor Bobby. Losing
his father like that. And now his mother."

"I tried to call him. He wasn't home. I'll try again later."

Ruth put her hand on Owen's arm. "Maybe we can help with the
arrangements. There's a new priest at Sacred Heart."

"Good idea." Owen leafed through the yearbook pages. "I think
I'd like to talk to a doctor about one of the loose ends that's been
bothering me. Is Tom McDougall still around?"

"Dr. Tom? He retired at least five years ago."

Owen turned the yearbook pages back to the football team and
found the photo he was looking for. In the center of the team layout
was a picture of a bulky tackle standing with his arms folded and
padded legs outspread, squinting out over high cheekbones that nearly
hid the earflaps of a flimsy leather helmet. Underneath the photo, the
legend read: "T. McDougall, Tackle." He showed the picture to his
mother.

Ruth smiled. "Dr. Tom was a handsome devil all right. Why do
you want to see him?"

"I thought I'd like to talk to him about head injuries."

"Oh, Owen. Were you badly hurt?"

Owen raised both his hands to ward off his mother's concern. "My skull's lots harder than whatever it was hit with. The county doctor says X rays of my head showed nothing." When his mother didn't react to the old Dizzy Dean joke, Owen added, "It's not about me; I want to ask about Mary Jewel's injuries."

"I'm sure Dr. Tom will be happy to see you. Remember when you had the measles and he came out to the house?"

"Mom, I was five years old."

"But he was always doing things for you boys. And he asks about you whenever I see him."

"I'll give him a call. Maybe I can see him before I have dinner with Robin."

"What time do you expect to be home?"

"You going to ground me if I'm late?"

"I'd like to know when to expect you, is all. I don't want any hanky-panky under my roof."

"Then we'll hank and we'll pank somewhere else."

"You always did."

"You weren't supposed to know."

"I'm your mother, Owen. I know everything."

Owen closed the yearbook and handed it back to his mother. "I'm beginning to believe it."

D<small>R</small>. T<small>OM</small> M<small>C</small>D<small>OUGALL</small> lived in a colonnaded house that backed onto the ninth hole of the Spring Hill Country Club. His front lawn was as flat and well-tended as the green in his backyard. The doctor answered the door himself. He had a shock of wavy white hair over a florid face, and looked as if he still might be able to play tackle for Denison. The doctor's right hand dwarfed Owen's as he clasped it and led him into a living room lined with floor-to-ceiling bookshelves.

"It's good to see you, Owen," the doctor said in the low, precise voice that Owen had always found reassuring as a child.

Through the door to the dining room, Owen could see three women about his mother's age seated around a bridge table. "It looks as if I'm interrupting you," he said.

"Nonsense. We were about to take a break. How can I help you?"

Owen outlined the details of Mary Jewel's accident and subsequent death. "First of all," he asked, "leaving aside the fact that George barely nudged the woman, is it even possible for someone to die of a blow received well over a week ago?''

The doctor sucked on the earpiece of his spectacles. ''A week is a long time. She could have had a subdural hematoma, a blood clot that eventually creates enough internal pressure to cause death, but that usually works itself out in two to four days. I've never heard of a case where it took more than a week.''

''Wouldn't she exhibit some symptoms?''

''Dizziness, perhaps incontinence. But you said she was wearing a neck brace. Maybe she reported these symptoms to her doctor.''

''The day after George hit her she was riding her bicycle up and down the countryside and traipsing all over Gobbler's Grade. Even after she got her neck brace, she was holding forth at the city council lectern and swilling beer by the pitcherful at the Oasis. If she was dizzy and incontinent, she hid it well.''

The doctor slid his spectacles into place and peered through them. ''So what do you think happened?''

Owen shook his head. ''I don't know. Maybe a heart attack. Maybe somebody clobbered her. God knows, she was an exasperating woman.''

''But Owen, it's a moot point. Any pathologist worth his salt could tell a fresh bruise from a two-week-old wound. And the signs of cardiac arrest are unmistakable.'' The doctor lowered his spectacles and peered over them. ''Who's the acting coroner?''

''A Dr. Johnston.''

Tom McDougall's bushy white eyebrows lifted a full inch above his spectacles. ''Don Johnston?''

''I think so. Is that bad?''

''We physicians have a reputation for protecting our own. But I'm retired now, so I'll tell you this. We used to say if you wanted to hide something from Don Johnston, the best place to put it was in a medical journal.''

''It gets worse, then. Dr. Johnston was the one who treated Mary Jewel Robertson after George bumped her.''

''And put her in a neck brace?''

''And sicced her insurance company on George.''

''And you're afraid he might adjust his autopsy to cover a fraudulent earlier diagnosis?''

''He might if he made a habit of helping patients bilk insurance companies.''

"Seems a bit extreme, even for Don Johnston." The doctor took off his spectacles and pointed them at Owen's chest. "Tell you what I'll do, though. There's an old colleague of mine from Saint Vincent's, Howard Sussman. He's a crackerjack pathologist. I'll arrange things between him and Sheriff Reader so that he consults on this case."

The doctor put his hand on Owen's shoulder and took a step toward the door, but Owen was slow to move. "Was there something else?" the doctor asked.

"You were at Denison with my dad. What can you tell me about him?"

The doctor tilted his head toward the ceiling and adjusted his eyeglasses, as if trying to focus on something on the second floor. "I barely knew your father then," he said finally. "We traveled in different circles. I was pre-med, he was engineering. I played football, he played basketball. Our paths rarely crossed."

"But it was a small campus."

"Oh, yes. And your father left his mark on it. He set a conference record his senior year. Scored eighteen points in one quarter. Most of them from the backcourt with a little waist-high set shot." The doctor flicked both hands upward from his waist to demonstrate. "Of course, the game's changed since then. Now any bozo coming off the bench can score that many dangling from the backboard."

"I never knew that. About the record, I mean."

The doctor focused on the ceiling again. "They called him Cat, I believe." He shook his head. "No, it was Alleycat. Alleycat Allison. He was catnip for the coeds."

The doctor removed his spectacles and rubbed his eyes, as if he'd seen too much, or told a patient more than he was sure of. "I didn't really get to know your dad until we both settled here in Barkley. He was a good man. He should have lived longer. If he had, he'd have been proud of both you boys. George taking his place as Highway Commissioner, and you with your graduate scholarship to Cal Tech. No question, he'd have been proud of you."

"It's nice to think that," Owen said. But he remembered the lost look on George's face as they bundled him into the treatment center, and thought of his own career flailings and flailings, and he wasn't so sure.

THE DINING ROOM of the Spring Hill Country Club had low beamed ceilings and dimmed lights that took the eyes of the diners to the floodlit greens and fairways outside its picture windows. Robin was wearing a black sheath set off by a single strand of pearls. From time to time she ran her finger along the strand, drawing Owen's attention to her aristocratic throat and the cleavage beneath it. He couldn't tell if the pearls were real, but he remembered that the cleavage certainly was.

As they finished dinner, Robin let her hand drift slowly from her necklace to her lap. "Did you ever dream when we were growing up that we might be eating dinner here at the country club?"

"I never thought much about the country club one way or another."

"Not even when you were caddying here?"

Owen looked out at the floodlit greens and hilly fairways. "Nope, it was just a golf course to me."

"That's because you didn't grow up on the wrong side of the tracks."

"You weren't on the wrong side of the tracks for very long. Once your dad started building roads, he could afford to move you out and buy up the tracks. And this club as well."

Robin laughed. "That's true. But they never really accepted Dad here. He was too rough and tumble for them."

"Your dad was a fearsome figure to me then."

"He would have been more fearsome if he'd known what we were doing up on Gobbler's Grade." Robin fingered her necklace. "You know what's scary to me, Owen? We're older now than our parents were then."

"That's scary all right."

"You never had any children, did you?"

Owen caught his napkin, which was slipping off his lap. Being childless was one of his biggest regrets. "No, we kept putting it off. I heard you did, though."

Robin's smile outshone her pearls as she reached into her purse. "Here's my Stephanie," she said, passing a photo to Owen.

The photo showed a pretty young girl kicking a shapely leg high over her head in the center of four kneeling chorus boys dressed up as ranch hands.

"She was Ado Annie in *Oklahoma*," Robin said.

"I can tell she's shy, like her mother."

Robin put the photo back in her purse. "I'm a good mother, Owen."

"I don't doubt it."

"It's not so easy raising a teenager nowadays. Especially when you're on your own."

"I know," Owen said. "I took care of a teenage boy last summer after his father died. It made me think I was missing something, not having one or two of my own."

When Robin didn't respond, he asked, "How long have you been divorced?"

"Nine years. Almost as long as we were married."

"What happened?"

Robin shrugged slightly, and one shoulder strap lowered to reveal the line of her black bra. "Nothing. Everything. Rudy had married the boss's daughter and was on track to take over the company when Dad retired. Dad had even promised it to him. When the time came, though, Dad gave Hager Construction to Eddie. Rudy left to form his own company. I went from being the boss's daughter to an aging wife whose father and brother had done him wrong."

"I'm surprised your dad would renege on a promise."

"It wasn't even very smart. Eddie's not up to running the company. He's botched a few jobs, and if he doesn't finish paving Gobbler's Grade soon, Hager Construction could go under."

"Because of the penalties?"

"He's losing five thousand a day there. But that's not all. He had to put up a bond equal to half the amount of the job. The state won't release it until it's done. So long as they don't release it, he doesn't have the capital to bond any more big jobs. And there's a sizable state bid coming up next month."

Owen poured the last of their wine into Robin's glass. "So he can't bid on anything else until he finishes Gobbler's Grade?"

"Nothing major. It's a winner-take-all game now. As the jobs and the bonds get bigger, the competition gets weeded out. There aren't that many local firms able to bond the big bids."

"So whoever spiked his equipment might have had more in mind than just vandalism."

"Like what?"

"Like eliminating the competition for next month's bid."

Robin looked as if she were lost in thought. The waitress brought their desserts, a dark chocolate decadence cake for Owen and a praline pecan pie topped with cinnamon ice cream for Robin. Both desserts were surrounded by a rich caramel sauce.

Owen picked at his cake with a fork. "It certainly looks decadent."

Something brushed against his inner thigh and he felt Robin's bare foot in his lap. He dropped his fork in the caramel sauce.

Robin fingered her pearls. "Let's talk real decadence."

Owen retrieved his fork with two fingers, looked quickly around the room, and licked the caramel sauce off the handle. "I don't know if I'm up for real decadence."

Robin's toes wriggled in his lap. "Oh, you're up for it, all right."

"Jesus, Robin. Take it easy."

"Don't tell me you haven't had a few fantasies about us."

"I haven't had a really good fantasy since Grace Kelly died."

Robin tilted her head back and looked down her nose at him. "Grace Kelly, huh? Well, I can do blond and aloof." She spotted something over Owen's shoulder, swore softly, and her toes stopped massaging his erection.

Robin's ex-husband appeared beside their table, wrapping a silk paisley scarf around a neck that already sported a bright red bow tie. He extended his hand to Owen. "I'm Rudy Slater," he said. "Don't bother to get up. If I know my ex-wife, she's got her foot in your lap right about now."

The foot withdrew suddenly, but the erection stayed. Owen remained seated and shook the offered hand.

"I listened to your little speech the other night," Slater said. "Too bad they decided not to widen the bridge."

Owen bunched his napkin on his lap. "I heard your talk, too. You didn't seem to care much one way or the other."

"We're servants of the democratic process," Slater said. "We build whatever the people want."

"Even if you know it'll cost a few lives?"

"There's no way to be sure of that." Slater dipped a finger into Robin's ice cream. She swatted at his hand, but he jerked it away quickly and licked his finger. "Umm, cinnamon."

"Bastard," Robin whispered.

"Well," Slater said. "I just came over to see how you were spending my alimony." He nodded in Owen's direction. "Nice to have met you, Allison."

Owen watched Slater leave the dining room. "I have to say that was a mood-shattering experience."

"Don't let that oily exterior fool you," Robin said. "Underneath, he's got a heart full of pure slime."

"How'd you two ever get together?"

"I've known him almost as long as I've known you. He was with Daddy from the beginning. That's probably why he was able to stand up to him."

Robin dipped her spoon into her ice cream and licked it clean. "Now, where were we?"

"Somewhere I wasn't sure I wanted to be," Owen said.

She turned her attention to her praline pecan pie. "Then we won't go back there."

IN THE CAR on the way home, Robin hunched over the wheel, staring straight into the oncoming headlights. "Look, this is hard for me," she said. "Maybe I'm not doing it right. I'm not looking for a lifelong commitment here. For now, I'd be happy with a live mind, a few laughs, some fondling, and a little tenderness. I happen to know you can deliver all those things."

"Maybe I'm the one looking for a commitment."

"Then I lied about that part." She looked over one nearly bare shoulder at him. "Are you? Looking for a commitment?"

"I'm not sure what I'm looking for."

"You used to know. How did that mantra go? Something about money, wealth, and power?"

Owen hadn't recited it since his high school days, but it came back to him immediately. "All I want is money, fame, wealth, power, immortality, six good laughs a day, and a blond nymphomaniac who owns a liquor store."

"I don't think you ever told me the part about the blonde. Would you settle for a brunette divorcee with part interest in a construction company?"

"Hell, I'd settle for six good laughs a day."

"But something's holding you back here. Is it your ex-wife?"

Owen remembered his earlier phone call with Judith. He missed her. There was no denying it.

Before he could reply, Robin continued, "I'm just looking for a way in here. Think of it as a free trial offer. I happen to know you can handle more than one relationship at a time. I had spies at Marquette, you know. You cut quite a swath through the female population there. How many were there? Ten? Fifteen?"

"That was a long time ago. I doubt if I even dated ten different girls. Nobody called me Alleycat Allison."

"There was that pom-pom girl. The one you spent your birthday with instead of me. What was her name?"

"Edie...Edie somebody." Owen found he couldn't remember her last name. "It didn't mean anything. You meant something. My wife meant something. I want it to mean something again."

"Don't you think it will?"

"I don't know. I'm not the same person I was then. You're not the same either. I'd like a chance to get to know the new Robin first." And a little more about how the new Owen differed from the old, he thought.

"There've been quite a few new Robins since we last saw each other. I've shed a husband, raised a daughter, made peace with my father, and fought off a few fortune hunters who thought Hager Construction is worth a lot more than Eddie's left us with." Robin flicked at her eyelash with her finger. "And one or two of those new Robins has done some pretty foolish things."

Owen traced his finger along her cheekbone. "I'll spot you five foolish things and two howling blunders and still pile up more regrets than you can list."

She captured his finger and nibbled on it. "You're sure I can't take you home tonight?"

"Not tonight."

She pulled her Mercedes up in front of Owen's house and turned to him. "But I'll see you again. You won't leave without seeing me?"

Owen saw the curtains move in his mother's bedroom. "I won't leave without seeing you."

"That's good." Robin slid across the seat and linked her hands behind Owen's head. "Now close your eyes and think of Grace Kelly."

Her tongue tasted of cinnamon, pralines, and promise.

NINE

Allegedly Deceased

"HOW DID SHE ever get her expenses up to thirty-five hundred dollars?" Owen asked the young insurance adjuster who was handling Mary Jewel Robertson's claim against his brother George.

"It's all right here, all thoroughly itemized." The young man smoothed his necktie, opened a manila file overflowing with loose sheets of paper, and turned it so Owen could examine it from his side of the desk.

The young man couldn't be much older than George's boy Billy, Owen thought, and already he was a budding bureaucrat. Owen ran his finger down the list of expenditures Mary Jewel had submitted for reimbursement. The big-ticket items were her three visits to Dr. Donald Johnston, assorted X rays, and a fitting for a neck brace. Together they amounted to $2000. After that, a seemingly endless list of incidental items brought the total up to $3500.

"What are you looking for?" the young man asked.

"Anything that smacks of fraud," Owen said. "I was with my brother when he hit Mary Jewel. He barely nudged her and she didn't complain of any injury that night."

"Dr. Johnston was quite thorough. All his forms were properly submitted."

"You do a lot of business with Dr. Johnston?" Owen asked.

"I can't speak for the other adjusters, but his office has always been quite helpful with my claims."

Owen scanned the items lower down on the list. "She bought two hundred fifty dollars' worth of painkillers."

"She went for brand names rather than the generics. Strictly speaking, we have no control over that."

"And a hundred and fifty dollars' worth of Ace bandages. That has to be enough to wrap a mummy or two."

"Ace bandages are an approved expenditure."

"And here's a hundred forty-four dollars for something called Depends. What's that?"

"I'm not quite sure." The young man turned the file toward him and fished through the supporting receipts. "Here it is: eight packages of absorbent pads at eighteen dollars each from Rexall Drugs."

"Diapers for adults," Owen said.

"She complained of incontinence."

"But eight packages would have to be, what? A month's supply?"

The young man adjusted his necktie. "Is there something wrong with that?"

"Sounds like a lot of crap to me."

OWEN STOOD IN FRONT of the incontinents display at the Rexall drugstore. The display stretched the length of a full aisle and filled all the shelves with large fluffy packets of products bearing brand names like Depends, Serenity, and Poise. There was even a generic brand manufactured by the drug chain. All products he had never heard of or given a moment's thought. He counted himself as lucky, although the faces of satisfied, active users smiling from the packages made incontinence seem like a minor inconvenience.

"Owen? Owen Allison?"

Owen looked up to see a rotund man extending a pudgy palm. The man's shirt had popped a button, and an expanse of white undershirt puffed out above his belt buckle. A plastic badge on his shirt pocket announced his name as Donny, and his position as Store Manager.

Owen shook the extended hand. "Donny?"

"Oh, hell, I wouldn't expect you to recognize me. Donny Samples. I caught for you second string the year we won the state championship. Finally made first string when Tom Goheen graduated."

"Of course. How are you?"

"Just fine." Donny thwacked his fist into an imaginary catcher's mitt. "Playing any ball?"

"Gave it up for tennis. How about yourself?"

"Slow-pitch softball, is all. Got the store in a coed league. Terrific for morale."

"I'll bet."

Donny crossed his stubby arms over his stomach. "Great to see you, Owen. What can I do you for?"

Owen pointed to the aisle-long display. "I was wondering about these adult diapers."

"Bladder-control pads."

"Bladder-control pads. They look like they come in pretty bulky packages. Do people usually buy more than one package at a time?"

"Usually one or two. One'll last you a week, easy. There's no shame to it, Owen. They're really popular items. What with the population aging and all. That's why we've got this whole aisleful. It's a little like buying toilet paper." Donny raised his eyebrows and shoved at Owen's elbow. "Come to think of it, it's a whole lot like buying toilet paper."

"But I buy toilet paper in bulk. Twelve rolls at a time. That's more than a week's supply."

"That's the way they're packaged." Donny pointed at the shelves. "These here items are packaged a week's worth at a time, and that's generally the way individuals buy 'em. Institutions, rest homes, places like that, they buy in bulk, and we just sell them right off the loading dock. You want me to give you a volume discount? Is that it?"

"No. I wasn't asking for myself."

"Like I said, there ain't no shame to it. Some folks do buy in bulk, though. Couple of weeks ago, Mary Jewel Robertson, God rest her soul, filled two shopping carts and pushed them through the checkout line. I figured she must have been a prodigious pisser. Turned out she was just a pain in the ass."

Owen sensed what was coming. "How's that?" he asked, to push Donny further into the story.

"Next day she returned 'em all."

"Every one? She didn't use any?"

"Well, now, Owen, we got a pretty liberal return policy here, but I assure you we don't take back used bladder-control pads."

"You know what I mean. She returned every package she bought unopened?"

"Every one. Along with a pile of Ace bandages and enough pain-killers to stock a hospital ward."

"And you gave her her money back?"

"Nothing was opened. I told you, we got a liberal return policy."

"Would you still have a record of that transaction?"

Donny shrugged. "We got a record of both transactions. We won't close our books till the end of the month."

"Can I get copies?"

"I don't know, Owen. It's company business."

"That's okay, Donny. They could be important, though. Just promise me you'll hang on to them until you hear from me or the sheriff."

"The sheriff?" I'm not getting anybody into trouble, am I?"

"No, Donny. You'll be getting somebody out of trouble." Owen shook his hand. "Great seeing you again."

"PRETTY GOOD detective work for an amateur," Sheriff Thad Reader said after listening to Owen's story. "What made you suspect she'd take all that stuff back?"

"I was there when George hit her. I knew she wasn't hurt. And I remembered Mom saying that Mary Jewel would squeeze a penny till Lincoln puckered. It just made sense that she'd try to wring every cent she could out of the accident."

The sheriff tilted back his office chair and rested one boot on his lower desk drawer. "Well, you probably saved the insurance company a little money. But just because Mary Jewel got a little creative with her claim doesn't mean she wasn't hurt."

"Oh, come on. I was there when she landed on her butt."

"So you keep telling me. But you didn't examine her. Doc Johnston did."

"Johnston's patients have more insurance claims than symptoms. At least let another pathologist take a look at her."

"I'm already doing that. Doc McDougall is sending somebody over at your behest. A Dr. Sussman. He should have something for us by the end of the day."

Owen stood to leave. "You can't really think my brother killed Mary Jewel?"

"Maybe not with his car."

Owen sat down again. He could see where the sheriff was headed. It was a road he hadn't yet let himself travel. "What's that supposed to mean?"

The sheriff scratched behind his ear with the tip of a well-chewed pen. "Think about it. If the accident didn't kill Mary Jewel, somebody did it deliberately. Your brother threatened her in public just before she died, and we don't know where he was that night."

"Hell, he doesn't even know where he was. He checked into the Creekside Cabins around three in the morning."

"A three-o'clock check-in doesn't clear him. He could have killed Mary Jewel and still made the motel by that time."

"Then I'll find out what bars he hit on his way there."

"Afraid that's my job." He raised the chewed end of his pen like a conductor ready to start a symphony. "Don't get me wrong, now. I appreciate your help. What you've given me is good stuff, but you've been about a half step slow in getting it. Nosing around a fresh murder can be dangerous, especially if you stay a half step slow. You found that out the other night. Best you leave it to us professionals." He brought his reclining chair upright with a sharp *thwack*. "Understand?"

"No, I don't understand." Owen raised his hands as if he were lifting a heavy weight, then let them drop to his lap. "I may be a half step slow, but it looks to me as if you haven't left the starting block. I may have been too late to save Dolores Cantrip, but I chased down the insurance fraud and found you a competent pathologist. Seems to me you need all the help you can get."

"We're not after the same thing here. I want you to stay out of it."

"Why aren't we after the same thing?"

"If Mary Jewel was murdered, I want to find out who did it. You just want to make sure your brother didn't."

"I don't see how that hurts your investigation."

"Suppose you found out your brother saw Mary Jewel after the town meeting. Would you tell me?"

"What makes you think I'd keep anything from you?"

"You already have."

Owen rose from his chair and planted his fists on the sheriff's desk. "You better explain that."

"You told me your father didn't own a gun."

The sheriff's statement hung in the air between them. Owen clenched his fists. He didn't know what to say. Finally, he blurted, "That was my mother," and regretted it as soon as the words were out.

"I didn't see you rushing to set the record straight."

Owen took two steps backward. "You've found Dad's gun."

"We've found a gun that looks to be your father's. We're still checking it out."

"Where? Where did you find it?"

"I'd rather not say. There are some things that just don't add up."
The sheriff waved his hand at the chair Owen had vacated. "Why
don't you sit back down and tell me what you know about the gun."

Owen reported what his mother had told him. That his father had
started taking the gun to work with him after receiving threats, and
that the gun had turned up missing after his father drowned.

"Who was threatening your father?" the sheriff asked.

Owen shrugged. "Mom didn't know. Could have been disgruntled
contractors. He'd made a lot of enemies and was about to testify
before a House Committee."

"Why wouldn't your mother tell me that?"

"You'll have to ask her. She has a hard time thinking clearly about
Dad's death. I've never known her to lie deliberately."

The sheriff chewed on the end of his pen. "All sorts of people lie
to me for all sorts of reasons. Usually, though, it's to cover something
up. Be helpful to know what your mother thought she was hiding."

Owen shook his head slowly, never taking his eyes off the sheriff.
"I'm sure I wouldn't know."

"See, that's another trouble with amateurs like yourself sniffing
around murder. You can't pick and choose what you find out. It all
comes out in a messy string, like puke from a sick puppy. Best to let
us professionals mop up. You go poking around, you're likely to dig
up some things that aren't so pleasant about your father and brother."
The sheriff pointed the chewed end of his pen at Owen and sighted
down it with his good eye. "Are you prepared for that?"

"I guess I'll have to find out."

OWEN CALLED GEORGE at the treatment center to get a list of bars
he might have visited in Barkley between the time he left the council
meeting and the time he checked into the Creekside Cabins. His
brother still couldn't remember where he'd been that night, but he
provided a list of bars that he'd visited at one time or another. The
list included every local bar that Owen had heard of and many he
hadn't, and was only slightly less inclusive than the Yellow Pages.

Before visiting the bars on the list, Owen rummaged through
George's Pontiac for clues to his brother's whereabouts on the night
in question. Given the cluttered state of George's office and garage,
his car was surprisingly clean. Road maps were stored alphabetically
in the pocket under the driver's window, and a black cup-and change
holder, empty of cups and change, straddled the transmission hump.

The glove compartment held only the owner's manual and registration, while the backseat looked as if it had never been used.

The trunk was just as pristine as the rest of the car, except for one item that caused Owen's breath to catch in his throat. A tire iron lay loose in the center of the trunk bed. Owen stared at it for a long time, afraid to pick it up, and afraid not to pick it up. Finally he reached for it and turned it over in his hands. It was a long hexagonal iron rod with one end bent, almost as an afterthought, and milled to accommodate lug nuts. He was relieved to see that it had evidently never been used, even for changing tires, and was ashamed of himself for thinking that it might have had some more lethal mission. He pitched the iron into the tire well and slammed the trunk lid down over it.

Owen started visiting the bars on George's list after dinner, hoping to find someone who'd seen his brother on the night Mary Jewel died. By closing time, the only person he'd found who remembered George was the bartender at the Oasis, the college hangout across the street from the council chambers. The bartender thought George had been in the bar when Mary Jewel and her friends were celebrating their victory, but he wasn't sure of the exact time. Since Owen and Ruth had stopped in at the Oasis shortly after the meeting without seeing George, he must either have left before they arrived or come after they had left. Either way, Owen reasoned, it didn't help George's case that the only bartender who remembered seeing him that evening was the same one who was serving pitchers of beer to Mary Jewel and her friends. He decided to do more checking before reporting anything back to Sheriff Reader.

THE NEXT MORNING'S newspaper carried the story above the fold on the front page.

ACTIVIST'S DEATH RULED MURDER

A coroner's investigation revealed yesterday that the death of Mary Jewel Robertson, local environmental activist, resulted from a blow to the head suffered shortly after she successfully led the fight to stop the widening of Barkley's Fifth Street Bridge. Sheriff Thad Reader announced that he is spearheading an investigation to find the person or persons responsible, and is confident that Ms. Robertson's assailant will be brought to justice.

The article went on to say that Mary Jewel was a familiar figure at local council meetings and to list the fights she'd led to safeguard

Barkley's endangered species, air quality, and open space. The last paragraph caught Owen's attention.

The murder was the third to be uncovered in the last two weeks involving individuals associated with highway construction in Raleigh County. Earlier this month, construction workers on Gobbler's Grade unearthed the bullet-riddled corpse of Raymond Cantrip, onetime assistant to former Highway Commissioner Wayne Allison. Just two days ago, Cantrip's wife Dolores was murdered by an unknown assailant at Shady Acres Rest Home. These deaths are a sad reminder of the days when West Virginia's highways were paved with kickbacks and corruption. (See Sidebar.)

The sidebar, headed HIGHWAY ROBBERY, chronicled the shady dealings of the West Virginia Highway Department from the late fifties onward. Owen scanned the initial entries.

●1959   Mingo County Five jailed for conspiracy to defraud government of Highway Department funds.
●1962   Blatnik Committee of U.S. House of Representatives investigates illegal right-of-way acquisition practices in West Virginia.
●1962   Prior to testifying before Blatnik Committee, Highway Commissioner Wayne Allison and Aide Raymond Cantrip disappear, allegedly deceased in floodwaters following dam washout.
●1968   Ex-Governor Banning, five others, indicted for bribery and kickbacks involving highway contracts.

The sidebar marched chronologically forward to the discovery of Ray Cantrip's body and the deaths of Dolores Cantrip and Mary Jewel Robertson, but Owen couldn't read the intervening entries. His eyes kept returning to the 1962 entry listing Wayne Allison and Ray Cantrip as ''allegedly deceased.'' Allegedly deceased! They'd lumped his father with the crooks who preceded him and the crooks who came after him. Hell, according to Sammy Earle, his father was responsible for jailing the Mingo County Five. But there he was, linked in a news story with those five and Governor Banning's band of highwaymen.

Owen crumpled the newspaper and looked around for a place to hide it so his mother wouldn't read it. Not seeing one, he tucked the paper under his arm and slammed out of the house, headed for the library. The least he could do was get the facts to set the record straight.

MARY ALICE HOGARTY smiled when she saw Owen enter the library and reached under her desk to produce a bound volume about two inches thick.

"I was hoping you'd come back," she said. "I got you a copy of the Blatnik Hearings from the Marshall Library."

Owen hefted the volume. "Pretty weighty material." Someone had placed yellow Post-it notes throughout the book, with comments on specific lines of testimony. Owen thumbed one of the yellow markers. "Did you do this?"

"All part of the service."

Owen opened the volume to one of the snatches of testimony Mary Alice had marked.

CHAIR:	You knew of one qualified appraiser in ten?
MR. JAMES CLARK:	Yes, sir.
CHAIR:	You then knew nine who were not?
MR. CLARK:	Very nearly nine.

On the yellow Post it note, Mary Alice had written, "Good Lord, 90% incompetence."

Owen closed the book and nodded. "Laboratory tests have conclusively shown that nine out of ten is ninety percent."

"It's all like that," Mary Alice said. "Full of incompetence and petty graft and corruption. It's ghastly. There was a reporter in reading it yesterday. She was appalled too."

"I just finished reading her piece. Appalling's the word, all right."

"I mean, when the Republicans were in, they filled the bottom slots with party hacks who could barely add, let alone appraise property. Then, when the Democrats took over, they cleaned house and filled those slots with their own nincompoops. The graft never stopped flowing, it just got diverted from one pot to another."

Mary Alice stopped suddenly, her forehead flushing under her red hair. "I'm sorry, I shouldn't get so worked up. You were in government for a while. Is it still that bad?"

Owen thought about the political appointees he'd known during his four years in Washington. "It's worse," he said. "Now they fill the top slots the same way."

"I found you some other references, too," Mary Alice said. She fitted her hand through the cuff of her metal cane and limped over to a clipboard holding a sheaf of copied sheets. Owen moved to help her, and she steadied herself against him as she flipped through the sheets of paper.

"Here's a great story Jack Anderson wrote in the Sunday Supplement in 1962." Mary Alice flipped to a sheet marked with one of her yellow Post-its and read, "The proper people of Ripley, West Virginia, rejoiced when they learned a new highway was scheduled to cut through a notorious bawdy house outside of town."

"I'm surprised the Highway Department didn't let the bawdy house stand and move the road," Owen said.

Mary Alice flipped the page over, swayed slightly, and clutched Owen's elbow for support. Her perfume smelled of lilacs. It was the same perfume Robin wore.

"They did better than that," she said. "They paid the madam four times what the property was worth so she could set herself up in fancier digs closer to town. Then it's rumored that the road commissioners took the balance of the overpayment out in trade."

Whores screwing whores, Owen thought. He was about to clean up his language and repeat the thought to Mary Alice when she suddenly stepped away from him and brought the clipboard up to cover her mouth. "Oh, Owen, I'm sorry," she said. "Your father was a road commissioner, wasn't he? I didn't mean to imply..."

Owen reached out and covered the hand holding the clipboard with his own hand. "It's all right, Mary Alice. My father wasn't one of the bawdy-house commissioners, or the bribe-taking commissioners, or the kickback commissioners, or the indicted commissioners." He took the clipboard from her hand. "And I'm hoping these articles you've pulled together will help me prove he wasn't. I really appreciate what you've done."

Mary Alice leaned on her metal cane. She looked lost without a book in her other hand to balance her weight. "Just ask if you need anything else."

"Don't worry, I will."

Owen took the clipboard and volume of hearings to a corner carrel and opened the report. The Blatnik Committee's official designation was "Special Subcommittee on the Federal Aid Highway Program of

the Committee on Public Works of the House of Representatives.''
Its hearings took place õver eight days in July, 1962, and focused on
right-of-way acquisition practices in West Virginia. Mary Alice's yellow notes marked a trail of rigged assessments, unqualified assessors,
bungled procedures, nepotism, and a political spoils system run amok.

Owen abandoned Mary Alice's paper trail and turned to the pages
documenting Sammy Earle's testimony. Sammy had been called as a
substitute for Owen's father and Ray Cantrip, and the Chair began by
expressing his condolences for the loss of these two public servants
and extending his sympathy to their co-workers and immediate family.
The Chair then opened the questioning.

CHAIR:	Mr. Earle, are you familiar with any of the following firms: Wilson Paving; Harding Asphalt; or Coolidge Construction?
MR. SAMMY EARLE:	No, sir, I am not.
CHAIR:	It would be fair to say that if you are unaware of them, they are not doing business in West Virginia?
MR. EARLE:	I believe so, sir.
CHAIR:	In fact, let the record show that these firms are not recognized as doing business anywhere in the United States. Can you tell us then, Mr. Earle, how it is that these firms were certified as bidders, for a sizable construction project on West Virginia Route Ten?
MR. EARLE:	No, sir, I cannot
CHAIR:	Yet these three nonexistent firms, certified by Mr. Raymond Cantrip, were the only recorded bidders for the Route Ten project except for the eventual winner, Hager Construction. It would appear, then, that Hager Construction had no effective competition for the job. Would you not agree, Mr. Earle?

MR. EARLE:	It would appear so, sir.
CHAIR:	Can you tell us how this could come about?
MR. EARLE:	I'm afraid not, sir. Perhaps Mr. Cantrip—
CHAIR:	Mr. Cantrip was scheduled to testify, but he is now answering to a higher authority. I'm asking you, Mr. Earle, if this practice of disguising non-competitive bids is common in West Virginia?
MR. EARLE:	I could not say, sir.

Owen inferred that the Committee had expected to get more definitive information on phony bid-rigging from his father or Ray Cantrip, but that Sammy either couldn't or wouldn't fill in the blanks. Owen wondered what his father would have said. What did he know? If he had testified, would he have blown the lid off the phony bidders? Or would he have been as uninformed and noncommittal as Sammy Earle?

Owen spent the rest of the day trying to look up information on the Mingo County Five, to verify his father's role in sending them to jail. All he had to go on was the year of their indictment, 1959. The state's newspapers had no indexing system at that time, so he started with the *Charleston Gazette*'s January file and scanned the first page of each edition. With Mary Alice's help, he worked his way through the end of April by the time the library closed, but he found no mention of the Mingo County Five or any road scandals in that county.

Frustrated, Owen rewound the microfiche reel and turned off the viewer. His eyes ached from staring at the back-lit images of newspaper pages on the viewing screen. He felt useless. His brother was under suspicion of murder, his father was being libeled in the press, and he couldn't even nail down a few simple facts. Maybe he ought to underline the word *failure* on his business cards.

Mary Alice patted him on the shoulder on her way out of the library. He nodded and thanked her for her help. Her perfume was the same as Robin's, but the way her sleeve brushed the nape of his neck reminded him of Judith.

TEN

Alleycat Allison

DOLORES CANTRIP'S funeral mass took place on a foggy morning in the same small church where the memorial service for her husband and Wayne Allison had been held thirty-five years earlier. Bobby sat alone in the front row beside the plain wooden casket, with Owen and his mother two rows behind him. A few parishioners were scattered around the dark mahogany pews. The only other face Owen recognized was Mary Alice Hogarty's. The rest of the small congregation looked like regular mass-goers, several of whom might have been attending daily mass ever since Owen and Bobby were altar boys. Their faces were weathered and sturdy, with deep-set eyes that had seen depressions, floods, mine disasters, and a hundred private miseries.

The young priest finished mass and descended to the lectern at the head of the casket. He quoted the Twenty-third Psalm, spoke for a while in generalities, and framed a few short sentences about Dolores Cantrip and her service to the parish. Then he paused, explained that he had been new to the parish when Dolores Cantrip entered the Shady Acres Rest Home, and apologized for not being able to say more of a personal nature. However, he invited any of Mrs. Cantrip's family or friends to come to the lectern and share their memories of her with the congregation. After issuing the invitation, he stepped aside from the lectern and waited expectantly.

No one moved. Owen glanced at his mother, who stared intently at the rosary in her hands. In the front pew, Bobby sat red-eyed and rigid, as if shell-shocked. Owen scanned the immobile faces of the congregation. The priest shuffled, edging back toward the lectern. One of the altar boys stifled a smirk.

Owen stood and walked slowly past the casket, gathering his

thoughts. The priest smiled at his approach as if he were the Second Coming. Owen gripped the sides of the lectern and looked down at Bobby. "I'm Owen Allison," he said to the congregation. "Dolores Cantrip was the mother of my friend Bobby Cantrip. When we were growing up, she always made me feel welcome in her home and shared whatever she had, especially her laughter. Her house was filled with laughter." He scanned the faces of the congregation and found his mother, who was still staring at her rosary. "She treated me like an adult, even when I didn't deserve it, and I think that helped me to grow up faster. She raised a good son, alone, under difficult circumstances. Her husband died too soon, and so did she. I hope they're together again, and I'm sure that wherever she is, there's laughter."

ON THE WAY TO the cemetery, Ruth sat quietly as Owen drove, following the hearse. Finally she said, "I suppose I didn't treat you like an adult?"

Owen was startled. "Oh, Mom. I was just winging it. I was thinking about you, really. I didn't actually know Bob's mother all that well."

Ruth patted the hand nearest her on the wheel. "I'm sorry. It was a good thing you did, talking up like that. I was proud of you. It's just…there was always something about that woman." She pursed her lips. "Well, she's at rest now."

Owen and his mother were the only members of the congregation to join Bobby and the priest and altar boys at the graveside. Owen hadn't visited the cemetery since he and Bobby were altar boys, and was shocked by its appearance. Most of the nearby gravestones had been vandalized. A statue of Christ overseeing the entryway was missing a hand and half a halo. Small wire cages erected to protect flowers had been tipped over, and the buds they had covered were uprooted. It didn't seem to be the tranquil resting place the priest was describing.

Bobby wept silently but uncontrollably as the casket was lowered into the earth. Afterward, he pulled himself together to shake Owen's hand and thank him for speaking at the service. "I wasn't expecting that open-mike thing," he said. "They never had that when we were altar boys."

"Old Father Hampton said the same words over every casket, saint or sinner, man or woman."

Bobby nodded, mimicking the old priest's drone. "Gone to their heavenly rest." He dropped the drone to say, "Look, I've got to see you. When's a good time?"

"Want to stop over right now?"

Bobby looked past Owen at Ruth Allison. "Not at your house. It's got to be alone. Let's have lunch at the Oasis. Soon as you can get there."

THREE PINBALL MACHINES were in full cry across the back wall of the Oasis when Owen arrived. Bobby sat in a corner booth, peeling the label off a half-full bottle of Bud Light. An empty bottle sat beside the one he was stripping. A plastic basket holding the remains of a half-eaten hamburger had been shoved to the far side of the booth, which was covered with the carved initials of students past and present.

When Owen sat down, Bobby lifted a shoebox from the wooden bench he was sitting on and placed it on the table. "I got this stuff out of Mom's safe deposit box," he said. "It's not a lot to show for a life."

"There's you."

"For a little while, anyway. But my life probably won't fill out the rest of this shoebox." Bobby reached inside the box and brought out a folded certificate with a gold-embossed seal.

"Mom's wedding license," he said, unfolding the document. "She was married on February seventeenth, 1952."

"So?"

"So she always celebrated her anniversary three months earlier, on November seventeenth, nine months to the day before my August seventeenth birthday. She claimed I was conceived on her wedding night."

"So three months went by before your father married her. So what? If you're worried that you're one-third bastard, don't. I've always figured the balance was more like fifty-fifty, and I haven't held it against you."

"It's just strange, is all. It's like I never really knew her." One of the pinball machines thocked out three free games, and the player released the flippers long enough to high-five an onlooker.

Bobby took a packet of letters from the shoebox. They were written on different kinds of stationery and tied with a red ribbon. "This is what I really wanted to show you. They're love letters."

Owen held up a warning hand. "Whoa, there. I don't want to read your mother's love letters."

"They're from your dad."

Owen stared at the letters. The pinball noise seemed to amplify and he wanted to press his palms against his ears to shut it out.

Bobby untied the ribbon and thrust the packet toward Owen like a magician forcing cards on a reluctant participant.

Owen pulled the top three letters off the stack. They were all signed "Love, Wayne," in his father's small, precise handwriting. "They're not dated," he said.

"What difference does that make?"

"He might have written them before he was married."

Bobby held up two pieces of pale blue stationery. "Here's one dated February fourteenth."

"Valentine's Day. There's one every year." Owen took the two scraps of thin blue paper from Bobby's hand and read the top of the second page.

I scratched a heart in your honor in the fresh asphalt on Horseshoe Bend. Sammy Earle threatened to smooth it over, but I fought him off. I'll bring you here to see it when the leaves turn this fall. There's no more beautiful sight in the world than Hawk's Nest and the New River Gorge. Unless it's your red hair on a white pillow.

Owen refolded the letter. "He talks about laying asphalt on Horseshoe Bend. He wasn't on the road laying asphalt after he got married. He had a desk job then."

Bobby thumped his bottle on the table. "What difference does it make? What difference does it make? You might care whether or not your dad was married when he wrote these letters, but I don't give a shit." He shoved the shoebox toward Owen with the bottom of his bottle. "What matters to me is that there are no letters here from my own dad. Your dad was the love of my mother's life, and the bastard broke her heart."

Owen returned the letter to the stack in the shoebox. He had wanted to know his dad. But this wasn't something he wanted to know. Was it too intimate? Or was the sheriff right that he was only looking for favorable evidence?

Owen nodded toward the box. "What else is in there?"

"Nothing much. A few savings bonds. The deed to the house she had to sell. An annuity from something called the Gray Eagle Trust she used to put me through college. A bracelet from your dad."

"How do you know it's from my dad?"

"He mentioned it in one of his letters."

"So you read all the letters?"

"Damn right. I wanted to know what my mother felt. What was important to her." Bobby shook the shoebox, and the letters bounced out onto the table. "Read 'em yourself. See how your father jerked my mom around. What's the matter? Afraid of what you'll find out?" He shoved two letters across the table to Owen. "Read 'em and weep."

Owen picked up the letters tentatively, as if they were cards dealt to a poker hand that was already a sure loser. Much as he might want to, though, he couldn't fold the hand with Bobby sitting across from him. He opened the top letter and began reading. The precise handwriting described the grading of a creekside road, passed along a joke from Sammy Earle, and recalled intimacies that left no doubt that his father and Bobby's mother had been lovers. The letter ended with his father counting the days until his return to Barkley.

Owen refolded the letter and placed it on the table in front of him, next to a carved heart gouged into the wood by some long-gone student. He tried to remember if he had ever written such a letter. He and Judith had rarely been apart during their short courtship, and he couldn't recall writing her then. And when they were married and on opposite coasts, the only correspondence he remembered was handled by lawyers. During his sophomore year at Marquette, though, he'd sent Robin variations on the same letter three times before admitting that the lack of an answer was her doing, not some foul-up by the postal service.

By the time Owen had finished reading his father's letters, he had divided them into two stacks. One stack contained letters that had clearly been written when his father was still a bachelor. The other, nearly equal in height, held letters that Owen was unable to date. He joined the two stacks together and handed them back to Bobby, who retied them with his mother's red ribbon.

"Well?" Bobby said.

"I don't know what to say. It's pretty clear I didn't know my father."

"At least you know who your father is."

The pinball noise racketed through Owen's thoughts. "You think my father might be your father?"

"There's nothing in that box from Ray Cantrip."

Owen tapped the stack of letters. "Well then, it ought to matter to you whether my father was married when he wrote these. For timing, if nothing else. And I think I know how to find out."

OWEN HAD PASSED THROUGH the outer gate in the maze of hedges surrounding Sammy Earle's house when a voice somewhere behind the hedge said, "Hey, there."

Owen stopped, startled. Sammy was kneeling off to the side of the path beside a sculpted pyracantha bush, pressing a short length of pipe into the ground. A shallow trench ran from the base of the pipe to the front porch of the house.

"Sammy," Owen said. "What in the world are you doing?"

"Installing an alarm system," Sammy said. "Gonna put an electric eye across that path right about where you're standing."

"Expecting burglars?"

"Can't be too careful. There was a mugging in town not two months ago. And Mary Jewel Robertson was killed right in her own home." Sammy stood up and brushed the dirt from his knees. "I guess what I'm really doing is keeping busy. You get to be my age, if you don't use it, you lose it."

"Can I help?"

"No, you're young enough so you're not in danger of losing anything." Sammy stepped over the small trench and joined Owen on the path. "Come on up to the house."

As they approached the house, Sammy nodded toward the front-porch steps. "How about we just sit a spell out here? Get you a beer?"

"That'd be fine. Where's Elizabeth?"

"Visiting her people in Princeton."

Sammy disappeared inside the house and returned with two bottles of Stroh's. He sat down beside Owen on the porch steps, handed him a bottle, and sighted along his own bottle down the trench he'd just dug. "Pert near, but not plumb," he said. "Now your dad, he could eyeball a plumb line."

"Tell me something else about my dad."

"What do you want to know?"

"They say he was called Alleycat Allison when he was in college. That he broke a lot of hearts."

Sammy pulled a pipe from his overalls pocket, filled it with tobacco, and tamped it down. "I didn't know your dad when he was in college." He lit the pipe and stared out through the smoke and flame.

"I don't mind telling you, though, we laid a lot more than roads when he first come here. Hell, you could have paved half the state with the rubbers we left behind."

"What about Dolores Cantrip?"

Sammy swallowed smoke, coughed, and stared at the bowl of his pipe. "What about her?"

"I hear she and Dad had an affair."

"Who told you that?"

"Her boy Bobby found some letters."

"Little heinie banger caused his mother enough grief when she was alive. You think he'd stop now that she's in her grave."

Owen wondered if he was the only one in Barkley that didn't know his best friend was gay. "Never mind about Bobby. Did Dad have an affair with Dolores Cantrip?"

The pipe bowl glowed red and Sammy exhaled a thin stream of smoke. "Dolores was a right pretty woman in those days. She and your dad had a little fling."

"Before or after he was married?"

Sammy took the pipe from his mouth and jabbed Owen's shoulder with the stem. "Look here, son. Your father didn't fool around after he got married. He met your mom, left the road, come here to Barkley, took a desk job, and settled down."

Sammy puffed on his pipe and leaned back against the porch step. "I mind the night of your dad's bachelor party. He and I stood together on the Fifth Street Bridge while he flung six packs of condoms into the river. Scaled them one at a time, like skipping rocks.

"Your mom was a mackerel snapper," Sammy said by way of explanation.

"Excuse me?"

"Oh hell," Sammy said. "You're old enough to remember meatless Fridays. Your mom was a Catholic. So was Dolores Cantrip, for that matter. They didn't hold with the use of condoms."

"I knew that," Owen said. It was one of the beliefs that had driven a wedge between him and the Church.

"Be thankful. Otherwise the best part of you might have wound up in a rubber in the river."

"That's a strong pro-life argument, all right." Owen set his beer aside. "Sounds like my dad had flings with more women than Dolores Cantrip before he was married."

"Son, you ever know a bee to dump all his pollen on just one flower? Or didn't your daddy give you that lecture?"

"I was only ten when he died, Sammy. We never got around to the birds and bees."

Sammy stared at his pipe bowl. "Sorry, I disremembered for a minute there."

Owen recalled the letters he had just read. "Did Dolores Cantrip think she was the only one?"

"Son, I imagine they all thought they were the only ones. We scratched hearts in the asphalt on every road we built. We weren't fools enough to put names in any of them."

"How did Dolores react when Dad married Mom?"

Sammy tapped his pipe against the side of the steps. "Never got over it. She found excuses to hang around the office. Finally took a job as secretary to Ray Cantrip. Married him eventually."

"I hear they had to get married."

Sammy stared at the sidewalk. "Nobody *had* to get married. Not even back then."

"But she was pregnant at the altar?"

"Could have been. Wouldn't have been the first. Won't be the last."

"And as far as you know, it was Ray Cantrip's child?"

"He's the one she married." Sammy glared at Owen. "Jesus, boy, what are you stirring up? Let the poor woman rest in peace."

Sammy's tone made Owen want to change the subject. "I read your testimony before the Blatnik Commission."

Sammy leaned back and took a swig of his Stroh's. "Been a lot of beer over the bar since I talked to them."

"Sounded like you didn't know much about those phony companies they used to rig Chuck Hager's bids."

"Well now, there's a difference between knowing, knowing for certain, knowing for telling, and knowing for swearing to."

"And you didn't know to tell?"

"Not to swear to, no."

"Did my dad?"

"I think your dad knew for certain and for swearing. I think he was fixing to blow the lid off the whole sorry business."

"But he died before he could testify."

"You saying there was a connection?"

"I don't know. But your testimony didn't blow any lids off, and then you went to work for Hager."

"Son, you're dipping your paddle in some pretty murky waters." Sammy glared again. "You better not be saying there was a connection between my testimony and my working for Hager."

"Were Hager's bids still rigged after you went to work for him?"

Sammy shook his head. "Not with phony competition. Once Chuck got a couple of contracts under his belt, he could win bids on his own. Everybody could see he was the best damn road builder in the state."

"But he still paid off the Governor?"

"Hell, that was the price of doing business back then. You wanted to play, you greased the Governor."

"But that all stopped when the Governor got indicted?"

"Oh, sure." Sammy jabbed Owen with his pipe for emphasis. "Nowadays, instead of putting the cash directly into his pocket, you make a campaign contribution."

WHEN OWEN RETURNED from Sammy Earle's, two patrol cars were parked across from his mother's house, one in front of George's Pontiac and one behind it. Two deputies were rummaging through the front seat of the Pontiac. The sheriff stood on the porch steps talking to his mother, who had a stricken look on her face. As Owen approached, she said, "Owen, thank God you're here. The sheriff wants to take George out of the treatment center."

"I didn't mind leaving him there when the charge was vehicular manslaughter," the sheriff said.

Owen took his mother's arm. "I thought the autopsy showed Mary Jewel didn't die as a result of the car accident."

"No," the sheriff said, "somebody bashed her skull with a blunt instrument."

"Then why are you still bothering George?" Owen asked.

"There's evidence he may have done the bashing. We're charging him with first-degree murder."

ELEVEN

Asphalt Atrocities

OWEN WATCHED the two deputies going over the front seat of his brother's Pontiac. "I assume you've got a warrant?" he said to the sheriff, who was standing beside Ruth Allison on her front porch.

Ruth shook her head. "Oh, my. I didn't think to ask."

The sheriff pulled two folded sheets of paper from his pocket. "One for the car, one for George. We've already picked up George."

Owen scanned the warrants. "You said you had evidence?"

"Your brother was seen outside Mary Jewel's apartment the night she was killed," the sheriff said.

One of the two deputies searching George's Pontiac opened the rear door and used a whisk broom to sweep something Owen couldn't see into a plastic bag.

"Seen by whom?" Owen asked the sheriff. "When?"

"One of my patrolmen stopped him around eleven-thirty in the evening. He was weaving between two lanes on Adams Avenue, a couple of blocks from Mary Jewel's house. When the officer recognized your brother as the Road Commissioner, he let him off with a warning."

The second deputy closed the passenger door of the Pontiac, adjusted his rubber gloves, and popped the car's trunk.

Owen tried to ignore the deputies' search and counter the sheriff's story. "We already know George was drunk. Being drunk two blocks from Mary Jewel's apartment hardly seems like grounds for arrest."

The deputy's head disappeared inside the Pontiac's trunk.

"The same officer saw George's car parked in front of Mary Jewel's house later that same night. He was passed out behind the wheel," the sheriff said.

The deputy pulled his head out of the trunk, hurried to the patrol car behind the Pontiac, and returned with a small black bag.

Owen could feel his argument growing weaker. "You find many killers sleeping off drunks in front of their victim's apartments? I mean, I've heard of killers returning to the scene of the crime, but how likely is it one wouldn't bother to leave?"

"A neighbor saw him pounding on Mary Jewel's door," the sheriff said. "He threatened her in public, then went straight to her house."

"Not straight," Owen said. "He stopped in at least one bar."

The deputy emerged from the trunk holding George's tire iron. "Look what we've got here," he said, holding the iron aloft and bringing it up to the porch.

"Oh my God," Ruth said.

The deputy showed the tire iron to the sheriff. It was covered with a thin white powder. "He wiped it clean, but there's one clear set of prints."

"Have them checked," the sheriff said.

"Don't bother, they're mine," Owen said.

"Got something you want to tell us?" the sheriff asked.

"I was looking in George's car for some sign of where he'd been the night Mary Jewel died," Owen said. "The tire iron was loose in the trunk and I threw it into the tire well."

"Tampering with evidence," the deputy said.

"I didn't see it as evidence," Owen said. "George hadn't been accused of anything."

"Don't give me that shit," the deputy said. "I suppose you wiped it clean before you put it away."

"Why would I wipe it clean and leave my own prints on it?" Owen asked.

"You smart-asses always make at least one mistake," the deputy answered.

"Oh yeah, that's from the *Crimestopper's Handbook,* isn't it?" Owen said. "I forget. Is it filed under 'smart-ass' or 'mistake'?"

"It's filed under 'cease and desist,'" the sheriff said. "Kyle, take that tire iron to the lab and see what they can find on it."

The deputy glowered at Owen and turned to leave the porch.

"If I really thought that was evidence against George, why wouldn't I just pitch it in the river?" Owen asked. He was beginning to wish that he had done just that.

"You don't believe he did it," the sheriff said. "If he's really innocent, you don't want to be destroying evidence."

"Do you believe he did it?" Owen asked.

The sheriff shrugged. "He's the best suspect we've got. Hell, he's the only suspect we've got."

"That wasn't what I asked."

"I've known George a long time," the sheriff said. "Sober, I don't think he could have killed her. But black-out drunks can do strange things."

"Not George," Ruth said. "I know George couldn't do that, drunk or sober."

The sheriff touched the brim of his hat and started down the porch steps. "I hope you're right, Mrs. Allison."

Owen took his mother's arm and led her into the house. "Don't worry, Mom, we'll get to the bottom of this." But he felt as leaden and empty of clues as the tire iron he'd left in George's trunk.

THE HEADLINES in the morning paper read HIGHWAY COMMISSIONER INDICTED FOR MURDER. Owen read the front page at the breakfast table, sipping tea and running a spoon through a bowl of oatmeal he didn't feel like eating. The lead story labeled Mary Jewel a "Macadam Martyr" and suggested it was her opposition to George's highway plans that led to her murder. A feature article on page 2 linked Mary Jewel's murder with past highway scandals, including Governor Banning's indictment, the jailing of the Mingo County Five, Owen's father's disappearance, and the recent discovery of Ray Cantrip's body. The article was laced with phrases like "asphalt atrocities," "pavement payoffs," and "concrete con games," and promised a week-long series on "the history of West Virginia's high-handed highwaymen."

Owen's stomach churned and he set his cereal aside. The reporter seemed more interested in alliteration than accuracy. She'd not only convicted George, but had lumped their father together with the crooks he'd jailed and the scandal-ridden Banning administration that had come after he'd drowned. It was too late to hide the paper from his mother, who had left it for him with the oatmeal and a note saying she was going to daily mass to pray for George.

Owen reflected that prayer was likely to be more helpful than anything he'd been able to do for his brother so far. His last-minute support for George at the public hearing hadn't swayed enough votes to swing the bridge decision. With his mother's help, he'd managed to get his brother into a treatment center, but that just made it easier for the sheriff to find him and take him out. Owen had left the tire iron where the sheriff could find it, and he hadn't been able to track George's whereabouts on the night Mary Jewel was murdered. The sheriff, though, had managed to piece together enough of George's movements to convince himself he had a murder case.

If it was too late to track George's movements; maybe he should try to find out more about Mary Jewel's. What had she been doing on Gobbler's Grade the night George hit her? It could be worth a trip back to the construction site to try to find out. And Robin could help him talk to her brother and his crew at the site.

He wondered briefly whether Gobbler's Grade was a logical place to visit, or whether he just wanted an excuse to call Robin. Who was he trying to kid, anyhow? What the hell, he didn't have to kid anybody. He didn't need an excuse to call Robin. He picked up the phone and dialed her home in White Sulphur Springs.

Robin told him she could pick him up in an hour, about the time it would take her to drive from White Sulphur to Barkley. She asked about George and the facts behind the *Daily News* article. Owen said the article was an "...egregious exercise in asinine alliteration at the expense of responsible reporting."

Owen waited for Robin's once-familiar laugh, but it didn't come. His attempt at parody had evidently died somewhere along the telephone lines. Maybe it just wasn't as funny as he thought. After a short silence, Robin said, "Sounds like George may have more problems than a reporter's style. You can fill me in when I see you."

His short conversation with Robin did nothing to relieve Owen's worries about George, but he looked forward to seeing her anyhow. He remembered the praline flavor of her parting kiss and rooted around the pantry for some cinnamon to make his oatmeal more palatable.

IT TOOK ROBIN nearly two hours to arrive at Owen's house. She showed up at the front door carrying a picnic hamper and wearing blue jeans and a plaid cotton shirt, with her hair swept back in braids that reminded Owen of hayrides, hoedowns, and long summer nights.

"I thought so long as we were going up Gobbler's Grade, we might as well make a picnic of it," she said.

"At the Knob?"

"Best view in the county."

"I always thought so. And most of the time I wasn't even looking at the landscape."

Gobbler's Knob sat on a cleared outcropping that overlooked Barkley and the Little Muddy River. A low stone wall formed a half-circle around a parking lot littered with crushed beer cans and condom wrappers. A bare foot of indeterminate gender could be seen propped on the dashboard of a dusty blue Mustang parked at the far end of the lot.

"I'd forgotten how grungy this place gets during the day," Robin said.

"The view hasn't changed, though."

Across the stone wall, the rock ledge pushed out about six feet before dropping steeply to the Little Muddy, which carved a jagged path between jutting, forested slopes. Barkley sat below them in the U of the river's horseshoe turn. The Fifth Street Bridge bisected the U, spanning not only the Little Muddy, but also railroad tracks on the Barkley riverfront and a bright splash of mustard grass in the lowlands across from the city.

Robin spread a teal-blue tablecloth on the top of the low stone wall. "The bridge doesn't seem like such a big thing from up here," she said. "Hard to understand all the fuss about traffic."

Owen sat on the wall and applied a corkscrew to a bottle of Chardonnay. "Harder to understand the concern about pollution. There's never been a day when you couldn't see all the way from here to Mingo County."

"We see pollution on TV and think we ought to worry about it."

Owen pulled the cork from the wine bottle and pointed it at the strewn beer cans. "You see litter on TV and nobody seems to worry about it."

"That takes a little more than talk at a public hearing."

"That's part of the trouble here. Everybody wants to save the world, but nobody wants to pick up the trash."

Owen poured two glasses of wine while Robin unwrapped a sandwich and handed it to him. He bit into the sandwich, and a bloodred sauce squeezed out onto his fingers.

"I hope you still like turkey and cranberry sauce," Robin said.

Owen licked the sauce from his fingers. "Love it. Are those orange rinds in it?"

"I remembered that's how your mother made it."

A dilapidated Chevy carrying two teenagers pulled into the parking lot, then left again when they saw Owen and Robin picnicking on the stone wall.

Robin cut an apple into sections. "Remember that picture I took of you standing on this wall?"

"I remember. You stood on the hood of my car to get the right angle."

"It made it look like you were balancing on the edge of the world."

Owen gathered his legs under him and stood up on the stone wall, holding his arms out like a tightrope walker. It was all right so long as he focused on the parking lot and didn't look down toward the river, but he knew he wouldn't dare take a step forward or backward.

"That's it. That's the pose," Robin said. "I've still got that picture."

Owen leaned forward and bent his knees until his hands could touch the stone wall. Then he eased himself down into a sitting position. "I must have been younger then."

Robin touched his hand. "We both were. We had some good times, though. If you look down on Barkley from up here, it's like nothing's changed."

Owen swallowed the last of his sandwich. "Up close, though, everything's changed. The Keith Albee's a multiplex. Bailey's is a Burger King. Ashbury's out of business. And George may be playing third base for a prison team if I can't find out what really happened to Mary Jewel."

"Isn't that the sheriff's job?"

"The sheriff thinks he knows what happened." Owen began packing the picnic utensils back into her hamper. "He thinks George is guilty."

On their way out of the parking lot, Owen noticed that the bare foot now propped on the dashboard of the dusty Mustang was adorned with an ankle bracelet and dark toenail polish. It moved like a slow metronome against the grimy windshield, waving good-bye.

AT THE CONSTRUCTION SITE on Gobbler's Grade, an asphalt roller with fierce eyes above the driver's cab and a painted red tongue encircling its forward cylinder appeared to be lapping the asphalt as it smoothed the roadway. A pickup painted like a circus wagon followed the roller, dropping orange cones in its wake. Two middle-aged women wearing black armbands stood in the shade of the nearby birch trees, holding hand-lettered signs reading HELL NO, WE WON'T GROW, and PAVE OVER THE HIGHWAY COMMISSIONER. Four construction workers sat in the shade a short distance away from the picketers.

The sight of the idle workers angered Robin, and she pounded on the door of the mobile home that served as the field office for Hager Construction. When Eddie Hager answered her knock, the first thing she asked was, "What the hell are those four guys doing lollygagging on our time?"

Eddie flushed red under his sandy hair. "I put them on so we wouldn't have any downtime during crew breaks."

"For Christ's sake, that's it?" Robin said. "They sit around until the regular crew breaks and run the rollers for a half hour?"

"They do more than that. I've got everybody on double shifts. We're in a penalty situation here. The quicker we finish, the quicker the bleeding stops and we get our bond back."

Robin pointed to the idle workers and shook her head. "That's no reason to run double shifts. At least stagger them so you're not paying overtime."

Eddie slammed the trailer door behind him, but he stayed on the top step so that he was a little taller than his sister. "Let me run the company, okay? Long as your checks make it to White Sulphur, you've got no complaints coming."

Robin clenched her fists as if she were about to use them, then let her hands fall to her sides. "Forget it. I didn't come here to argue."

"Just why did you decide to grace us with your presence?"

Robin turned to Owen. "You remember Owen Allison? He's got some questions about the night we were vandalized."

Eddie stepped down to ground level, but he didn't offer to shake hands with Owen. "You were out here that night, weren't you?"

"Just after it happened, yes."

"Well then, you know more than I do."

"I was hoping to talk to your foreman."

"Jimmy Joe's on the grader."

"Call him over," Robin said. "There's no shortage of men to run the equipment."

Eddie ignored his sister. "What is it you want him for?"

"I want to know what he saw that night," Owen said. "I also want to know who stands to gain from your downtime."

"The state, that's who. We're paying five grand a day in penalties."

Robin shook her head. "Besides the state, Eddie."

"Hell, you know that. Your ex-husband. If we can't get our bond back, we can't bid the New River job against him."

"Surely he's not your only competition?" Owen asked.

Eddie shrugged. "There's a couple of other firms might could handle it. These new guys, DPR Construction. Maybe one other. But Rudy Slater's the front runner. And he's in tight with the Dragon Lady."

"Who's that?" Robin asked.

"Alicia Fox," Owen said. "George's boss at the Transportation Department."

"That's right," Eddie said. "That woman's a real ball-buster. I hear she practices on billiard balls. I'm surprised you don't know her, sis. You two have a lot in common."

"I can think of two I'd like to bust right now," Robin said. "If I thought I could find them."

Owen stepped between Robin and her brother to calm the confrontation. "Maybe you could let us talk to your foreman."

Eddie shouted to one of the workers sitting in the shade, telling him to spell Jimmy Joe on the grader.

"That takes care of one of them," Robin said. "Now if we could just find work for the other three. Maybe we could make signs and let them picket the picketers."

"Give it a rest, sis," Eddie said. But he walked over to the three remaining workers and gestured up the hill where the roller had disappeared. The three men rose, dusted themselves off, and followed the trail of orange cones over the hill.

One of the cones alongside the freshly rolled asphalt was pitted and discolored. Owen picked it up and examined it. The logo on the underside of the base said "WorldSafe" and showed a smiling world globe wearing a traffic cone for a hat.

"This one of the biodegradable models?" Owen asked.

Eddie spat on the ground. "That's one of them, yeah. The state made us use them and most of the batch didn't make it through the winter. That one's going to have to go soon too."

Owen held the cone up and showed the logo to Robin and Eddie. "Must not have occurred to anyone that the cone hat looks like a dunce cap."

"It must've been dunces thought of the idea in the first place," Eddie said. "That's what the state gets, always giving jobs to the low bidders."

They heard the whine of truck gears downshifting, and Jimmy Joe Cresap cleared the hill and ground to a stop in a mud-splattered pickup truck. When Owen explained what he wanted, Jimmy Joe offered to drive Owen and Robin back to the site where the body had been found and the trucks vandalized. As they jounced along the unfinished road, Owen asked the foreman what he remembered about the vandals.

"Didn't get a real good look," Jimmy Joe said.

"What were they wearing?"

"Jeans, windbreakers. One guy had a sailor's cap, the other was wearing a baseball cap with a big C. Chicago or Cincinnati, I can't tell them apart."

"Neither of them was dressed in black?"

"Nah, just regular outfits. They both had black gook smeared on their faces, though. Like centerfielders or wide receivers."

Jimmy Joe pulled into the clearing where the equipment had been vandalized. The yellow tape that had marked Ray Cantrip's grave lay sagging and twisted by the roadside. The grave itself had been filled in and paved over.

"So I pulled in right here," Jimmy Joe said. "And my lights swept over these two guys. One of 'em, the guy in the sailor cap, was over by the dozer. The other guy was a little ways back from the edge of the woods. They both jumped when they saw me pull up."

"Where was the guy in the woods?" Owen asked.

Jimmy Joe pointed. "Over there. About where they found the gun."

Owen tried to keep his voice as matter-of-fact as Jimmy Joe's. "They found a gun?"

"Oh yeah. A couple of days later. It was buried pretty deep, but those metal detectors picked it up. Cost us another half day of downtime while they fussed over it."

"Show me."

Jimmy Joe walked Owen and Robin past the first row of birch trees to a triangle of yellow tape stretched between three trees. In the center of the triangle a mound of dirt had begun to seep back into the hole it came from.

"So they found a gun," Owen said. His mind kept returning to that fact like a needle in the groove of a broken record.

"Yeah, like I said. It looked like it had been there awhile."

Owen made a conscious effort to think of another question. "And the guy with the baseball cap was somewhere around here?"

"Pretty close. When he saw my lights he ran for his buddy."

"What else can you tell me about them?"

Jimmy Joe shrugged. "Not much. I don't think they were young kids, though."

"Why not?"

"Way they moved. They were none too spry. I almost caught them, even after I stopped to load up."

"And they got away down that fire trail?"

"Yeah. I couldn't get a clear shot. Not that I would have tried to drop them."

"And there were only two of them?"

Jimmy Joe scratched at his sideburns. "You know, when I pulled in, I thought my lights flashed on a third person. But there were only two of them ahead of me on the fire trail."

"Where did you think you saw the third person?"

"Up a ways in the woods. But it was pretty dark. I probably just imagined it. The two I chased were the only ones I really saw until you came along with your brother."

"And that was the first time you used the shotgun?"

"I said I was sorry about that."

"No harm done. Mind if we look around a little?"

"Hell, it's not my land. Want me to stick around?"

"We don't want to keep you from your job, Jimmy Joe," Robin said. "We can find our own way back."

Jimmy Joe touched the brim of his pink Hager Construction cap and drove the pickup back down the hill.

Robin watched the pickup disappear. "The sheriff's been all over this site. Do you really think you'll find something, or did you just want to get me alone in the woods?"

Owen smiled. "You're the one that sent Jimmy Joe away." He walked over to the yellow tape that marked the hole where the sheriff had unearthed a gun. He had to assume it was his father's gun. "I'm just trying to understand what happened here that night."

Robin joined him at the yellow tape. "What night? The night somebody spiked our gas tanks? Or the night somebody buried Bob Cantrip's dad?"

"Both. But let's start with your gas tanks. I'm pretty sure Mary Jewel was up here that night."

"You think she was one of the vandals Jimmy Joe ran off?"

"No. She was wearing black from head to foot." Owen skirted the edge of the birch trees looking for the bittern nest Mary Jewel had identified for the TV cameras. When he found it, he said, "I think she was up here planting this nest as a ploy to stop your construction job."

The nest was soggy and empty of eggs. Robin toed it with her sneaker and one side collapsed inward. "Doesn't look like anybody's home."

Owen squatted beside the nest. "Not anymore. It didn't work for the bittern or for Mary Jewel."

"So why do you care about it?"

"I think she saw something up here that night."

"Like the vandals?"

"Like the vandals."

"And that somehow got her killed?"

Owen restored the crushed side of the bittern nest. "It's a good working hypothesis." He stood up. "Problem is, you probably don't kill somebody just because they've seen you spiking a gas tank."

"Maybe something more happened here."

Owen stared at the soggy yellow tape. "Something more did happen. Thirty-five years ago." He took Robin's hand. "Let's take a look at the fire trail."

The fire trail the vandals had used as an escape route scraped downhill through thick undergrowth before it intersected a gravel road that widened as it took them back uphill to the main highway. When they followed the gravel road back downhill past the fire trail, it narrowed into a footpath that wound around tree trunks and squeezed between limestone formations before coming to a stream of clear spring water.

Owen jumped the stream and held his hand back for Robin. She took it and jumped after him, splashing her trailing toe in the water. Her wet shoe left a clear imprint in the dirt path. Next to her footprint was the caked and crumbling impression of a bicycle tire.

Owen knelt to look at the nearly faded tire track. "I'd be willing to bet this is Mary Jewel's bike."

"Do you think the sheriff knows?"

"If he doesn't, he soon will."

They followed the path for another fifteen minutes, scraping under low-hanging birch branches and finding three more tire imprints that hadn't been worn away by the weather and other hikers. The trail finally opened out onto the highway just down the road from Robin's parked Mercedes and about a half mile from the spot where George had bumped Mary Jewel into the ditch.

"That hike made me hungry," Robin said as she opened her car doors. "How about dinner?"

Owen dusted himself off and picked briers out of his jeans before settling into the passenger seat. "I don't think I'm quite up for the country club."

"Are you up for Johnny Angelo's?"

"You mean he hasn't turned into a franchise or a multiplex?"

"Not a chance."

"Sounds perfect."

THE RED-CHECKERED tablecloths at Johnny Angelo's pizza parlor looked as if they hadn't been changed since Robin and Owen had been there in high school.

"I had my first pizza here," Owen said. "Square, with thin crisp crust and Johnny's spicy sauce. Ever since then, round ones just don't look right to me."

Robin poured them both beers from a plastic pitcher. "We came here on our first date, remember?"

"I remember. I was so nervous I couldn't eat."

"You kept excusing yourself and going to the john."

"I thought I was going to throw up. But I never did."

"As I recall, you got over your nervous stomach."

"I just learned to hide it better."

"You hide it well." Her knee pressed his under the table. "We had some great times here, didn't we? Remember when Johnny laid out free pizzas for everybody after you won the state championship. You pitched some game."

Owen tried to recall the celebration and couldn't. "You know, I think I'm wired all wrong," he said. "I love baseball. Loved playing it. Still love watching it. But when I think about those high school games, I barely remember winning the championship. Instead, I remember the year before, when I walked that guy with the bases loaded to take us out of the playoffs."

"It was a bad call."

"It could have gone either way." He could still see the pained look on his catcher's face as he turned his head away from Owen while the winning run crossed the plate.

"You must remember good times too. What about us? What do you remember about us?"

"Those letters you never answered when I was at Marquette."

"That's the wrong answer." She ran her nails lightly over the back of his hand. "We were just up on Gobbler's Knob. I want you to close your eyes and tell me what you remember about the two of us up there."

Owen closed his eyes, smiled, and shook his head. He knew he ought to lie, but he told her the first thing that he remembered. "The night you told me you thought you were pregnant."

"You're a sick man. Do you remember what we did when my period finally came?"

"Oh, yes. I remember."

"That's a start, at least." She nodded toward the last square of pizza. "Finish your dinner. I'm going to wire you for a whole new set of memories."

ROBIN KEPT TESTING HIM in the car on the way home. "Fifth grade. Sister Mary Fidelis. Great times. What do you remember?"

"Losing the county spelling bee. I left an *I* out of 'ellipsis.'"

"How could you do that?"

"Beats the *I* out of me."

Robin shook her head and smiled. "Boy Scouts. You made it to Eagle. What do you remember?"

The clutching hand in Gauley River flashed into Owen's mind. But he couldn't tell her about that. Instead he said, "Ray Cantrip caught me forging my dad's signature on some merit-badge affidavits."

"I can't believe you. You're really a hardcase."

"It's not that I don't remember the good times," Owen said. "But when you spring a topic on me like that, the memories that pop up, that are most vivid, are the times I screwed up royally."

"They write psychiatric texts on people like you."

Owen smiled. "My memories are the least of my worries. You think I'm dysfunctional?"

Robin moved one hand from the steering wheel to Owen's thigh. "God, I hope not. I do have a few other tests in mind, though."

Owen felt the beginning of an erection. "Umm, I don't want to tell you where to put your hand, but didn't you just miss our turn?"

Robin's hand massaged his inner thigh. "Nope. I'm taking you to my lab in White Sulphur for a thorough examination."

"All the way to White Sulphur and back tonight?"

"The examination I envisioned requires an overnight stay."

"Oh, Jesus, I can't tonight. They just packed George off to jail and I haven't seen Mom all day. I better not leave her alone tonight."

Robin removed her hand and returned it to the steering wheel. "Are you trying to tell me something here?"

"Just that I need a rain check. Maybe we could spend a weekend in White Sulphur?"

"This weekend?"

"This weekend."

Robin made a U-turn in the middle of the block. "I guess I could reschedule your exam."

Robin turned a corner and pulled up in front of Ruth Allison's house. "I'll pick you up right here at noon on Friday."

"I'll be ready."

She returned one hand to Owen's thigh. "Bring your tennis racket, bathing trunks, and a box of condoms."

"Sounds like an athletic weekend."

The fingers of her other hand played with the hair at the nape of his neck. "Maybe I better tell you what those items are for. Otherwise, that mind of yours might conjure up images of double faults, drowning, and impotence."

Owen saw the curtains move in his mother's living room. "That's okay. I think I can figure it out."

Her lips nibbled his earlobe. "Maybe a little demonstration is in order. One picture is worth a thousand sperms."

Owen's voice thickened. "I think sperm is already plural."

Robin ran her fingers lightly over his crotch and found the zipper on his jeans. "Just a little preview of coming attractions."

A blinding light filled the front seat of the car, followed by a loud thumping on the passenger window.

Robin's head jerked up. "What the hell?"

A flashlight beam lit up Owen's lap. The voice behind the beam said, "Lady, if that zipper doesn't come back up in five seconds, there's going to be another asphalt atrocity in tomorrow's paper."

The flashlight burned red circles into Owen's cornea. He couldn't see, but he recognized the voice. He leaned forward and felt for the button that lowered the passenger window.

The sticky river air entered the car as the window slid down. "Robin," Owen said, "I'd like you to meet my ex-wife Judith. Judith, this is Robin Hager."

TWELVE

Antique Iron

JUDITH PACED the living room, waving the still lit flashlight as if she were trying to direct an artillery barrage somewhere in Owen's vicinity. Her black carry-on suitcase stood next to the stairs where Ruth Allison sat clutching her quilted robe around her.

Judith looped the flashlight so the beam made an arc on the ceiling and landed on Owen's head. "Your brother's in jail, your mother's half crazy with worry, and what the hell do I find you doing?" The beam dropped to Owen's crotch. "For Christ's sake, finish zipping up your fly."

Owen struggled with his stuck zipper. The flashlight beam returned to his face, and he shielded his eyes with one hand and looked at his mother. "You called her?"

Ruth Allison drew her arms tightly around her breast and nodded.

Judith swung the flashlight beam again so it arced on the wall behind Owen and struck his face. "Of course she called me. Your brother needs a lawyer. That's what I do. It's obvious why it didn't occur to you to call me. It's obvious why you only called once in the past two weeks."

Owen cleared the zipper jam and closed his fly. "It's not what you think."

"The hell it's not," Judith said. "That woman was well on her way to doing the Clinton curtsy. Are you going to tell me she was just blotting her lipstick on your collar?"

Owen shifted from one foot to the other, dodging the flashlight beam. "I mean, that's not all we were doing. We spent the day—"

"I don't care how you spent the day. I saw how you were ending it."

Ruth moved on the staircase. "Son, I think you better quit while you're behind."

"Listen to your mother," Judith said. "Her generation's response to infidelity was to reload."

"Infidelity!" Owen struggled to keep from shouting. "Look who's talking infidelity. We're not married. Haven't been for four years. And I'm not the one who was unfaithful when we were."

Judith slammed the flashlight down on an end table, toppling Owen's high school graduation picture. "That's it. I'm out of here. Find George another lawyer." She stalked over to her suitcase and fumbled at the pull bar.

Ruth rose on the staircase and put a slippered foot on Judith's suitcase. "Children, please. I need you. George needs you. Both of you."

Judith jerked up the pull bar, dislodging Ruth's foot. "Ruth, you weren't out there. She had his zipper at half-mast."

Owen moved between Judith and the door. "Oh, yeah. That's right. Tell my mother. Tattletale."

Judith straightened. "And he had the nerve to apologize to her. For my behavior."

Ruth sat back down on the stairs. "Oh, Owen, how could you? And with that woman."

Owen unclenched his fists and opened his hands, palms outward, toward the two women. "You're right. I'm sorry."

"You're sorry," Judith repeated. "Sorry about what? Sorry I interrupted you? Sorry you didn't get your ashes hauled? Sorry you're embarrassed?"

Owen took a step toward Judith and put his hand on the suitcase pull bar. "No. You're right. You and I were working toward something. I knew that. I'm sorry. I blew it."

"It looked to me as if your girlfriend was the one about to blow it."

Owen leaned toward Judith and said in a stage whisper, "Now, honey, 'blow' is only an expression."

Judith lowered her head, trying to hide a tight smile. Owen thought he could feel the tension leaking out of the confrontation.

Ruth looked from Owen to Judith. "Did I miss something?"

"It's an old joke. Or at least an old punch line." Judith shoved the pull bar back into her suitcase. "All right. I accept your apology."

"Thank God that's settled." Ruth stood and put her arm around

Judith's shoulders. "Now, Owen, so long as Judith is here helping us, I don't think it's fair for you to see that other woman."

Judith nearly laughed. "Owen's a big boy now, Ruth. He can do whatever he wants."

"No, Mom's right," Owen said. "I'll postpone the weekend we'd planned."

"Postpone? Weekend?" Ruth said. "Why see her at all?"

"Mom. She's an old friend."

"Her father was no friend of your father," Ruth said. "And she's a source of discord. Not to mention temptation."

Judith smiled. "And didn't you always say the best way to get rid of temptation was to yield to it?"

"No," Owen said. "I think Oscar Wilde said that."

"And didn't he go to jail for overworking his penis?"

"I think it was his mouth he overworked," Owen said. "But I get the message. Until we get this all settled, if I do see Robin, I'll steer clear of temptation."

Ruth tightened her grip on Judith's shoulder. "I still think you shouldn't see her at all."

"It's all right, Ruth. If there's one thing I know about your son, it's that he'll keep his word or die trying." Judith nodded toward Owen's crotch. "Just in case you are tempted, though, let me tell you, from now on, whenever that little sucker sees the light of day, it better be peeing." She raised her hand and made a quick snipping motion with her fingers. "I've still got my diploma from the Lorena Bobbitt School of Marital Relations."

It occurred to Owen that Judith had crossed the line from outrage to amusement at his discomfort. It also occurred to him that he was glad to see her. But he was damned if he was going to tell her so.

JUDITH CAME INTO the breakfast room the next morning wearing her navy-blue lawyer suit and carrying her black leather briefcase. "Time to go see my client," she announced.

"I thought you might want to," Owen said. "His car is gassed up and ready to go."

Without pausing to sit, Judith pulled three cinnamon rolls free from the pan Ruth had baked, folded them into two napkins, and dropped them into her briefcase. "George'll appreciate these," she said. Then she poured herself a mug full of coffee, took a quick sip, and nodded to Owen. "Let's go. I'll drink this on the way."

Owen slipped behind the wheel of George's Pontiac and put the key in the ignition as Judith laid her briefcase on the front seat. Instead of getting in the car, she patted the front seat and ran her finger over the dash. "This car's immaculate. Where'd you find the tire iron?"

"In the trunk."

"Show me."

Owen popped open the trunk and pointed to the place where he'd seen the tire iron. "The cops have it now," he explained.

"And you tossed it into the well over here?"

Owen nodded.

Judith sat her coffee mug in the center of the trunk and tugged at the strap on the false bottom of the tire well. "Did you look in here?"

Owen shook his head.

Judith lifted the false bottom and stood aside. "Maybe you should."

A hand jack encased in a molded and sealed plastic form was fitted snugly into the tire well. Alongside the jack, in the same sealed plastic casing, was a tire iron much smaller and lighter than the one Owen had found and the police had pulled from the trunk two days earlier.

"The iron the police have isn't even George's," Owen said.

Judith replaced the false bottom and reclaimed her coffee mug. "You don't know that. But at least it didn't come with this car."

GEORGE SAT SLUMPED in a metal folding chair across the interrogation table from Owen and Judith. Crumbs from the rolls Judith had brought dotted the front of his gray prison pajamas and collected in the crease above his stomach, but he made no move to brush them off. "Jude, honey," he said. "I just don't remember."

Judith took her time writing on her yellow legal pad. "Try again, George. Anything you can tell us will help."

George shook his head once, slowly. "I remember talking at the hearing. I remember waking up in the motel. But I don't remember anything that happened in between."

"But you didn't kill Mary Jewel?" Owen said, half as a question, half as a statement.

George stared into space and shrugged. "I don't know. How can I tell? I believe I had it in my heart to kill her."

Judith glanced sideways at Owen. "God help us if we're going to be prosecuted for what's in our hearts."

Owen stood and walked to the barred window. "We drove your

Pontiac over here, George," he said. "It handles really well. When was the last time you had a flat?"

George kept his eyes focused on his lap. "Never have flats anymore. Those new radials last forever."

Owen returned to the table. "But when's the last time you remember having one?"

George shifted slowly in his chair, causing crumbs to drop from his stomach crease to his lap. "I can't remember that either. What difference does it make?"

"You fix your flats yourself?"

"Hell no. That's what Triple-A is for."

"So you never bought a tire iron?"

George blinked once, but continued staring straight ahead. "Why would I buy a tire iron if I never had a flat?"

"The police found a tire iron in your car," Judith said.

George seemed to ponder her statement. Finally, he said, "Every car on the road has a tire iron. They're standard equipment."

"Your Pontiac had an extra one," Owen said. "Any idea how it got there?"

George ran one hand through his thinning hair. "No. I can't help you with that either. I guess I'm just no good to you at all."

In the car on the way home, Judith reviewed the notes on her legal pad. "Jesus, Owen. He was like a zombie."

Still shaken by his brother's appearance, Owen squeezed the steering wheel to keep his hands still. "I liked him a lot better when he was a nervous, chain-smoking alcoholic. Before he agreed to take the cure. One of those twelve steps must have been a lulu."

"You think it's some sort of withdrawal shock?" She closed her legal pad. "He was just no help at all. And he's not going to make a very good impression on a jury."

"We've got to get him out of there. What's next on the legal agenda?"

"I'll have a talk with the D.A. Why don't you tell me about the extra tire iron. What did it look like?"

"It was just a long, heavy, hexagonal rod. It looked as if the tip had been bent over as an afterthought and milled to fit a lug nut. It looked old and black..." He remembered the weight of it in his hand. "And lethal."

"But you think it was old?"

"It was big and kind of clunky. Not modern and streamlined like the one in the trunk now."

"Too bad there's not an antique registry for tire irons."

Owen pressed his foot down on the accelerator and the Pontiac jumped forward. "Let's go pick up Mom. I think she'll know where to find one."

THE BANNER over the gravel road leading down into the parking lot read WEST VIRGINIA'S LARGEST FLEA MARKET. At the end of the road, a lot the size of a football field was parked full of vehicles ranging from dented pickups held together with strapping tape to brand-new Lincoln Town Cars. Three Quonset huts set side-by-side stretched the length of the parking lot. A grease-spattered grill in front of the first hut vended hamburgers, hot dogs, and sodas to a smattering of bargain hunters seated at wooden picnic tables. Twenty rows of hubcaps stacked waist-high in five-deep columns lined the concrete walkway leading to the other two huts.

"Your dad used to bring us up here for auctions," Ruth said. "It wasn't nearly so big then."

"I remember the hubcaps," Owen said. "I could barely see over the stacks."

"Too bad Mary Jewel wasn't killed with a hubcap," Judith said. "Looks as if we could find one from every car in Christendom right here."

Inside the Quonset huts were rows and rows of booths with vendors selling everything from antique andirons to used kitchen appliances. Judith started looking for tire irons in the first hut, while Owen and Ruth went on to the third. They passed displays of porcelain poodles, tin trays bearing images of the Last Supper, lidless popcorn poppers, delicate pincushion dolls, purses and wallets made of road-kill pelts, antique medicine bottles, twelve card tables of jumbled household goods, sculptures made of coal, and racks of used audiotapes carrying six different classifications of country music before coming to three bins filled with lug wrenches, crowbars, and tire irons. The third bin had a hinged glass cover that locked on one side. Under the glass cover, between a lug wrench bearing a "Wheeling Steel" monogram and a crowbar with a bottle opener on one end, Owen recognized the hexagonal tire iron he had seen in George's trunk. It lay on its side and had an orange decal reading "Union 76" on one of its six facets.

Owen asked the booth's proprietor, a lanky man with slick black hair that hung stiffly above the collar of his plaid work shirt, if he could see the tire iron.

"You a collector?" the man asked.

"No, just interested."

The man fished a string of keys out of the pocket of his bib overalls and opened the glass case. "Well, buddy, you sure picked yourself a beaut. This here item's rare as a Mingo County virgin."

"What makes it so rare?"

The man lifted the tire iron from the case and cradled it in his arms. "What makes anything rare? They didn't make many of them to begin with, and these here dee-cals kept rubbing off the ones they did make. 'Sides that, it's a genuine antique."

"How old is it?"

The man handed the tire iron to Owen. "Twenty-five, thirty years at least."

A man and woman wearing matching maroon baseball caps saying "His" and "Hers" stopped and nodded gravely at the news of the tire iron's age. The idea that it might be considered an antique didn't seem strange to anyone but Owen. He hefted the tire iron and handed it back to its owner. "How much do you want for it?"

The man gazed at his tire iron, studied Owen, scratched at his nose, and said, "I could let you have it for forty bucks."

Owen reached in his hip pocket for his wallet when his mother grabbed his arm.

"Owen," Ruth said, "what on earth are you doing?"

"I'm buying that tire iron. It's the same as the one in George's car."

"Not for forty dollars, you're not." She addressed the man holding the tire iron. "We'll give you twenty."

The man shook his head. "Can't do that, ma'am. It's still got the original dee-cal." He held the iron so Ruth and Owen could see inside the hexagonal cavity. "And looky here. This hole's black as Rastus's rectum. Not a mark on it. This baby ain't never seen no lug nut."

"Well, we'll just look around for one that has," Ruth said. She took Owen by the arm and led him away from the booth.

Owen stopped in the middle of the aisle, out of earshot of the tire iron's owner. "Mom, that's the one we need."

"It's not going anywhere, Owen. But forty dollars is just too much.

I grew up during the depression. Back then, forty dollars was a week's wage.''

"It's not a week's wage anymore. And I wouldn't know where to look for another one.''

"These people expect you to barter. Let me tell you what your father would have done. You want it for twenty, right?'' Ruth rummaged in her purse for a twenty-dollar bill. "Take this twenty, fold it up so he's not sure how much is there, and put it in his hand. Make sure he takes it. Then, when he sees it's only twenty, tell him that's as high as you're willing to go. Believe me, he'll give you that tire iron rather than part with the twenty.''

Owen took the twenty, folded it in quarters, and went back to the man with the tire iron. "What else can you tell me about that iron?''

The man shrugged. "Not much, except you could look till Beelzebub's baptized and not find another in as good as shape as this one.''

Owen held out the folded twenty. "Anybody else around likely to know about them?''

The man took the twenty in his free hand. "Old Bob Shinko at the Union 76 Truck Stop off Route Sixty. He knows antiques and he's been running that stop ever since they built it. He won't have one of these babies in cherry condition, though.'' He unfolded the bill. "There's only twenty here.''

"That's as high as I'm willing to go.''

"Man, that's a real screwing.''

"Take it or leave it.''

The man weighed the twenty in his right hand and the tire iron in his left. "All right, it's yours.'' He laid the tire iron gently on the glass case, pulled a crinkled sheet of bubble wrap out from behind the counter, and wrapped it tightly around the iron. "Just don't tell nobody you got it from me at that price.''

Ruth wore a smug "Mother Knows Best" look as they searched the other two Quonset huts for Judith. They found her at a side booth in the middle hut, bent over a display case filled with blown glass figures.

Judith waved them over. "Come see what I've found.''

She pointed to the blown glass figure of a dolphin arcing out of a blue glass sea. The top level of the display case held other glass animals, all created with sweeping abstract curves. Owen recognized the plump body of the least bittern he'd looked up in the library, along with a breeching whale and the curled form of a sleeping squirrel. The lower shelf of the case contained figures from a nativity scene, with a kneeling madonna hovering over an infant in a glass manger.

"Aren't they exquisite?" Judith said.

"Real works of art," Owen agreed.

"I can't decide between the dolphin and the small bird."

The young woman behind the display case stepped forward. "They're part of Mario's endangered species suite."

"Pick one and it will be my treat," Owen said.

"All right, then. The dolphin."

"How much is it?" Owen asked.

The young woman took the dolphin out of the display case. "Thirty dollars."

Ruth stepped forward. "Will you take twenty? Owen, you've got a twenty you can give her, don't you?"

The woman hesitated. "I'm afraid I couldn't take less than twenty-five."

"Make it thirty-five," Judith said.

"Judith, dear," Ruth said. "I don't think you fully understand the nature of this negotiation."

Judith put her hand on Ruth's forearm. "Oh, Ruth. This figurine would go for ten times that amount in California. As far as I'm concerned, the artist deserves as much as he can get. Besides, it's Owen's guilt money. Pay the woman, Lothario."

The saleswoman smiled as Owen reached for his wallet. "That's all right, I'll take the original thirty."

"What can you tell me about the artist?" Judith asked.

"His name's Mario Etchivario. He works at Pilgrim and moonlights making these figurines."

"Pilgrim Glass," Owen explained. "It's outside Huntington. There's a Blenko glass factory about a mile from here. West Virginia's famous for its glassware."

"I'm not surprised," Judith said. "Everyone seems so good at blowing things."

"It's only an expression," Owen said.

"Not with molten glass, it's not."

They watched as the young woman packed tissue paper around the clear glass dolphin. Owen ripped a strip of bubble wrap from the shank of his tire iron and handed it to her. "Here," he said. "What you're wrapping is a little more delicate than what I'm carrying."

On the way out, Owen stopped at the audiotape booth and paid four dollars for two used Kathy Mattea tapes. He opened Judith's package and placed the tapes in the bag alongside the glass dolphin. "Just another sample of a home-grown state product."

BOB SHINKO'S OFFICE was on the second floor of the Union 76 Truck Stop off Route 60. A corner window overlooked the service bay where two eighteen-wheelers were taking on diesel fuel. Shinko, a friendly balding man with a budding paunch, stood at the window and nodded toward the two fueling trucks. "Used to have to watch the operation pretty close, make sure nobody was skimming cash. Now it's all plastic. Couldn't cheat us if you wanted to." He returned to his desk and asked Owen, "What can I do for you?"

Owen peeled the bubble wrap away from his flea-market tire iron. The minute the "Union 76" decal was exposed, Shinko came out from behind his desk to examine it. He took it back to the window, ran his eyes up and down the length of the iron, and inserted his index finger in the nut cavity. When the appraisal was finished, he handed it back to Owen, saying, "That's in really good shape. Where'd you find it?"

"Flea market near Milton."

"Mind telling me how much you paid for it?"

Owen considered inflating the buying price, but he felt faintly foolish paying what he had for a tire iron. "Twenty dollars."

Shinko whistled with appreciation. "Helluva deal. I know a guy got seventy-five for one wasn't in as good a shape as this."

"What makes it so expensive?"

"You mean you paid twenty dollars for a tire iron and didn't know how rare it was?" Shinko shook his head in wonder. "Listen here, fella, I've got a binfull of irons downstairs I'll sell you for ten bucks apiece. Better yet, I'll trade you ten of them for that little baby you've got in your hands."

"Just tell me what makes it so rare."

Shinko opened the lower drawer of his desk, pulled out a straight length of black hexagonal iron, and plopped it on his green desk blotter. "Thirty, maybe thirty-five years ago, we used to give these away to truckers."

"What is it?"

"Tire thumper. Man drives an eighteen-wheeler in here, he don't want to put a pressure gauge on every tire. But a good trucker can give a tire a solid whack with this and tell whether it's got enough air."

Shinko picked up the straight piece of iron and whacked it against his palm. "We ran into a couple of problems, though. One was, our decals didn't stick too good. But, hell, we figured truckers would remember where they got their thumpers."

He laid the iron back on his desk. "Other problem was more serious. OSHA, that's the Occupational Safety and Health Administration, got on our case. Claimed we were giving away lethal weapons. Ordered us to stop."

"Were they lethal?"

"Well, hell yes, if somebody decided to thump a noggin instead of a tire. But that's true of Coke bottles and bowling pins, too, and you don't see OSHA shutting down Coke or the Academy Lanes."

"I mean, were there cases reported where somebody'd been killed with one?"

"None we knew of. But that didn't stop OSHA. So we were left with a lot of iron bars on our hands, until some bright boy in the front office got the idea of crimping the ends and gouging out a nut-hole. All of a sudden, we had tire irons to giveaway."

Owen smiled. "Amazing. And it worked?"

"For about four months. Then the shit really hit the fan." Shinko took Owen's tire iron and rolled up his shirtsleeve. "Lemme show you."

Shinko fished a thick rubber band out of his desk drawer, nestled Owen's tire iron against his inner forearm, and ran the rubber band up his arm until it caught just under the bent lip of the iron and held it fast against his arm. Then he rolled his sleeve back down and buttoned his cuff. "What we'd done, see, was create a concealed weapon."

He dropped his arm to his side. The tip of the tire iron barely protruded under his shirt cuff. "Wasn't too long before a maverick trucker took out a cashier at our Macon truck stop using one of our own irons, hidden just like this. Didn't kill him, but it numbed him out pretty good."

Shinko rolled up his shirtsleeve, carefully worked the rubber band down around Owen's tire iron, and returned it to him. "By now, OSHA was all over us like flies on shit. They threatened us with fines and lawsuits if we didn't recall everyone of these irons."

"And did you?"

"How the hell could we? It wasn't like we registered the names of the guys we gave them to. We sure as shit stopped making more, though."

"And that was, what? Twenty-five years ago?"

"About that."

"And you gave them away to truckers?"

"Truckers, heavy-equipment workers, anybody who came to our truck stops and wanted one. Giveaway only lasted about four months. That's why one like this, with the decal and all, is so rare."

Shinko bent down and opened his lower desk drawer. "Story has a happy ending, though. Fellows in the front office put their heads back together and come up with this." He withdrew a short, stubby baseball bat exactly the same length as the tire iron. The bat had the familiar Hillerich and Bradsby label. On the barrel of the bat where you'd expect to find a major leaguer's signature, though, was an orange imprint reading "Union 76 Tire Thumper."

"What you call a real win-win solution," Shinko said. "OSHA was happy and we solved our decal problems."

"So the feds didn't see the baseball bat as a lethal weapon?"

"No more than Coke bottles or bowling pins or other symbols of the American way. I hear they even gave us an award for our cooperation and ingenuity."

Owen laughed. "Just another fine example of your government at work."

JUDITH WAS SITTING on the couch in Ruth's living room and leafing through clippings describing Mary Jewel's death and George's arrest when Owen returned from the truck stop.

"So how do you think the tire iron got into George's trunk?" she asked after listening to Owen's tale of OSHA and the limited-edition tire irons.

"I think the killer planted it there to implicate George. He said he'd never seen it when he was sober. And what are the odds a blackout drunk is going to lay his hands on a tire iron that was only manufactured for four months twenty-five years ago?"

"Who else had access to the car?"

"Barb and Billy. But why would they need a tire iron? There was one in the car already."

"We can check on them easily enough. You said they only gave the tire irons to truckers?"

"Mostly to truckers. And people with heavy equipment. Like construction workers."

"Or highway departments?"

"Whose side are you on?"

"Yours, Owen. But you're only seeing one side of this. You think our brother's innocent, so you believe him when he says he never saw the tire iron, and you see the iron's scarcity as some sort of evidence of his innocence."

"And you don't?"

"That's not the point. If he's lying to you, or if a jury thinks he's lying to them, then the tire iron isn't any kind of alibi at all. It's a sign of premeditation."

"Come here. Come here. Quick," Ruth called from the breakfast room.

Owen and Judith hurried to join Ruth, who was pointing to a small TV set balanced precariously on top of a tin bread box. Alicia Fox stared at them from the TV set.

"She's suspended George without pay," Ruth said.

"And she called a press conference just for that?" Judith asked.

As if to answer Judith's question, Alicia announced, "For years in the past, the Office of the West Virginia Highway Commissioner has been a seedbed for kickbacks and corruption. I want to make it plain that this administration will not tolerate any hint of wrongdoing in the office. The muck stops here."

"Sanctimonious bitch," Judith said. "Whatever happened to 'innocent until proven guilty'?"

"What's the point?" Owen asked. "He can't work when he's in jail anyhow."

"George may get out on bail," Judith said. "And even if he doesn't, the suspension will freeze his benefits. He won't be able to draw sick leave or vacation pay."

"It'll just lay George low," Ruth said. "He was so proud of following in his father's footsteps. And Barb and Billy can't live without his salary."

"I'll look into it," Judith said. "State employees must have some rights."

"It'll just lay George low," Ruth repeated.

Owen looked at Judith. Neither of them wanted to tell Ruth that when they'd left George in jail that morning, he looked to be as low as he could possibly go.

THIRTEEN

The Scene of the Crime

GEORGE'S DISMISSAL AS Highway Commissioner shared the front page of the next morning's newspaper with a blaring headline that announced MURDER GUN LINKED TO FORMER HIGHWAY COMMISSIONER. The article accompanying the headline put the worst possible interpretation on every aspect of the thirty-five-year old murder of Ray Cantrip and the recent killing of Mary Jewel Robertson, referring to the "mysterious disappearance of murder weapon owner Wayne Allison following the Cantrip death," and the "...indictment and incarceration of just-deposed Commissioner George Allison following a public argument with murdered environmental activist Mary Jewel Robertson." The reporter even brought Owen into the picture, noting that he was "...first on the scene following the suspicious death of Cantrip's widow."

Owen tossed the front section of the paper onto the breakfast table. "The story ranks the Allison clan somewhere between the Borgias and the James boys."

Judith set down her coffee and picked up the newspaper. "Which James boys? Henry and William, Frank and Jesse, or the English kings?"

"The ones who robbed, raped, and pillaged," Owen said.

"That only lets Henry and William off the hook."

"It's outrageous," Ruth said. "Can't we sue for slander?"

"If it's published you have to sue for libel," Judith said. "But they've stacked enough 'allegedlys' and 'supposeds' in the story to stave off any lawsuits. Besides, what they're saying is basically true. Owen's dad was never seen again after Ray Cantrip died. George did threaten the Robertson woman in public. And Owen nearly interrupted Dolores Cantrip's killer."

"But when you string it all together like that, we sound worse than the Mafia," Ruth said.

Owen picked up the phone. "I'll call the sheriff," he said. "The bastard's got no business leaking the gun story. Besides, I want him to show us Mary Jewel's apartment."

Judith reached out for the phone. "Better let me lay some legal lingo on him. As George's attorney, I'm entitled to look at the apartment. And the sheriff may not appreciate being called a bastard by a member of the notorious Allison clan."

THE SHERIFF LED Owen and Judith into Mary Jewel Robertson's small apartment. The three of them shared the cramped living room with her black bicycle, a sofa enclosed in a clear plastic covering, three mismatched wooden chairs, a barren coffee table, and a wallful of paperback books organized neatly on stacked wooden shelves. The top shelf of the bookcase held four of the glass figurines Judith had admired at the flea market, and she took Owen's arm and nodded her head in their direction.

"The place is pretty much the way we found it," the sheriff said. "She had no next of kin."

"Spare but neat." Judith ran her finger over the top shelf of the bookcase. "Dusty, though. It looks as if something's missing from this shelf." She pointed to an oblong indentation in the thin film of dust covering the shelf. "See. It looks like there was a fifth figurine here."

The sheriff shrugged. "My boys didn't find anything."

"Where was the body?" Owen asked.

"There. In the doorway." The sheriff pointed to the doorway separating the living room from the kitchen.

The narrow kitchen barely accommodated a gas stove, an old-fashioned refrigerator topped by a ceramic crown, a sink, and a white drop-leaf table with two matching chairs. Two coffee mugs sat empty on the table, and a dented aluminum teakettle covered the front burner of the stove.

"Teakettle boiled over," the sheriff said. "By the look of it, she'd invited her killer in for a cup of tea."

"There was no sign of forced entry?" Owen asked.

The sheriff shook his head.

"She'd hardly have asked George in for a social visit," Owen said.

"Can't tell," the sheriff said. "Maybe she was feeling magnanimous after her victory."

"Mary Jewel was about as magnanimous as Snow White's stepmother," Owen said.

"Were there any fingerprints to indicate George was in here?" Judith asked.

"Got a set from the doorpost outside that belonged to George. Nothing in here."

"Any other prints in here?" Owen asked.

"Just Mary Jewel and the women from her protest group," the sheriff answered.

"What about the murder weapon?" Judith asked.

The sheriff blinked and scratched the brow over his glass eye. "We're not entirely sure about it."

"Don't be coy," Owen said. "You didn't hesitate to tell the press that the murder weapon in the Cantrip case belonged to my father."

"I didn't approve the release of that information," the sheriff said.

"What's done is done," Judith said. "What killed Mary Jewel?"

"A hard, straight rod wrapped in one of those kitchen towels." The sheriff nodded toward a single striped dish towel dangling from a bar at the side of the sink.

"So you don't really know whether it was the tire iron from George's car," Owen said.

"His tire iron had traces of fibers that matched the towel hanging there."

"That towel and a thousand others like it," Owen said.

The sheriff shrugged. "I told you we weren't entirely sure about the weapon."

"You said you weren't entirely sure about the weapon in the Cantrip case, either," Owen said. "Does that mean my father's gun might not have killed him?"

"No. There's no doubt where the bullet came from."

"Then what worried you?"

"Where we found the gun. There were signs somebody had started digging before my deputies got a hit on their metal detectors."

"So the gun might have been planted recently?"

"No, we checked that. The gun had definitely been in the ground for thirty-five years."

"In the ground at Gobbler's Grade?"

"That's what the lab boys tell me."

Judith left the kitchen and entered the small bedroom, which was a tight fit for a twin bed, a three-drawer dresser, and a nightstand. Posters with pictures of polar bears hung on two of the walls, while a window in the third wall looked out on a narrow gravel alleyway.

Judith picked up a check register from the nightstand. "This woman wrote checks for everything. There's a string of ten checks that are all under five dollars." She sat on the bed and began copying figures from the checkbook onto her notepad. "What did she do for a living anyhow?"

"A little temp work here and there," the sheriff said. "She set herself up as a charity and cadged donations for her lobbying."

"Her deposits aren't much bigger than her checks," Judith said. "Ten dollars here, twenty dollars there."

"Probably donations from private citizens," the sheriff said.

"Here's one for two thousand dollars from something called the Gray Eagle Trust."

"Could be for temp work. Either that, or she found herself a corporate sponsor," the sheriff said. "We're checking that out."

"Two-fifty a month to rent this apartment," Judith said, taking in the bedroom with her eyes. "What a sad, cramped life."

"She was a sad, cramped woman." Owen turned to the sheriff. "She must have had other enemies besides George?"

"None that threatened her in public."

"Here's a check for eighty dollars to Mario Etchivario," Judith said.

"Your glass sculptor," Owen said.

Judith smiled up from the bed. "Think that could be a clue?"

"Sounds as if you'd like to check it out," Owen said.

"When the going gets tough, the tough go shopping," Judith said.

"This time, you buy your own bauble," Owen said.

Judith rose from the bed and closed her notepad. "Oh, you're not done paying yet."

Owen picked up a telephone book from the bedside stand. "We probably ought to check out the Gray Eagle Trust as well. There's something familiar about the name." He leafed through the business numbers and the yellow pages. "It doesn't seem to be listed in the Barkley directory."

"Could be a Charleston firm," the sheriff said. "Mary Jewel did a lot of business in the capitol."

"I guess we've got no choice but to start with the sculptor," Judith said.

OWEN AND JUDITH stood on a glass-enclosed catwalk overlooking two large furnaces at the Pilgrim Glass Company. Workers in brown overalls captured small gobs of molten glass on the ends of long iron tubes which they delivered to aproned blowers who sat in semicircles around each furnace and blew, twirled, and shaped the gobs into recognizable forms. The heat from the two furnaces was a palpable force that pulsed upward through the catwalk.

A short round man wearing a blower's apron over his smudged brown overalls appeared at one end of the catwalk. He removed his safety goggles, leaving dark circles around his eyes, and said, "You wish see me? I'm Mario Etchivario."

"I saw your glass animals and loved them," Judith said. "I wanted to meet the man who made them and find out how to buy more."

The man smiled, showing a gold tooth under his dark mustache. "I make. Pilgrim sells. Flea market sells. I sell. I give you best deal, though. Which pieces you like?"

"I saw four pieces at Mary Jewel Robertson's home."

The smudged circles around the man's eyes narrowed. "You friend of Mary Jewel?"

"No," Judith said. "I just saw the pieces at her home."

"Hard woman," Mario said. "I sorry she die, but she a hard woman."

"Hard how?" Judith asked.

"She try to, how you say, chew me down. I don't chew good. Better you know that."

Judith raised an eyebrow. "But you sold her the pieces?"

"I sell. Pilgrim sells for forty dollars. Flea Market sells for thirty-five. I sell for twenty-five. She want for fifteen."

"Which pieces did you sell her?"

"I tell her for twenty dollars I sell her flawed, how you say, secondos."

"Seconds."

"Yes. I sell seconds for twenty dollars. She say only fifteen. She keep coming back. Finally I sell streaked squirrel for fifteen. Big mistake."

"How a mistake?"

"She want more at same price." Mario rubbed his thumb rapidly against his first two fingers. "More, more, more. Only for fifteen dollars. She keep coming back. Hounding." He folded his arms across his apron. "I sell no more at that price."

"What happened?"

Mario shrugged and wiped his hands on his apron. "One day she come with open checkbook. Say she will pay twenty dollars apiece for all seconds. I sell what I have. I so happy to be rid of her, I sell one primo at secondo price."

"Which pieces did you sell her?" Judith asked.

Mario counted off the animals on his stubby fingers. "Dolphin, whale, bird, bunny. She already have squirrel."

"The whale," Judith said. "The whale was missing from her apartment."

"Would you recognize the whale you sold her?" Owen asked.

"Of course. It had small bump on back. I was careless with scoop."

"Would you sell me a whale?" Judith asked.

"Primo or secondo?"

"Primo. And my friend here will be happy to pay full price."

IN THE CAR on the way home, Judith held the translucent whale up to the light. "The man's a real artist. Why do you think the whale was missing from Mary Jewel's shelf?"

"Maybe the killer wanted a souvenir."

Judith hefted the whale. "It's big enough for a weapon."

"If it were a weapon, why wouldn't the killer have planted it in George's trunk instead of the tire iron? Maybe Mary Jewel gave it away as a gift."

"She doesn't strike me as a very giving person. Maybe she just broke it by accident."

"If she did, she would have been back bargaining with Mario."

"Except she didn't have to bargain anymore, because she'd just gotten a two-thousand-dollar infusion to her bank account."

"That's what we experienced analysts call a lead," Owen said.

"That's what we legal experts call a remarkable grasp of the obvious."

OWEN'S MOTHER and his friend Bobby were waiting on the porch when Owen and Judith pulled into Ruth's driveway. Ruth stayed seated on the slat-backed swing as Bobby rose to meet them. "I'm glad you're home," Ruth said. "Barb called. She needs George's car.

And George's boss wants somebody to clear the stuff out of his office."

"Sounds like Alicia Fox expects George's suspension to be permanent," Owen said. "Tell Barb I'll bring the car and help clean out the office."

"And that's not all," Ruth continued. "Barb wanted to remind you that you promised to go rafting with George and Billy on the Gauley this weekend. Since George can't make it, she's hoping you'll take Billy. It's his birthday."

"Rafting on the Gauley," Bobby said. "Now that brings back great memories. Best time of my life."

"Didn't somebody drown there when you were little?" Judith asked.

"A boy named Berry," Owen said. "I couldn't save him."

"You're not still beating yourself up over that, are you?" Bobby asked.

Ruth rose to join them and took Owen's arm. "But you got a lifesaving medal." She reached out and drew Bobby close as well. "You both did."

Owen shrugged free of his mother's grasp. "But only one of us saved a life."

"You never told me you got a medal," Judith said. "Just that you couldn't save him."

"I couldn't," Owen said.

"Bullshit," Bobby said. "You did everything you could. Tell them what happened."

"Yes, Owen," Ruth said. "What you remember doesn't sound like what we were told."

Owen sat uneasily on the stone porch railing while Ruth joined Judith on the slat-backed swing and Bobby leaned against a white wooden column. "It was only a couple of months before our dads died," Owen began. "The rivers were starting to run high and my dad thought it would be fun to shoot the rapids on the Gauley River. This was before there were organized trips, and Dad wanted to stake out a roadbed near the mouth for his surveyors.

"Dad and Ray Cantrip took Bobby and me down the Gauley in a rubber raft. We cleared most of the tough rapids and stopped to camp just above Big Lick Falls. Bobby and I were gathering firewood by the river while Dad and Ray were up above setting up the campsite."

Owen could see the river in his mind's eye, rippling along with little hint of the whitewater above and below. "Bobby was closest to the river, and he saw it first. A kayak had overturned upriver, and two heads were bobbing in the middle of the current. They were kids, not much older than us, and neither of them was wearing a life vest. One of the kids was a strong swimmer, and he cut through the current toward our shore."

Owen remembered Bobby's dad, too far away to help, standing on an overlook and shouting, "Stroke! Stroke! Stroke!" to the swimmers. With each "Stroke!" he thrust his fist high in the air, then paused a beat, caught his breath, and pumped his fist again to the cry of "Stroke!" It wasn't clear whether he was timing the swimmer's strokes, or whether the boys in the water actually heard him, but each forward thrust of the first swimmer's arms soon matched the cadence of Ray Cantrip's shouts.

"It was obvious the second boy was in trouble. He'd reach out of the water with one hand, flail and splash around, then clutch at the air with his other hand." Owen's right hand clutched involuntarily. "But he was splashing, not swimming. By the time the current carried them past us, the first swimmer was close enough for Bobby to reach him with a long oak branch."

"I just stood on the shore, held on to a tree with one hand, and put the branch where he could get it," Bobby said.

"The other boy was still in the middle of the current when Bobby pulled the first swimmer in," Owen said. "And I just stood there watching."

"Bullshit," Bobby said. "You went in after him."

"I went in," Owen said. "But I waited too long before I did." He could still hear Ray Cantrip's cadence count. How many shouts of "Stroke!" had he heard before he went in? Four, certainly. Maybe five.

"The current carried me along, but I was too far behind him. I waited too long."

"You might have drowned yourself," Ruth said.

Owen went on as if he hadn't heard. "Dad took a side trail down to the water and fished us both out just below the Big Lick rapids, but the boy had been in too long. He'd swallowed too much water." He could see the boy's head lolling on his father's chest as he carried him back to the campsite. The boy might have been asleep, except for the streak of blood over his eyebrow and the mud-caked leaf embedded in his left ear. 'I might have saved him if I'd started sooner."

"You might have started sooner and still not saved him," Judith said. "You were ten years old and you risked your life to save somebody you didn't even know. And you let it haunt you. God, you're exasperating. You beat yourself up for things a normal person would be proud of. Isn't that right, Bobby?"

Bobby arched his back against the porch column and raised both eyebrows. "Define normal."

"Judith's right, Owen," Ruth said. "You can't save everybody. We're proud of you just for trying."

"You're my mother. It's in your job description to be proud of me," Owen said. "The Berry boy's mother probably would see things differently."

"Do you want me to call Barb and tell her you can't make the raft trip?" Ruth asked.

"God no. I already promised to go. Besides, I haven't had a chance to talk with Billy since George was indicted."

"If you go, I'll go," Judith said. "We'll make it a family outing."

"Oh, shucks," Bobby said. "Count me in too. Even though I still can't swim anymore than the sixty feet it took to qualify as a minnow at the Barkley YMCA."

"Sixty feet will get you to solid ground on the Gauley," Owen said. "But don't you teach traffic school on weekends?"

"They've shut me down," Bobby said. "You remember the old joke: You know why they had to cancel all of West Virginia's drivers' ed courses?"

Owen and Bobby recited the punch line in unison. "The mule died."

"That can't be a problem with your class," Owen said. "As long as you're teaching, there's always at least one ass available."

"Oh, that's good. I'd use it in class if I still had a class."

"Sorry," Owen apologized. "You told me the state was putting all the traffic schools up for bid. Did you lose?"

"I just bid on Wayne County. They decided to award all the state contracts to a single bidder. It was all rigged."

"Winner take all," Owen said. "It's happening all over. It's easier for a bureaucrat to deal with one contract, even if it's a crappy one."

"Why not just hire yourself out to the winner?" Judith asked. "They're bound to need good teachers."

"I can't make a living doing that. Besides, they won't let me do my jokes. They've got handbooks you have to follow to the letter.

And they charge an arm and a leg for them. That's how they get their profit." Bobby picked absently at a Band-Aid on his cheek. "On top of everything else, they won't pay my medical."

Owen looked at the Band-Aid. "You all right?"

"For a while. It'd be nice to be employed, though."

"What did you mean when you said the bid was rigged?" Judith asked.

"The state put a cap on the profits from each class so they wouldn't be ripped off," Bobby said. "But they required that all materials be produced on recycled paper, so that only a couple of local firms could make the handbooks. The winning bidder's just a front for a big paper manufacturer. They rack up their real profits by overcharging for materials. The little they get for running classes is just gravy."

"How can they get away with that?" Ruth asked.

"Welcome to West Virginia, Mom," Owen said. "Phony corporations are a time-honored tradition here. Just read the *Blade*'s blurb on Governor Banning and his buddies."

"But they jailed Banning's cronies back in the sixties," Ruth said.

Judith rose from the swing and faced Bobby. "Maybe your paper tigers can be caged too. Do you know who they are?"

"Edutech's the name of the front," Bobby said. "The paper manufacturer's WorldSafe. For all I know they're the same people. There may be others I don't know about."

"WorldSafe's the logo on those biodegradable traffic cones," Owen said. "Somebody made a bundle off the state on those too."

"That's the place to start, then," Judith said. "Let's find out who's pocketing WorldSafe's profits."

"They're not the only corporate officers we need to run down," Owen said. He stopped short and stared at Bobby.

"What's the matter?" Bobby asked. "Did I miss something?"

"No, I did," Owen said. "Something I should have seen earlier. Do you still have that shoebox of your mother's?"

"It's in the trunk of my car."

"Bring it up here."

Bobby looked at Ruth Allison, then back to Owen. "Is that smart? I mean, there's all that personal stuff."

"Oh, hell," Owen said. "I'm not interested in her letters. Bring up the rest of it. The financial stuff."

As Bobby went down the steps to his car, Ruth asked, "What's going on?"

"Bobby's mother left him some papers," Owen said. "Her house deed, insurance records, and the trust fund she used to pay for his college education."

Bobby returned with the shoebox. "What is it you're looking for?"

Owen could see that Bobby had left his father's love letters in the car. "Your college tuition payments. Or whatever records are in there. You said your mom got the money from a trust."

"Yeah. Some trust I'd never heard of."

"The Gray Eagle Trust," Owen said.

"The same fund that paid Mary Jewel two thousand dollars," Judith said.

"Right," Owen said. "I should have made the connection before this."

Judith took his arm. "Forget it. We just saw her checkbook this morning. You're not even a day late. That's well within the grace period."

Bobby handed Owen a packet of single sheets held together with a paper clip. "Here they are."

Owen spread the sheets on the stone porch railing. There were four in all.

Ruth bent over the first sheet. "Oh my God."

Each sheet was a copy of a thousand-dollar check drawn on the Gray Eagle Trust for the education of Robert Cantrip. Each was made out to Wheeling College. And each bore the tight, crabbed signature of Rudolph J. Slater.

"So who's Rudolph Slater?" Judith asked.

Owen gathered up the sheets and returned them to Bobby. "Robin Hager's ex-husband."

FOURTEEN

Tale of a Whale

THE CLOCK OVER the massive oak doors leading to Rudy Slater's office read ten twenty-five. Owen and Judith had been waiting in Slater's outer office since ten o'clock, when they had scheduled an appointment to discuss what Judith had advertised as "...a few details of the case of my client George Allison." In one corner of the outer office, a tall curving counter sculpted from black marble shielded a nail-filing receptionist and word-processing secretary from the temptation to interact with anyone waiting for an appointment. Owen judged that his own cramped and littered office back in California could easily fit in the space behind Slater's reception counter and reflected that his consulting business could probably fit in a post-office box if he didn't get back to it sometime soon.

When the clock read ten thirty-five, a buzzer sounded and the receptionist put away her nail file, came out from behind the marble counter, and led Owen and Judith into Slater's office.

Their footsteps echoed off the polished wood floor as they approached Slater, who sat behind a smooth ebony desk in a windowed alcove overlooking the Little Muddy River. When they neared his desk, Slater rose and waved his hand toward two plush chairs covered in brown suede.

The shiny inlaid wood under his feet reminded Owen of a basketball court and he declined the offer of a seat, saying, "No, thanks, I'll just stand here at the free-throw line."

When Slater frowned, Owen explained, "Your office. It's big enough to be a basketball court. You ought to be able to handle a half-court game easily."

Slater turned his frown into a thin smile without showing any teeth.

"Oh yes. I see. The decorators wanted to partition this space, but I wouldn't allow it. It seems to impress clients."

"I've always thought size doesn't matter," Judith said. "It's quite an office, though. Quite a building, too."

"Thank you." Slater smiled again, still without showing any teeth. "Well now, Ms. Allison," he said, drawing out the Ms. so it sounded like a bee's buzz, "As I told you on the phone, I don't know how I can help your client, but I'm happy to give you a few minutes of my time." He leaned back against his ebony desk. "I know that Mr. Allison here is the defendant's brother. I assume you must be related to George Allison as well."

"I was his sister-in-law."

"Was?"

"Owen and I are divorced."

"That's a shame. I know that they say a man who defends himself has a fool for a client. I don't know what they say about a man who's defended by an ex-sister-in-law."

"They say he's fortunate," Owen said. As Judith smiled and nodded, he pressed on. "I sort of expected to find an office for the Gray Eagle Trust here in your building," Owen said. "Aren't you affiliated with them?"

Slater's thin smile disappeared. "The trust has no office. It's a fiduciary convenience." He went behind his desk and slid open a drawer. "Rather like a cash drawer."

"Mary Jewel Robertson cashed a check from the Trust just before she died," Judith said.

"Mary Jewel relied on the kindness of her supporters," Slater said. "I'm proud to say the Trust was one of them."

"Why not just donate in the name of Slater Construction?" Owen asked.

Slater slid the desk drawer shut. "To keep tongues from wagging. A donation from a construction company to an environmentalist could be construed as a bribe."

"You'd given her other donations then?" Judith asked.

"I'm not sure. It wouldn't surprise me. She'd been around a long time. Her passing was a terrible loss for the community."

"How long has the Trust been around?"

"At least as long as my construction company," Slater said. "We use it primarily as a vehicle for donations and other indirect transactions."

"That might otherwise be construed as bribes," Owen said.

"In the eyes of some beholders, perhaps," Slater said. "I assure you, there's nothing at all illegal about it."

"Just a vehicle for your charitable impulses," Owen said.

"I see we understand one another," Slater said.

"About twenty-five years ago, your charitable impulses extended to my friend Bob Cantrip," Owen said.

Slater's jaw dropped just enough to show an even line of teeth. "That was sometime ago. I don't believe I recall your friend."

"You paid his tuition to Wheeling College."

Slater nodded. "Oh yes, I remember. There was a time when we established a scholarship fund for deserving students."

"What made Bobby Cantrip deserving?" Owen asked.

"As I recall, his father was thought to have died in public service. Fighting a flood, I believe."

"My father died in the same flood," Owen said. "You didn't give me a scholarship."

"Perhaps you should have applied."

"Bobby Cantrip doesn't remember applying."

"His mother must have applied for him."

"Why wouldn't she tell him about it?"

"I can't explain that. Perhaps she viewed it as charity. You know how these West Virginians are about charity."

"Then it was charity, not a scholarship?" Owen asked.

"When you're on the giving end, scholarships are charity," Slater said. He ran his hand under his desk drawer and his telephone rang almost immediately. "I fail to see how any of this helps your client."

"We have more than one client," Owen said.

"So do I," Slater said, rising and walking over to the phone. "That's likely to be one of them now. I think we're done, don't you? Perhaps you can show yourselves out."

On their way out, Owen stopped fifteen feet short of the tall oak doors and mimicked a quick left-handed jump shot from the key. While Judith waited, he followed the imaginary shot with his eyes, then shook his head. "Clanked it," he said. "Can't even make my fantasy shots anymore."

THE ASPHALT parking lot of Slater Construction baked under the early-afternoon sun. Stenciled lettering announced that the parking place nearest the rear door was RESERVED FOR RUDOLPH SLATER. The space marker itself had been painted over and widened to accommodate a gray-green HUMVEE.

"Jesus Christ," Owen said. "A Hummer. How much does one of those things cost?"

"Sixty, maybe seventy-five grand. Our Mr. Slater is doing all right for himself."

"He's a smooth son of a bitch," Owen said. "But Robin says he's lower than a snake's jockstrap."

"Ex-wives don't always make the best character witnesses. You might be surprised to hear some of the things I've said about you."

"Spare me," Owen said. "Slater lied to us about not remembering Bobby. He remembered how Bobby's dad died without any prompting."

"It's been in all the papers lately. Why do you have it in for him? Is it because he married your old girlfriend?"

"Could be that. Could be the size of his office. Or because he drives a car that costs more than I'm likely to make this year. Mostly, though, it's because he's tied into the troubles with both my dad and brother and I think he's a lying scumbag."

"That doesn't make him a murderer."

"It doesn't make him innocent, either." Owen ran his hand over the boxy rear of Slater's Hummer. "Maybe we should stir things up a little."

"What do you have in mind?"

"Remember when you left Buster Junior in my TR-6 as a present before we were married?"

"It was supposed to be a surprise. But he got scared and peed on the upholstery."

"The car was locked. I never could figure out how you got in."

Judith batted her eyelashes. "The wiles of woman."

Owen tried the door handle on the Hummer. "Think you could do it again?"

"You're going to get a puppy to pee in Slater's Hummer?" Judith made a clucking noise with her tongue. "That's so immature."

"I had in mind leaving him another kind of present."

"What kind?"

"One of Mario's whale sculptures."

"You want to sacrifice my whale? Don't be an Indian giver."

"That's hardly a politically correct response."

"Don't be a bestower of indigenous American artifacts, then. And don't dodge the issue. What about my whale?"

"We'll get you another one. Mario likes you."

"Well, it's not surprising. You can tell from his sculptures he has excellent taste."

BACK AT THE parking lot an hour later, Judith balanced a gift-wrapped sculpture and an overnight case on her lap while Owen looked for an empty space. "Try to park as far away from Slater's Hummer as you can get."

When Owen found a space, Judith hopped out and used her nail file to let the air out of the left rear tire of their rented car. "Now call Triple-A," she said.

"You sure this will work?"

"Unless I've lost my touch. All you have to do is pretend you don't know me."

"I can handle that. Is there some way to make it retroactive?"

"Be careful what you wish for." She wiggled her fingers in a short good-bye. "I'll get changed and wait inside until the rescue truck comes."

Within twenty minutes of Owen's call, a yellow tow truck pulled up and a stocky young man in a matching yellow jumpsuit with the name "Billy Jack" monogrammed on its breast climbed down and saluted him. "In trouble, huh?" the young man said.

Owen nodded toward his left rear tire. Billy Jack got down on his knees and inspected it gravely. "Not so bad," he announced. "It's only flat on one side."

"Maybe you could help me rotate it so the other side's down."

Billy Jack studied Owen, considering the possibilities. "Nobody's ever suggested that before," he said. "But I think we better put your spare on just to be safe."

"Whatever you say. You're the expert."

Billy Jack was turning the last nut on the spare when Judith materialized at his side. "Thank God you're here," she said. "Can you help me for a minute?" She turned to Owen. "Listen, it'll only be a tiny minute, I promise."

Owen stared at Judith. She'd exchanged her navy-blue lawyer suit for a tight red dress, put on lipstick to match the dress and done something to her eyes to make them dark and inviting. She turned her newly made-up eyes on the mechanic and tugged at his arm. "Just come with me for a minute," she repeated. "And bring your tool kit."

Billy Jack rose and gave Owen the questioning look of B'rer Rabbit facing the brier patch.

Owen shrugged and said, "Go ahead, I'm in no hurry," but Judith was already leading Billy Jack away, clasping his elbow with one hand and using the other to gesture with the gift-wrapped sculpture.

The mechanic returned five minutes later, shaking his head and smiling. "Some looker, huh? Wanted to leave a present for the guy in the Hummer, so I got her into it. Said she was married to him, but she wasn't wearing any ring I could see." He knelt down and tightened each of the nuts on Owen's spare all over again. "Man, she can park her slippers under my bed anytime."

Owen watched Billy Jack stand and toss his tire iron into the rear of the tow truck. He considered telling the mechanic Judith didn't wear slippers to bed, or anything else for that matter, but thought better of it.

ON A HILL above the parking lot, Owen trained binoculars on Slater's Hummer while Judith used the passenger mirror to adjust her lipstick. "The mechanic didn't believe you were married to Slater," he said.

"Of course not. That's what made it work."

"Man was fantasizing about your bedroom slippers."

"Can you be more specific?"

"That's all he said. I've got his number if you'd like to call him."

Judith blotted her lipstick and readjusted the mirror. "That's all right. He already gave it to me."

Owen put down the binoculars. "What'd you do to your eyes?"

"Just a little extra eye shadow. It's my new going-out face. You like it?"

"It's...umm...exotic. I don't think I've seen that dress before, either."

"A gal has to come prepared."

"Prepared for what? A brothel opening?"

"You wish." Judith reached out and tapped the binoculars. "Better pay attention to business. Here comes our man."

Owen trained the binoculars on Slater. "Where'd you put the whale?"

"Right in the driver's seat."

Slater opened the Hummer and started to get in, then stopped with his hand on the door handle.

"He sees the package," Owen said. "He's unwrapping it."
Slater threw the unwrapped whale onto the car seat as if it had burned his hand.

"It's upset him," Owen reported. "He's looking around the parking lot. He probably senses he's being watched."

"It's a good thing we're in this rental car. If he did kill Mary Jewel, he'd recognize George's Pontiac."

"He won't look up here. We're too far away."

They watched Slater climb behind the wheel and start his engine. Owen turned on his ignition at the same time. "I'll pick him up at the lot exit and follow him," he said, easing down the hill. "He didn't act like he'd just gotten a gift from a friend."

"Neither did you when you found Buster Junior."

Slater drove off parallel to the river, then made two abrupt right turns.

"He's circling back to cover his tracks," Owen said.

"Or to see if somebody's following him," Judith said. "Stay well behind him."

"One good thing about a Hummer. It's so wide we can let a dozen cars get between us and still see him."

Slater made two more right turns, taking them back to the river road. Owen followed, keeping at least two cars between himself and the Hummer. As they passed the outskirts of the city, the Hummer made a sharp right down an unmarked gravel road hemmed in by barbed wire on one side and high weeds and straggling rows of cattails on the other.

Owen braked without following Slater down the gravel road. "There's no way out of there. It leads to an abandoned boat slip. He's bound to see us if we take the car in." He opened the driver's door and slid out from behind the wheel. "I'll follow him in on foot. If he comes out before I do, give him a head start and tail him. I'll find a phone and get in touch with you at home."

"Be careful."

"Don't worry. I'll keep out of sight."

Owen hurried down the gravel road, staying close to the high weeds and cattails on his left so that he could use them for cover if he needed to. The cattails nearest the road had been bent and broken by the jutting bed of the Hummer.

The road soon narrowed to a rutted dirt path, and Owen stopped to listen. He could smell the river, but he couldn't hear it. Unlike the Gauley, the Little Muddy was wide and smooth and didn't announce its meanderings. The only sounds were the incessant chirping of crickets and a random clicking noise he didn't recognize.

He left the pathway and picked his way through the broken cattails toward the river, hoping to find a spot where he could watch Slater and the Hummer without being seen. Before finding one, he heard a distant splash and the sudden roar of an engine. The roar increased, and he dived for the cover of the deeper weeds, landing on his hands and knees in a murky slough as the Hummer sped by in reverse.

Owen heard the Hummer brake quickly and he splashed deeper into the slough. He didn't think he'd been seen, but he couldn't be sure. He knelt silently in the murky water, listening to the cadence of the crickets and the faint ruffle of a breeze in the high grass. Finally a car door slammed, and he heard gravel pinging against the Hummer's undercarriage as it backed out to the highway.

Alone with the crickets, Owen waded back to the rutted dirt road and followed the wide Hummer tracks down to the river. They stopped just short of the two leaning posts and rotted, half-submerged planks that marked the remains of an abandoned boat slip. The post anchoring the near side of the slip was freshly scarred, as if someone had pounded it with a crowbar. A sliver of glass glinted in the dirt near the foot of the post. It was a shard from the tail of the whale they'd left in Slater's Hummer.

SHERIFF READER tilted back in his desk chair and swiveled his good eye slowly between Owen and Judith. "Lemme get this straight. You want me to drag the Little Muddy for some busted glass whale you put in Rudy Slater's Hummer?"

"I'm betting you'll find more than one busted whale there," Owen said.

"What if I did? What'd that prove? That Slater's an art critic?"

"It'd prove Slater was the one who took Mary Jewel's whale," Judith said.

"It might suggest that, Counselor," the sheriff said. "I don't see it would prove it beyond a reasonable doubt."

"It's a pretty strong suggestion, though," Owen said.

"You got any idea of the manpower it takes to drag that river?" the sheriff asked.

"Use a diver then," Owen said. "The pieces have to be within a couple of hundred feet of the slip."

The sheriff leaned forward and clasped his hands together on his desk. "You two have been watching too much TV. Maybe Jim Rockford and Jessica Fletcher operate that way. But I got me a real police force here."

"At least question Slater," Judith said.

The sheriff held up his right hand, palm outward, as a stop sign. "Hold it right there. Rudy Slater draws a lot of water in this state. I'm not going to question him about a killing just because he may or may not have pitched a glass whale you left in his car seat into the Little Muddy."

"He did pitch it," Owen said. "Or whatever was left of it. There's no doubt about it."

"But you didn't see him do it," the sheriff said.

Owen held up the shard from the whale's tail. "I heard the splash. I found this piece."

"You're holding that piece of glass up like it means something," the sheriff said. "Hell, he could have busted up the whale right there in the parking lot in front of God and everybody and it wouldn't prove a damn thing."

"Think about it," Judith said. "What would you do if someone left a present on the seat of your car? Wouldn't you take it home with you? Or at least try to find out who left it?"

"You've got to admit his behavior was suspicious," Owen said.

"Curious, maybe," the sheriff said. "But not necessarily suspicious. Suspicious is a murder weapon in your brother's trunk after he's threatened Mary Jewel in public."

"Why do you keep getting stuck on the evidence against my brother?" Owen asked.

"Why do you keep gliding right over it?" the sheriff said. "I told you once, this is a job for professionals. You keep on blundering around, you might could get hurt. I can't be responsible for your safety."

"Is that a threat?"

The sheriff rose from his desk. "Son, if I decide to threaten you, you'll know it. You won't have to ask."

FIFTEEN

A Cushion for the Electric Chair

ALICIA FOX POINTED to the three tiers of cardboard boxes lining two walls of George's office. "You can start by taking those boxes," she said to Owen and his nephew Billy. "I assume that all belongs to George. I've already claimed the state's property, except for the furniture."

Owen nodded toward the large wooden drafting table that dominated the cramped room. "That table was my father's."

"Unless you can produce a bill of sale," Alicia said, "I have to assume it's state property."

"I don't have a bill of sale," Owen said. "But I doubt that it's state property. There can't be any others like it in the building."

"I'm sure it's one of a kind," Alicia said. "But unless you can establish ownership, it stays in this building."

"Then I'll buy it. How much do you want?"

Alicia bristled as if Owen had offered to bribe her. "I can't set the price. Any sale would have to go through the surplus-property office. It will take time and paperwork."

"If you've got the paperwork, we've got the time."

"I can't possibly get to it today." Alicia turned in the doorway and swept a regal arm over the office. "At least remove the rest of this clutter." She slapped her hand against her side like a commander completing a salute and disappeared down the hallway.

The sloping drafting table was the only empty surface in George's office. Stacks of paper topped the cardboard boxes and filing cabinets, rows of texts and manuals lined the shelves of two bookcases, rolled blueprints were stacked like cordwood under the drafting table, and George's desk was nearly invisible under an avalanche of loose papers and typed reports.

Billy wheeled a black dolly through the door, nearly crowding Owen out of the room. "I don't see how Dad could work in all this mess."

"It's not mess to him." Owen started loading loose papers into an empty box. "I'll pack. You haul."

A device that looked like a paper punch with distended circular jaws dangled by a chain from the drafting table. Billy hefted the chain. "What's this thing?"

Owen inserted a piece of paper between the jaws of the device and squeezed. When he pulled the paper free, it bore an embossed seal whose raised letters read:

APPROVED BY
WAYNE M. ALLISON
COMMISSIONER OF
HIGHWAYS

"Grandpa's seal. Cool," Billy said. "I never knew him."

"I barely did myself. He died when I was ten."

"How old was my dad then?"

"About fourteen."

"So he got to make all his decisions for himself from then on."

Owen began sorting papers from the top of George's desk into neat stacks. "Not quite. Your grandmother was there to help."

"Did she make him become an engineer?"

"Nobody made your dad do anything. He had a mind of his own. And engineering didn't come easy for him."

Billy wrestled a box loaded with books onto the dolly. "It's not coming easy for me, either. But he doesn't want me to switch to poly sci."

"He thinks it'll be easier for you to find a job with an engineering degree."

Billy loaded another box onto the dolly and looked around the office. "But I don't want an engineering job. He still treats me like a child."

Owen remembered Ruth leading him around the flea market. "That may never change."

"So I want to change majors. But I still want him to approve. You know?"

Owen ran his fingers over the raised letters of his own father's seal. "That's another thing that probably won't change."

"So what do you think I should do?"

"It's your life. Now's the time to experiment. While all your options are still open." Owen remembered his own first year in college. All promise and potential, until life's choices and a few failures narrowed his options. He helped Billy load a third box onto the dolly. "I'll talk to your dad if you want."

"What do you think he'll say?"

"I don't think he'll raise much of a fuss. Your approval is important to him too. Right now, though, his mind is on other things."

Billy held the top box and tilted the dolly back onto its wheels. He'd started to haul the load out of the room when he stopped in the doorway and said, "Do you think Dad killed that woman?"

"Of course not. Do you?"

Billy's shoulders slumped against the dolly. "I don't know. He could be a pretty mean drunk."

"Mean how? Did he ever hit you?"

"No. I knew to stay out of his way. But he let Mom have it once. Seems like they were always arguing. The neighbors called the cops a couple of times."

The news came as a double shock to Owen, for what it said about his brother and for what it meant to Judith's defense. "So there's a record of domestic violence?"

"The cops never took him in. Just calmed him down."

"But there'll be a record of the calls."

Owen realized his concern must be showing in his face, since Billy rushed to defend his father, saying, "Don't get me wrong, he's a great dad most of the time. We have lots of fun. He still takes me to the Reds' games. And rafting. I'm really sorry he's going to miss tomorrow's trip down the Gauley." Billy backed the dolly out of the office. "I'm glad you're coming, though."

Owen continued packing in silence, trying to reconcile Billy's new information on George with the brother he'd grown up with, who'd taught him to drive, lay off the outside curve, and never draw to an inside straight. In the meantime Billy took several dolly loads of boxes from the office to the car in near silence, finally announcing that the car was full and that he was going to drive the first load home.

After Billy left, Owen went on sorting, finding a storage box full of leather-bound journals that had belonged to his father. The top journal contained a day-by-day log of construction progress on the winding road that led from Barkley up to Lookout Point over the Gauley River. He marked the box and set it aside so that he could review the journals in more detail when they'd finished clearing George's office.

Owen was telescoping rolls of highway plans into a mailing tube when Judith appeared in the office doorway, smiling like the Cheshire cat and hiding both hands behind her.

"I wasn't expecting you until this evening at George and Barb's," Owen said.

Judith leaned against the doorframe, keeping her hands out of sight. "I couldn't wait. I stopped off at the library to see what I could find on those three corporations."

"WorldSafe, Edutech, and the Gray Eagle Trust."

"The librarian was quite nice and very helpful. Until I signed a request slip and she realized I was your ex-wife. Then things got a little chilly. You're not bonking her too, are you?"

"It was either that or pay the overdue fines."

"At least that would show a little class. I still don't know what you see in your friend Robin."

"You didn't come early just to be catty," Owen said. "You could have saved that for later. What have you got behind you?"

"Well, your friend at the library is still working on the Gray Eagle Trust. It was set up some time ago." Judith came into the office, took her hands from behind her, and presented Owen with a moldering traffic cone. "But we hit pay dirt with WorldSafe and Edutech. Guess who's the CEO of both?"

Owen set the traffic cone on his head like a dunce cap. "I give up. Who?"

"John Philip Crane."

Owen racked his memory. "Is that supposed to mean something to me?"

"That's just what I said. But then your librarian friend earned her pay. What would you say if I told you John Philip Crane was the husband of Alicia Fox?"

Owen grinned and took the traffic cone off his head. "I'd say we can unpack all this stuff."

OWEN AND JUDITH walked past Alicia Fox's secretary without bothering to have her announce them. Alicia was on the phone in her office, sitting behind a polished wooden desk large enough for a landing field. When they entered, she put her hand over the phone's mouthpiece and said, "I'm afraid I'm busy. If it's about that drafting table, I told you you'll have to go through channels before it can leave the building."

Owen plopped the traffic cone on the near corner of the polished desk. "I don't think that drafting table is going to leave the building just yet."

Alicia whispered, "I'll call you back" into the mouthpiece, hung up the phone, and pointed a long lacquered nail at the crumbling cone. "What are you doing with that traffic cone?"

"Tracking its genealogy," Owen said. "So far, we've traced its parentage to the WorldSafe Corporation, whose father is John Philip Crane. A name that should be familiar to you."

Alicia drew herself up straight in her chair. "WorldSafe won that contract in an open bidding competition."

"After your friend the Governor pushed through legislation mandating environmentally friendly construction materials," Judith said.

"Much like the bill mandating the use of recycled materials in all state education programs," Owen added.

"Those laws helped the environment," Alicia said.

"And just happened to lead to big contracts for your husband's firms." Owen slid the dilapidated cone across Alicia's desk until it stopped in front of her chair.

Alicia moved her chair to peer around the cone. "Those contracts were won in open competition. It's all perfectly legal."

"Perhaps," Owen said. "We're looking into that. But with all the attention the press is giving to highway scandals, I don't think the Governor would like to see anyone connect the dots between those ludicrous traffic cones and his Transportation Commissioner."

"Especially after she's been on TV denouncing past scandals and announcing that 'the muck stops here,'" Judith added. "Nice phrase, by the way."

Alicia swept the traffic cone off her desk and into her wastebasket. "How much do you want?"

Owen raised his eyebrows to Judith and said in a hurt tone, "She thinks we want money. Wouldn't that be illegal?"

Judith clucked her tongue. "Definitely illegal."

Owen turned to Alicia. "You've assured us there's nothing illegal going on. We wouldn't want to set a precedent." He paused. "We'd just like a few favors."

"What favors?"

Owen raised one finger. "First, reinstate my brother George."

"The man is in jail."

"We don't think he'll be there much longer," Judith said.

"What reason would I give for reinstating him?"

"Make up something," Judith said. "Pressure from the state employee's union. Clause B of his employment contract."

"What's Clause B?"

Judith rolled her eyes toward Owen. "The Sanity Clause."

Owen took a thick stick of chalk from the blackboard and held it like a cigar while wiggling his eyebrows. "You can't fool me. There is no Sanity Clause."

Alicia glared. "I fail to find this amusing."

"Millions of Marx Brothers fans would disagree," Judith said.

"Give any reason you'd like," Owen said. "Just reinstate George. And while you're at it, go back to the Barkley Board of Supervisors. Explain that a review of George's impact report has caused you to rethink the state's position on bridge lanes."

"Don't be absurd. I can't do that."

Owen went behind Alicia's desk, retrieved the traffic cone from the wastebasket, and showed her the WorldSafe logo. "I think you can. The vote was close last time. You should be able to swing them the other way."

"And if I can't?"

"Then look for this traffic cone on the front page of the *Charleston Gazette*."

Alicia slowly shook her head. "This is ridiculous."

"We're not done yet," Owen said. "A friend of ours, Bobby Cantrip, lost his job running Wayne County's traffic schools when you gave the statewide contract to Edutech. We'd like you to see that he gets his job back, along with full medical benefits."

"I can't do that. I have no control over the hiring practices of state contractors."

"The Board of Directors of Edutech is remarkably similar to WorldSafe's," Judith said. "We're confident you'll find a way."

Alicia wrote Bobby's name in her Daytimer. "This is blackmail. Suppose I do what you're asking. How do I know you won't go to the press anyhow?"

"You don't," Owen said. "But you can be damn sure we'll go if you *don't* do what we've asked."

"And no matter what you do, if my research turns up anything illegal about those contract awards, I'll be bound as an officer of the court to make it public," Judith added.

"So you better hope those contracts are as legal as you say they are," Owen said.

Alicia returned the traffic cone to the wastebasket. "Will that be all?"

"For now," Owen said. "We'll let you know if there's more. In the meantime, we'll just leave George's things in his office. It's still a little cramped in there, though. You might want to move him into a bigger space when he returns."

OWEN AND JUDITH returned to George's cramped office to see if Billy had returned. There was no sign he'd come back to load more boxes.

"Jesus," Owen said. "I haven't felt this good since I've been back. It's like we're finally making some progress."

He took the adhesive-backed visitor's pass the security guard had stuck on Judith's lapel and used his father's seal to stamp

APPROVED BY
WAYNE M. ALLISON
COMMISSIONER OF
HIGHWAYS

in the center of the badge. Then he returned it to her lapel and kissed her on the cheek. "Couldn't have done it without you."

Judith didn't move during the small award ceremony. "I wish I felt as good about it as you do."

"What's the matter?"

"The woman was promoting good causes. Causes I believe in. And we blackmailed her."

"Oh, come on. Being for good causes doesn't make you a good person. Jeffrey Dahmer recycled. Mussolini promoted mass transit."

Judith smiled. "And Oedipus loved his mother."

"The woman is bilking the state. She may have found a way to do it legally, and she may be doing it in the name of the environment, but she's no different from the frauds who used to rake off Interstate funds in the name of progress.''

"I guess I'm disappointed, is all. I keep expecting more from women who make it up the ladder.''

"What? You take away the glass ceiling and give women the same opportunities as men, you think they'll steal less?''

"I admit I'm a little irrational on the subject. It's like your thinking the Reds have a chance every summer.''

Owen squeezed Judith's shoulder. ''Well, it took a woman to catch Alicia. That should be some consolation.''

Owen tried calling Billy at home and got no answer. ''Let's leave a note for Billy and drive down to Barkley. I can't wait to see George's face when we tell him about Alicia.''

GEORGE'S FACE after Owen described the scene with Alicia Fox looked very much like George's face before Owen began talking: gaunt, glum, and haggard.

Owen paced the county jail's interrogation room, embellishing the story. ''Don't you see, it's no wonder she didn't want anybody talking about those cones.''

George slumped in his metal chair. ''Yeah, I can see that now.''

"Not only did she agree to reinstate you,'' Judith said, ''she'll reopen the bridge hearing.''

"And if there's anything else you want from Alicia, we just have to ask for it,'' Owen added.

George waved in the direction of the barred window. ''Can she get me out of here?''

"We're working on that,'' Judith said.

"I don't mean to sound ungrateful,'' George said. ''But so long as I'm here in jail, getting my job back is about as comforting as an extra cushion on the electric chair.''

"Get the electric chair out of your mind, George,'' Judith said. ''Nobody's talking about the death penalty. Even if you did kill Mary Jewel, you were clearly drunk at the time.''

"There's no chance George killed Mary Jewel,'' Owen said.

George stared at his hands, which dangled limply between his legs. ''They tell me I left fingerprints on her front door.''

"But not inside,'' Owen said. ''We think you were sleeping the booze off in your car when someone killed her.''

George pinched his forehead as if he were trying to squeeze out clues from the murder night. "I just don't remember."

"Do you remember assaulting Barb?" Judith asked.

George dropped his hand from his forehead and gaped open-mouthed at Judith.

"Oh, come on, Judith," Owen said. "There's no need to go into that."

"If I'm going to defend him, there is," Judith said. "There are police reports. You said at least two. The prosecution is bound to use them."

"I never hit her," George said. "Just shoved her around a little. We were yelling. The neighbors called the cops."

"What were you yelling about?" Judith asked.

George shrugged. "Money. Billy. My job. Take your pick."

"But you were drunk," Owen said.

"Of course."

"And you still remember it?"

"Barb won't let me forget it."

"The point is, you remember it," Owen said. "If you killed Mary Jewel when you were drunk, don't you think you'd remember that too?"

George's shoulders slumped and his head lolled forward, shaking slowly. "I just don't know. I don't remember knocking on Mary Jewel's door. But I must have done it. I do remember shoving Barb." His head stopped shaking and sank even lower. "Jesus. Now everybody will find out what a shit I've been."

Owen put his arms around George's shoulders from behind and pulled him upright. "You're only a shit when you're drunk, and you're working on that." He clasped both his brother's shoulders tightly and whispered in his ear, "As for everybody finding out, that's just not going to happen. We'll get you out of this mess before it ever comes to trial." Even as he said the words, he realized he had no clear idea how to make them come true. But he knew he had to deliver on his promise.

OWEN AND JUDITH drove from the jail to George's house, where Owen helped Billy sort George's boxes into two stacks: one that would be stored at home and one that would be taken back to the state office building. When they finished sorting, Billy left to celebrate his birthday with friends and Owen joined Judith and Barb in the kitchen. Judith sat at the kitchen table snapping fresh peas into a bowl, while Barb stood at the counter assaulting a tomato with a paring knife. When Owen got a beer from the refrigerator and offered to help, Barb handed him the knife and tomato and began laying out lunchmeat to make sandwiches for the next day's raft trip.

"I'm not surprised George isn't being much help to you," Barb said, lining up eight slices of bread and attacking each in turn with a knife and butter. "He dithers and worries so much it paralyzes him sometimes."

"That's not fair," Owen said. "He's in a pretty tough spot right now."

"He got himself there," Barb said. "And dithering has always been his first response to any new situation."

Judith snapped open a peapod. "You're the same way, Owen. You remember your failures and forget your successes, so you're slow to start anything until you're sure, and slow to change anything once you've started."

Owen ran his thumb along the knife blade, testing its sharpness. "I prefer to think of myself as prudent and steadfast."

"I prefer to think of myself as blond and big-busted," Judith said. "But my mirror doesn't agree."

"At least *you* could change with a little peroxide and padding." Owen smiled and added quickly, "Not that anyone would want you to change."

"I don't get it," Judith said. "You learn from failure on your job. Why don't you do it in your life? Instead, you carry it around like those lead weights they use to handicap horses. And half the things you think are failures, anyone else would count as successes."

"Well, I'm ready to learn from my failures," Barb said. "One way or the other, I'm leaving George once this mess is settled."

Owen stopped slicing and steadied the knife against the cutting board. "Give the guy a chance, Barb. His biggest problems disappear when he's sober and he'd started taking the cure before the sheriff jailed him. If nothing else, the jail will dry him out."

"He started the cure once before. I'll be more impressed if he ever finishes it," Barb said. "Divorce isn't the end of the world. Look at the two of you. You're divorced and you get along better than George and I ever did."

Owen looked at Judith, waiting for her to say something. Judith stopped shelling peas and stared back at him. "We're not exactly poster children for divorce," Owen said finally.

"Mistakes were made," Judith said. "Before, during, and after we separated."

The tone of regret in Judith's voice reminded Owen that they, both of them, were skating over waters that held deep hurts, and the ice was thin in spots they never expected.

SIXTEEN

The Devil's Staircase

OWEN AND JUDITH SAT on an uprooted tree that clung tenaciously to the sandy soil where the curving Gauley River had gouged a shallow beach. Owen's nephew Billy sat cross-legged in front of them while Bobby Cantrip stood next to the river itself, stirring the clear edge of the flowing water with a stick that turned the submerged pebbles into tiny bouncing mirrors. All four wore T-shirts, sneakers, and cut-off jeans, with the only difference in their outfits being their T-shirt slogans and choice of headgear. Owen and Billy wore maroon Cincinnati Reds baseball caps, with Billy's sweat-stained version turned backward so that tufts of brown hair poked through the adjustable band. Bobby wore a white navy watch cap, while Judith had braided her hair and tied it up with a red bandanna.

Their guide, Kim Stark, a wiry, tanned brunette wearing a white visor and T-shirt advertising Stark's River Runners, sat on the edge of a black rubber raft and cradled an oar on her lap as she ran through her pre-trip safety lecture. "Wear your life vest at all times," she said, pulling on her orange life jacket. "If the raft flips, or if you fall out, point your feet downstream and let the current carry you. Don't try to get back into the raft. You don't want to come up under it or be caught between the raft and a rock."

For Owen, the guide's talk conjured up uncomfortable images of clutching hands and water-choked lungs. He didn't remember his father giving any pre-trip advice, other than to "...hang on and paddle." But rafting hadn't been an organized activity then. He imagined that Kim's fear-inspiring lecture was a legal requirement, like the release forms they'd all signed earlier at her mobile office.

"If you do go in," Kim was saying, "hang on to your paddle. It adds an extra five feet to your reach." She grasped her own paddle easily by its handle and held it out to Billy, who shook hands with the flat blade. "And it costs us an arm and a leg to replace them if they're lost."

"Above all," she continued, "if you do go in, don't panic. With your life vest on you can make it through any of the rapids on this river. Just remember to float on your back and point your feet downstream." She pointed her paddle at the river, which was about fifty yards wide at the curve. "And you can make shore easily in the calm pools between the rapids."

Two kayakers rowed by and waved at Kim's outstretched paddle. Owen saw that they were both wearing life vests, unlike the boys in his nightmares.

"Any questions?" Kim asked.

"Tell them what to do if they get Maytagged," Billy said.

"It doesn't happen often," Kim said, "but sometimes the river creates a hole and the eddies can suck you in, just like you were going down a drain."

"Or were caught in the spin cycle of a washer," Billy said.

"Thank you for sharing that with us, Billy," Judith said. She shaded her eyes and looked at Kim. "What do we do then?"

"Just hold your breath," Kim said. "It may suck you in, but it will spit you right out."

"What if we spring a leak?" Bobby asked.

Kim touched the four rounded corners of the raft with her oar. "The raft has four separate air compartments. If one of them goes, it will still float. It'll just be hard to maneuver."

When there were no other questions, Kim announced it was time to get into the water. Owen approached the raft and made an elaborate show of inspecting each of its four sides.

"What are you looking for?" Bobby asked.

"A warning from the Surgeon General," Owen said. "After listening to that safety lecture, I'm sure OSHA must require a warning label somewhere."

"They used to nail the labels on," Bobby said. "But they finally figured out that hurt more than it helped."

Billy laughed and, for the third time since they arrived at the inlet, thanked Owen, Judith, and Bobby for coming with him. "Mom would have come," he said, "but after riding the rapids once she never wanted to do it again."

"That's not exactly a ringing endorsement," Judith said.

With two on a side, they picked the raft up and walked it into the river. Owen's feet tingled with the unexpected chill of the water.

"Why do I keep thinking of *Deliverance?*" Judith asked.

Bobby raised his voice an octave. "Oh my goodness, can we expect to meet some burly mountain men?" He let his wrist go limp and pointed at Kim. "Y'all be sure and point them out to me now, won't you, sugar?"

Kim smiled professionally and held the raft while the four of them climbed aboard. Owen straddled the left rear of the raft behind Billy, while Bobby sat behind Judith on the right side. Kim hefted herself into the stern, where she could support either side and steer the raft through the rapids. It occurred to Owen that he and Bobby were seated exactly where their fathers had been the day the kayak overturned upriver.

"All right," Kim announced, "we have a little time to get the feel of the river. Just use nice even strokes and let the current carry us along."

Owen's oar clacked off a submerged rock, stinging his hands like an inside fastball. Once they were in deeper water, though, he matched his strokes with Billy's long, even pulls, and they soon settled into an automatic rhythm.

On the other side of the raft, Owen could see Judith pulling strongly in the lead position. Behind her, though, he heard Bobby's paddle splatting the water and felt the spray raised by his choppy strokes. The raft began to drift to the right.

"Get with the program there, sailor," Owen said to Bobby. "Just because we don't have a plank for you to walk doesn't mean you're free to fluff stroke after stroke."

"There's nothing wrong with my strokes," Bobby answered. "I can switch hands masturbating without missing a beat."

In front of Owen, Billy laughed and missed a stroke. With Judith and Bobby pulling on the other side, the raft came back around.

Owen felt the raft move with the current and remembered his father telling him they were a part of the river when that happened.

On either side of the river, steep layers of scarred limestone began to rise up. As the layers increased in height, Owen had the sensation that they were gliding down an escalator. Soon both banks were inaccessible and the raft was hemmed in by reddish brown walls streaked with traces of dark shale.

"All right, you're going good," Kim shouted. "Now let's try back-paddling."

Everyone but Bobby managed the shift. He splashed water and swore.

"Pretend you're switching hands," Owen said.

"It doesn't feel the same," Bobby answered. "The oar's just not thick enough."

"That's enough," Kim shouted. "Let's go forward again."

Small ripples appeared in the water and Owen heard a soft, remembered rumble. The raft rounded a curve and the rumble increased to a dull roar.

"That'll be Widowmaker Falls," Kim announced.

"Oh, great," Judith said over her shoulder to Owen. "Lucky we're not married anymore."

"Don't worry," Owen said. "Divorcee Drop is just about a mile farther on."

After the next curve they saw it. In the center of the river, white-water foamed and splattered against a looming rock shaped like the spine of a brontosaurus.

"That's Razorback Rock," Kim said. "Steer to the left of it. See, where the current's creating the rapids."

The roar increased and the raft picked up speed. Owen matched Billy's long hard strokes, and the raft veered to the right, heading for the spine of the rock.

"Right side, pick it up," Kim shouted. Owen could sense her adjusting behind him, adding her paddle to those of Bobby and Judith.

Still speeding toward Razorback Rock, the raft began to turn into the current. Too close, Owen thought. We're too close to the rock. He lifted his paddle out of the water, preparing to backpaddle.

At the lip of the falls, the raft scraped the edge of the rock. Kim pushed off the rock with her paddle, and the raft fell into the foaming white spray.

Owen heard a mixture of shouts and screams, one of them his.

The raft hit the surface with a jarring thud that jolted Owen forward into Billy. Then it righted itself and squirted free of the rapids into calm water.

Judith raised her paddle overhead with both hands. "Whooee, that was great."

Owen slid backward and lodged his right foot under the rear thwart so he wouldn't slip forward again. Across from him, Bobby did the same with his left foot and gave him a thumbs-up sign.

"All right," Kim said. "It could have been worse. Next time let's try paddling together."

The current picked them up and they rowed steadily through calm water. On their left, the gorge wall fell away to a steep slope covered with trees and bushes. Owen could see trails in and out of the underbrush near the top of the slope.

"My God, it's beautiful," Judith said.

Small ripples appeared on the calm surface and a soft roar reached the raft. Around the next curve the roar grew louder and two large rocks loomed in the distance, funneling whitewater between them. Owen remembered the rocks. The kayak with the two boys had overturned there.

"That'll be the Devil's Staircase and Big Lick Falls," Kim said.

"Who thinks up these names?" Judith asked.

"Whoever does it has an oral fixation," Bobby said. "I can hardly wait to see Big Lick Falls."

Billy laughed out loud, missed another stroke, and the raft lurched to the left.

Owen felt a sharp sting along the calf of his submerged left leg. A loud pop exploded under him, followed by a hissing noise. His side of the raft collapsed and he was in the water, his right foot still lodged under the rear thwart.

The raft swung catty-corner to the current, dragging Owen with it.

"Right side, backpaddle," Kim shouted. But the right side had become the raft's leading edge, propelled by the force of the water rushing through the collapsed quadrant.

Water filled Owen's mouth. He sputtered and struggled to release his foot from the thwart. He bent double, reaching for his captive sneaker, but the raft kept pulling it away from him. He kicked at the thwart with his free foot. He took a deep breath and stretched backward, steeling himself for a massive thrust forward, when he felt something poking against his right hip. He twisted and saw through the foam that Kim was holding her paddle out to him. He grabbed the blade and with Kim's help pulled himself onto the flooded floor of the raft.

Owen coughed up water and hugged the thwart, preparing to free his foot, when he heard Kim yell "Jump!"

Billy and Judith disappeared into the foaming river. Owen lifted his

head to see the lead rock coming at him. He heard Kim splash into
the water, ducked his head, and held tight to the thwart.

The raft slammed against the rock and rode up onto it, crushing
Owen's forearm between the thwart and the black rubber.

Water pounded against him. His fingers trembled, and he tried
clenching them and flexing his forearm. Nothing appeared to be broken. The force of the current had wrapped the raft around the rock,
pinning him upright against the rubber floor.

Fighting off panic, Owen, inhaled deeply, bent beneath the pounding water, and jerked his foot free of the sneaker that was stuck beneath the thwart. He found a foothold on the raft and was about to
edge around the rock into the falls when something kicked his side.

Bobby was above him, still straddling the inflated upper side of the
raft. He pounded at the black rubber between his legs as if he were
riding a bucking bronco. "I'm stuck, Owen," he shouted over the
roar.

The lips of the raft's still-inflated right side caught the rushing water
and pinned Bobby's leg between the rock and the rubber floor. He
was high enough on the rock so that he was in no immediate danger
of drowning, but something had to be done to free his leg. Owen
tugged at the thwart, trying to pull the raft away from the leg, but the
pounding river held it fast.

"Looks like I'm between the wreck and the hardplace," Bobby
shouted.

Owen's teeth were clenched too tight to smile. He held on to the
upright thwart with one hand and used the other to grope in his soggy
cutoffs for the pocket knife attached to his key chain. Still grasping
the thwart, he opened the knife with his teeth.

"You're not planning to amputate, are you?" Bobby asked. "Not
with that little thing."

Owen raised the knife and attacked the upper lip of the raft, punc-
turing it just behind Bobby's seat. The seat burst with a loud pop, air
wooshed out, and water cascaded over the collapsing rear quadrant.

With no counterforce against the rear of the raft, the raging current
caught the front lip of the raft and slid it slowly around the rock.

"Oh shit, it's going over," Bobby shouted.

Owen grabbed Bobby's belt and heaved backward, pulling him free
of the raft as it slid into the falls. Then he held tight to the belt and
struggled to point his feet downstream as the two of them bounced
between the rocks and followed the raft down the Devil's Staircase.

SEVENTEEN

The Sorriest Thing I Ever Did

OWEN THUDDED AGAINST Bobby and bounced off a submerged rock as the rushing water poured the two of them down the Devil's Staircase. He fought to hold on to Bobby's belt and keep them both afloat as they caromed from rock to rock. His feet hit bottom, jolting the air from his lungs, and he struggled to hold his breath and claw toward the surface when they popped free of the rapids into the clear downstream water.

Treading water with one arm, Owen shifted his grip from Bobby's belt to his life vest, which had bunched up around his ears. Bobby's eyes were closed and his head lolled against the orange collar of the vest. A deep gash ran from his left eyebrow to his earlobe. Owen shook his head, blinked his eyes to clear them, and saw arms waving from the canyon wall farther downriver. He paddled toward the waving arms, dragging Bobby's dead weight behind him.

As Owen neared the riverbank, Kim swam out to help. She took Bobby from him and backpaddled expertly to the shallow beach, a narrow limestone shelf rubbed smooth by the lapping river. Owen paddled after her, watching as Judith and Billy waded in to drag Bobby out of the river.

Kim laid Bobby on his back and leaned over him to check his breathing. Owen couldn't tell from her expression whether Bobby was still alive. He moved closer, shouldering his way between Judith and Billy. Kim knelt beside Bobby, pinched his nose, and blew into his mouth. Then she thumped his chest and leaned back as water spritzed up from his mouth. "He's still breathing," she announced. "Just swallowed a bellyful of the Gauley."

Kim smoothed Bobby's hair away from the gash over his eyebrow. "We better do something about that."

"I'll take care of it," Owen said. He stripped off his T-shirt, folded it into a cold compress, and bound it tight to Bobby's head with Billy's T-shirt.

"Looks like you've had experience doing that," Kim said.

"Worked at Saint Vincent's Hospital the summer after I got out of high school," Owen said. He didn't tell her he was an operating room orderly who rarely had to bandage patients. He'd seen the emergency room nurses do it often enough, though, and as long as he could contain the bleeding, he didn't want to broadcast the fact of Bobby's AIDS.

Kim scanned the limestone wall behind them, which rose in steps at an angle of about sixty degrees. "Long as he's out, we'll never get him up that wall," she said. "Better go up ourselves and call in a copter."

"Why not just flag down the next raft over the falls?" Owen asked.

"That's a nasty gash on your friend's head," Kim said. "I don't think we should subject him to more bumpy rapids. Besides, it's at least two hours down the river to civilization. It won't take me a half hour to make the top and find a phone."

"I'll wait here with Bobby," Owen said. "Judith, why don't you and Billy go with Kim?"

Judith looked up the sloping limestone face. "I think I'd rather wait with you."

"It's not so bad as it looks," Kim said. "I've climbed out of here before." She looked from the steep limestone steps to the river. "Here comes the raft."

The black raft floated sluggishly on the current, dragging its deflated stern like a wounded whale.

Kim splashed into the river. "Better try to salvage it." Owen and Billy followed her in and they dragged the raft back to the limestone shelf where Bobby lay.

Kim spread the raft on the shallow shelf and poked at it with a slim oak branch. "Never had a blowout before." The point of the stick lodged in a hole at the side of the raft just under where Owen had been sitting.

Owen bent to look at the hole, which was the size of his little finger. He lifted the raft's deflated stern and inspected the underside. "There's another hole here," he said, "just under the first one." He remembered the sting he'd felt just before the raft had exploded under him and looked at the back of his leg for the first time since he'd gone into the water. A laser-straight gash cut diagonally across his calf, starting just below his knee. The gash ended at mid-calf, near the spot where his lower leg had been clamped against the raft as he rowed. The same spot where he now poked his finger through the rent rubber.

Owen stood and scanned the steep canyon wall across the river. There was no sign of movement from the river's edge to the trees lining the top of the craggy limestone. "I think somebody took a shot at us."

Judith's head jerked up. "Where from?"

Owen pointed at the opposite canyon wall. "Up there. Somewhere."

Judith followed Owen's pointing finger up the steep limestone wall and looked at him skeptically. "Come on. Nobody could get up there."

"It was back upriver. When the raft exploded. That's what did it."

Judith looked to Kim for confirmation.

Kim bent over the raft and examined it. "Something went in the top and out the bottom right here. I've never seen a blowout like this before. But I've never been shot at before either. Who the hell are you people?"

"We're sitting ducks, that's who we are." Judith looked again at the steep wall across the river. Sunlight burned through the trees lining the edge of the cliff. "If somebody can get up there, we're sitting ducks."

Owen fought down a feeling of panic. "That's why the three of you better start climbing out right now."

"So you'll be the only duck in the shooting gallery?" Judith asked.

Owen pointed at the gash in his leg. "I'm the one they're shooting at anyhow. Somebody thinks I know too much."

"About what?" Kim asked. "What the hell's going on here?"

"I know everything you know," Judith said to Owen.

"All the more reason for you to get out of here," Owen answered. "If a sharpshooter does make it to that cliff face, he won't get both of us."

"This is about Dad, isn't it?" Billy said.

Kim looked from Owen to Judith to Billy. "Dad? Who's Dad?"

"I'm defending Billy's father on a murder charge," Judith explained. "We think the real murderer is shooting at us."

Kim clambered up onto the waist-high limestone ledge. "Then the man's right. We better get out of here."

"Can't we do something for you and Bobby?" Judith asked Owen.

"Help me move this raft to make a shelter for Bobby," Owen said. "Then get the hell out of here."

Grunting and straining, they moved Bobby next to the canyon wall and propped the inflated bow of the raft over him to shield him from the sun and sharpshooters. Then Billy and Judith climbed up on the first ledge with Kim, who found a toehold and moved one level higher.

Judith hesitated before following Kim upward. "At least move around a little," she called down to Owen.

Owen tried to grin reassurance. "I'll bet you say that to all the boys."

"I just think you ought to give him a moving target."

"Don't worry about me," Owen said. "Go."

Owen watched as Kim, Judith, and Billy worked their way slowly up the steep, craggy slope, moving from one jutting limestone ledge to the next. He scanned the opposite wall, looking for any sign of movement. Judith was right. He was a sitting duck. He wondered whether it was true that you wouldn't hear the bullet that killed you. He certainly hadn't heard the shot that capsized their raft. Just the pop as the raft exploded.

Owen checked on Bobby, still unconscious under the makeshift rubber tent. He considered crawling under the tent himself to hide from whoever might be shooting at him. If somebody was watching, though, that would just endanger Bobby as well. But if somebody with a gun was watching, why wouldn't he have fired already?

Maybe there was no way to get to the top of the cliff across the river. He tried to estimate how long it had been since the first shot was fired. Time was dragging now, but it couldn't have been more than fifteen minutes ago. The sniper would have to work his way downstream parallel to the river to get in another shot. Could he have done that already? It depended on the terrain, and Owen had no idea what it was like up there.

He slid into the water, shivering against the cold, and watched the climbers. Kim and Billy had just cleared the high-water mark where a scattering of scrub oaks provided the first sign of green on the limestone facing. Judith lagged behind, but finally reached the oaks, which could provide cover if anyone started shooting. But who would be shooting at them? Who had known they would be on the river today? Just their immediate family. He was sure they hadn't told Rudy Slater or Alicia Fox. But Judith and he had discussed the trip while they waited in Slater's outer office. Could he have overheard?

Owen waded out of the water and checked on Bobby, who was still unconscious. A raft full of laughing paddlers thudded down the Devil's Staircase, followed closely by another. The lead raft rowed over to see if he was all right. He told them there'd been an accident, but that help was on its way.

At least he hoped help was on its way. He couldn't see the climbers from the ledge where Bobby lay, so he waded back into the river to get a better sight angle. From the middle of the river, he could barely make out Kim, Billy, and Judith. They were about to disappear into the woods that topped the limestone facing. Judith turned and waved before entering the woods. He waved back from the water, wondering if he would ever see her again.

Owen started to return to the ledge where he'd left Bobby when it dawned on him that, just as he couldn't see the climbers reach the canyon crest from Bobby's ledge, a sniper on the opposite cliff wouldn't be able to see him as long as he hugged the shoreline below it. He ducked underwater and swam across to the opposite bank, surfacing only once. When he reached the bank, he swam along it until he found an outcropping that would both shield him from any snipers and provide a clear view of Bobby's ledge across the river.

The sun shining over the cliff above Owen left a horizontal shadow just under the ledge that held Bobby and the sheltering raft. Owen made up his mind to cross the river and check on Bobby when the shadow crept up high enough to cover the raft. He judged that would take about fifteen minutes. While he waited, he wondered about the sniper. He could have taken his shot and left the cliff face. Or he could have tried to follow them along the edge of the cliff. But what if he'd come down to the river instead? How long would that take? He couldn't come down these cliffs, it would have to be upstream. So it would take at least thirty minutes just to get down to the river. And then he'd need a raft to come after them. Say another half hour to get to the Devil's Staircase. That's at least an hour. Before long, though, Owen would have to worry about rafters as well as sharpshooters. He hoped the helicopter would come before that happened.

A shower of pebbles from the cliff above Owen bounced off his outcropping and caused endless patterns of expanding bull's-eyes to ripple on the water's surface. Startled, he left his shelter to look up at the edge of the cliff, but he could see nothing but a circling hawk.

When the time came to check on Bobby, Owen edged along the overhang until he was directly across the river from the raft sheltering his friend. He took a deep breath and swam underwater as far as he could, surfacing twice before reaching the opposite ledge. He pulled himself up quickly and hurried, hunched over, to the shelter of the raft. No shots rang out. The only sounds he heard were his own rapid heartbeat and the distant roar of the Devil's Staircase.

Bobby was still unconscious. Owen unwrapped his makeshift compress, scuttled to the river, dipped it in the cooling water, and hurried back to the raft, where he wrung out the compress and returned it to Bobby's pale forehead. He took his friend's hand and said, "Hang in there. Help's coming." There was no response.

Owen held Bobby's hand a little longer, but he couldn't free his mind of the possibility that someone with a rifle was making his way to the opposite cliff. By staying on Bobby's side of the river, Owen was endangering both of them. He released his friend's hand and swam underwater back across the river to the safety of his overhang.

Owen floated on his back in his shelter, marveling at the calmness of the river between the roaring rapids upstream and downstream. Two kayakers cleared the upstream rapids and waved as they rowed by. He waved back, remembering the two that had capsized years ago. What was it like to drown? he wondered. He tried to see how long he could hold his breath underwater. He found he could barely make it for a minute. While he was counting one thousand-one, one thousand-two, he remembered the head of the drowned boy resting on his father's chest. He made it to one thousand fifty-five before surfacing. He tried it again, but couldn't stay under for a full minute. This time when he surfaced, he heard a mechanical chopping noise under the roar of the falls. The noise grew louder, and a helicopter appeared where the hawk had been circling earlier.

SHERIFF THAD READER came in on the helicopter that carried Bobby and Owen out. After inspecting the beached raft, he called ahead and had a deputy meet them at the hospital with a jeep and a change of clothes for Owen. When the emergency room medics assured them that Bobby's chances of survival were good, Owen and the sheriff set off with the driver in search of a location that might give a sniper a clear shot at rafters heading for the Devil's Staircase. They crossed the Gauley on a steel truss bridge and started uphill on a lonely mountain road that wound through a dense forest of black birch. Trees cut out most of the late-afternoon sun as the jeep jounced off the narrow pockmarked asphalt road onto an even narrower gravel pathway.

"At this rate, we'll run out of road before we get anywhere near the top," Owen said.

"Just wait," the sheriff answered. "You can't judge a road by its ruts."

The jeep thudded into a deep pothole that bounced Owen off his seat. Almost before he'd regained it, the jeep rounded a corner and the road widened to a smooth four-lane highway. A painted earth mover and a backhoe from Hager Construction sat on either side of the asphalt. Just beyond the equipment, a sign welcomed them to Grandview Estates.

"What's going on?" Owen asked.

"A little private development," the sheriff said.

"Why aren't Mary Jewel's people protesting this?"

"It's too hard to get to. Besides, the road is private. They're building it from the top down just to keep the protesters at bay."

The jeep passed a colonnaded brick mansion in the final stages of construction. Farther along, a wide foundation was being poured for another home. Then, just as suddenly as it began, the short road ended in a circular cul-de-sac surrounded by a waist-high stone fence topped by iron pickets.

Sheriff Reader tapped the driver's shoulder and he stopped the jeep. "Wait'll you see this," he said to Owen.

The stone fence commanded a view of green wooded hillsides climbing from the canyon walls of the Gauley River. The steel truss bridge where they'd crossed the river was visible well below them. Beyond the bridge, the Gauley wound its way between canyon walls and sloping green hillsides.

"It's spectacular," Owen said. "Who owns all this?"

"Movers and shakers. Word is, your man Slater has a plot of land up here."

"Why am I not surprised?"

"You can't see the Devil's Staircase from here. We've got to drive a little and hike a little."

They returned to the jeep and followed a dirt road that branched off from the overlook. The sheriff tapped the driver again and he pulled off the dirt into the shade of tall birch trees. "We'll use shank's mare from here.'' He adopted a down-home twang for Owen's benefit. ''That's hiking for you city fellers.''

''City feller? I grew up around here.''

About a hundred yards ahead of them on the dirt road were tracks where another vehicle had pulled off to park. The tracks were wider than a normal wheelbase.

''Looks like a Hummer parked there recently,'' Owen said.

''That or somebody's wide-body,'' the sheriff said.

''Maybe you ought to have your men take an imprint of the tread.''

''Son, you trying to tell me how to do my job?''

''Aren't you worried it might be Slater's Hummer?''

''If it is, he's the one ought to be worried.'' The sheriff nodded to his deputy, who took a black tool kit from the back of his jeep. Then he led the way downhill through the densely packed evergreens.

Following the sheriff through the trees, Owen could hear the steady roar of the Gauley River rapids in the distance. When shafts of sunlight began to poke through the trees in front of them, the sheriff slowed and held up his hand to Owen.

''Careful now, that first step's a bitch.''

The trees ended abruptly at the edge of a jutting limestone precipice. Far below, in the distance, Owen could see the Devil's Staircase, where the rapids had impaled their raft.

''How close were the rapids when you got hit?'' the sheriff asked.

''Not too close. We were still practicing our strokes.''

The sheriff pointed a stick at the calm waters far below. ''Whoever did it could have lined you up from here.'' He sighted along the stick and made a soft popping noise with his lips. ''Wouldn't have been too tough a shot.''

Owen pointed downstream at the Devil's Staircase. ''We wrapped ourselves around that rock after the raft blew.''

''That's a lot tougher shot from here,'' the sheriff said. ''Shooter'd have to traverse the edge of the canyon to get closer. Likely take him a while.'' The sheriff began walking along the edge of the canyon as if he were stalking prey down below.

''We weren't on the rock long.''

''Good thing. Shooter might have been able to catch up with you.''

''After we went over the falls, though, we must have been on that shallow bend at least an hour. It seemed like forever, once I knew somebody was stalking us.''

''From here, you can see beyond the falls. It's too tough to traipse that far along the edge, and the road starts back downhill just beyond where we parked. Like as not he packed it in.''

The sheriff knelt and examined the base of a birch tree. "Somebody's been here recently."

"How can you tell?"

The sheriff pointed at a broken tendril. "Busted twig's still green. I'll get Vonnie Lovisa up here to look around. He could track a tick through a dust storm. Might be he can tell us more about who's been here."

"So you'll look into it?"

The sheriff rose, tilted his head until the brim of his Mountie's hat almost touched his shoulder, and stared at Owen. "That surprise you?"

"Don't get me wrong, I appreciate it. The other day, though, you didn't seem to take my problems seriously."

"The other day you brought me the tail of a glass whale. I can't get too worked up over a busted geegaw." He pointed his stick at the gash on Owen's calf. "Today, though, somebody shot at you. Now that's got my full and undivided attention."

"So you'll check out Rudy Slater?"

"He know you were going to be on the river?"

"We didn't tell him. But we didn't keep it a secret either."

"'Pears to me you're the one not taking things serious enough,'' the sheriff said. "You got somebody riled to the killing point and you're still poking around."

"You want me to stop?"

"You know damn well what I want. I want you to leave the poking to the folks who get paid for it."

"Even if I wanted to, it's a little late for that. Somebody already thinks I know too much."

"And do you?"

"I told you everything I know."

"Well, tell me again, slow. And from the start. That wound on your leg just improved my hearing."

THE BEDS IN Bobby's ward at Saint Vincent's Hospital were enclosed by gray curtains that left little room for visitors. When Owen pulled aside Bobby's curtain, he found his friend slumped halfway down the slanted headrest, as if he hadn't the strength to sit upright.

His puffy eyes were nearly closed, and his head was wrapped in a bandage that didn't quite cover the strawberry lesion on his cheek.

Owen drew the curtain closed and hesitated, not sure whether Bobby was awake or asleep.

Bobby lifted his right hand slightly without raising his wrist from the covers and said in a hoarse whisper, "'S okay, Scout. Come on in."

Owen's concern showed in his voice. "Are you all right? Can I get you anything?"

The right hand lifted again, then dropped feebly to the covers. "Wantcha do something," the faint voice said.

Owen took Bobby's right hand in his and bent over the bed. "Just name it."

"Someday," Bobby whispered, "when you're up against it and it seems like you'll never laugh again"—he turned his head slowly and gave a hollow cough that caused his clammy hand to squeeze Owen's—"I want you to go in there with all the jokes you've got." He drew a shallow breath that sounded like a sob. "And tell one for the Tripper."

Owen grinned broadly and pulled his hand free. "That speech plays better with the Notre Dame fight song in the background."

Bobby laughed a full-throated laugh that announced his instant recovery and sat upright. "Had you going there for a minute, though, didn't I? Admit it, Scout, I had you going there."

"It was the little cough that gave you away. You turned your head as if a doctor were holding your balls to check for a hernia."

"What do you think, though? Wasn't that a good George Gipp?"

"That wasn't even a good Ronald Reagan."

"I forget how to do Ronald Reagan."

Owen pointed his forefinger at Bobby and brought his thumb down like a pistol hammer. "Now, *that's* a good Ronald Reagan."

Bobby laughed again and Owen marveled at how easily laughter had always linked the two of them, even at the worst of times.

Bobby's laughter faded, and he said, "They tell me you saved my life."

Owen's knees were pressed against the bed, but he could still feel the ward curtain chafing against his back. "Once we got you off the rock, your life vest did all the work."

"Don't be so damn modest. It's a short-term deal at best."

"What'd your doctor say?"

"Said I was crazy to go rafting in my condition."

Owen stared at the lesion on Bobby's cheek. "And how is your condition?"

"Worse than yesterday, but better than tomorrow."

Judith poked her head through the curtain. "Your mom told me I'd find you here." She squeezed inside the curtain and stood by Owen. "How's the patient?"

Bobby shifted on his pillow. "The grim reaper's still in a holding pattern."

"Did you learn anything with the sheriff?" Judith asked Owen.

"A wide-body had been parked near where the shooter stood. It looked like a Hummer's tracks."

Bobby raised his fist and let it fall back to the bed. "That son of a bitch Slater. He's in this up to his crotch."

"Was it Slater?" Judith asked.

Owen shrugged, "Seems likely. There aren't that many Hummers around. And he's got a lot in a plush new development nearby. The sheriff's checking the tread marks."

"Sounds like real progress," Judith said. "While you and the sheriff were on your wilderness adventure, I spent some time on the phone with your old flame."

Owen leaned back into the curtain. "Robin? Why did you do that?"

"Your librarian friend hit pay dirt with the Gray Eagle Trust. Guess who's a founding partner?"

"Rudy Slater," Bobby answered.

"We already knew that," Owen said.

"Guess who else," Judith said.

"Not Robin," Owen said.

"No, her father. He and Slater set it up when they were both with Hager Construction."

"So why call Robin?" Owen asked.

"I called her father to get a line on the Trust. She answered the phone."

"And?"

"She said she'd talk to him and call you back. She didn't seem to want to talk to me."

"You didn't exactly part on friendly terms the last time you two met," Owen said.

"You think she still holds that against me?"

"Why not? I do."

Judith shook her head and smiled. "You men. You're so touchy when someone interrupts your little pleasures."

Bobby laughed. "Wasn't it Will Shakespeare that said, 'There's many a slip twixt zip and lip'?"

ROBIN CALLED OWEN at home that evening. His mother took the call and brought him the phone, frowning with disapproval and mouthing the word "Robin" to Judith.

With the two women watching him, just answering the phone felt like an act of betrayal to Owen.

Robin sounded preoccupied, as if there was more on her mind than the phone conversation. "Owen. Daddy said he'll talk to you. But it has to be alone. Can you drive down tomorrow?"

"Why alone? I'd like to bring Judith at least." And maybe even the sheriff, he thought.

"It has to be you alone. You'll know why when he talks to you. He's not been well. The best time to come is four o'clock, after his nap. You can stay for dinner. And of course, spend the night if you want." She paused, then added, "We could finish what we started."

Owen remembered the feel of Robin's hair against his cheek and her mouth on his neck. He was conscious that Judith was watching him from across the room, and stared back at her. She crossed her eyes and grimaced.

"I don't think I'm up for that," he said into the receiver.

"You were up for it before your ex-wife pounded on the windshield."

"That's the trouble with ex-spouses," Owen said, loud enough for Judith to hear.

"Sounds like you still have feelings for her."

"Don't you have feelings for Slater?"

"A feeling I'd like to strangle him."

"Hold that thought," Owen said. "I'll see you tomorrow."

Judith watched Owen hang up the phone and asked, "What's the word from your fevered past?"

"Robin's set it up for me to talk to her father before dinner tomorrow. But she wants me to come alone."

"Oh, right. Someone's trying to kill you and you're going to march off alone to meet with a prime suspect."

"Robin's not a suspect."

"That's only because you can't see past your penis where she's concerned. Think about it, Owen. Her father's Trust is connected with the victims of two killings thirty-five years apart.''

"That's her father. That's not Robin.''

"Maybe I missed something. Isn't he the one you're going to see?''

"I can't believe he's a killer.''

"We'll put that on your tombstone. What was that little exchange on the phone about ex-spouses?''

"Robin inquired about your health.''

"Well, tell Robin her health is of concern to me, too. Be sure to ask her about communicable diseases.''

"I doubt I'll have the opportunity. Or the inclination.''

"From what I saw of her, she'll see to it you have both.''

THE HAGER ESTATE in Greenbrier County was nestled in the crook of a shallow creekbed across from a private golf course. Gleaming white wood columns framed a porch flanked by two redbrick wings at the end of a long manicured lawn. The driveway Owen used to approach the estate skirted the lawn and the west wing and ended in a parking lot beside two tennis courts.

Robin met him in the parking lot wearing a white tennis outfit. She kissed him warmly and led him inside to a library with dark oak paneling and two walls of books in leather bindings that looked as if they'd never left the shelves. A third wall held a display of dueling pistols and pictures of a young Chuck Hager in the cockpit of a jet fighter, sitting with a pig-tailed Robin and her little brother Eddie on the treads of a pink bulldozer, and posed in a leather bombardier's jacket with two other pilots at the bar of an officer's club in Korea. Owen thought he recognized one of the other pilots in the picture when Robin reentered the library with her father.

Owen wasn't prepared for what he saw. Chuck Hager sat stiffly in a wheelchair, his lap covered with a bombardier's jacket like the one in the picture. His hair was steely white, and the right side of his craggy face seemed to be immobile, with half his mouth stretched into a permanent grimace.

The left side of his mouth managed a smile as he held out his left hand. "Owen. It's good to see you. You look just like your daddy.''

Owen took the hand, which felt stiff and unyielding. "I was just looking at your pictures. Isn't that Ted Williams with you in the officer's club?''

Hager turned his head awkwardly to focus on the picture. "Yep, that's Teddy Ballgame. We flew together in Korea. Fished a little afterwards in the off-season. Good man. Great hitter. Would have been the greatest ever if he hadn't lost all that time in the service.''

Hager turned his head back to Owen. "I hear Teddy had a few health problems himself sometime recent.'' He raised his right fist slightly and let it fall back on the arm of the wheelchair. "Nothing so bad he's in one of these, though.''

"I'm sorry,'' Owen said.

"Hell, boy. No need to be. It could be a lot worse. Robin has taken care of me pretty good. Can we get you a drink?''

"Just tonic will be fine.''

"Bourbon and branch for me, honey.''

Robin fixed their drinks at a sideboard and put a straw in her father's. He took the glass in his left hand, raised it slightly to Owen, and took a long sip through the straw. "Yep,'' he said. "She takes care of me pretty good.''

Owen sipped his tonic, then broke the silence by saying, "I was hoping you could tell me a little about my father.''

Hager moved the straw aside with his tongue. "You want to know whether he was on the take, like the papers are saying.''

"Was he?'' Owen felt as if he was betraying his father just by asking the question.

"Hell no. The newspapers got it all wrong. Wrong as wrong could be. I'm here to tell you your dad was an honest man. Couldn't be bought, bribed, or bedded.''

Owen felt a vast sense of relief. "But you tried?''

"Hell yes, we tried. We tried with everybody. That was the way you did business then. You had to grease palms to get jobs. But your dad wouldn't grease. And he fired them that would. It like to froze me out. Here I was, back from Korea, with two young kids and a yardful of government-surplus earth movers. In debt up to my eyeballs, and I couldn't get a construction job to save my ass.''

"So how'd you get started?''

"We found a way in.'' The old man turned his head toward Robin.

Robin handed him his refilled glass. "You promised you'd tell him, Dad.''

Hager stared into his glass. "All right. But it's not to leave this room. Anybody ever asks me, I'll deny it.''

"There's at least one murder involved,'' Owen said. "You may be asked under oath.''

"There's no murder involved in what I'm going to tell you. There's a death, and there's people should be called to account for it, but there's no murder I know of. And I'm asking you, man to man, to help me keep it bottled up."

Owen's tonic tasted bitter. "I'll do my best."

Hager took a long pull at the straw of his drink. "We couldn't get no work, so Rudy Slater and me, we spent our time painting the equipment so you couldn't tell it was government surplus. Rudy was fresh out of school, full of piss and vinegar, and he got the idea of painting faces on the bulldozers and backhoes." He turned the live side of his face toward Robin. "You kids liked it, so we kept it up."

Robin nodded. "Tell him, Dad."

Hager's left eye squinted as if he were looking into the past. "Rudy was keeping company with Rose Haley, one of Tom McDougall's nurses. Woman's tongue was looser than a hospital gown on an anorexic. Turned out Ray Cantrip was seeing the doc about his sperm count. He'd had mumps as a child. Couldn't shoot nothing but blanks."

Owen's hand shook enough to rattle the ice in his drink. "So Ray Cantrip wasn't Bobby's father."

"Not a chance."

"And you used that against him?"

Chuck Hager stared down into his drink and started talking into it. "That was Rudy's idea. Ray's wife cut quite the social figure in Sacred Heart Parish. Rudy figured they wouldn't want it known that somebody other than Ray had dipped his wick to get Bobby."

Owen recalled his father's letters to Bobby's mother. "Did Rudy know who did?"

The old man hunched his good shoulder in a half-shrug. "If he did, he never told me. All we really needed to know was that Ray wasn't anybody's daddy. Once we had his dead balls in our pocket, we started getting state highway jobs."

"Did my father know Ray was steering jobs your way?"

"He knew somebody was rigging bids. I don't think he ever suspected Ray. Hell, he put Ray in charge of keeping things on the up-and-up."

Owen finished his drink and set his glass down carefully. If his father had found out, would he have been angry enough to kill Ray? It didn't seem likely. Still, something had made him think he needed to carry the gun that shot Ray. "What about the Gray Eagle Trust?" he asked.

"The Gray Eagle Trust," Hager repeated. He gave another half-shrug with his left shoulder. "Hell, that was just our little front. Rudy Slater set it up back when we started so's we could cut checks for folks without putting the Hager name on them. Cut a few for Ray Cantrip, as I recall."

Hager sipped at his straw. "Back then, every state road inspector got two checks. One from the government and one from the contractors he was inspecting."

He finished his drink and held it out to Robin for a refill. "We didn't play that game, though. We greased the system to get the jobs, but once we got them we gave good value. Built the best damn roads in the state. Most of them still carry traffic."

Robin refilled his drink and brought him a fresh straw. "Tell him what happened to the Trust."

Hager stirred the drink with his straw, then curled the left side of his mouth down so it matched the frozen right side in a full-fledged frown. "We went along just fine for quite sometime. Then I come to find out Rudy was using the Trust to skim money for himself. He started bribing inspectors to look the other way so's he could do a half-assed job and pocket the savings."

His face still in a frown, Hager continued, "I come across a road over to Harker's Bend that was one of our jobs. Asphalt so thin the ruts showed through." He shook his head. "I never would have put my name to a road like that.

"Well, sir, I looked up the inspector and asked him what was going on. He said Rudy had paid him off. Acted real surprised I didn't know."

Hager's right fist began to tremble on the wheelchair arm. "At first, Rudy denied there was anything going on. When he seen I had the word straight from the inspector, though, he admitted it. Said the competition was all doing it, so's it was the only way we could keep up. Well, that was a bold-faced lie. He was the one keeping up. I never seen a penny of his kickbacks, buy-offs, and skim money."

Flecks of white formed at the dead corner of Hager's downturned mouth. He shook his head. "I don't know. You work with people. You think you know them. You expect them to do you right."

Robin wiped the white flecks off her father's mouth with a napkin. He bowed his head and continued, "I told Rudy we was quits. Told him I never wanted to see him again, even though he was married to my daughter. That's when things got ugly.

"Rudy said he had records of what we'd paid out of the Trust all the way back to our start-up days. Bribes we'd laid out to get our first jobs, invoices we'd overcharged, inspectors he'd bought off so's he could skim money for shoddy work. Said he'd go to the Highway Commission, make a clean breast of it. Claim it was all my idea."

The old man swiveled his wheelchair to face Owen. "Well, hell. My name was on the door. I couldn't have people thinking I was responsible for shit like that washboard road on Harker's Bend. I bought him off. Put enough money in the Trust so's he could start his own firm, then let him take it all. We let on like he left because I promoted Eddie over him, but that's not the way it happened. He blackmailed me and I gave in."

"Rudy even told me he left because of Eddie," Robin said. "I never knew the truth until now."

"That's the way he wanted it, honey." Hager shook his head slowly. "Hell, I should of fired the son of a bitch outright and let the chips fall where they may. Should of used the blackmail money to patch up the roads he'd butchered. Should of repaired Harker's Bend myself."

The old man took a deep breath and let it out in a series of short, guttural spasms. "Well, a bushel of should ofs ain't worth a peck of dried horse turds."

Hager slumped back in his wheelchair. "I don't know what I was thinking. Maybe that Rudy'd take it out on Robin if I fired him outright. Or maybe that I couldn't start over if folks thought Harker's Bend was my doing. Or maybe that Harker's Bend wasn't all that bad. Sure it was rutted like a washboard, but the ruts ran with the road, so it didn't give a bad ride."

The left side of Hager's mouth trembled, anchored by the frozen frown on the right side of his face. "Well, the ruts didn't bother cars none, but I hadn't reckoned on motorcycles. A boy named Jimmy Easter, his daddy worked for me off and on, took Harker's Bend at fifty miles an hour, caught his front wheel in a rut, lost control, and laid his bike down. He skidded twenty feet on his belly and took out a road sign with his helmet. Was in a coma three months before he died. Bankrupted his daddy and drove his momma to despair.

Hager's right fist jerked upward and fell back to the wheelchair arm. "A whole family flushed down the tubes, all because I didn't have the balls to face up to Rudy Slater, fire him outright, own up to his shenanigans, and patch up his graft-rotten roadways.

"Let me tell you, paying that bastard off to keep him quiet about what I ought to have owned up to anyhow..." The old man's good left eye glazed over and he fixed it on Owen. "Well, it was the sorriest thing I ever did."

EIGHTEEN

Soul Sickness

OUTSIDE THE HAGER MANSION, fireflies were just beginning to dot the broad expanse of lawn with incandescent mating signals. Inside, Owen paced the library without trying to find a wall switch to illuminate the darkening room. The dinner with Robin and her father had been interminable. The old man bowed his head and chewed silently with the live side of his jaw, saying little, evidently embarrassed by having said so much before dinner. Owen picked at his food, his stomach jumping, trying to digest the certainty that Ray Cantrip wasn't Bobby's father, and had betrayed Owen's father to keep that fact secret. One or both of those facts must have figured in Ray's shooting, but Owen was at a loss to know how. Robin attempted to make small talk for a while, then gave up and tried to get through the ordeal as quickly as possible.

Robin joined Owen in the library after putting her father to bed. She motioned him toward the overstuffed chair where he'd sat earlier, handed him a cup of tea, and said, "Daddy's mortified. He never thought anyone would find out."

The teacup rattled against his saucer and Owen silenced it by balancing both on the arm of the chair. "Why'd he decide to tell me?"

"He doesn't have much time left. I think it's been eating at him for sometime. And the newspaper attacks on your dad set him off."

"How long have you known?"

"I called you as soon as he told me."

"It's hard to make any sense out of it."

Robin looked out the window at the fireflies. "It's why Daddy gave Hager Construction to Eddie and shut out Rudy. That never made any sense to me. But knowing Rudy, it's his to believe he'd blackmail Daddy."

The room grew steadily darker. Owen said nothing. He couldn't come to grips with the fact that the man who'd led him in the Cub Scout Pledge, taught slipknots, and shouted ''Stroke!'' to struggling swimmers wasn't Bobby's father. It left too many questions unanswered.

Robin turned from the window and broke the silence. ''Do you think, maybe, Bobby suspected?''

''That Ray wasn't his father?'' Owen shook his head. ''Not while we were growing up.'' But he couldn't help remembering Bobby's reaction to the shoeboxful of Wayne Allison's love letters. ''Later on, maybe,'' he added, thinking the letters certainly gave Bobby reason enough to doubt his parentage.

Robin sat on the arm of the overstuffed chair and toyed with the hairs at the nape of Owen's neck. ''I take it you won't be spending the night?''

Owen's neck tingled under Robin's touch, and he could feel the sensation starting to spread. He captured her hand in his own, brought it to his mouth, kissed her fingertips, and answered her question. ''No. I don't think so.''

Robin removed her hand from his. ''Does that mean you're getting back together with your ex?''

It was a question he'd avoided asking himself, but the answer came instinctively. ''I'm going to work on it.''

''Wasn't she unfaithful when you were married?''

''We were two different people then. On different sides of the country.''

''Like you and me in different colleges?''

''Something like that.'' Owen winced at the memory of his younger self dropping letter after unanswered letter into the silent maws of the mailboxes in front of the Marquette post office.

''Why give her another chance?'' Robin asked, putting enough emphasis on the word ''her'' to let Owen hear the unspoken ''and not me?''

Owen answered with the first thing that came into his mind. ''She makes me laugh. Always did. Still does.''

''That's funny. That's what I used to say about you.''

''We're not laughing now.''

''It's been a hard evening.'' Robin let her hand rest on Owen's shoulder. ''For all of us.''

Owen took her hand in his. ''I thank you for it anyhow. It helps me to know my father wasn't bought off. Even though it's hard to believe about Ray Cantrip."

"He must have been a sorry man."

"Not to Bobby. And not to me." He gave voice to the question that had been poking at the edge of his consciousness. "Speaking of sorry men, did Rudy Slater ever play around on you?"

"Rudy?" She loosed a short, sharp laugh that turned the corners of her mouth downward. "He'd much rather screw a business partner than his wife. If he played around, it was with bids, brokers, and tax returns."

"Do you have a recent picture of him?"

"Why? Are you lining birdcages or decorating dartboards?"

"Neither. But he's involved somehow in Mary Jewel's death and I think he's been shooting at me. And he knows more about Ray Cantrip than anybody else. I want to show his picture to a few of the other people involved. See if they recognize him."

"Shooting at you? My God, Owen. Has someone been shooting at you?"

Owen rolled up his pant leg and showed Robin his scar. "On the Gauley River. Last weekend."

"That's not Rudy's style. He'd lie, cheat, and steal, but I can't imagine he'd involve himself in murder." Robin rose from the arm of the chair. "I'll get you a picture."

As she left the room, Owen stood and moved toward the door. The nape of his neck still tingled from Robin's touch, and he didn't want to be sitting when she returned.

Footsteps echoed on a long stairwell and Robin entered with a picture of Rudy Slater. "It's one of the last ones I took before the divorce," she said. "But it's at least nine years old."

"Still looks like him," Owen said. "Right down to the bow tie. How long has he been wearing those?"

"Ever since he saw one on George Will."

Robin tucked the photo in Owen's inside vest pocket, patted it, and kissed him lightly on the lips. "All right, Mr. Straight Arrow," she said, linking her arm in his and leading him toward the door. "I'm giving you six months to work things out with your ex. If you're not back together by that time, I'm coming after you."

"Why six months?"

"That's how long the doctors have given Daddy."

"I'm sorry," Owen said. He took her in his arms and held her.

Robin's cheek was moist against his. "I hope you find what you're looking for," she whispered.

ON HIS WAY HOME, Owen stopped at the nursing home where Bobby's mother had been killed and showed Rudy Slater's picture to the nurses on duty. When none of the nurses on the three-to-eleven shift remembered seeing Rudy in the nursing home, Owen decided to wait for the 11 p.m. shift change to question late-shift nurses. The nurse in charge of the shift was Beverly Bryan, an old high school classmate. Beverly, a slim brunette whose appearance had changed little since graduation, told Owen that Dolores Cantrip had few visitors other than Bobby.

Owen showed her the picture of Rudy Slater. "What about this man?"

Beverly used the glasses looped around her neck to examine the photo. "That's Robin Hager's ex-husband, isn't it?"

When Owen nodded, Beverly handed the photo back to him and shook her head. "Never saw him here. There was one old guy. Kind of spry. Wore a funny hat, like a beret. He came a couple of times. Enough so we teased Dolores about having a boyfriend."

Beverly stared at the pale green walls and nibbled the earpiece of her spectacles. "Your mom came once or twice, but I suppose you knew that." She let her spectacles dangle from their neckpiece and focused her eyes on Owen. "I've been working the late shift for the last month. You really ought to talk to the nurses on the day shift."

"They come on at seven?"

Beverly nodded. "I'll set it up for you. Meantime, why don't you go home and get some sleep? You look as if you could use some."

OWEN ARRIVED HOME a little after midnight to find Judith waiting up for him. She was wearing black slacks and a gray sweatshirt and had one bare foot tucked under her on the couch as she made notes on a yellow legal pad.

When Owen entered, Judith set aside the pad, checked her watch, and said, "Well, at least you didn't spend the whole night."

Owen sank into an upholstered chair across from the couch. "No."

Judith leaned forward on the couch. "So?"

Owen sank deeper into the chair. "So?"

"So what was so important little Miss Quiver Lips had to see you in person?"

"I promised I wouldn't tell."

"Get serious. Somebody's trying to kill you. This is no time to be a Boy Scout."

The words "Boy Scout" reminded Owen of Ray Cantrip and Bobby's uncertain parentage. "No. Don't even ask me. I can't tell you."

"I'm defending your brother on a murder charge. If it's important I need to know."

"It's important. But not to George's defense."

Judith shook her head so that her brown hair skimmed her shoulders. "I should be the one deciding that." She scrutinized Owen's slumped posture. "You look like you could use a beer."

Owen half-nodded and said something that sounded like "Ummph."

Judith left the room and returned with a glass and a bottle of Henry Weinhard's. "You know what happens to people who withhold information in B movies, don't you?" she said, pouring the beer into the glass and handing it to Owen. "They die in the sixth reel gasping, 'The murderer is...arrgh.'" She clutched her throat and fell backward onto the couch, legs splayed in simulated rigor mortis.

Owen managed half a smile. "I'll write it all out and put it in a sealed envelope. You can open the envelope if I don't make it past the sixth reel."

Judith recovered from her mock death and sat upright on the couch. "Whatever it was, it got to you."

"It got to me."

"And did Robin get to you as well?"

Owen sipped his beer. "Not in the way you're implying."

"How, then?"

"She gave me a deadline."

"For what?"

"To get back together with you."

Judith looked as if she might simulate rigor mortis again. "Just how long is this deadline?"

"Six months."

"And what happens if this little reconciliation takes longer than six months?"

"She hinted the field might become more competitive."

"Competitive in what way?"

"She wasn't specific."

"That must have taken some restraint on her part." Judith leaned forward on the couch. "Knowing you and deadlines, you'll probably wait until the last minute before making any kind of move."

"There's a real art in recognizing the precise last minute before it passes you by."

Judith rose from the couch. "Ever thought of starting early?"

"It goes against my grain," Owen said. "I'm not sure I could manage it."

Judith set aside his beer and took him by the hand, pulling him up from his chair. "I think I might be able to help you with that problem."

As Judith led him toward the stairs, Owen whispered, "Shh. We don't want to wake Mother."

"Don't be silly," Judith said. "It'll make her night."

THE CORNERS OF Ruth's mouth nearly met her earlobes as she bustled around the kitchen the next morning, fixing pancakes, brewing tea, and cutting up fruit for Owen and Judith. Setting a cup of tea in front of Owen, she asked, "What did you learn at Greenbrier yesterday?"

"Chuck Hager had a stroke. The doctors give him six months."

The smile left Ruth's face for the first time that morning. "That's six months and thirty-five years more than your father had."

"I don't think Hager had anything to do with Dad's death," Owen said.

"Maybe not," Ruth said. "But he was a part of the whole dirty system that threatened him."

The telephone rang and Ruth answered it. She handed the phone to Owen, mouthing the words, "Sheriff Reader."

The sheriff got right to the point. "Thought you'd like to know," he said. "We checked Slater's Hummer. His tires didn't match the tracks left by your sniper."

Owen said "Shit" softly into the phone. Both Ruth and Judith stared at him.

"Thought you'd also like to know," the sheriff continued, "Slater has two Hummers. One's his, the other's a company car. Neither one has treads matching the tracks we found. My deputy did say, though, that there were at least two brand-new tires on Slater's personal Hummer."

"Think he changed them?"

"Seems a mite extreme. Like getting a new car when your ashtray's full. Be a lot easier just to cover his tracks on the spot."

"If he did change his tires, there'll be prints of the old treads on the river road just outside the city limits. Where he dumped the glass whale."

"I'll look into it," the sheriff said. "Sounds like you're still poking into this mess. Where do you plan to be today?"

"I haven't decided," Owen said. Actually, he planned to visit Bobby and return to the nursing home, but he didn't feel like advertising his whereabouts, even to the sheriff.

"Well, wherever you are, watch your back."

STANDING WITH JUDITH next to Bobby's bed in the hospital ward, Owen filled his friend in on his conversation with the sheriff.

"Would Slater really do that?" Bobby asked. "Buy new tires, I mean. Wouldn't it be a lot easier just to sweep away the tire tracks?"

"Money means nothing to somebody like Slater," Owen said. "Time is everything. It's a lot easier to buy new tires than to risk being caught covering your tracks at the scene of the crime. Or to be sure you've covered *all* your tracks."

Bobby picked at some gray lumps of oatmeal in a plastic dish on a lap tray. "That son of a bitch."

"Maybe that's why he took the whale," Owen said. "Maybe it had his fingerprints on it."

"Come again?" Judith said.

"The missing whale's been bothering me," Owen said. "If he killed Mary Jewel, why would he take the whale from her apartment? It could be, though, that he'd handled it."

Owen continued, imagining the scene. "Slater goes to see Mary Jewel with the tire iron up his sleeve. He wouldn't be wearing gloves, so he's careful not to touch anything. She invites him in, fixes tea, shows him the loot she bought with his first blackmail payment. Maybe even hands him the whale."

"Why's she blackmailing him?" Bobby asked.

"She saw him vandalizing Hager's equipment on Gobbler's Grade," Owen said.

"That hardly seems like a motive for murder," Judith put in. "Two grand is pocket change to somebody like Slater."

"Maybe there's more, I don't know," Owen said. "Anyhow, she turns her back to fix tea and he clobbers her. He wants to leave as quick as he can, remembers the whale with his fingerprints, and pockets it instead of wiping it clean."

"That could have happened," Judith said. "Or he could have taken it planning to plant it somewhere to incriminate someone else."

"Then why hasn't it turned up?" Bobby asked.

"Because one of the first things he sees when he gets outside is George, asleep in his car," Owen said. "So he leaves the real murder weapon in George's trunk and ditches the whale, which he doesn't need anymore."

"It all fits," Judith said. "But we've got no hard evidence."

"So the son of a bitch is going to get away with it?" Bobby asked.

"We're just brainstorming, Bobby," Owen said. "We've got no real proof."

"Brainstorming, bullshit," Bobby said. "The son of a bitch was paying her off and he killed her. And he's got enough money and juice to get away with it. I'll bet he killed my mom, too."

"Why do you think that?" Judith asked.

"He was paying her off for some reason, same as Mary Jewel," Bobby said. "That's how I got my college tuition paid. Mom must have known something."

"About what?" Judith asked.

"About how my dad was killed." Bobby flailed his arms around, knocking over his lap tray and its contents. A mound of red Jell-O slid to the floor, where it quivered on the olive-green tile. "You got enough juice, you get whatever you want. You get the jobs from the state. You get the Air Force commissions. You get to sniff the rich heinies, bark with the big dogs, play the comedy clubs, and chat with Leno and Letterman."

Another swipe of Bobby's arm sent the lap tray clattering to the floor "And me," he said, collapsing back on his pillow. "Look at me. I couldn't even keep the Just 4 Laughs Traffic School open."

Owen took his handkerchief and wiped off the beads of sweat forming just under the bandage around Bobby's forehead. "Alicia Fox will see that you get your job back. And you're still funnier than all the rest of them put together. You can spot anybody two pratfalls and three fart jokes and still get more laughs than Uncle Miltie on Tuesday night."

"Yeah, that's me," Bobby said, his head sinking into the pillow. "Too funny for words. Too funny for Wheeling College. Too funny for the Jesuits. Too funny for the Air Force. Even too funny for traffic school.

"Never would have busted out of those places if I'd had old Rudy Kazootie's bucks," Bobby continued. "How old was Slater when my dad died, anyhow?"

"Twenty, maybe twenty-one," Owen said.

Bobby raised his right hand from the bed and pointed his index finger at Owen. "So he could have killed Dad, too."

"Being of voting age when your father died hardly constitutes incriminating evidence," Judith said.

"Bullshit," Bobby said. "He's been getting away with it all his life. Somebody's got to stop him."

Owen thought Bobby's single-minded pursuit of Rudy Slater would grow even more heated if he knew Slater had been instrumental in blackmailing Ray Cantrip, but he didn't see any point in breaking his promise of silence to Chuck Hager. Bobby didn't need to know about the blackmailing. And there was still one big unanswered question surrounding his parentage.

"All right," Owen said, drawing back the curtain around Bobby's bed. "I'm going back to the nursing home to see if anyone on the day shift remembers seeing Rudy Slater visit your mother."

"What makes you think he would have visited Mom?" Bobby asked.

"Something must have set the killer off. Whatever your mom knew about your dad's murder, she'd known for thirty-five years without being killed."

"The discovery of the body could have set the killer off," Judith said.

"Still, wouldn't you think whoever it was would check on Bobby's mom before he killed her? To see whether she was really a threat?"

"She wasn't a threat to anyone," Bobby said. "She was a sick, rambling old woman. You can dance around it all you like. We all know Slater did it."

Owen put his hand on Bobby's forearm. "We don't know he did it. We suspect he might have. It's not the same thing."

Bobby pulled his arm free of Owen's grasp. "By God, I'm not going to let him getaway with it."

BEVERLY BRYAN HAD prepared the day-shift nurses for Owen's visit, and each nurse gave Owen roughly the same answer. Not one of them had seen Rudy Slater visiting the nursing home.

Owen stopped for lunch at Angelo's Pizzeria and picked up a *New Yorker* and the latest Michael Connelly paperback for Bobby. When he got to the hospital to deliver them, the desk nurse headed him off, a look of professional concern on her face. "You're Mr. Allison, aren't you?" she asked.

When Owen nodded, she took him by the arm and lowered her voice. "Your friend's gone."

"Where?"

"We don't know." She kept her voice low and adopted a scolding tone. "He really shouldn't be running around after that bump he got."

"How long has he been gone?"

"I'm afraid we don't know that, either." She reached into the pocket of her cardigan and pulled out a folded envelope. "He left this for you. On his bed."

Owen took the envelope to Bobby's rumpled bed and drew the curtain, shutting out the nurse. The envelope contained three folded slips of paper. The first was half of an ornately lettered missal page that had been folded many times and bore the stains of a leather wallet on its creases. It was the page he and Bobby had salvaged from their fathers' joint memorial service and consecrated with the blood of their promised friendship. Bobby had smeared a yellow highlighter over four Latin words from the Pater Noster: *Dimitte nobis debita nostra.* Forgive us our sins.

The second slip of paper was a folded, yellowing copy of the newspaper clipping that followed their bridge escapade, headlined DID OWNER OF COAT, SHOES FOUND ON BRIDGE END LIFE?

The third slip of paper was a copy of a quatrain from a poem by A.E. Housman, hand-lettered on the back of a hospital prescription sheet.

> And if your hand or foot offend you,
> Cut it off, lad, and be whole
> But play the man, stand up and end you,
> When your sickness is your soul.

Owen felt a sickness welling in his own soul as he pieced together the message Bobby had left him. He stuffed the crumpled slips of paper into his pocket, flung back the curtain surrounding the bed, and hurried down the corridor toward the elevator.

As he approached the desk nurse, she asked, "Did he say where he's going?"

Without slowing his pace, Owen answered, "Not in this life-time." The nurse shouted after him, "He really shouldn't be walking around."

He won't be if I don't get to him soon, Owen thought. He punched the elevator button and, when it didn't arrive instantly, took the stairs two at a time, ran to his car, and burned rubber out of the parking lot heading for the Fifth Street Bridge.

OWEN PULLED UP and parked on the far side of the Fifth Street Bridge. A steady stream of cars crossed the bridge in either direction under a high, bright, mid-afternoon sun. There were no crowds, no gawkers, no ambulances. Maybe he wasn't too late. Or maybe there was nothing to be late for. Maybe it was all a joke, just another one of Bobby's pranks.

Owen started walking across the bridge toward Barkley. He hadn't gone more than ten feet when he saw Bobby on the opposite sidewalk, near the middle of the span. He was wearing a sailor's watch cap with the brim turned down to cover his bandages, and he wasn't alone. Walking beside him, arms crossed tightly across his chest, was Rudy Slater.

Bobby was gesturing broadly with his arms, sending semaphore signals that Slater seemed unable to decipher. His arms stopped wind-milling when he spotted Owen, and he punched the air with his open palm as if to say "Go back." Owen ignored his signal and started to cross both lanes of traffic to reach the two men.

Just as Slater looked up to see Owen coming, Bobby grabbed him by the collar with his left hand and slapped him hard across the face with his right. Slater raised his hand to strike Bobby, who stumbled backward, still holding Slater's collar, until his back was against the bridge railing.

Owen waited for a gap in the traffic and started running toward the two men. Slater struck Bobby hard across the face, bending him back-ward over the bridge railing. Bobby screamed for help, tightening his grip on Slater's collar with one hand while fending off blows with the other.

Owen saw with sudden, certain clarity what Bobby was doing and knew that he couldn't make it to the two men in time. He stopped in his tracks and reversed direction, trying to get off the bridge and into the river. Near the end of the span he leaped over the railing and scrambled down the crumbling embankment.

Above him, Owen saw Bobby, bent backward over the bridge rail, put his arm around Slater's neck, arch his back, and bury his face in Slater's throat. Slater screamed and struck at Bobby, beating at his head with both fists.

Horns blared, brakes screeched, and car doors slammed. Owen lost his footing, fell hard on his backside, and slid downhill in an avalanche of gravel. He came to a stop, lurched to his feet, and ran to the riverbank in time to see Bobby clear the railing and fall, arms flailing, forty feet into the Little Muddy.

NINETEEN

Drowned Loves

OWEN SHUCKED HIS SHOES, stripped off his shirt, dived into the Little Muddy, and counted each breath as he stroked toward the spot where Bobby had gone under. By the time he reached the midpoint of the bridge, he had inhaled eighty mouthfuls of air. Those were eighty breaths Bobby hadn't taken, eighty seconds he'd been underwater without surfacing. Owen gulped down a great lungful of air, held his breath, and dived for the bottom of the river, searching for his friend. The murky water stung his eyes and clouded his vision, so that everything looked as if it were floating inside a dirty cup of milky coffee.

Owen came up for air and saw Bobby's white sailor cap floating about fifty feet downstream. He dived under again and swam toward the cap, peering through the murk toward the sandy river bottom. The white blob of Bobby's bandaged head drifted into view, followed by his body, which was twisted into a cramped fetal curl. Owen grabbed him by the collar and kicked upward toward the filtered sunlight. When he broke through the surface, he shifted his grip to clasp Bobby under his armpits and backpaddled toward the riverbank.

Owen dragged Bobby headfirst onto the muddy bank, laid him on his back, and tried to remember the CPR technique Kim Stark had used after pulling Bobby out of the Gauley. He tilted Bobby's head back, pinched his nostrils shut, and blew into his mouth. It was like trying to inflate a stiff balloon with a slow leak. When there was no response, he pounded on Bobby's chest, shouting, "Breathe, goddammit, the joke's over." The only answer was the distant wail of sirens.

Owen jacked up the pace of the CPR routine, alternately pounding Bobby's chest and blowing into his mouth. He pressed his ear against his friend's soggy chest, hearing nothing. Checking for a pulse, he saw that Bobby's fist was closed tightly around Rudy Slater's red bow tie. One end of the tie had been looped under the band of Bobby's wristwatch, and it pained Owen to think that his friend had spent the final minutes of his life making sure that the evidence he'd concocted against Slater wouldn't wash away. He cradled Bobby in his arms, hugged him fiercely, and rocked back and forth, whispering, "God-damn fool" over and over into his dead ear until the sheriff arrived.

OWEN DROVE HOME and showered, sitting motionless on the floor of the stall and allowing the water to pelt him until it turned from hot to tepid to cold. The pounding spray submersed him in memories of his dead friend: Bobby measuring off the sixty-foot tadpole test in the YMCA pool; Bobby shouting "Fuck you, world" in the rain on the Fifth Street Bridge; Bobby rafting on the Gauley River; Bobby float-ing facedown in the Little Muddy. If he'd been a half minute quicker, Owen thought, his friend might still be alive. But he knew that wasn't necessarily true. Bobby hadn't wanted to be saved. He'd orchestrated his own death with an elaborate ritual to implicate Rudy Slater. Owen had seen it coming on the bridge, but he still had trouble compre-hending it.

Owen had promised to give Sheriff Reader a statement at his office, and he left a note asking Judith to meet him there. When he got into his car, he saw that its passenger seat still held the *New Yorker* and the Michael Connelly mystery he'd bought to take to Bobby at the hospital. Looking at the undelivered gifts, he realized how little he knew about his friend. The magazine and mystery were gifts Owen would have liked for himself, but what would Bobby have liked? The two of them had started out life in the same place and ended up in the same place, geographically at least, but their intervening paths had been vastly different. Bobby seemed to have gotten so little of what he wanted out of life, but Owen had only the sketchiest idea of what that was. One thing was certain: he'd wanted Owen to support the illusion that Slater was responsible for his drowning. Knowing what he knew, Owen wondered whether his support would stand up under the sheriff's questioning.

THROUGH THE WINDOW of the sheriff's office, Owen could see Rudy Slater standing next to a tall, beefy man in a tailored suit whose large hands nearly engulfed a slim leather briefcase. When the deputy on duty interrupted to announce Owen's presence, the sheriff came out of his office to ask Owen to wait until he'd finished with Slater. On his way back, he left his office door ajar, so Owen could hear the conversations inside.

The sheriff himself couldn't be seen through the office window, but Owen could hear his voice clearly. "You know I can't release your client, Harley. Eight eyewitnesses swear they saw Rudy Slater here attack a man and shove him off the Fifth Street Bridge. We're still questioning other people, but every witness seems to agree on that point. Your client attacked a man, and the man's dead. I've no choice but to hold him until Judge Stapleton can set bail tomorrow morning."

The tall lawyer responded in a level, fluid voice, "My client was provoked, Thaddeus."

"The little shit hit me and pulled me over to the rail," Slater said.

"And why were you on the bridge with him in the first place, Mr. Slater?" the sheriff asked.

Owen could see Slater's jaw muscles tighten as he considered his answer. "He called me. Said he had certain information. Information vital to my well-being. He wanted to meet someplace where we couldn't be overheard. He suggested the bridge."

"But you'd never met the man before?"

"Not to my knowledge," Slater answered. He looked through the office window, saw Owen waiting outside, and pointed at him. "There. That man. Allison. He saw it all. Ask him what happened."

The sheriff appeared at the office door and beckoned Owen inside. "You were on the bridge when this dustup started?"

Owen nodded.

"Tell him what you saw," Slater commanded.

Owen considered his options and elected a half-truth. "I saw you hit Bob Cantrip,"

Slater looked from the sheriff to his lawyer and back to Owen. "It's a put-up job, isn't it? By God, I saw him wave to you. You're in on it. You're both out to get me. I was set up."

"Why would I be out to get you, Slater?" Owen asked.

The question stopped Slater for a moment. Owen could see him weighing his response, thinking what was safe to say. "In my office, you as much as accused me of bribery. Your friend certainly must have had something against me."

"My friend is dead," Owen said. "You shoved him over the bridge railing."

Slater rubbed his neck. "He bit me. By God, the man bit me. I ought to be tested for typhus."

"Test for AIDS, too, while you're at it," Owen said.

"I beg your pardon?" the lawyer said.

Owen took a certain grim pleasure in delivering the message. "Bobby had AIDS."

Slater wilted visibly and collapsed into the wooden chair next to his lawyer. "They set me up," he said, rubbing at his neck. "The two of them."

Seeing Slater's reaction, Owen felt momentarily ashamed of the pleasure he'd taken in delivering the news about Bobby's AIDS. He considered telling him that saliva wasn't a very effective vector for transmitting the disease, remembered that Slater had undoubtedly shot the raft out from under himself and four other people, and kept his mouth shut.

Slater pointed at Owen from his seated position. "I'll get you, you son of a bitch."

The sheriff moved between Slater and Owen. "You better go back to waiting outside," he said to Owen.

JUDITH ARRIVED while Slater and his lawyer were still in the sheriff's office. She hugged Owen and said, "My God. I can't believe Bobby's dead."

Owen took Judith outside where they couldn't be overheard.

Standing beside a stone lion on the courthouse steps, he told her what happened on the bridge, finishing by saying, "I was about two minutes too late."

"So Bobby staged all that to get Slater?"

Owen shrugged. "Apparently."

"Did we drive him to it, do you think? With all speculations about Slater's guilt?"

"Life drove him to it. Who knows what triggered it."

"But it's not right. Slater could be innocent."

"So could O.J. Simpson, but I wouldn't bet the farm on it."

"Is the sheriff moving to prosecute?"

"The sheriff's with Slater and his lawyer right now. It looks as if Slater will be spending the night in jail."

"But Slater didn't kill Bobby. He really was set up."

"As far as I'm concerned," Owen said, "It's like getting Al Capone for income tax evasion. Slater deserves to be jailed."

"It's not the same thing. Al Capone really did evade the income tax. Slater didn't kill Bobby."

"The sheriff has lots of eyewitnesses who swear they saw him push Bobby off the bridge."

"Are you saying you're willing to let their stories stand?"

"I'm certainly not willing to volunteer a counterstory."

"But Bobby provoked Slater. We don't know what Slater might be guilty of, but we ought to be putting him away for his real crimes, not some misguided prank."

"It's hardly a prank. Bobby sacrificed himself to get Slater." Owen remembered the bow tie looped around his dead friend's wrist. "As far as I'm concerned, it was his dying wish."

"So you're willing to perjure yourself to grant that wish?"

"I won't lie outright. But I won't poke holes in Bobby's story."

The sheriff appeared on the top steps of the courthouse, accompanied by Slater's lawyer, who wagged a finger in the sheriff's face and said, "Thaddeus, if you ever expect to get reelected in this county, you'd best release my client."

The sheriff closed his fist over the lawyer's finger and bent it backward until the man winced and dropped his briefcase. "Harley, if you don't want to spend the night with your client, you better think real hard about what you say to me."

The lawyer reclaimed his finger and his briefcase and backed down the three stone steps to the street where Owen and Judith stood. He turned to say something to the sheriff, thought better of it, and disappeared down the street.

The sheriff held the oak door open. "Your turn," he said, motioning to Owen and Judith.

The sheriff showed Judith to the same chair Slater had used and found a second chair for Owen. When they were both seated, he said, "Slater tells me he was set up."

"So I heard," Owen said.

"Says your friend provoked him, then jumped off the bridge."

"So he just happened to be pounding on a potential suicide in full view of your eyewitnesses?" Owen shook his head in disbelief. "Sounds pretty far-fetched to me."

"Your friend was going to die anyhow," the sheriff said.

"We're all going to die," Owen said. "I wouldn't shorten my life deliberately on the off chance Slater might be blamed."

The sheriff dropped a fresh tape into a vest-pocket tape recorder and set it on his desk in front of Owen. "Tell me what you saw," he said, turning on the recorder.

"Bobby and Slater were walking across the bridge," Owen said. "Bobby was waving his arms and talking. Slater was mostly listening."

"Was Bobby on drugs?"

"He'd just come from the hospital," Owen said. "You'll have to ask them."

"Did he hit Slater?"

Owen stuck with the half-truth he'd used earlier. "Slater hit him."

"That wasn't exactly what I asked. Did Bobby attack Slater first?"

"He was waving his arms. He may have grabbed Slater to make a point. I wouldn't say he attacked him."

"So you saw it all, right from the start?"

"Not all," Owen said. "I was watching cars, dodging traffic to try to reach them."

The sheriff's good eye stared off into the distance, as if he were trying to read a flashcard in the next room. "And did you?"

"No. Slater backed Bobby against the rail and started pummeling him. When it looked as if Bobby might go over the edge, I went for the riverbank instead."

The sheriff jotted something in a spiral notebook. "How'd you happen to be on the bridge in the first place?"

"I was looking for Bobby. He'd left the hospital, and the nurse said he shouldn't be wandering around in his condition."

"But why look on the bridge?"

Owen guessed that the sheriff might already have talked to Bobby's nurse. "He left me an envelope."

"What was in it?"

"Personal things. Things he'd carried in his wallet for sometime. A missal page from our fathers' memorial service and a newspaper clipping about the bridge. That's why I went to the bridge."

"But no suicide note?"

Owen thought of the Housman poem. "No suicide note."

"So your friend left you a few personal mementos and went off to meet Slater on the Fifth Street Bridge." The sheriff shifted his attention to Judith. "What do you think, Counselor? Think I have enough of a case against Slater to hold him overnight?"

"Well," Judith answered, "it's second-degree murder at best. Whatever happened doesn't sound premeditated."

"Not on Slater's part, anyhow," the sheriff said.

"What do you mean by that?" Owen asked.

"I mean, loony as it seems, it sure sounds like your friend set Slater up."

"So you're going to turn Slater loose?" Owen asked.

"I didn't say that." The sheriff flipped open a folder on his desk and tapped the typewritten sheets in it with his pencil. "There's more going on here. You were right about his tires. The tracks on the river road matched the tracks above the Gauley."

"So he changed his tires after he shot at us."

"He changed his tires," the sheriff said. "But he's got property up there overlooking the Gauley. And tire tracks near his property don't mean he shot at you."

"But you put that together with his checks to two murder victims, and it starts to look pretty suspicious," Owen said.

"He says those checks were charitable donations. And in any case, the amounts involved are chump change to a man like Slater."

"Who knows what Slater considers chump change?" Owen said. "His ex-wife claims the only reason he ever let loose of a dollar was to get a better grip on it."

"Well, ex-wives don't make the best character witnesses," the sheriff said, looking at Judith. "And I think you'll agree, Counselor, that the evidence we're talking about is so flimsy that if you were wearing it, I'd have to arrest you."

"Is that a legal analysis or a sexist comment?" Judith asked.

The sheriff smiled. "Probably just wishful thinking." The tape recorder clicked softly, and he picked it up, flipped the tape over, and reinserted it.

"Do you record all your interviews?" Owen asked.

"Anything that's likely to be important."

"Did you record the interview you had with Dolores Cantrip just before she died?"

The sheriff nodded. "Yes. But I told you, she was pretty spaced out. Nothing she said made much sense."

"Can we listen to it?"

The sheriff took a small cardboard box from his desk drawer and rummaged through it, coming up with a miniature audiotape. "Here it is. But I don't know what you expect to get out of it." He inserted the tape in his pocket recorder and pushed the PLAY button.

The recorder produced the sheriff's voice, whispering the date, location, and time, and giving Dolores Cantrip's name. There was a scraping noise, as if a chair or table were being dragged across a linoleum floor, followed by Dolores Cantrip's voice: "I was expecting Sheriff Brennan."

Bobby's mother's voice filled Owen with an immense sense of loss. Another scraping noise came from the tape, followed by the question, "What have you done with Sheriff Brennan?"

"Sheriff Brennan's not around any longer, ma'am."

"Will he be coming?"

"Not this afternoon."

The tape hummed softly for a few seconds. Then the sheriff's voice said, "I'd like to ask you about the night your husband died. What can you tell me about that night?"

"There was a flood. The dam burst and there was a flood." Dolores Cantrip's voice had a rasp that grated on Owen's heart. "I lost my love." Her voice dropped to a throaty whisper. "He drowned."

The tape whirred and popped, and Owen imagined the sheriff moving the recorder closer to Dolores Cantrip. "He drowned," she repeated. "My love drowned."

"No." The sheriff's voice seemed to come from inside a tunnel. "He was shot."

"Not shot. Drowned."

"No. He was shot and buried. Remember, your son Bobby told you. Just after they dug up his father's body."

"Bobby's father wasn't buried." The fading voice took the tone of a patient kindergarten teacher. "He wasn't shot. He wasn't drowned. Where's Sheriff Brennan?"

"There," Owen said. "Play that last part again."

The sheriff rewound the recorder. "She's confused," he said. "First he's drowned. Then he's not. Then he's not buried. She can't keep it straight."

The sheriff punched a button and the patient voice rasped again, "Bobby's father wasn't buried."

Owen reached over and shut off the recorder. "She said that same thing when Bobby told her they dug up Ray Cantrip. That his father wasn't buried." Owen stood up. "She's not confused. She's talking about two different people. Maybe even three."

"How three?" the sheriff asked.

"Her love. Her husband. Bobby's father." Owen held up three fingers and counted down. "One drowned. One shot." One finger still pointed upward. "And one may still be alive."

Owen picked up the tape recorder. "Will Dr. Sussman be doing an autopsy on Bobby?"

"I haven't ordered one," the sheriff said. "We know how he died."

"Order one," Owen said. "You want to know whether he was on drugs." He popped the tape out of the recorder. "And I'd like a DNA sample for a paternity test."

TWENTY

One More Son of a Bitch

THE LABYRINTH OF TREES leading to Sammy Earle's house cast moving shadows in the chill twilight. Tree frogs burped to announce Owen's slow, careful approach as he ducked hanging limbs and skirted bramble bushes. He stopped in front of the bush that hid the head of the burglar alarm he'd helped Sammy install, steeled himself for what was to come, and stepped into the path of the infrared beam.

Sirens blared. A crossfire of searchlights caught Owen in their glare and beat back the tree shadows. He stopped and shielded his eyes against the fiery blaze. The sirens wailed to a stop and Sammy's voice came from inside the house, "Just come on ahead real slow with your hands where I can see them."

"Jesus, Sammy. It's me, Owen. Turn off those damn fireworks."

The twin barrels of a shotgun wedged the screen door open and Sammy peeked around the doorsill. "Owen. Why don't you rattle before you strike? You like to give a man the shivering shits." The gun disappeared inside the house and Sammy stood full frame in the doorway, motioning Owen forward with his arm and calling, "Come on up, boy."

As Owen entered the dimly lit living room, Sammy propped the shotgun next to his grandfather clock, switched off the searchlights, and started to punch the code reactivating the alarm into the panel of buttons beside the clock.

"Leave it off, Sammy," Owen said. "You don't need it anymore. Rudy Slater's in jail."

Sammy stopped punching buttons and turned his back on the wall panel to face Owen. "What's that got to do with my burglar alarm?"

"I think you only put it in to protect yourself against Slater."

"Slater's no threat to burgle my house. That'd be like Willie Sutton knocking over a Seven-Eleven."

"You're not afraid of being burgled, Sammy. You've lived here, what, fifty years without an alarm? I'll bet you didn't lose so much as a teaspoon to burglars in that time."

"Why'd I put the alarm in, then?"

"You tell me."

"Sounds like you're about to tell me." Sammy folded his arms across his chest and leaned against the wall where he'd propped his shotgun. "Well, go right ahead. Man's itching to tell something, it's no trick to make him tell it. The trick is to shut him up."

"And Rudy Slater's been shutting people up lately. My guess is he's been shutting up anybody who knew anything about Ray Cantrip's death. And that includes you, Sammy. That's why you hot-wired this place."

Sammy tilted his head back and peered at Owen through half-lowered eyelids. "And just what has Rudy been saying in his cell?"

Sammy's cagey response convinced Owen that he had something to hide. "He's been saying lots of things," Owen answered. "And he's not the only one. Dolores Cantrip had something to say too."

"Dolores Cantrip's dead," Sammy said. "And nothing she's said for the last three years has made a lick of sense."

"If you listened close enough you could make sense out of it. She said Bobby's father wasn't drowned or shot or buried. We thought at first that was just a sick old lady's ravings. But now I think she was really saying that Bobby's father is still alive. What do you think of that?"

Sammy shrugged. "I think it's just a sick old lady's ravings."

"I don't. I think a DNA test will show you're Bobby's father."

Sammy's shoulders slumped. He turned his back on Owen and made a show of adjusting the hands on the grandfather clock. "And what makes you think that?"

"Dolores was a lovesick woman hanging around Dad's office. Which was right next to your office. You're the right age, and you're proud of all the places your pecker's probed. You spent a lot of time with Bobby and me after our fathers died. And the only man anybody remembers visiting Dolores Cantrip in the county home sounds a lot like you."

Sammy turned to face Owen. "I offered to pay for an abortion."

"She was Catholic, Sammy."

"I was afraid she'd go to your dad. But she was too shamed to tell him."

"How'd she wind up with Ray Cantrip?"

"He'd taken her out a few times. She dangled the bait and he jumped at the chance to marry her."

"So you stood by and let him raise your child."

"Cut me some slack here, Owen. I helped look after both you boys after your daddies died."

"Tell me about Ray Cantrip's death, Sammy. What happened the night he died?"

"What makes you think I know?"

Owen reached over Sammy's shoulder and punched the bank of alarm buttons with his fist. The siren squealed and died. "You put that alarm in because you're afraid of Slater. You know what he's been doing to keep people quiet. You didn't even bother to ask me why he's in jail."

Sammy shrugged. "Man was juggling so many dynamite sticks, don't see it matters much which one blew up on him."

"Bobby," Owen said. "Bobby was the one that blew up on him. Slater killed your son. Pushed him off the Fifth Street Bridge."

The only reaction Sammy gave to his son's death was one of curiosity. "Why in hell would Slater do that?"

"My guess is, Bobby told Slater he had proof Slater killed both his parents. He goaded Slater into killing him in front of witnesses."

Sammy shook his head slowly. "Little pecker-puller had more balls than I gave him credit for."

"Tell you what, Sammy," Owen said. "You refrain from calling Bobby a pecker-puller and I'll try to forget you don't seem to feel a bit sorry he's dead."

"Boy's been dead for years. I saw them sores on his face. Faggot flags."

"Will you for Christ's sake drop the name-calling. If you knew he had AIDS you must have kept track of him."

"Hell yes. I watched him botch up the seminary and the Air Force. And I got Slater to pay his way through Wheeling College."

"Why would Slater do that? He's about as charitable as a Ponzi scheme."

"You guessed right. It was hush money over Ray Cantrip's death."

"Tell me what happened, Sammy."

"Your dad found out Ray had been taking money to steer jobs to

Hager Construction. He was going to fire Ray and blow the whistle on Hager and all the other construction grifters sucking at the state teat.''

"In his testimony to the Blatnik Committee.''

"That's right. But the flood hit just before the hearing. Your dad and I drove a state pickup to the busted dam. He told me about Ray. He was all tore up over it. The other grifters, they was all skimming before Wayne took over the Highway Department, and he'd cleared most of them out. But Ray was your dad's right-hand man. His pissing around splattered your dad as well as the Department.

"It was the last straw for your dad. Contractors had been threatening him ever since the hearings were scheduled. Threatened Ruth and you boys too. He showed me some of the letters. Kept them in the glove compartment. Along with his gun.''

Sammy patted the shotgun he'd left leaning against the grandfather clock, and Owen saw that the twin barrels had been sawed off, leaving two shiny metallic circles at the tips of the matched black cylinders.

"By the time we got there,'' Sammy continued, "the water had broke through and anything that wasn't nailed down was running with the river. Two cows caught in the current disappeared downstream when we pulled up. Ray was already there, toting sandbags, and your dad went to help him. Rudy Slater was there too. He'd moved his equipment down, and I took over one of his painted bulldozers.

"Like I told you, the storm was a real toad-strangler. There was times I couldn't see beyond the dozer blade. When the storm let up a little, I could see your dad and Ray Cantrip downstream of me, one on either end of a sandbag. The hood of your dad's slicker had blown back, and it looked like he was yelling at Ray. Ray'd pull on his end of the bag and your dad would pull back, like they was having a tug-of-war with it. Finally, Ray dropped his end and took off, leaving your dad dragging the sandbag by two of its ears.''

Sammy scratched at his white widow's peak. "Now I'm just guessing, mind you, but I'll bet your dad told Ray what he knew and what he was fixing to do. I lost sight of your dad for a while as Rudy and I piled earth, him with his backhoe and me with the dozer. Maybe fifteen minutes went by before we crested a little rise and I saw a sight I'll never forget.

"Your dad had tethered himself to a fence post with a rope and edged his way into the floodwater to free a little boy who'd ridden a tabletop into a barbed-wire fence. While your dad was working his way along the fence crosswise to the river, Ray Cantrip come up and hacked away at the tether and the barbed wire with the blade of a spade. The tether and the fence ripped loose and the flood carried away your dad, the boy, and the barbed wire.''

Owen staggered backward as if caught in a flood himself and sank into an overstuffed couch. "So Ray Cantrip killed my dad?"

"He didn't think anybody saw him. Until he heard my bulldozer and turned to see me and Rudy Slater watching him. He just stood stock-still, his yellow slicker billowing in the wind. Then he flung the spade into the river and took off running.

"I left the dozer and took off after him, but he got to his car and drove away before I could catch up. I took the state pickup and followed as best I could. There wasn't but a few roads open, and pretty soon I could see his taillights blinking through the rain. I had a pretty good idea he was headed home, so I hung back and let him think he was getting away clean.

"When I got to his house, his car was parked in the driveway. I blocked the drive with the pickup, so he couldn't get away, and took the gun out of the glove compartment.''

"My dad's gun."

Sammy picked up the sawed-off shotgun in his right hand. "I figured I was dealing with a killer, you know." He held the gun aloft like a pistol. "I scoped out the situation through the window."

Sammy stared out through his own window, as if he were watching the thirty-five-year-old scene. "There he was in his living room, dripping floor water and hugging my boy Bobby. The son of a bitch had sold out the Department, killed my best friend, and there he was hugging my boy.''

Owen winced at what was coming. "His boy, Sammy. He raised him, remember?''

"And look how he turned out.'' Sammy spun away from the window. "I went in through the back way, shushed Dolores, and got her to take Bobby to the bedroom. Then, when Cantrip was alone, I went in after him."

Still holding the shotgun aloft like a pistol, Sammy strode to the center of the living room. "I swear to God I didn't plan what happened next. I just wanted to take him to jail. But he come at me. Wild-eyed, like he had a death wish.'' Sammy lowered his right hand and pointed the shotgun at Owen. "It was like the gun had a mind of its own.''

Doubt and fear welled in Owen as he stared into the twin barrels.

"Jesus, Sammy. It was you." He'd suspected that Sammy knew something about Ray Cantrip's death, but not that he'd killed him. Had Sammy been involved in the other deaths as well?

Owen's voice seemed to snap Sammy out of a trance. He sat down on the arm of the couch and rested the shotgun on his lap, still pointing its barrel at Owen. "It's like your daddy said. There's always one more son of a bitch than you counted on."

"What about Rudy Slater?"

"Slater had followed me to Cantrip's house. He come through the door right after the gun went off. I know just how Ray felt at the river. Just for a minute you think you can get away with it. That nobody saw you. But then you look up, and somebody's staring right at you. And your mind flip-flops like a landed fish."

"But it was self-defense. He'd killed my father. He came at you. Why not just give yourself up?"

"Ray was unarmed. I had a gun." Sammy patted the stock of the shotgun. "It would be hard to plead self-defense. Rudy helped me see that. He convinced me to hide the body."

"Of course Rudy would want to hide the body. A trial would expose the whole dirty story, including his blackmailing."

"There was that, sure. Dolores didn't want that either. Her name would have been smeared for good."

"And your name too, for abandoning Bobby."

"Rudy made that point too."

"And you didn't want to risk a trial."

"I didn't want to risk jail."

"So you decided to bury Cantrip."

"The three of us decided. Rudy, Dolores, and me. We planted him under Hager's construction site on Gobbler's Grade. Rudy paved over him first thing next morning. Everybody assumed the flood got him."

The shotgun lay absently across Sammy's lap. He seemed to have forgotten it, but Owen couldn't be sure. He measured the distance across the couch to the two barrels. "What about my father's gun?"

"We buried it in the woods well back from the roadway. That turned out to be our biggest mistake. When they found Ray's body, they started sweeping the area with metal detectors. The gun was far enough away so they didn't find it at first, but we figured it was only a matter of time."

Sammy shifted on the arm of the couch and the twin barrels dipped so they pointed at the cushion between him and Owen. "We decided to dig the gun up and pitch it into the Little Muddy, like we should have done in the first place."

"And spike Hager's equipment at the same time."

Sammy nodded and the gun barrels bobbed. "That was Rudy's idea. A little payback for passing him over. It would slow Eddie down, maybe keep him from finishing the job in time to bond his next bid against Rudy. Besides, it gave us an excuse for being up on Gobbler's Grade in case anybody saw us."

"And Mary Jewel Robertson saw you."

"We sugared the gas tanks we could get open. I went off to spike the rest while Rudy dug up the gun." Sammy shook his head. "Neither of us finished. Jimmy Joe Cresap showed up and we were lucky to get away. Come to find out, though, Mary Jewel had been watching us. God knows what she was doing up there at that hour."

"Nesting."

"Well, that woman was tough enough to hatch rocks. She went right after Rudy. Wanted hush money to keep from telling anybody we'd spiked Hager's equipment."

"Two thousand dollars."

"Rudy paid it right off. No more trouble than emptying lint from his pockets. She didn't stop there, though. She'd seen Rudy digging for the gun, and she was up on Gobbler's Grade when the sheriff's men finally found it. She put two and two together and figured Rudy was after more than a little payback for Hager Construction."

"So she upped the ante."

"Well, hell. The crime had gone from vandalism to murder. She asked for a hundred grand."

"That's a lot of money to buy silence."

"Rudy could've raised it easy. He figured he wasn't really buying silence, though, just paying on a short-term lease. Mary Jewel'd be back for more. Once she'd got a taste for it, she'd sure as shit want second and third helpings."

"So he killed her?"

"Cold-cocked her in her own apartment. Left the murder weapon in your brother's car."

"He told you this?"

"He acted like he was doing me a favor. Mary Jewel knew I was on Gobbler's Grade with him. It was only a matter of time before she'd come after me too. The only reason she went to Rudy first was because he had deeper pockets.''

''And a tire iron up his sleeve.''

''She hadn't counted on that.''

Owen shook his head slowly. ''Sammy. Sammy. You knew George was innocent. And you were going to let him stand trial without saying anything?''

Sammy bowed his head and the gun barrels drooped a fraction of an inch. ''Rudy threatened to kill me if I talked. That's the real reason he told me about Mary Jewel. It was kind of like a warning.''

The shotgun barrels were now pointing more toward the couch than toward Owen, but he calculated the conical spray of pellets would still do more harm to him than to the upholstery. ''And Dolores Cantrip. Was that another warning? She was a delirious old woman, for Christ's sake.''

''Not so delirious,'' Sammy said. ''Not if you listened close to what she was saying. And Rudy was afraid someone would do just that.''

''So he killed her too?''

''Dressed up like a doctor. Nobody at the nursing home noticed him. Not until you busted in on him, anyhow.''

Owen inched forward on the couch so that he was within an arm's length of the gun barrels. ''Sammy. You have to tell the sheriff what you just told me.''

Sammy lifted the gun from his lap and leveled it at Owen. ''I'm too old to do time.''

Owen's right hand began to shake and he clutched the couch fabric to steady it. ''You won't do time, Sammy. If it happened the way you said, Cantrip's death was self-defense.'' But what if it hadn't happened that way? ''Just put the gun down.''

''You shouldn't have come back, Owen.''

''You don't want to shoot me, Sammy. I'm Wayne's boy. Remember? You were his best friend.''

''That's why you shouldn't be talking about going to the sheriff.''

''I don't have to, Sammy. He's right outside.'' Owen opened his jacket to show him the sheriff's tape recorder. ''We've been recording this talk. He's been listening in.''

''The sheriff can't be outside, Owen. He would have tripped the alarm.''

''You shut it off, remember?'' Owen nodded to the alarm panel behind Sammy. ''Take a look.''

Sammy rose, keeping the shotgun trained on Owen. Owen rose with him, closing the distance between himself and the gun.

Sammy made a quarter turn and glanced quickly over his shoulder, trying to catch sight of the alarm panel. The gun moved with his head, and Owen leaped forward, clamping both hands on the barrels and shoving downward.

The gun exploded and pain seared through Owen's right foot. He went down, wrenching the gun away from Sammy, who crumpled and fell beside him.

Sammy writhed on the floor, clutching his left leg just below the knee. "My leg. I've shot off my leg."

Owen tested his own right leg. His pant leg was shredded and his foot was numb where pellets had penetrated his shoe, but he could support himself on his heel. He hobbled over to the phone, dragging the shotgun with him.

Sammy's left leg jerked spasmodically. His foot flapped free like a marionette's. "Don't turn me in, Owen," he said through clenched teeth. "I never would have shot you. I was your father's best friend. I helped raise you."

"You should have raised Bobby. He was my best friend and you orphaned him twice. Once when you wouldn't marry his mother, and once when you killed the man who did." Owen lifted the phone and dialed 911.

"The sheriff isn't outside?"

"No. But he will be soon."

Sammy moaned. "You son of a bitch. You bluffed me."

Owen gave the address to the dispatcher and put his hand over the mouthpiece. "That's me, Sammy. The son of a bitch you didn't count on."

TWENTY-ONE

I Would've Saved Him If I Could

OWEN PICKED GEORGE UP at his home to drive him back to the alcohol treatment center at Saint Vincent's Hospital. His brother had packed everything he thought he'd need for a four-week stay into a small carry-on bag.

George heaved the carry-on bag into the trunk and slid into the passenger seat. "One night of freedom and it's back to a different cell."

"But the nuns make better landlords than the sheriff's deputies, and they'll let you out in a few weeks."

"Don't think I don't appreciate that." George reached out and squeezed Owen's shoulder. "If it weren't for you, I might still be a long-term tenant of the sheriff."

"I'll see that you get the family discount for my services. Did you talk to Billy?"

"Yeah. He's changing majors. But if he can't find a job when he graduates, I'm sending him to live with you."

"That'd be all right. He's a good kid." Owen glanced sideways at his brother. "What about Barb?"

George made a show of looking in the backseat. "You don't see her in this car, do you?"

"She'll be there when you get out," Owen said with more conviction than he felt.

"I don't think so. It's like we don't even speak the same language anymore. She talks that fucking counselor lingo. You know. 'Get in touch with the child inside you.'"

"No. I don't know. We skipped counseling and went directly to divorce." Owen shook his head. "It wasn't the smartest thing I ever did."

"Well, Barb's got the lingo down pat. She's in direct contact with the child inside her, the teenager inside her, the mother inside her, and the wife inside her. None of them want anything to do with me."

"What about you? What did you tell the counselor?"

"That the child inside me was a deaf mute."

"I can see where he couldn't do much with that."

"I told him how I felt, though. Shit, I still feel the same. It's like I'm a part of this movie experiment I read about. They show the audience a close-up of an actor on the screen. Then they cut to a picture of a cuddly baby. Then they show the actor again. And the audience marvels at how well the actor portrays tenderness. Then they show a dead dog. And cut back to the actor again. And the audience marvels at how well the actor portrays revulsion. But the close-up of the actor never changed. See, it was exactly the same in all three shots."

Owen nodded. "There's a word for that experiment. Some Russian name."

"Yeah, well. I told this counselor, what I feel is, that the picture of me in Barbara's mind has gotten switched somehow. But I haven't changed. I haven't changed."

"And what did the counselor say?"

"He wanted to know how the child inside me felt about that."

Owen laughed. "I'd say it's time to get another counselor."

"Shit," George said. "This place I'm going to is wall-to-wall counselors. The child in me won't stand a chance."

"Give it a try, George. You come out dry, that'll be a big change. Maybe even big enough to switch the picture in Barb's mind back to where it was."

They passed through a construction zone marked by two rows of traffic cones and a diamond-shaped orange sign saying CONSTRUCTION WORKERS—GIVE 'EM A BRAKE. There were no workers in sight, but extra cones were stacked beside a Porta Potti. Two of the stored cones were pitted and discolored. Owen pulled over, jumped out of the car, picked up the two discolored cones, and put them in George's lap. "Souvenirs," he told his brother. "Just in case Alicia gives you a hard time when you get back to work."

At the hospital, a short, white-robed nun led the two brothers to George's room, a small, spare cubicle with a neatly made bed, a slat-backed wood chair, a desk under the lone window, and a picture of the Sacred Heart on the wall.

When the nun left, George plopped his small bag on the bed. "Just a tad tinier than the sheriff's digs, don't you think?"

"The difference is, you've got the key to the door here." Owen put a pitted traffic cone on either end of the desk. "These will add a little color." He turned to leave.

George stood in the doorway. "We never did get to a Reds game."

"A lot of things got in the way. Maybe you and Billy can take in one for me."

Owen held out his hand. George took it, pulled him into an awkward embrace, and whispered, "Thanks, little brother," into his ear.

Owen felt a dampness against his cheek. He pulled back and said the first thing that came into his head. "Well, lay off the outside curves and the inside straights."

George flicked at his eyelash with a knuckle. "That's what I told you when you went away to college."

"Best advice I ever got."

"Best advice I ever gave."

Owen stopped halfway through the door. "Hang in there. We're all rooting for you."

George nodded. Standing in front of the spare desk, flanked by two dilapidated traffic cones, he looked to Owen like a goalie dreading a penalty kick in a pick-up soccer game.

WHEN OWEN returned home, he found Judith and Ruth on the living-room couch sorting through a jumble of post-flood clippings and photographs.

"I never got around to organizing these in a scrapbook," Ruth said. "Judith is helping me do it now."

"How is George?" Judith asked.

"All right, I guess," Owen said. "His new room's not much bigger than his old cell."

"He'll get through it," Ruth said. "And Barb will stick by him when he gets out."

"I don't know," Owen said. "Barb's not cutting him much slack."

"She doesn't see what he's going through." Ruth held up a picture of her father, seated on the tractor he rode into eternity. "I never saw it with your dad or your grandfather either."

"Grandad? He had the farm. It was permanent job security."

"Farming looks easy when all you see is your grocer's produce bin. The farm was a constant worry. You never had to wait out a wet winter with your life savings tied up in seed.''

Owen recalled the photo of his grandfather in his too-tight tuxedo staring grimly at the wedding photographer. "I'm sorry. I didn't realize. It was a silly thing to say."

"Don't apologize. I told you. I didn't see it when my father was alive. You didn't see it when your dad was alive. Billy doesn't see it with George." Ruth reached out and flicked Owen's arm with a photograph. "And if you'd get busy and give me more grandchildren, they wouldn't see how hard you work and worry either."

Owen rested his hand on Judith's shoulder. "A grandchild's not a solo undertaking."

"I didn't mean 'you' as a singular noun."

Judith patted Owen's hand. "I'm ready anytime. It's that plural 'you' that's a bitch to work out."

Suddenly embarrassed, as if she'd pushed too far into personal territory, Ruth fished around in the early pages of the scrapbook and took a picture from its corner mounts. "Believe me, it's worth whatever you have to work out." She showed the picture to Owen and Judith. It was a black-and-white snapshot of Ruth and Wayne Allison, each bent at the waist, each holding one upraised arm of young Owen, whose bare bowed legs and bootied feet barely touched the ground.

"You were so eager to learn to walk," Ruth said to Owen. "You'd pull yourself up on the couch, push off, fall on your little tush, laugh, and keep doing it until you made it from the couch to the coffee table."

Judith leaned back on the couch and looked up at Owen. "See. You were learning from failure way back then."

"Now I've matured," Owen said. "I've decided to try to learn from success instead."

Judith shoved playfully at his hand. "It'll never work. You'd have to succeed first."

"Stop it, you two," Ruth said. "I'd say you've been pretty successful lately. George is in treatment and Rudy Slater's in jail." She examined a photo and let it drop into her lap. "And I finally know what really happened to your father."

Owen watched as Judith slid across the couch and hugged Ruth. He recalled the awkward embrace he'd just shared with George and marveled at Judith's ability to move instinctively to comfort his mother.

Ruth dabbed at her eyes and handed Owen the photo from her lap. It showed his father with his arm around Sammy Earle. Both men wore plaid work shirts and knickers that bloused overhigh-topped work boots. Wayne Allison towered at least a foot over Sammy, who was leaning against a pair of pole-mounted tourist binoculars.

"They took that picture at Lookout Point," Ruth said. "Your father was so proud of that road. It was the last one he built before we were married. He carved a heart in the asphalt in my honor."

Owen hoped it wasn't one of the anonymous hearts Sammy had boasted the two men had left on every road they'd built. "What's the latest on Sammy?" he asked Judith.

"He's still in jail. They haven't decided how to charge him yet."

"When they do, could you defend him?"

Ruth straightened on the couch. "Owen, how can you ask that?"

"Mom, he was the father of my friend."

"Not a very good father."

Owen tapped the photo. "He was also a good friend of my father."

Ruth took the photo back. "He's a vile little man. He kept quiet all these years, when he knew what really happened."

"Mom, he couldn't talk without incriminating himself. He did what he did to avenge Dad."

"So he says."

Judith interrupted. "Of course I'll defend him if he needs it."

"Does that mean you'll both be staying?" Ruth asked. "The two of you make such a good team."

"I was planning to leave right after Bobby's memorial service, but I'll stay if you need me," Owen said to Judith.

Judith shook her head. "You've got to get back to your consulting business. Besides, I know everything you know."

"You keep saying that," Owen said, "but it's just not true. You don't know who played third for the Cincinnati Reds in 1985, how much asphalt goes into a mile of road, or where Betty Lou Weiler was tattooed."

"Knowing Betty Lou Whoosis was tattooed in Philadelphia won't help Sammy's defense," Judith said. "I know everything you know about his case. Besides, he may not need a defense. There's a good chance they'll give him immunity if he testifies against Rudy Slater. That way they solve two fresh murders just for letting a stale one slide."

Ruth handed Owen another photo. "Here's the last picture ever taken of your father."

The grainy black-and-white photo showed Wayne Allison up to his ankles in mud, bending over to lift one end of a sandbag. His face was barely visible under the hood of his slicker. The other end of the sandbag was held by Sammy Earle.

Owen stared at the photo. "Who took this?"

"A photographer from the *Gazette*," Ruth said. "They never ran it because you can barely make out your dad's face. The *Gazette* man gave it to me after the memorial service."

Owen pointed to the photo. "That's Sammy Earle on the other end of the sandbag."

"Oh, yes," Ruth said. "You can see him clearly. The wind's blown his hood back away from his face."

Owen leaped up from the couch. "You're right, Mom. He's a vile little man." He started for the door.

"Where are you going?" Judith asked.

"I need to make some phone calls. Then you and I are going to visit Sammy and the sheriff."

Judith set aside the photo album. "Do you still want me to defend him?"

"No. I want you to help me bury the little bastard."

SHERIFF READER showed Owen and Judith a transcript of the statement Sammy had provided after he'd been booked. Word for word, it was virtually identical to the story he'd related to Owen just before his capture, in which he'd confessed to killing Raymond Cantrip.

"He's offered to help us convict Rudy Slater," the sheriff said. "If he does that, I don't think the D.A. will press too hard on the Cantrip killing. After all, Sammy had just seen Cantrip kill your dad, and Cantrip wasn't the most upright of citizens."

Owen showed the sheriff the picture of Wayne Allison and Sammy Earle handling sandbags at the edge of Eight-Pole Creek. "As it turns out, neither was Sammy. Let's go talk to him."

Sammy Earle sat wedged in the corner of his cell, his left leg encased in a thigh-high cast that was propped awkwardly on a rolled blanket at the foot of his fold-down cot. Two wooden crutches leaned against the wall next to him.

"Got some visitors, Sammy," the sheriff announced. "Don't bother to get up."

Sammy didn't smile, either at the sheriff's forced humor or at Owen's and Judith's entrance.

"You remember my ex-wife Judith," Owen said, standing in the middle of the cell. "She's a lawyer. We think you might need one." Sammy nodded from his cot. "I told them I killed Ray Cantrip. I'm ready to take whatever comes from that. The son of a bitch killed your dad. Cut him down in the middle of the worst flood I ever seen. I watched him go under. I would've saved him if I could. I want you to know that, Owen. He was my best friend. I would've saved him if I could."

"I appreciate your saying that, Sammy. I just wanted to go over a few points in your story." Owen took the transcript from the sheriff's hand. "First off, it was Ray Cantrip who helped Dad with the sandbags?"

Sammy shifted uncomfortably on his cot. "That's right. I told you that already."

"Was there anybody else helping? Anybody else who might have seen what happened?"

"Nope. We'd brought the sandbags in our pickup. We were the first ones to arrive."

"But you didn't help with the sandbags. You took over the bulldozer, so you don't know what happened between Ray Cantrip and Dad that led up to the killing."

"I just know what I seen from the dozer."

"And after that you followed Cantrip home." Owen checked the transcript of Sammy's official statement. "You say the sight of Cantrip holding your boy Bobby enraged you. You say, 'The son of a bitch had sold out the Department, killed my best friend, and there he was hugging my boy.'"

"That's right. I couldn't stand the sight of the son of a bitch."

"What I don't understand, Sammy," Owen said, "is how you knew Cantrip had sold out the Department."

"Your dad told me. While we were driving out to the flood."

Owen leafed through the transcript. "And you say here Rudy argued if Ray's body was found, the whole story would come out and you'd be smeared for abandoning Bobby."

"There was that, yes."

Owen snapped the transcript shut. "But how did Rudy know Bobby was your son? Chuck Hager didn't know."

Sammy slumped back into the shadowed corner of his cell. "Rudy was a bright guy. He put two and two together. Just like you."

"And you confirmed it for him?" Owen asked.

"I didn't deny it."

"You were on pretty good terms with Slater, then?"

Sammy shrugged in the shadows. "All right, I guess."

"But you worked for the State Highway Department. And Rudy worked for a struggling start-up road builder looking to find his way into some state contracts."

"Rudy found his way in through Ray Cantrip. On account of what Rudy and Chuck Hager knew about Cantrip."

"But why would you confide in Rudy?" Judith asked.

"What the hell is this, Owen?" Sammy asked. "I thought you wanted to find me a lawyer?"

"No. I said I thought you needed one," Owen replied. "I just talked to Chuck Hager on the phone. He says you figured out that Cantrip was rigging their bids. Instead of going to my dad or the Attorney General, though, you went to Hager and demanded to go on the pad too."

"Hager's a dotty old man. Since his stroke, half of what he remembers ain't so. And the other half might not have been."

"Hager's pretty sure about you, Sammy. And my guess is Rudy Slater will back him up."

"It was Cantrip sold us out," Sammy said.

"But you were happy to ride on his coattails," Owen said. "And that's not all you did, is it?"

Sammy's voice squeaked out of the shadows. "What do you mean?"

Owen picked up one of Sammy's crutches by its slim footpiece and swept it back like a baseball bat. "You killed my father, you sorry little shit."

Sammy seized the remaining crutch and held it in front of him like a shield. "I told you how your father died."

The sheriff stepped up behind Owen and grabbed the handgrip of the crutch he was brandishing. Owen released the crutch and took a step toward Sammy. He was surprised to find that he could still control his voice. "You told me the man sandbagging with Dad cut his lifeline when he edged out into the floodwaters."

Sammy cowered behind his crutch. "That was Ray Cantrip."

Owen took the picture of Sammy hefting a sandbag with Wayne

Allison from Judith and thrust it in the prisoner's face. "Bullshit. It was you."

"Ray Cantrip cut your dad loose," Sammy said. "I disremembered about helping out with sandbags before Ray spelled me and I took over the dozer. I told you how it happened. Why don't you believe me?"

"I believe it happened the way you told it. Except I believe you were the one who chopped my dad's lifeline, not Ray Cantrip. Dad found out both of you were on Hager's pad. He was going to testify before the Blatnik Committee and send you both to jail."

Owen stepped back and handed the picture to the sheriff. "I believe Ray Cantrip saw you kill Dad. He took off for his house and you followed him. You killed him to keep him quiet. Not to avenge Dad."

"What I told you was true. Ask Rudy Slater."

"Rudy didn't see what happened. He only knows what you told him. And you told him the same story you told us. It's what you told Dolores Cantrip too. She never would have helped you hide Ray's body if she hadn't thought he'd killed the love of her life."

"You can't prove any of this."

Owen took Judith's briefcase. "We've got the picture of you handling sandbags, which contradicts your sworn statement. We've got Chuck Hager's testimony that you were on his payroll." Owen reached into the briefcase and pulled out a leather-bound journal. "And we've got my father's logs. You remember these, Sammy. He kept daily logs when he was in the field with you. And he went on keeping them after he took a desk job. He knew you'd sold out."

Sammy stared at the leather journal. "Still don't prove I killed him." He looked past Owen at the sheriff. "You want my testimony against Slater, you'd best forget about all this."

The sheriff shrugged. "We can nail Slater without you. We've got evidence placing him at Mary Jewel's and at the site where he winged Owen here."

Owen thrust the leather journal into Sammy's stomach as if he expected the prisoner to take an oath on it. "And if Slater didn't kill Dolores Cantrip, you're the next most likely suspect. Her nurses remember seeing you visit her."

Sammy cringed and scuttled backward on his cot. "I never could've killed Dolores. She was the mother of my boy."

"That certainly wouldn't have stopped you. We know how you felt about Bobby." Owen handed the journal back to Judith. "But you know what, Sammy? We don't have to prove you killed Dad. You've already confessed to killing Ray Cantrip. And by the time we've finished telling our story to that jury, they're not likely to let you off easy. You're eighty years old. The Cantrip killing alone will keep you behind bars for the rest of your life.''

The sheriff took out his glass eye, polished it on his sleeve, returned it to its socket, and froze it on Sammy. "Course, if you were to tell us what really happened, show us none of it was premeditated, it might go easier.''

Sammy slumped forward. "It all happened so fast. Wayne was out along that fence. The fence posts were creaking, ready to let loose. I just helped them along. I barely thought about it.''

The crutch Sammy had used as a shield slid off his cot and clattered to the concrete floor. "When I saw your dad go under, I wanted to go in after him. He was my best friend. I chased along the bank, but the river was running too fast. I would've saved him if I could.''

IN THE CAR on the way home, Judith pulled the leather journal from her briefcase and looked through it. "This just records how many miles of asphalt they laid each day on Horseshoe Curve. There's nothing here about Sammy and your dad.''

"I just grabbed the top journal from the stack,'' Owen said. "I'd looked through all of them. Dad never wrote anything about Sammy and Chuck Hager. Or Ray Cantrip either. But I wanted to have something of Dad's in that cell.''

"So you were running a bluff.''

"I'd bluffed Sammy once before. He was a cringing little asshole with a cruddy hand. It's no real trick to bluff a man who's holding crappy cards.''

"Remind me never to go up against you in a serious game.''

"Are you kidding? You already have. I lost big time.'' Owen reached out and took Judith's hand. "But I'm ready for a rematch.''

TWENTY-TWO

One for the Tripper

BOBBY'S BRIEF WILL left all of his possessions to Owen and asked that his body be cremated. Although he dreaded the task, Owen, followed by the sheriff, drove to Bobby's run-down rooming house to sort through his inheritance. Bobby's equally run-down landlady met them in the same tattered gray housecoat and rubber flip-flops she'd worn on Owen's last visit, although the copy of the *National Enquirer* she brought to the door with her this time appeared to be new. The sheriff explained their mission and departed, leaving the landlady perched like a vulture at the door of Bobby's garage apartment, ready to pounce if Owen claimed any of her own furnishings as part of his friend's meager estate.

Under the watchful eye of the landlady, Owen grouped Bobby's possessions on the linoleum floor of his dark, wood-paneled living room, stacking books from the cinder block-supported shelves, packing clothes into plastic garbage bags, and sorting magazines, videotapes, and a few pots, pans, and dishes into cardboard storage boxes. The landlady let him know that the only furnishings belonging to Bobby were a television set, a VCR, a card table, and four folding chairs.

Owen consigned the TV, VCR, card table, chairs, and kitchen items to Goodwill, along with all the clothes and about half the books and videotapes. For himself, he kept a box of books that included volumes of poetry by A.E. Housman and E.A. Robinson, essays by Thurber and E.B. White, and biographies of W.C. Fields, the Marx Brothers, and Woody Allen; videotapes of a few fifties musicals, including *Singin' in the Rain*; and a life-sized bust of W.C. Fields that had been designed as a cookie jar. While the landlady clucked her disapproval, he filled a large plastic bag with an assortment of homoerotic videos and magazines. These he deposited in the trash, not so much because he shared the landlady's disapproval, but because they were sad evidence of the loneliness of Bobby's solitary existence.

The only personal papers Owen could find were Bobby's passport, his high school and college diplomas, and four handwritten letters from someone who signed himself Skipper. The most recent letter was over

five years old. Owen put these few personal effects into the shoebox Dolores Cantrip had left Bobby containing Wayne Allison's letters and the college payment receipts from the Gray Eagle Trust. He recalled Bobby's gibe that his own life wouldn't fill out the rest of his mother's shoebox and was saddened to find that to be true. There was little or no satisfaction in the fact that the books, tapes, and cookie jar Owen was taking for himself expanded his friend's legacy to two full storage boxes.

After paying Bobby's landlady for two months' back rent, Owen left her and stopped at Reger's Funeral Home to make arrangements for the cremation. A pale middle-aged man at a desk flanked by two lit candelabra took down the details and asked if Owen would like to purchase a cinerary urn from their Sacred Sepulcher Series. Owen declined, saying that he had already arranged for a receptacle to hold the ashes of the deceased. When the mortician raised an eyebrow so far it disappeared under his drooping forelock, Owen explained that the receptacle was a hollowed-out sculpture of William Claude Fields. He didn't want to shatter the solemnity of the surroundings by admitting that the sculpture had begun life as a cookie jar.

"And is Mr. Fields a relative of the deceased?" the mortician asked.

"In a way, yes," Owen answered.

THE MEMORIAL SERVICE for Bobby Cantrip was held in the same Catholic church where the funeral masses for his father and mother had been held, thirty-five years apart. The current pastor agreed to hold the service, even though he explained to Owen that he wouldn't offer a funeral mass for a lapsed Catholic who had opted for cremation.

A few more mourners attended Bobby's memorial service than had been present at Dolores Cantrip's funeral mass. Owen sat with Judith and his mother in the front pew on one side of the center aisle, while Robin sat alone on the other side. Owen recognized roughly half of their high school graduating class of thirty-eight students scattered throughout the church. Mary Alice Hogarty, the librarian, sat alone in a middle pew, and just before the service started, Owen saw Sammy Earle, escorted by the sheriff, hobble in on crutches and take a seat in the rear. In a concession to the secular nature of the memorial service, the bust of W.C. Fields containing Bobby's ashes sat in a niche to the right of the altar, under the outstretched hand of the Infant of Prague. It was a touch Owen was sure Bobby would have appreciated.

After leading the mourners in a hymn, the priest read the Twenty-third Psalm, recalled the recent funeral of Bobby's mother, and repeated many of the same generalities Owen remembered from that service. Then, just as he had at Dolores Cantrip's funeral, the priest stepped down from the lectern and invited the family and friends of the deceased to share their memories with the congregation.

This time Owen was prepared. He took over the lectern, introduced himself, and said, "Bobby Cantrip was my best friend. He had a hard life and a harder death, but he enriched the lives of those around him with laughter."

Owen saw Judith smiling encouragement from the front pew. "Few men choose the way they will die," he continued. "Bobby always told me, 'I want to die peacefully in my sleep, like my grandfather.'" Owen paused, trying to time the next sentence the way Bobby would. "Not screaming, like the passengers in his car."

Judith laughed out loud, and Robin stifled a giggle. There were a few titters scattered around the rest of the congregation. But most of the mourners stared blankly up at him, and the church was soon shrouded in silence. Ruth Allison bowed her head and covered her eyes with her hand. Seeing his mother embarrassed made Owen glad he hadn't promised to tell more than one for the Tripper.

Owen gripped the lectern hard and fought the urge to hide behind it. "That joke was a little like Bobby's life. Out of place, outlandish, outrageous, and in questionable taste. But, I think, funny just the same.

"He never failed to make me laugh. Thirty-five years ago, we served as altar boys at a funeral mass for our fathers in this very church, and he made me laugh. In high school, whenever I blew a ball game, lost a girlfriend, or fluffed a test, he made me laugh. To my regret, I lost touch with him for a long time, but whenever I saw him, he made me laugh. Less than an month ago, he told me he was dying. And, by God, in the next breath, he made me laugh."

Owen's voice cracked, and he knew he couldn't continue much longer without breaking down. "He made me laugh," he repeated. "I never knew till now how much that meant to me. And I never told him. I'm not laughing now. But wherever Bobby is, I'm sure he's laughing still."

Owen held up the thin volume he'd carried to the lectern. "Bobby had kept this book of poetry by A.E. Housman with him ever since high school. Before he died, he left me a handwritten copy of a stanza of poetry from the book. There's another stanza here that I think fits this occasion." Owen opened the book and read,

> "Lie you easy, dream you light,
> And sleep you fast for aye
> And luckier may you find the night
> Than ever you found the day."

Owen closed the book and returned to his seat, where his mother took his arm and patted his hand.

Robin followed Owen to the lectern and somehow fashioned a graceful memorial out of Bobby's Elvis interview, a prank that Owen knew had mortified her at the time. Judith went next with a story about the bedroomful of balloons Bobby had left for Owen and her on their wedding night. The congregation finally warmed to the humor of the speeches and responded by chuckling in most of the right places.

A few other high school classmates recalled memories of Bobby. Then the priest returned to the lectern, led the congregation in "Lord of the Dance," and brought the service to a close.

Owen, Ruth, and Judith were the last of the mourners to file out of the church. When they reached the vestibule, Ruth took them both by their arms and said, "What you said in there, I just want you to know, it made me proud of both of you. And of Bobby, too. I'll miss him. And I'll miss having the two of you around."

"If I stay any longer, I won't have a business left," Owen said.

"I'm glad you came, though," Ruth said. "George is out of jail and in treatment. Rudy Slater is out of commission and in jail, and you closed the book on your father's death and Ray Cantrip's killing."

Owen led the way out of the dark vestibule and shielded his eyes against the sun. "I was too late to save Bobby and his mother, though."

Judith took his hand. "Stop it, please. You got Bobby over the Devil's Staircase. You found his father's killer. You can hardly be thinking you failed him."

"I called him my best friend and I barely knew him," Owen said. "That's failure enough."

RECALLING THAT Bobby had said some of his happiest childhood memories were of the Gauley River, Owen put the cookie jar with his friend's ashes into his rented car the next day and drove alone up the winding mountain road to Lookout Point. He continued past the private road that led to Grandview Estates and parked in the public overlook, where a man was hoisting his young son to look through a pair of pole-mounted tourist binoculars. They were the same binoculars that Sammy Earle had leaned on when he posed with Owen's father for Ruth Allison's camera. Owen left the bust of W.C. Fields on the front seat of his car and walked to the waist-high stone wall that marked the edge of the overlook. An iron picket fence sat solidly on top of the wall. Nearly a thousand feet below, the Gauley River flowed easily between the moist limestone walls that channeled it, foaming and splashing, over Big Lick Falls and down the Devil's Staircase.

At the base of the stone wall, a florid heart had been scratched into the asphalt of the parking lot. A crude arrow pierced the heart, but there were no initials identifying either the original artist or the object of his affections. Owen remembered his mother's pride in the heart his father had carved at Lookout Point and felt a tug of resentment at Sammy Earle's boast that neither he nor Alleycat Allison had been fool enough to put anyone's initials in the hearts they'd left on the roads they'd built.

The only other car in the parking lot belonged to the young father, who was trying to coax his son down from the stone wall, where he was running a stick along the iron pickets. Owen walked over to the tourist binoculars they had abandoned and was about to insert a dime when he saw another heart etched in the asphalt between the base of the binoculars and the restraining wall. This heart bore the initials WA and RE, for Wayne Allison and Ruth Evans. A tight, precise hand had surrounded the initials with lower-case letters that spelled out the message

alWAys
adoREd.

Owen smiled and whispered, "Sorry I doubted you, Dad," into the pole-mounted binoculars.

The father encircled his son's stomach with both arms, pulled him down from the stone wall, and carried him back to their car. As he passed Owen, he said, "Some view, huh?"

Owen pretended to look through the binoculars, but he could see only the heart at their base. "Some view," he agreed.

After the father and son had left, Owen retrieved the cookie jar from the front seat of his car and climbed up on the overlook's stone wall. Leaning over the iron pickets, he removed W.C. Fields' cracked hat and swept the jar in a tight arc over the edge of the gorge. Ashes streamed from the jar in loose ribbons that spread and thinned as they drifted downward, disappearing in the wind before they reached the flowing river.

Owen returned the lid to the cookie jar, then jumped down from the wall and watched the river wash over Big Lick Falls. Well beyond the falls, the Gauley's waters joined the New River to form the Kanawah, which flowed to the Ohio and on to the Mississippi, finally reaching the Atlantic through the Gulf of Mexico. Owen thought the ocean made a far grander resting place than the cookie jar he had just emptied or the shoebox Bobby had contemplated for himself.

Across the river, at the base of the gorge wall, the tip of a thin sapling thrust upward through the current. From where Owen stood, it looked like a human hand. In the distance, the play of light and the flowing water caused the hand to wave. Owen waved back, tucked the empty jar under his arm, and trudged away from the river toward his waiting automobile.